Surrender

Alec's smile disappeared and he relaxed his savage hold on her, lifting lean, brown fingers to caress her damp cheek and trace lightly over her lips. Juliet felt at once helpless when his fingers touched her skin, dangerously weak so near his strength. Try as she might, she could not stop her lips from trembling, and the tremor seemed to echo throughout her entire body. He toyed with a strand of hair which had blown across her cheek, then his hand freed the rest of her long, chestnut hair and lingered there to stroke the downy softness at the back of her neck. In utter confusion she lifted wide, golden eyes to meet his gaze.

His mouth bent to take hers gently, then with increasing passion, deliberately coaxing a sweet response. Her mind counseled her the folly of such surrender, but she was powerless to still the sudden desire he stirred within her. . . .

For Honor's Lady

Rosanne Kohake

AVON
PUBLISHERS OF BARD, CAMELOT, DISCUS AND FLARE BOOKS

FOR HONOR'S LADY is an original publication of Avon
Books. This work has never before appeared in book form.

AVON BOOKS
A division of
The Hearst Corporation
1790 Broadway
New York, New York 10019

Copyright © 1984 by Rosanne Kohake
Published by arrangement with the author
Library of Congress Catalog Card Number: 83-91200
ISBN: 0-380-85480-5

First Avon Printing, January, 1984

AVON TRADEMARK REG. U. S. PAT. OFF. AND IN
OTHER COUNTRIES, MARCA REGISTRADA, HECHO EN
U. S. A.

Printed in the U. S. A.

WFH 10 9 8 7 6 5 4 3 2 1

To my husband David who believed

Foreword

1730

Young Lawrence Hampton lay motionless on his bunk, making careful plans for the future while everyone else lay deep in sleep. He was different—better—than the common sailors or even the youthful first mate, Adam Barkley, whose snores drowned out the creaking of the ship as it rocked on the gentle sea. He was meant for far greater things than they—for a fine house and servants and the respect that was due a successful man. Yes, he was certain that money bought everything, and more money bought more of everything. One could never have enough of the stuff! He had been one of hundreds of young street thieves in Liverpool, youths forced by poverty and utter desperation to crime, but he had not been so foolish as to waste his meager "earnings" on a brief respite from the hunger which gnawed at his belly. Not Lawrence Hampton!

He had boarded this ship a few weeks earlier with slightly less than half fare, relying on a convincing bit of self-salesmanship for the remainder. Captain Thompson was usually quite adept at turning away the would-be sailors who amassed at port cities with empty pockets, hoping to reach the colonies and a new life, so it was no small feat when Hampton talked his way on board without prior sailing experience. The past weeks at sea, the old captain had done his best to break the landlubber, but the boy had tackled even the most difficult and degrading of jobs with energy and had completed them with efficiency. The ship had been only a few days out of port, however, when the extent of Hampton's greatest talent came to light. Selling himself into service for the initial price of entry into a game of cards, he had proved

1

himself a master at the subtle art of deception and had exhibited a shrewd and almost uncanny knack for recognizing a bluff.

When the inevitable accusations of cheating had reached the captain, Hampton had been barred from the games for the remainder of the voyage and placed under the watchful eye of the first mate. These past few days he had amazed Mate Barkley with his tremendous drive, his ability to work day and night at the most physically demanding of chores with no sign of fatigue. In return, Barkley had amazed Hampton with stories of the New World, of the countless people arriving every day, of the new money being made and spent on nearly everything that could be imported.

But there was more: the most lucrative business of all, the business of piracy! The letters of marque and reprisal issued by all major governments made it technically legal to plunder and destroy, and Hampton meant to do a lion's share of both as he clawed his way to the top. He would have it all some day, he thought confidently. A house and land; a name and wealth and respect—and damn anyone who stood in his way!

The Colony of Virginia, 1743

Alexander Farrell's sharp brown eyes flickered over his son's new suit of clothing—the fashionably unbuttoned coat with turned-back collar and cuffs, tailored of deep brown satin and flaring from the waist; the long floral-design waistcoat, which hid all but a few touches of the fine cambric shirt beneath; fitted breeches fastened tightly at the knee; white hose and broad-toed buckled slippers. Jerome had taken his time preparing himself for this visit, he thought, noting also the powdered wig rolled at the ears and tied in a queue at the back of his neck. He seemed quite anxious to speak his mind, for all he politely endured his father's scrutiny. Alexander could hardly help but notice the way his son's thumb and forefinger nervously tested the curved edges of his tricorn hat.

"You had something you wished to see me about, Jerome?" Alexander asked in his richly timbred voice, which had always commanded total respect.

"Yes, Father," Jerome answered, wishing that his own voice were deeper and more impressive. But then, he was not yet nineteen, and he planned to be every bit as successful when his years matched his father's two score and five. "I have met a woman and I wish to marry her," he stated rather bluntly.

Alexander frowned and cleared his throat, instructing his son to take a seat opposite himself. The older man leaned forward, and his folded hands rested on the desk while he considered his youngest son. Why, he was still just a boy! How could he best explain to Jerome that marriage was an important step for a man, a turning point in his life? He could well imagine the woman the boy had become enamored of—some pretty young actress trouping through Williamsburg during the season, bedded by the entire student population at William and Mary. He probably wished to wed the woman before the company's final performance in town!

Bracing himself for the worst, Alexander put the question to him. "Does this woman have a name?"

A dreamy look in his eyes, Jerome softly and almost tenderly answered the question. "Colette Mignon Rocheau DuFaux."

Alexander's eyes lit up the slightest bit. His son was hardly the fool he had feared! Colette DuFaux was staying in Williamsburg with his close friends the Randolphs, so he was familiar with the young woman and with her background as well. She was the descendant of French Huguenots who had emigrated earlier in the century, victims of religious persecution and the Camisards War. The years in Virginia had been profitable ones for the ambitious immigrants, who had added to their land holdings yearly and had reaped the benefits of the cheap slave labor and a steady rise in tobacco prices. Her father had planted a stretch of land just west of the fall line and had amassed a substantial fortune within the past decade or so, though the greater part had been spent on building and furnishing an extraordinary manor house, which had recently been destroyed in a tragic fire. "Ciel," Heaven, they had called it, but it had turned into Hell when Colette's entire family had perished in the fire. Now she was alone.

Alexander lifted a quill from its holder and idly stroked its softness. He could easily understand a man's preoccupation with the lovely French woman, though at fifteen she was just barely that. She was already tall and slender, with perfect, dainty features and a milky white complexion, to which her jet-black hair and polished ebony eyes made a brilliant contrast. And there was something more about the girl that had caught Alexander's fancy. The just less than arrogant tilt of her chin, the fearless way her dark eyes had of meeting another's, the unwavering ease with which she handled herself—all told him that somewhere just beneath the beauty and grace was real strength of character, something that Jerome Farrell sorely lacked. The girl had title to all that land, though it was not being worked now and the slaves had been sold to finance her extended stay in town. Although many of the Tidewater planters were certainly not partial to the French, Colette spoke English perfectly and was welcome in the best of homes.

He replaced the quill pen and once again settled folded hands on the desk, taking a second look at his rather ordinary son.

"Have you spoken with this woman?"

"At several parties," the youth responded, "and balls as well. I have danced with her innumerable times, and I am certain that she finds me . . . interesting."

"She is very young, Jerome," Alexander began, thinking that his son was only one of scores of young swains in Williamsburg to interest Colette DuFaux, and certainly not capable of winning her heart.

"But she has no one now, Father," Jerome interrupted, obviously truly sympathetic of her situation, "and she dislikes the city. She wants to return to plantation life—she told me that she did!"

"Well, it seems that the two of you have spoken then," Alexander said, a trifle more encouraged by the remark. "And do you believe that Miss DuFaux finds you . . . interesting enough for marriage?"

A deep crimson spread over Jerome's face all the way to the start of his powdered wig.

"Yes, I do, Father. We . . . we have talked about the future, and we share many of the same dreams."

"Would you work her father's lands and rebuild the house that once stood there?"

"No, Father. I would sell the lands and build a new house, hopefully on the western lands you recently patented on the

Rappahannock. I was much impressed by the beautiful rolling hills."

A slow smile began on Alexander Farrell's lips and crept into his eyes as well. His youngest son was growing up—and it seemed like only yesterday he had celebrated his breeching day!

"Have you a name picked out for this home you plan to make for your bride?"

"Yes, sir!" answered Jerome, barely able to contain his excitement, for his father's approval was apparent in his expression. "We shall call our home 'Beau Rêve,' Beautiful Dream . . . with your blessing, Father," he added.

He was so very young, thought Alexander, and yet the world belonged to the young. With a woman like Colette DuFaux and a prime tract of Virginia soil to begin with, perhaps his son would have his beautiful dream after all.

Part I
New York, 1775

Chapter 1

The promising warmth of early April woke the City of New York from the dormancy of a long, cold winter. Open-sided, stone market houses along the East River were crowded with people buying the necessary commodities of life, while unusual specialty shops along Pearl Street and Hanover Square also bustled with shoppers, everyone enjoying the mild spring weather. The sun spread its welcome warmth on the shoreline of Manhattan Island, heavily fringed with wharves and slips in close succession; on the countless comings and goings of seafaring men; on longshoremen busily scurrying about the docks. A shimmering circle of gold reflected on the surface of Collect Pond, the favorite social gathering place of wintertime, now deserted of its avid patrons.

Odds and ends of the city's beginnings were yet interspersed throughout the island, particularly in the southernmost sector, which was brightly spattered with multicolored and diverse styles of buildings. Though the tidy patterns of New Amsterdam had long since disappeared, a few of the one-and-one-half-story, stepped-gabled houses of yellow Holland brick still remained. For the most part, the three-thousand-odd houses of the city were red brick or frame with red tiled roofs, built one next to another, each boasting a meager dash of greenery for a rear yard. Where once a barricade of wooden planks had marked the northern border of a diminutive Dutch settlement, several fashionable residences and thriving businesses now lined Wall Street.

The wealthy of the city had built their grand houses at various sites according to propriety and taste, Broadway being a logical choice for many of the elite. A prosperous banker, Edgar Church, had constructed an imposing mansion there, quite near the Trinity Episcopal Church. Fluted white columns supported the stately three-storied structure, which frequently hosted lavish parties, for the Churches were well-known for their elegant style of entertaining. But on this gladly received first day of spring, the house stood basking peacefully in the sun.

Streets of cobblestone with walkways along one side were vastly improved from their rutted, muddy predecessors, where livestock had once run freely in the city proper. Sunlight glinted on an impressive gilded statue of King George III, solemnly erected less than five years before in Bowling Green, the city's first park. The nearly thirty churches that served the residents of the city cast long shadows with their steeples and cross-supporting spires in the early morning sun.

On a rise of land to the north stood a massive L-shaped brick structure, simple yet dignified in design, set well back from the main road on a long, curving drive. Built by Lawrence Hampton, the merchant, its grounds and adjacent stables were much less confined than its urban counterparts.

Roughly equivalent in size to the Church home, it was rarely the scene of a party, though it was a frequent stop for Hampton's business associates—a motley group that often included slovenly sailors as well as refined gentlemen.

On this fine morning, a handsome young man of perhaps twenty left the house on a spirited black stallion. Juliet Hampton stared out the parlor window on the brilliant spring day at the figure of her brother on horseback, shrinking quickly as he galloped off. She sighed deeply as unbidden memories of another bright spring day flooded her mind. It had not been so very long ago when a younger boy had gone off riding and she had followed.

She smiled, thinking of that strange little creature, unruly hair blowing in every direction (despite Rachel's best efforts to keep it tightly braided), running, laughing, tossing stones, and climbing trees with boys her own age. Her smile deepened as she recalled riding her very own spirited mare, Ginger. Juliet had been a splendid equestrienne at the age of seven and a half; she had manuevered a horse with the best of the male riders twice her age. And she had been proud of her accomplishments, encouraged by a brother one year her senior.

She ran her hands over the pleasant light blue pattern printed on her chintz dress. How different she was from that girl in her memory! Every strand of her thick chestnut hair was neatly curled and arranged according to the dictates of fashion. Her voice no longer pealed in unleashed laughter or was raised to shout at her friends. Instead she spoke in a soft, cultured tone; wore a practiced, social smile. Childish effervescence had been replaced by mature restraint, and the temper for which she had been notorious had been quelled beneath a facade of serenity.

Juliet turned around slowly and walked toward the oversized portrait of her mother, which covered the greater part of one wall. She stood beneath its gilded frame, looking up at the lovely woman captured there. Claire Farmington Hampton had been an exceptionally beautiful woman, and the artist had painted her auburn hair, her delicate brows and lashes, her straight and slender nose, and her smoothly curving lips with amazing accuracy. It was none of these, however, that held Juliet captive; nor was it the startling resemblance she bore to the woman depicted on the canvas. It was something in the eyes, Juliet thought, in those golden eyes that were somehow void. Instead of mirroring spirit and life, they merely covered an emptiness with their smile. They were haunting, those eyes, and they conjured up more memories long forgotten.

So very little time had been spent in this parlor, she thought, looking away from the painting and studying the various objects, which had remained here unchanged all these years. She paused at the large chair of mahogany and green brocade fabric, running a finger over its textured softness. She could imagine her mother sitting here, her back perfectly straight and never touching the chair's back, her chin held high, her hands working a fine piece of stitchery. She had spoken softly, in a voice that was pleasant though without expression, to a small mirror-image who could not sit still for more than a moment.

"Juliet Cecilia, you simply must learn to sit tall, like a lady. Hold your head up, dear."

Then she would sigh at the futility of tutoring such an unlikely pupil on femininity.

"You want your father to be proud of you, do you not? Then you simply must try harder. Now, where is the sampler we started?"

Juliet remembered staring helplessly out the window at the young boys who were so lucky—they were encouraged to do exactly as they pleased! She had looked down at her sampler and frowned. It was the third item she had worked on, and far from being like the pleasing handiwork her mother produced, it was filled with careless mistakes and would hardly have won her father's praise. Juliet simply had not had the patience for such time-consuming trivialities! If she was to win her father's approval, it would certainly not be with a needle.

How she had longed to be like Robert! He was so lucky, she had thought, wincing as her lack of concentration caused her to prick her finger. She had brought the injured finger quickly to her mouth, earning a disapproving glance from her mother, who had sighed once more and shaken her head.

"Juliet, please, please try. Your father simply does not know what to make of you."

Claire had risen from her chair then, and moved closer to Juliet, who sat on a low stool very near the large window. She had bent low, and her long slender fingers had reached out for her daughter's waist. Juliet's face had beamed in warm expectation for a moment—until she realized that her mother intended not an encouraging hug, but merely to straighten the yellow sash on her daughter's dress and to smooth the folds of the skirt flowing about the stool. . . . Even after all this time Juliet felt the pain and disappointment of that moment.

She drew a deep breath and stared dreamily out the window. Closing her eyes, she could almost feel the crisp, exhilarating breeze that had caressed her face as she rode on Ginger that day. For months she had secretly defied her mother's orders and even Rachel's sternest punishments, leaving the house every chance she found. She had grown so tired of trying to be like Mother! So bored with practicing her posture and her soft, polished voice; with working on her sampler and pounding on the spinet! Her father had never even noticed her efforts. And why should she work so hard at being like Mother? she had wondered, when Mother was obviously not the object of Father's affection. But if she could be like Robert . . . So many times Father had taken Robert special places, shared secrets with him, boasted among his friends that his son did thus and so, or put a firm arm around his shoulder while Juliet looked on in envy. If only she could be like Robert, then surely her father would love her, she had thought.

Juliet's smile was bittersweet as she remembered how earnestly she had plotted to be a boy. Her plans had been permanently put to rest, however, when Claire Hampton had come to this very room and chanced to see her daughter outside in a horse race with four of her brother's friends. The fact that she wore Robert's cast-off clothing and rode Ginger astride had been enough to drive Mistress Hampton to despair. But when Juliet had beaten them all and shouted taunting remarks back at them—well, it was surely more than a mother was meant to endure! That very evening she had insisted that Juliet be sent away to school.

How vivid the memory of that night years before, when she had faced her parents in this same room. She had stood proud and tall, and although a million butterflies had fluttered in her stomach, she had given no sign of her fear. When Mother had related the story to her father, Juliet had actually expected him to be pleased. He had always been proud of Robert when he won a race or was the best. Instead her father had frowned and stared at his young daughter with anything but pride. Juliet remembered how hard it had been to hold back the tears. She could still hear her mother's soft, monotonous voice, ". . . and I believe that Aunt Cecilia is correct. A young lady must receive proper training if she is ever to marry well. There is a fine school near her, and arrangements can be made immediately for Juliet's enrollment, providing you concur. I have given the matter much consideration, however, and I feel that there is actually very little choice."

How Juliet had prayed that her father would refuse to send her away! But seeing the look on his face she had known at once that her prayers were in vain.

A confused little girl had been packed off to England, a

child who had failed and did not understand why. Even now Juliet did not realize that her father's love for Robert was merely an extension of the love he had for himself, that his pride in him was only pride in one more successful business venture.

On arrival in England, Juliet had met her great aunt Cecilia for the first time. She was a shorter, thinner woman than Juliet's mother, with light silver hair and faded blue eyes, yet in words, actions, and expressions they were nearly identical! Their voices were so very much alike—cool and reserved, never nervous, never laughing, never once raised above the proper level; exactly the opposite of her own voice, which so often betrayed her emotions.

Cecilia had taken Juliet on a long tour of the house, ending with a rather tedious history of the Farmington ancestors traced back even prior to the Norman Conquest. There were several who had distinguished themselves in valorous service to the king and a few who had married royalty. The seven-year-old had listened politely until the lecture's end, but had then asked what difference all of these old men made to her. Cecilia had come very close to displaying her shock at the inanity of such a question, but after a short sigh and a remark about the barbarous state of affairs in the colonies, she had managed an appropriate reply.

"One's blood is of utmost importance," she had said, "for it determines who and what a person is." She had not been able to answer Juliet's questions about her father's blood, however, stating simply that ". . . the Farmington heritage is sufficient cause for acting with the honor and dignity befitting one of high birth."

She had been enrolled at St. Bride's, a very small, very strict school whose students were girls from wealthy families. The rigid discipline and regimentation had a quieting effect on Juliet's spirit; she had learned what was expected of her and had meekly conformed with those expectations. Arrogance and indifference were subtly encouraged by her aunt, and Juliet unconsciously began to assimilate the haughty airs of a Farmington.

After nearly seven years of school, a subdued, quiet girl of fourteen was called home when her mother fell seriously ill.

Claire Hampton never saw her only daughter again, for Juliet arrived in New York a few weeks after her death.

It had been so strange to come home after having spent half her life away. Her father had been exactly as Juliet remembered him, though his hair had become lighter and interwoven with silver; but Robert had grown so tall and handsome that she scarcely recognized him! Juliet would never, never forget the way he had run to embrace her, or how he had smiled and told her that she was beautiful.

A few weeks later at the Churches' Christmas party, her heart had been broken when she discovered Robert's devotion for shy, pretty Frances. Frances Church of all people! The pale, proper little porcelain doll she had despised ever since she was three! Juliet had choked back her tears and had been very sure she wanted to die—until Allan had asked her to dance. Frances's brother, Allan, was blond, handsome, and very mature—nearly eighteen years old! He was charming and attentive, and while her father watched them with a proud smile, Juliet had fallen hopelessly in love. Before she returned to school in the spring, Allan promised her he would write.

For eight agonizing months Juliet had waited for his letter, but finally her patience had come to an end. Her cheeks burned as she recalled the letter she had written to him, spilling out her deepest feelings, never doubting for a moment that he felt exactly the same. It was totally beyond her comprehension that the short time they had spent together had already been forgotten by him. Two months later a letter had arrived, but it had hardly been the missive Juliet had dreamed of receiving.

". . . Allan Church was married last week to a lovely girl from Boston," Robert had written. "I am certain that you and Mary will become good friends when you return. . . ."

Juliet's lips curved into a reluctant half-smile as she slowly paced the parlor. She had been very sure her life was over when she had read those words, and to this day she knew them by heart. The tears she had cried seemed so silly now! She was certain she had not cried at all since then.

Not long afterward, Lady Margaret Medford, by far the wildest, most undisciplined young lady at St. Bride's, had invited Juliet to her home for a holiday. Juliet had accepted the

15

invitation at the urging of Aunt Cecilia, though she had little in common with the girl, whose interest seemed confined to a single subject—the opposite sex. Lady Margaret was not a beauty, but neither was she unattractive; she was most certainly an expert at the art of flirtation and was anxious to share her expertise. She had noted Juliet's obvious assets and spent most of their time together coaching her friend on how to entice a man. Juliet had listened with polite disinterest to her earnest council, finding much of her advice quite amusing.

It was during one of several visits to Medford Manor that Juliet had been introduced to Lady Margaret's older brother, Lord Harold, who was the opposite of his sister in every conceivable way. Whereas she was sophisticated, he was naive; while she listened to no one and made her own set of rules, he was timid and proper, and hardly took a breath without consulting his mother or Margaret; while she toyed with several men's hearts at one time, he was shy and attracted little feminine attention, in spite of a title and a sizable inheritance. Harold was not an ugly man, but his skin was pale, his flesh loose and unmuscular. Even his voice betrayed his weakness of character, though it was tinged with a well-practiced arrogance.

Juliet stopped her thoughtful pacing and walked to the wall opposite her mother's portrait, where other portraits flanked either side of the massive mahogany mantel. Frowning, she lifted a forefinger to trace the mouth of her brother, so expertly captured in the painting. Robert would not like Harold, she knew, but then, she did not like Frances. At least Harold would not demand too much of her after their marriage, she thought.

Harold had agreed that the wedding would take place in New York, though his mother had not favored the idea while England buzzed with talk of trouble in the colonies. Juliet planned to make her wedding the largest and most exciting social event in anyone's memory. She would show them all—Allan and Frances and Robert, and most especially her father—that she was not the rejected little girl everyone remembered. She was better than all of them! Her father would be bursting with pride when his daughter married a name, a title, and wealth!

She looked up at his portrait, at the firmly set jaw, at the steel-blue eyes, but even on tiptoe with her head held high, she was unable to stand tall enough to meet the level of his gaze. An odd feeling came over her, a feeling of sadness and yearning as she stretched in an effort to look him squarely in the eye. . . .

The dainty timepiece on the mantel chimed the hour of twelve, interrupting Juliet's flow of thoughts. Could it be that she had been daydreaming that long? Robert would be back before she even changed her dress!

She hurried out of the room, shutting the door soundly on all thoughts of the past.

Chapter 2

Robert stood tapping his foot, arms folded across his chest and an irritated frown creasing his brow. You'd think anything as trivial as a hair ornament could be chosen in a matter of minutes, he said to himself, all but losing his temper. It vexed him further when Juliet asked his opinion for the twentieth time, then grimaced and discarded his selection along with the black velvet bows she had been considering. It was only when he threatened to leave the shop without her that she frowned into the looking glass and held each item in her hair one last time, reluctantly choosing a golden-brown shade of ribbon that came close to matching her eyes. He barely took the time to pay the clerk before impatiently ushering her out of the shop, and he let out a snort the moment they reached the sidewalk.

"It must take you every bit of two days to pick out a pair of slippers! And fabric for a gown? Why, I believe I could just leave you here in town and stop back after the better part of a month!"

Juliet's face lifted slowly, her eyes narrowed and bright with annoyance. "Is it so difficult to understand why I want to look my best at the Churches' party?"

"Yes, it is, considering that Lord Harold will not even be there."

"I am not interested—" She caught herself just a bit too late to retract the statement, but she drew a deep breath and began again in a calm and proper tone. "It is my first party since coming home and—"

"Exactly who is it you want to impress?" Robert interrupted.

"Everyone!" she answered simply. "I don't want anyone to think of me anymore as the black sheep of the family."

"I never thought of you as that."

"Well, everyone else did!" Juliet insisted. "I want to show them all just how wrong they were!"

Robert scoffed. "I hardly think that a hair ribbon will change anyone's opinion of you, Juliet."

"It's part of the image I want to project, Robert—a small part, granted, but every detail is important."

"And is Lord Harold a detail?"

The hard glint in Juliet's eyes gave evidence to her rising temper. "Robert, what I do with my life is my own affair. But you might at least reserve judgment until you meet the man."

"I don't need to meet him, sister dear. My judgment of the man is based entirely on your feelings—and those are quite obvious to me."

Juliet stopped in mid-stride and turned, braced for an argument. "Lord Harold is from a very old and very fine family, and I am quite honored by his proposal of marriage. There's not a single man in the colonies who could match his credentials! And each and every unattached woman in New York will be green with envy when I march him down the aisle."

"Like an innocent lamb to the slaughter," Robert concluded.

"Hardly that," Juliet answered, raising her chin a notch. "He happens to be very much in love with me."

"A pity, Juliet, that the love is not returned."

"Do you dare to question my devotion?" she asked incredulously.

"Juliet," Robert answered with a smile, "I know you too well."

They stood facing one another on the busy sidewalk, oblivious of the people brushing past.

"Oh, no you do not! I am not the little girl who left New York ten years ago, or even four! I am a woman now, and I am soon to become Lady Medford."

"Well, I beg your pardon, M'lady, but I much prefer the old Juliet—the one who did not act like such a snob!"

"A snob!" she burst out. "You drooling simpleton! Don't you realize that this marriage will make you the brother of a titled gentleman?"

"Thank you, but I would still prefer to keep the sister I once knew. I rather liked her."

He was impossible! Juliet thought. He absolutely refused to be impressed! Her angry stare made no mark on his congenial disposition, and when her eyes strayed to the left, she encountered a second countenance, likewise unaffected by her iciest stare. Robert turned and followed her eyes to the man leaning leisurely against a storefront, watching them with obvious interest even now, after he had been noticed.

The color rose in Juliet's cheeks as he held her eyes, a striking figure in his casual but well-made clothing. Skin-tight breeches of soft buckskin, with knee-high boots of the same soft brown, joined a dark leather jacket that flared from a narrow waist. A contrasting crisp white linen shirt was opened to reveal what Juliet considered a rather vulgar display of the thick black hair on his chest. It was unusual clothing, for most men who wore leathers and skins were frontiersmen whose breeches and jackets were noticeably ill-fitting. The better dressed gentlemen wore their well-cut and tailored suits of silk, satin, or broadcloth, never animal skins. Still, it was not the clothing that held her attention, but the dark-skinned face of fine chiseled features, utterly masculine. His hair was thick and black as coal, and his eyes were so dark that they, too, were almost black, with a look that was piercing and at the same time nonchalant, a look that she found intriguing and compelling. She vaguely realized that she was staring, but she was reluctant to take her eyes from his. There was something about those bright, expressive eyes, something in the way they appraised her matter-of-factly, the way they boldly held hers far longer than what might be considered proper. When he lifted an expectant brow and his lips curved upward in a slow, knowing smile, Juliet gasped and turned indignantly away. He had no right to look at her with such familiar regard, and she had no intention of standing there enduring inspection like a sack of goods before being purchased. To her dismay, Robert closed the distance between himself and the stranger and offered him a warm greeting. Then he retraced his steps, leading the man to Juliet's side and introducing him with a wide smile.

"Juliet, this is Alexander Farrell, a cousin of Allan and Frances Church from the colony of Virginia. Alec, this is my sister, Miss Juliet Hampton."

Alec's long brown fingers closed lightly about the hand Juliet offered him, and he touched it briefly to his lips. His mouth was warm against her skin, and it sent a strange tingling sensation up her arm. As her eyes locked with his darker ones, she felt a burning in her cheeks, and for the first time in many years she found herself at a loss for words.

"It is indeed a pleasure to meet you, Miss Hampton," he said smoothly. "I have heard so many things about you . . . and they are obviously all true."

Juliet liked the sound of his voice, so deep and rich and manly, and the lazy drawl fell pleasantly on her ears. Then he smiled a taunting sort of smile that sent an odd shiver up her spine. He was quite handsome when he smiled, she thought. She was about to thank him for the compliment when it suddenly struck her that the stories cousin Frances had told him were probably a good deal less than complimentary. Before she could make a more appropriate reply, Robert was extending him an invitation to join them.

"I was about to take Juliet to the Ranelegh for some suitable refreshment. Will you join us, Alec?"

This came as a surprise to Juliet, who had thought him in a hurry to see her directly home. Alec readily accepted the invitation, and the three began to walk along the flat stone sidewalks and cobblestone streets the short distance to the Ranelegh.

New York was dotted with countless taverns for men only, but the Ranelegh was a newer type of establishment—a pleasure garden, which copied the popular originals in London, with flowers, greenery, and pleasant surroundings designed to appeal to a feminine clientele. The three young people had been seated but a few moments when a short, stocky man in seaman's garb searched out Robert to summon him to the docks on a pressing matter of business. He rose to excuse himself, insisting that Juliet and Alec stay and enjoy their tea and pastries, in spite of Juliet's protests. He assured her that he would only be a moment with Father. She stifled a sigh of

22

reluctant resignation. Robert was leaving her to entertain an utter stranger in a place she had never even been before, a stranger whose dark eyes she found unexplainably disturbing. She was not accustomed to being observed so candidly by a man, though she knew that most men thought her to be quite pretty. Gentlemen she had known in the past had gazed upon her in open admiration, but it was not admiration she saw in those handsome black eyes. There was an awkward silence after Robert had parted their company, and she grew increasingly uncomfortable under Alec's stare, which took in every inch of her from hair to hemline.

"Isn't this a lovely place?" she remarked, for lack of something better to say. Her lips curved into a practiced smile, which she knew he must find attractive.

"Is it?" he returned after careful consideration, raising his brows and smiling with a hint of a challenge.

She was caught offguard by his reply. "Uh, yes! I mean . . . well, it is a glorious day! And the flowers and the shrubs and—"

He interrupted her rush of words. "Actually, all of this"— he gestured leisurely at their surroundings with an upturned palm—"brings to mind the majority of women I know." He drew a lengthy breath and leaned back in his chair while he thoughtfully chose his words. "Artificial . . . useless . . . misplaced . . . yet very well kept."

Juliet's eyes widened in surprise, and she felt more than a little insulted. How disgustingly arrogant he was to make such a caustic comment—and to a lady whom he hardly knew at all! She was stunned into silence while she tried to collect her thoughts, which was difficult to do under his unwavering scrutiny. Even as they were served the locally made herbal tea, popular here because of the general public's objection to imported tea, Alec's eyes were fastened on her.

Juliet remembered hearing about the "Boston Tea Party" and about New York's own unloading of the tea ship *London* in the harbor a little over a year before. In England the two incidents had been viewed as disgraceful exhibitions of colonial impertinence, but Robert had seen them as glorious examples of the colonists' love of liberty. He had zealously written her about the Liberty Poles that were put up at Bowling Green, torn down, and put up again; about hanging and burning effigies of public officials who tried to force the people to accept the hated tea; and about other unpopular rulings opposed by a rowdy group called the "Sons of Liberty." Now she was reminded of those letters by the terrible brew that was served as a substitute for the beverage she loved. Robert had done his best to explain it, but Juliet could not understand why everyone was so opposed to the new laws, which actually meant cheaper tea!

She watched as Alec prepared his cup and stirred it thoughtfully, then took a long sip of the steamy brew, and though she had definite misgivings about further conversation with him, her curiosity finally got the better of her. She drew a deep breath and dared to ask, "Exactly what was it that you heard about me, Mr. Farrell?"

As he lowered his cup and leaned back in his chair, Juliet realized that he was watching her as closely as ever, and that he almost seemed amused by what he saw. His answer was slow and deliberate, and his eyes were narrowed in an expression that confused her.

"I heard that you were quite beautiful . . . and that you were away at school for several years." He paused while Juliet, disregarding that strange look in his eyes and basking in the glow of his compliment, chose a pastry. She knew how to handle compliments; indeed, she had come to expect them. He was raising his cup to his lips when he added as an afterthought, "And I heard that you could outride, outclimb, and outthrow nearly every man in this town."

She was just about to take a bite of her pastry, but her mouth promptly closed at his remark. She blinked and stared at him, amazed. "Where on earth did you hear all that?" she blurted out.

"Then it's true!" he responded swiftly. "I had thought it quite impossible, but now that I've met you—"

"Wait a moment!" Juliet interrupted him firmly. "Someone—Robert, I assume—told you some very exaggerated stories about a long, long time ago. I do not race horses anymore, or throw stones, and I most certainly do not climb trees!" She frowned at him in annoyance for a moment before lifting her chin high and looking away. She'd had quite enough of his inane discourse, and she intended to let it go no further.

"A pity!" returned Alec with a pained sigh.

Juliet did her best to hide her exasperation. She concentrated all of her attention on her tea, sipping at it daintily and trying not to wrinkle her nose at the odd taste it left in her mouth. There was something very different about Alexander Farrell, she was thinking, and she did not like whatever it was. He actually seemed to enjoy her vexation, and his behavior seemed calculated to further it.

"Are you here on business, Mr. Farrell?" she asked, broaching what she hoped was a safe subject. She thought that indeed he must be, for no one could actually enjoy such tactless company as his.

"In a manner of speaking, Julie," came the smooth reply, which continued without a pause though Juliet choked on her tea at his casual use of her first name, "and it is also a social call on the Church family."

How she would enjoy putting this impudent bore in his place! But she was momentarily at a loss as to how to do exactly that, so with a good deal of effort she forced a smile, in the interest of maintaining her aura of serenity.

"Exactly how are you related to them?" Surely it was a distant relationship to the well-mannered Church family!

"My father and Elizabeth Church were brother and sister, Julie."

His insolence was infuriating! And his eyes were every bit as taunting as his words!

"It seems that every family has one black sheep," she muttered through clenched teeth.

Her words were not quite audible, but Alec caught the general drift of her comment and laughed outright until several people at surrounding tables turned to stare. Juliet flushed a painful pink, and she sank a bit lower in her chair, hardly happy with the attention she and Alec were receiving.

"You are wondering, though you are far too much of a lady to ask," he said to her total embarrassment, "how could this rogue be related to such a proper Episcopal family? I am not afraid to tell you the truth." He leaned very close to her and directed her to do the same with a wriggle of his index finger. Juliet glanced about nervously before leaning timidly in his direction. She was absolutely certain that he would say something scandalous, but she was extremely curious about what that something would be. "My blood is not pure," he confided in a whisper. "My mother is French, you see, and there is probably a bit of savage thrown in somewhere, who is to say? It matters very little, actually, no matter what you may have been told."

He smiled at her, and she drew back immediately, not liking the way he easily dismissed her arrogance. "What I have been told is hardly applicable where you are concerned, Mr. Farrell. I can judge your behavior for myself!" she stated tartly.

He looked at her then, for a long, hard moment, and Juliet found it quite impossible to look away. "I certainly hope so, Julie," he said softly.

That rich masculine voice caressing her name completely unnerved her; and those dark, penetrating eyes! "Please do not call me that!" she pleaded uncomfortably. She shook her head and did her best to resume her haughty demeanor. "I did not ask you to call me by my first name, and I wish that you would not," she amended nervously. She picked up her cup and downed the last of the putrid-tasting liquid. He looked very much like a small boy playing in the mud, Juliet thought, enjoying himself all the more for his mother's irritation.

"Ah, but it's such a lovely name!" he was saying. "Juliet . . . the name of a star-crossed, romantic young girl. I remember, let me see, about"—he paused, calculating—"four years ago, my cousin Allan got a very interesting letter from a girl named Juliet."

Juliet's face went absolutely livid with a mixture of rage and humiliation. Her letter to Allan had been read by a stranger who actually remembered after all this time! She clenched her teeth and gripped the empty cup so tightly that her fingers turned white; even so, he continued sighing wistfully.

"Ah, the girl who wrote such lovely thoughts was so filled with love and passion! A girl after my own heart . . . as well as Allan's."

"Girl, indeed, Mr. Farrell!" she ground out with her last bit of control. "I was but fourteen at the time, and a mere child. I believe that nearly everyone does things in his youth of which he would rather not be reminded."

"Sometimes, Julie, growing up is according to everyone else's rules when it ought to be according to one's own. Then perhaps the actions of one's youth would not be so painful a remembrance."

He spoke in earnest, and she noticed that his eyes were suddenly touched with regret, but she was far too angry to be interested in what he was trying to say. Fortunately Robert returned to end the uncomfortable conversation at that point, and much to her relief, further discourse was limited to mutual acquaintances, politics, and business. Juliet barely said a word.

On the way home she was quiet, trying to sort out her feelings, for Alexander Farrell had upset her more than she liked to admit. He had made her angry, yes, but that was only a part of it. He had also made her feel very unsure of herself, as if he could see right through what she said and did to what she really thought and felt. It troubled her to be so affected by a total stranger, and try as she might she could not reason away her uneasiness.

"You're awfully quiet, Juliet," Robert teased.

"Am I?" she said absently.

"Yes, you are. I don't suppose you might be a trifle taken with Alec?"

Juliet glared at him, appalled at the suggestion. "Robert really! If you must know, I found his company disagreeable, and I most certainly do not look forward to seeing him again."

"Most women find him very attractive," he remarked innocently.

Her eyes narrowed. "Oh, I'm sure they do!" she retorted. "Perhaps I am not so taken with appearances as most women."

"You do agree he's handsome then. He's wealthy, too, I am told. . . . Inherited quite a bit of land in Virginia—"

"Robert," she snapped, "I am not interested!" Robert shrugged, and was silent but Juliet noticed the mischievous grin that tugged at the corners of his mouth.

Chapter 3

The Churches' beautiful white-pillared house was lit with a thousand candles, and no expense had been spared for this evening's gala affair. There were two long tables in the dining room filled with tempting exotic dishes of all kinds, and simple fresh fruits and vegetables, as well as succulent beef and ham. An excellent orchestra sent sweet strains drifting in the air, and the music and light seemed to touch everything. Each guest was in his finest clothes, and the bright colors of silks, satins, and velvets spilled onto the ballroom floor as couples kept time with the music.

Robert escorted Juliet inside the entrance hall where Edgar, Elizabeth, and Frances Church stood welcoming guests into their home. Elizabeth embraced Juliet, saying that she could scarcely believe she was the same little girl who had gone off to England just a few years before. Frances told her that her gown was the prettiest she'd ever seen, but Juliet noticed that her attention was focused more on Robert than on the latest fashion. Robert, too, seemed to have eyes only for the lovely hostess, but until her duties were fulfilled he would have to concentrate on his sister and the other guests.

They walked to the ballroom, the largest room in the house, which was crowded with the orchestra at one end, dancing couples throughout the center, and groups of people talking and observing in what space remained. The left side of the room had three doors that had been opened wide, allowing for the free movement of air and perhaps, for some, a moonlight stroll in the garden. The right side of the room had three identical doorways, which opened to a large dining room and two smaller parlors. One parlor was set up for the men who preferred to play cards or engage in games of chance. Strong alcoholic refreshments were served here. The other merely provided a relatively quiet and comfortable setting for conversation.

Juliet spotted Allan almost immediately, looking handsome as ever in a cream-colored satin suit and a frilly white shirt. Next to him stood a small, dark-haired woman whom Juliet surmised was Mary, his wife. Studying her from across the room, Juliet wondered what it had been about Mary that had won Allan's heart. Robert gave her no time to think, however, propelling her across the room and proudly introducing her to the young couple.

"Mary, this is my sister, Juliet. Allan, you remember Juliet?"

Allan smiled, and his gaze flicked over the young woman who stood before him. "I can hardly believe it! Why, you really are all grown up!" He stared a moment longer before remembering his manners. "Oh, may I introduce my wife, Mary. Mary, Miss Juliet Hampton."

The two women nodded and smiled politely.

"I understand that you are a father, Allan," Juliet commented.

"You are correct," he answered, his face beaming with pride. "Little Edgar is not yet two years old, and already he is talking as well as his father."

Everyone smiled at that.

"He looks quite a bit like him, too," Mary added in a soft, timid voice.

"I have been told he's a beautiful child," Juliet said.

"Indeed he is!" came the reply from behind her. She turned her head at the sound of the vaguely familiar voice, but when she confronted that handsome dark face and mocking half-smile, she flashed him her coldest stare and turned pointedly back to Allan.

"Juliet, this is my cousin from Virginia Colony, Alexander Farrell," Allan said. "Alec, this is Robert's sister, Miss Juliet Hampton."

"I believe we may have met before, Miss Hampton," he

said, taking her hand and touching it to slightly smiling lips. "Have you ever been to Virginia?"

In spite of the annoyance that churned within her, the touch of his lips kindled a strange warmth, and Juliet pulled her hand away as quickly as possible to be rid of the odd sensation as she answered him with feigned innocence.

"No, I have never been to Virginia, nor have I any desire to go there. I've heard that the place is quite overrun with ill-mannered savages." Then she added every bit as sweetly, "Perhaps we met in England. I've just recently returned from there, you see." The ill-bred clod had probably never been out of the colonies, she thought with a smug smile. From the corner of her eye she could see the puzzled expression on Robert's face as he stared from one to the other, trying to figure out this game. To her surprise, Alec replied smoothly to her question, obviously unaffected by her comment about his home.

"I have been to England several times, Miss Hampton, but cannot recall having met you there . . . Perhaps it was France. I find it a much more civilized state, at any rate, don't you agree?"

Juliet did not answer him this time; she merely glared at him in the hope that he would back down. He did exactly the opposite. Turning to Robert, he smiled and asked ever so graciously, "You wouldn't mind if I borrowed your lovely sister for this dance, would you?"

Robert eagerly gave his consent, completely ignoring Juliet's hostile look, and Alexander took her firmly by the arm and led her to the center of the room. She had no choice but to endure his company, unless she wished to make a scene.

"You look absolutely radiant this evening, Julie," he said at a pause in the music.

Juliet seethed beneath a poor excuse for a smile. "How dare you call me by my first name when I asked you not to?"

"Ah, it's difficult for us 'savages' to remember such social amenities, particularly when dancing with such a lovely lady," he taunted.

Juliet took a deep breath and frowned as she faced her partner, who bowed to her as the music continued. He was a handsome devil, she was forced to admit, and his movements were fluid and quite graceful, unusual for a man of such height and muscle. Except for her father and Robert, she had never before met anyone she could not silence with her coldest stare or turn away with a sharp remark, and she was certainly not about to admit that she had been bested by this . . . this . . . half-breed, no matter whose cousin he was!

"Shall we call a truce, Miss Hampton?" He surprised her with the question and had her full attention when he continued. "I intended to be charming this evening, but I am afraid that your dazzling beauty quite made me forget myself."

Juliet wrinkled her nose in distaste. How could he sport such as earnest expression while saying something so absurd? He certainly did look like a gentleman, dressed in an excellently fitted suit of fine beige broadcloth trimmed in deep brown velvet. Indeed, Juliet noticed a great many females staring at him with open admiration and a few with inviting smiles. But she was not so impressed by appearances as they! She lifted her nose into the air and scoffed aloud, "I rather doubt that it is possible for you to be charming at all, Mr. Farrell."

"Oh, but you are wrong, Miss Hampton! My own dear mother assured me that I am most charming," he announced solemnly. "And Mother is always correct!"

Juliet suddenly found herself unable to suppress a grin. A picture of a little old woman patting Alexander Farrell on the head and telling him how utterly charming he was—why, it was ludicrous! She could imagine Harold in such a scene, but certainly not Alec!

"You can smile! I was beginning to worry about that!" He flashed her a truly warm grin in return.

"You are impossible!" she conceded.

"So I've been told. . . . I noticed that Robert escorted you to the party this evening."

"Yes," she answered, copying the bored tone in his voice. "My fiancé is in England, but we plan to be married here in New York this autumn. Perhaps you have met him—Lord Harold Medford?" She lingered for half a moment on the word "Lord," assuring herself that he noted the title.

"I don't believe I've had the pleasure. But then, I met so many people in so short a time while I was traveling that it was impossible to remember all of them. I tried to concern myself with the more important ones."

With that remark the dance ended, and he returned her to Robert before she could think of an appropriate rejoinder.

"Your brother has extended to me an invitation to your home for midday meal tomorrow," he said to her after thanking Robert for the dance. "I shall look forward to seeing you then."

He abruptly excused himself from the group and withdrew, leaving a confused pair of amber eyes staring after him. Though she hated to admit it, she was sorry to see him go. He had managed to make her feel totally unsure of herself, of the impression she may have made, and yet, there was something about him. . . . Perhaps it was his total lack of concern for what others thought and did. What had he said the other day about rules? He was obviously a man who made and followed his own and let the rest of the world go to the devil. A smile curved her lips as she considered what her life would be like if she did exactly the same. She had long since given up her dearest pursuits to please her father, had even planned a marriage she hoped would gain his approval. But all of this was as it should be, she resolved, for after all, she was not a man and was not expected to have a mind of her own. Realizing that the conversation was moving briskly around her, Juliet put her thoughts aside and made an effort to be charming, witty, and gracious.

During the remainder of the evening there were several young men who asked Juliet to dance, and a pair of them who found themselves absolutely captivated, barely leaving her side for a moment. But it was Alec who claimed the last dance after having been absent the entire evening. Again he did not ask for the favor; rather, he walked directly to her side and with a terse "I believe this is my dance," effectively dismissed the others who had hoped to claim it as theirs. Juliet meekly complied, doing her best not to appear eager.

The crowd had thinned considerably by this time, but there were still a few women about the room whose eyes followed Alec as he moved to the music. When he acknowledged such flirtation with a quick glance, a half-smile, a slight nod, Juliet became quite annoyed and began to wonder if he had asked her to dance to draw attention to himself. She had not seen him with anyone else the entire evening, though she would rather have died than admit that she had been following his actions. She completely lost her temper when a generously rounded redhead fixed a blatantly obvious stare on Alec and suggestively stroked the jeweled necklace that hung low at her breasts. A moment later Alec returned the look and let his lips curve into a sensuous smile.

"It would seem, Mr. Farrell," Juliet hissed, "that you have several admirers who might have appreciated this dance far more than I!"

"Really?" he answered in feigned surprise. "I hadn't noticed." He turned his head to flash the redhead another, wider smile.

"Well, perhaps you had better open your eyes!" Juliet retorted.

All at once she commanded his full attention, his dark eyes holding hers as he answered in a low voice, husky and masculine. "I have, Julie, and that is precisely why I am dancing with you."

Her arrogance melted in the face of his intoxicating stare, and an unexplainable warmth tingled instantly inside her. Even when the music stopped she hardly noticed, so hypnotic was the attraction in those shadowy eyes. Alec broke the spell with a polite bow and curt farewell, leaving Juliet staring after him. In spite of herself, she could not wait to see him the next day.

Chapter 4

It was well into morning when Juliet woke in a room already bright with strong yellow sunshine. She lay in bed a moment longer, enjoying the pleasant warmth as she stretched her arms high above her head and pointed her toes until her muscles tingled. With a reluctant sigh she rose from the comfort of her soft bed, torn between the desire to relax a while longer and an eagerness to put such a glorious day to good use. As she splashed the last traces of sleep from her face with a cool bit of water, she became aware of several deep, muffled voices ascending from downstairs. She had cautiously opened her door a crack to hear who might be visiting so early in the day when Rachel appeared, shaking her head. With a chastising look she opened the door just far enough to admit herself to Juliet's room, then closed it again soundly.

"There be visitors at the house this morning, and no reason to be peeking about when you not be properly dressed."

"Who's here?" Juliet asked anxiously, remembering at once that Alec was expected.

"Visitors for your father and Master Robert, and none of your concern," Rachel said evasively.

With resigned obedience, Juliet took a seat before her vanity and allowed Rachel to arrange her hair in curls, securing each one in a full, becoming style with practiced expertise.

A tall, slender woman with smoke-gray hair and cool blue eyes, Rachel had been in service at Hampton House for as long as Juliet could remember. She had been hired as a governess for a young girl who had shown the need for a firm disciplinarian, but when her stringent rules and cold supervision had proved ineffective and Juliet was sent away to school, Rachel had assumed other duties, assisting the mistress of Hampton House. Claire Hampton had been an excellent organizer and had ruled the house with both an iron hand and a silken glove, drawing the best performance from each and every servant. Dismissals had been all but unheard of, for Claire had chosen well from those who applied for positions and had made certain that each knew exactly what was expected of him or her.

After Mistress Hampton's death, however, Juliet's father had taken charge of the household as he might have a business that was failing because of poor management. Chaos had quickly resulted. Disregarding the subtle considerations his wife had always shown them, he ordered his servants about like a tyrant, brooking no impertinence and allowing for no mistakes. Many of those who had joined the staff over a decade before resigned; a good many others were dismissed for real or alleged indiscretions, without regard for a spotless prior record of service. Even now Hampton's depositions remained swift and fatal to a servant's career. If he felt that anyone had tried to take advantage of him in any way, he would see to it that the same person found no future work in New York.

Juliet knew nothing of Rachel's past, for she was a bitter woman who had learned long ago to trust no one save herself. She had been an attractive young woman when she secured her position at Hampton House, and from the very beginning she had admired Lawrence Hampton, whose steel-blue eyes spoke to her of strength and power. He had been a generous employer because she had performed her duties well, and when he expected nothing more, her admiration grew. In the years following his wife's death, Rachel became totally dedicated to serving him, to aiding him in the running of the house, to keeping him dutifully informed of everything that might interest him.

Now that his daughter had returned home from school, Rachel acted as Juliet's personal maid. This was not to her liking, as she had never been fond of the girl and considered her a headstrong, unladylike piece of baggage, for all she seemed to have tamed in the years away. In Rachel's opinion, it would be better for all concerned if Juliet did marry this no-bleman she had laid claim to and left Manhattan for good.

"Who is it?" Juliet inquired again, trying hard not to let her growing curiosity show.

With a frown and a small sigh her maid finally answered. "It be Captain Barkley and Mr. Farrell."

Juliet's face broke into a smile. "Alec—" To her utter aston-ishment, the name came naturally to her lips. "I mean, Mr. Farrell is here already?"

Rachel's frown deepened, leaving Juliet no doubt that she had caught the slip. The maid's words were clipped, and her tone carried her disapproval. "You have slept late, Miss Ju-liet. It is well after eleven o'clock. Your mother was always awake and about no later than eight." Rachel seemed to enjoy reminding Juliet of the differences between her and her late mother.

But this morning Juliet refused to allow the woman to af-fect her good mood. It was a beautiful day, and she did not in-tend to waste it, and the presence of the man who had made such an intriguing impression on her the evening before made her all the more anxious to maintain her placid de-meanor.

When her hair was nearly finished, she studied her reflec-tion, with a small, satisfied smile curving her lips and light-ing her eyes. Rachel caught the look and shook her head in disgust.

"You'd better be getting no ideas about Mister Alexander Farrell! He be no gentleman—you can see that right enough by the look in his eye! You'll be getting into trouble if you toy with the likes of him!"

"I am hardly 'toying with the likes of him,' " Juliet laughed, thinking how impossible it would be to trifle with someone like Alec.

"Take a good bit of advice and stay away from that man. He means trouble—his kind always does," Rachel warned Juliet sternly. "He's got the devil's eyes! Black as sin, and that means nothing but trouble, you can take my word. Your mother would never have trusted anyone with looks like that, and I do not believe your father trusts him, either."

Juliet sighed, not wishing to argue the point. "You're right,

Rachel. He's not the type of man I would want to confide in," she said honestly.

"Just don't be forgetting Lord Harold will be coming soon enough, and it wouldn't do to have him greeted by malicious gossip."

"There will not be any gossip, I can assure you. And you needn't remind me of Harold; I remember him quite well!"

Lowering her eyes to prevent any further show of her thoughts, Juliet studied her perfectly manicured fingers, then drummed them gingerly on the vanity. Rachel had managed to quell her spirits somewhat, and before she succeeded in doing so totally, Juliet withdrew into silence. Now that she thought about it, there was really no reason Alec's presence in her home should mean anything to her—but it did. A spark of nervous anticipation refused to be smothered in spite of its absurdity. Something about the man was magnetic, and it attracted Juliet more than she cared to admit. There was an excitement, perhaps even a fear of being challenged. Alexander Farrell accepted no one on face value, and he had hardly been convinced that Juliet was what she purported to be—a well-groomed and properly arrogant young lady. A part of her was afraid of his adept perception, yet another part was elated at the recognition.

After much deliberation, Juliet chose a lovely gown of off-white chintz printed with bright yellow flowers. Yards of material flowed in tiny pleats from a deep point at the center of a tightly fitted bodice. The demure squared-off neckline complimented her long, sculptured neck, and the off-white fabric was becoming to her pink and ivory complexion. Pleased with her reflection in the large looking glass, Juliet lost no time in leaving Rachel's company.

She descended the stairs a bit faster than had been her habit of late, listening to the voices rising from her father's study. She paused at the foot of the stairs and considered for a moment what to do. It would be proper to wait in the parlor, to patiently work on the needlepoint that she still despised so, but she was curious about what was being discussed so heatedly in the study, for she could hear Robert's voice rising shrill with emotion. She took careful steps down the long hall until she stood before her father's study, where the thick door was opened slightly, permitting her to see about a quarter of the room. She pressed herself against the wall and strained to hear the conversation.

It was Captain Barkley who spoke the first words she heard clearly, while helping himself to the decanter of Madeira on a table in Juliet's scope of vision.

"Smugglers deserve justice, to be sure! They near got away with murder a few years back!" He smiled and directed a strange look at her father before he continued in earnest. "But these commissioners in Boston—they not be after justice! They be after bribes, and the law protects them from their crimes. What about we?"

Juliet frowned, perturbed at the subject of their conversation. Men! All they seemed to care about sometimes was war and politics. Robert's letters had been full of this type of talk. Still, this was a trifle more interesting than Robert's letters had been. . . .

"If a man's property can be taken away from him, things have gone too far,'" Robert insisted. "And it's not only our ships, it's our homes as well. We are forced to house Crown troops in our own homes if so ordered. And when our assembly tried to protect us from such a ridiculous law, they were stripped of their power—as if Parliament had appointed them in the first place! It's time we took a firm stand!"

Her father spoke slowly and cautiously, as it had always been his custom to do. "I agree that things have gone too far, but it's absurd to think—as some of you seem to—that we could actually wage a war with England. It's impossible for a million reasons! First, we have no army. Oh, I know we could gather together a group of untrained volunteers, but our militia would hardly be fit to contend with the entire British army! Second, we have no navy. Britain's navy is the finest. Can you imagine what a blockade would do to the colonies? We'd be shut off from the rest of the world! Third, if through some strange quirk of fate we did manage to win a war, what could we do? How could we survive? Certainly not as a separate entity! The basis of our existence is trade with the motherland. The furs, the grain, the lumber, the tobacco—all need to be shipped somewhere. Without our ties with England, our products would have no market, and we would be forced to do without the cloth and manufactured goods we desperately depend on!"

She could see Robert's eyes burning in anticipation of answering his father's challenge. "Our economic dependence is mutual to a great degree, Father. And I, for one, find it impossible to sit back and wait for better times! We have rights as Englishmen, though Parliament seems intent on taking them away. As far as our military strength, your assessment is correct. We have no army as such, yet I know of many men ready to fight before they will submit to this tyranny! And do not forget, Britain will be forced to import all her men and guns, while we merely have to"—he paused to sport a cocky grin—"beg, borrow, or steal what's already here."

"Robert, your youth is painfully obvious," his father sighed. "It is idealistic to want to die for a cause, and it's usually a wasted death." He sipped at his wine, and Juliet proudly recognized the careful reorganization of his thoughts when he spoke again, coolly, convincingly. "The colonies don't have a chance, even if they all banded together—which in itself is an impossibility. We are different peoples with different life-styles. We in New York have nothing to tie us to, say, the planters in Virginia, except our English heritage. If we separate ourselves from that, what have we to bind us but our geographic borders—which have caused more arguments than any tax England has levied on us yet, I might add. I readily supported the nonimportation agreements, but my loyalty cannot permit me to go beyond that point."

For the first time Juliet recognized Alec's deep, lazy drawl, which carried none of the agitation that was evident in Robert's voice. "The colonies are different," he conceded. "Our life in the Tidewater and the Piedmont areas is different from the one you live here in the city. And there have, in the past, been differences between us—petty squabbles over boundaries and such. Yet in this cause I have seen a great deal of agreement, wherever I have been. There are men in every colony who refuse to accept the fact that their elected representatives can be stripped of their power by an order of Parliament, as happened right here in New York. Just a few weeks ago in our own Virginia assembly, a man named Patrick Henry said it well." He hesitated for a thoughtful moment, as if to remember the man's exact words. " 'Is life so dear or peace so sweet as to be purchased at the price of chains and slavery? . . . I know not what course others may take, but as for me, give me liberty or give me death!' "

For a long space of time the room fell silent under the weight of such emotional words. Even Juliet was surprised at the feelings that swept through her as Alec spoke. He continued then, in his casual tone, directing a question at her father.

"Could it be, Mr. Hampton, that the turning point of your loyalty is related to profit?"

Juliet saw her father's eyes narrow as he studied Alec, surprised and caught off guard by the direct accusation. Robert looked from one man to the other, and when his father did not respond he turned to Alec.

"What exactly do you mean?"

"I mean that for some—namely those who had warehouses filled with goods already imported from England—the ban on trade was hardly a patriotic gesture. It made those goods all the more valuable."

Giving Robert scarcely a moment to digest this revelation, he continued to rebut the arguments Hampton had put forth. "You are correct in saying that we cannot wage a war with England easily and without great sacrifice. But I believe that at this particular point in time, there are living more great men than any of us may realize. Men capable of organizing an army, with the help of France and Spain, and perhaps, with some luck, creating a new nation." He stopped and drew a long draft of wine from the glass he held in his hand.

In the uneasy silence that followed his speech it occurred to Juliet that Alexander Farrell was actually a rebel! A traitor! The man was talking treason!

"I am sorry, gentlemen," her father said at length, "but it's nearing noon and I fear that my daughter may be deeply offended if we keep to ourselves any longer. I am quite sure that everything has been arranged for our midday meal. Shall we retire to the dining room?"

Somewhat dazed by all she had heard, Juliet realized with a start that the men were leaving the study, so she lifted her skirts and hurried to the bottom of the stairs just as the door opened wide. With her hand resting lightly on the bannister, she managed to look as if she had just made a graceful descent. The gentlemen greeted her as they exited, and she accepted Robert's arm to be escorted to the dining room, pretending not to notice Rachel, who stood scowling and shaking her head at the top of the stairs, having witnessed the entire episode.

During the luncheon, Juliet managed to keep the attention of everyone at the table, wittily embellishing stories about her years spent away at school. It was Robert who suggested a ride in the countryside following the meal, a suggestion vetoed by her father, who claimed to have pressing business with Captain Barkley.

So it was that Juliet, Robert, and Alec set off on that warm spring afternoon. Juliet had not been riding since her return home, and she was thoroughly exhilarated at giving her mare a free rein. Though she still missed the control of riding astride, she had adapted well to the less comfortable and more proper seat and preferred an even more spirited animal to show off her skill in riding like a lady. She eyed Alec's horse enviously. What a beautiful specimen he was! A stallion, long and lean, with well-defined muscles and an elegant style—the type of animal she had often dreamed of riding to the very limits of his strength.

They rode north for well over an hour, far out into the countryside. When they came upon an absolutely perfect setting of rolling green grass, a few trees filtering the sun's silver rays and a small stream babbling by, they dismounted to rest the horses and silently drink in the lush beauty of nature, breathing deeply and stretching their cramped muscles. Several moments had passed when Robert suddenly made a lame excuse about wanting to see the view from the next hill, then departed without giving anyone else a chance to join him.

Surprised by his rather obvious ruse to leave her alone with Alec, Juliet could not help but wonder if Alec had asked him to arrange the entire scheme. She watched her brother gallop off with a smug smile on his face, then she turned to find that Alec was walking along the brook and seemed intent on throwing pebbles into the water. Obviously he was not the one who arranged this, she chafed silently. She trudged along in his path to a spot where several large trees bent very near the water's edge. Alec stared distantly at the rushing water, alone in his reflections, though Juliet did her best to pry into them.

"Does this place remind you of home?"

"Yes and no," he replied with unmasked disinterest. He did not even bother to look at her and made no attempt to continue the conversation.

Juliet shrugged, having failed to get his attention, and perched herself on a long, flat rock to study Alec's lithe movements in his casual leather and buckskin clothing. It suited him, she thought, better than the laces and silks that were the vogue. He was lean yet broad-shouldered, with an easy grace and natural arrogance that reminded her of a lion, not a peacock, like some of the men she'd known. With a suppressed giggle, she pictured Harold, with his pale skin, his rounded stomach, and his generally less than virile physique, in an outfit of skins and leather. She had never been physically attracted to Harold, but then, so few men had ever appealed to her that way. More than once she had been left completely unaffected by a young man whose mere physical appearance had driven Margaret to distraction.

Juliet's trivial musings fled at once as Alec turned and his eyes found hers. He came to take a seat very near her, and one thought alone suddenly surfaced—she was very much attracted to Alexander Farrell.

Black eyes studied her familiarly, drifting over the entire length of her slender form before returning to meet her gaze. With effort she forced herself to remain aloof and casual under his regard, resisting an impulse to check her hair and smooth her skirt. His continued scrutiny augmented her anxiety until at last she could stand no more. She rose to her feet and took a few steps, glancing about nervously for some sign of her brother's return. But Robert was nowhere in sight, blast him! And he'd put her in this predicament on purpose!

She drew a long, steadying breath and squared her shoulders, turning with renewed resolve to face Alec. When she found him less than an arm's length away, she struggled to suppress a gasp of surprise, for his movement had been so quiet and stealthy that she had been completely unaware of it. With a quick shuffle she retreated instinctively to a more proper distance, a good deal of her determination fading as she made her withdrawal.

"Now why do you suppose," he questioned her thoughtfully, "your brother left us here all alone?"

He closed the distance between them with a single step, and just as quickly she backed away.

"He wanted to see the view from the next hill," she answered with a quivering smile. She felt completely devoured by the look in his eyes, and for a split second she actually considered running away. But it was not in Juliet's nature to admit to fear or defeat, so she stoically stood her ground—or tried to.

"Can you not think of another more . . . interesting reason?" he asked, again advancing a step.

Juliet's eyes widened as she once again withdrew, only to find her back to a giant old oak tree. Before she had recovered enough to sidestep the barrier, Alec's arms took up position on either side of her, effectively trapping her against the rough bark.

"A more interesting reason?" she asked, swallowing hard.

He nodded. "Yes. Something perhaps Robert feels was lacking in your education in England."

He leaned his weight against the tree, his face dangerously close to hers. She gulped and pressed herself hard against its bark, finding his nearness almost suffocating.

"Well?" he whispered, his lips by her ear. The rich timbre of his voice sent a sharp tingle up her spine.

"Well what?" Juliet managed weakly, feeling none of her usual assertiveness. She suddenly found it impossible to draw an even breath! Her eyes darted nervously from the piercing black eyes to the well-defined mouth to the broad chest only inches away from her own heaving breast.

"Julie," he murmured huskily. He shifted his weight to a single arm and casually dropped the other to rest on the deep curve of her waist.

She actually felt faint when he touched her, and the sound of her name rolling smoothly off his tongue was purely and simply sensuous. Her heart fluttered violently like a feather in the wind; she felt her limbs go limp. She could give no reason for what was happening to her, but she knew that it had certainly never happened before and would probably never happen again.

A tremor shook her every nerve when he bent forward to press a warm, lingering kiss to the side of her neck, and her eyes shone at once with a new brilliancy, rivaling the beauty of newly polished gold. Alec took hold of her shoulders and gently pulled her close, his lips hungrily tracing the outline of her ear. Over and over he murmured her name, his mouth moving on to her temple and brushing over her cheek.

He was in no hurry to kiss her. On the contrary, he seemed to tarry until she had long anticipated the feeling before he did so. When her entire body was actually trembling in giddy expectation, his lips touched hers—toying, playing, softly testing, gently extracting a response. He withdrew the slightest bit; she was swift to close the gap until she was leaning full against him, her hands resting on his chest.

Encouraged by her response, Alec quickly retrieved the lead, working his tongue through her warm, yielding lips. He kissed her then in so thorough a manner that her knees felt far too flimsy to support her spinning head. She knew a tingling confusion as her arms found their way to a more secure hold around his neck, while Alec's mouth became even more persistent, destroying her attempts to catch her breath. She was completely unarmed under such an assault. The madness took hold like a fever, and she returned his kiss with a desperate longing for something she did not comprehend. For a long, wondrous moment she felt totally a woman, alive with a newly awakened need. She surrendered unconditionally to that need, and there remained not a single rational thought in her mind. When his lips pulled away from hers, she did not even recognize the mocking gleam in those handsome, smiling black eyes.

"And I thought you might slap me! Poor Harold!" he sighed.

Juliet stared up at him, her eyes still soft and urgent with longing. "Oh, Alec, please don't joke!" she whispered anxiously.

"Julie, dear," he chided, kissing her again, this time a brief, paternal peck. "Ladies don't do any more than we've already done . . . not unless they are married, that is. Perhaps after you and Harold are wed, we might . . ."

It took a moment for full realization to dawn, and then a raging red blaze of anger burst from her, like a rocket in the sky.

"Oh!" she shrieked, pushing him away with every ounce of strength she could muster. "You . . . you . . ."

"Ah, ah!" He waved a finger in front of her. "Remember, ladies know of no appropriate language to use at a time like this. But I would ask you to remember the offer I made, after you are married to the honorable lord. You might feel quite differently about things then. You do still plan to marry Harold, don't you?" He hesitated, watching her for a moment, but she was seething with such fury that she was unable to answer.

"I thought you did," he said coolly, quite unaffected by her murderous stare. "The trouble with you, Julie, is that you expect to be petted, pampered, and treated like a china doll. Nothing in your life is important enough to fight for, to give up for. You, my dear, are a spoiled brat who wants nothing more than to keep on being spoiled.

"I am certain that your fiancé is very rich, very proper, and I'm certain that he can make you very happy. I also know that you don't care a fig about him—you proved that to me just a few moments ago. So I offer you this advice, Julie. Marry him and leave here. Go back to England before the war starts, or you'll find yourself caught somewhere in the middle. You might even have to make a choice between your family and that title you're so interested in adding to your name." This outburst was bitter, emotional, and it flamed Juliet's anger.

"There won't be any war!" she said, trying to conjure up a confidence she was far from feeling. "Why, the colonies haven't an army, much less a navy," she continued, repeating part of what she'd heard that morning. "And besides, even if there were a war, my father is not stupid enough to be a part of it!"

"Perhaps not," he conceded. "But Robert is."

Her angry glare disappeared as she suddenly considered that possibility, and her brow drew together in a worried frown. "But he wouldn't! Robert has everything!"

"Oh, yes! Why should he risk his money, his future, his life for such a hopeless cause? I'll tell you why, Julie, though I doubt you'll understand. Because Robert is a man who believes in something beyond his own little world, and he is willing to risk everything for what he believes in. Because money and luxury are not now, nor have they ever been, so important to him that he would compromise himself for them.

Because, dear Julie, that is not what life is all about, no matter what you may think."

He gave a short, bitter laugh. "I thought perhaps you were still in love with Allan, that you'd planned to marry out of loneliness. But I was wrong. You obviously don't love anyone or anything except yourself!"

Tears stung her eyes at his cruel words, and at that moment she hated him more than she'd ever hated anyone in her life. She had never before shared a kiss with a man beyond a chaste farewell with Harold, and she had not allowed herself to feel anything for anyone since Allan. Now this man had stirred a passion inside her that she had never known existed and had proceeded to betray her feelings! If Robert had not ridden up at that moment, she was certain that she could have killed Alec Farrell with her bare hands.

The ride home was void of the laughter and exuberance that had filled the group when they first rode off. Hardly saying a word, Juliet excused herself promptly and marched directly to her room. But it was much easier to part Alec's company than it was to be free of his strange hold on her, and long hours later she was still trying to reason away the weakness she had felt in his arms.

Chapter 5

Only a few short weeks following the Churches' party,
the City of New York received news of the first fighting of the
war. In Lexington and Concord, two small towns near Boston,
a surprisingly well-organized system of warning sentries and
local militia had proved itself willing and able to face the
British troops. Patriots in New York, who had begun to organize their discontent the previous year by sending delegates
to the Continental Congress and setting up several committees, now made haste to take over local government. The Customs House was seized, and arms, stolen from British military stores throughout the city, were distributed to those who
supported the cause. While Boston became a city at war with
the British, New York became a city at war with itself, as a
great number of its citizens held fast their loyalty to the
Crown.

The differences that occurred almost overnight now that
actual fighting had begun amazed Juliet. The men who had
peacefully debated politics at social functions no longer did
so. Loyalists avoided associations with patriots, and patriots
in turn avoided loyalists. Women began talking of the consequences of war, each solemnly repeating what opinions she
had been told to adopt by her menfolk. Distrust and suspicion
were everywhere; everyone lived in fear of the coming war.
Worst of all for Juliet, Hampton House became a battlefield
in its own right, with Robert and Father arguing endlessly,
morning, noon, and night. At first Juliet had strained to hear
their discussions, and had even pressed her ear to the door of

her father's study, not wanting to miss a single word. Now, a few weeks later, she descended the stairs and turned resolutely away from the sound of still another heated argument, walking instead into the empty parlor. Try as she might to keep her concentration on her long-neglected stitchery, the angry voices penetrated.

"There is such a thing as justice, Father."

"And such a thing as stupidity," her father returned. "You know nothing of what life is really about, Robert. I suppose that's my fault—you've always had everything money could buy. But take my word, you do not want to know what it is like to live without wealth."

"That is the only thing that really matters to you, isn't it?" Robert accused bitterly. "Alec was right—your only loyalty is to profit."

"I am loyal to the King, but I admit that I am also loyal to myself. That is something you must learn, Robert, that you owe your first loyalty to yourself, not a cause."

"And how can I be loyal to myself if I do not do what I know is right?"

"You only think war is right because you've listened to those hotheaded radicals—the Sons of Liberty, or whoever. Listen to *me* now! No one respects poverty; no one respects a failure. Self-respect is bought and paid for, and it won't come from fighting in some ridiculous war."

"You talk as if I were a child, Father," Robert protested. "I'm not! I can decide for myself what is right and wrong."

"And I suppose what is right is fighting in a fool's army? If there were an even chance that you could succeed, I might at least be able to understand. But we are talking about the entire British army, not to mention the navy! I cannot believe that you would be such a fool!"

No longer able to endure the tedious work or the endless stream of hostile words, Juliet retreated to her room. There she assembled the clothing she would wear to pose for Mr. Blackmoor, a highly respected artist her father had commissioned to do her portrait.

Jason Blackmoor was a rather eccentric and temperamental man who worked only under specified conditions. Apparently his patience had been spent in building a reputation for himself as an artist, for now he accepted only subjects he felt merited his talents, demanding that they pose stoically for as long as the natural lighting was just so, or whenever he felt himself appropriately inspired. He was a slight man, dark of skin, with a straight, almost pointed nose, extremely thin lips, and large, expressive eyes that often seemed ready to burst from their sockets. He could bellow like a giant and was never intimidated by anyone, even those of far greater stature than he. The sittings had proven difficult, but Juliet had resolved to endure them, for her portrait would be the only remembrance of her at Hampton House when she left for England.

She laid her gown out on the bed, carefully stretching each tiny fold that fell from the waist as she smoothed the deep blue fabric. The fine silk was a magnificent blend of blue and silver trimmed demurely in cream-colored lace, though the cut of the gown was anything but demure. Juliet had purchased it and several others just prior to leaving England, and though she had fallen in love with the fabric, she had felt quite uncomfortable in its revealing lines. She had considered ordering the seamstress to alter it to something more conservative, but at Margaret's insistence had finally accepted and paid for the gown as it was. She had chosen a more modest gown the day Mr. Blackmoor had come to do preliminary sketches, but when Rachel had offered some slight criticism of the color, Juliet had changed to the blue in a fit of temper, knowing her maid would object to it even more fiercely than the other. Later she had found cause to regret her hasty decision when she encountered Robert's wide-eyed stare and a matching look from her father, though neither had made any comment. Margaret would be proud of me, anyway, she thought wryly, sighing away her own misgivings and calling for Rachel to help her.

The maid entered her room promptly, eyed the dress she had laid out, and flashed Juliet her usual disapproving frown before helping her out of her chintz morning dress. Juliet took a seat before her vanity and watched Rachel's skilled fingers arrange her hair in a mass of curls high atop her head. Saying not a word when she had finished, the slender gray-haired woman lifted the gown from the bed and carefully dropped it over the newly arranged coiffure. Nimble fingers worked the numerous fastenings at the back and smoothed the deep blue folds that fell from the tightly fitted waist, while Juliet idly fingered the delicate flounces of lace that trimmed the ends of snug-fitting half-sleeves.

The clock in the upstairs hall chimed twelve times as her toilet was completed. It would be another hour before the artist began his work, Juliet thought with a sigh. She watched without interest as Rachel gathered up her discarded clothing and returned each item to its proper place, then dismissed her as soon as she was finished with the task. When the door had closed behind her, Juliet stepped before the full-length looking glass to study the woman who returned her stare. Thick, shiny hair framed a delicate face; eyes shone bright and clear beneath jet-black lashes. Ivory shoulders and a daring expanse of creamy skin were laid bare above the lace-edged blue, leaving little of the full contours of her breasts to the imagination. Juliet frowned at the incongruity of such enticing attire and the vulnerability in her warm brown eyes. She lifted her chin and lowered the lids of her eyes, allowing her lips to curve at the corners into a tempting smile, then letting it deepen to one of blatant seduction. As she appraised the alien reflection, a fantasy of ebony eyes caught hopelessly in the trap of that smile danced through her mind. How sweet the taste of her revenge could she bait Alec with such a smile, tempt him until he begged for her favors, then turn him arrogantly away. The smile faded, and she scolded herself for thinking again of the man who so obviously despised her.

She had made a very bad mistake forgetting herself in his arms that afternoon, a mistake she vowed never to repeat. He had awakened a part of her that she had never even known existed, an untamed part that craved the warmth and excitement she had felt at the touch of his mouth on hers. Since that day, she often woke at night from deepest slumber for no apparent reason, disturbed by a penetrating feeling of loneliness, an overwhelming desire to be held and loved. She dared not question why it had been Alec who had drawn such feelings from within her, while other men had left her unaffected. She would only admit that it would give her pleasure to hurt him, to awaken the same desires in him and then to cast him aside. But that was only a fantasy, for Juliet had come to realize fully the hypnotic effect of those black eyes and wisely planned to stay clear of his company. She had refused Frances

Church's repeated invitations to tea, fearing a confrontation with the man, and planned to excuse herself for as long as Alec remained in New York. Perhaps it would be the one good thing to happen if there really was a war—surely then he would be gone for good! But then, so might Robert . . .

With a thoughtful frown she walked to the window and pulled aside a dainty lace curtain, observing her father as he left the house. She let out a long sigh of relief. At least there would be a measure of peace until he returned.

Juliet descended the stairs and walked to the last and largest room in the west wing of the house. The room had always been a favorite of hers, especially when the dark-green draperies were drawn back from the many paned windows that covered the greater part of three walls, as they were now. Mr. Blackmoor arrived several minutes early as had been his custom, and positioned Juliet just so, lifting her chin so that light and shadows fell in a manner identical to the day before. She forced herself to hold the exacting pose, concentrating on trivialities to help pass the time and to keep her face void of all expression. She counted how many breaths she took, how many times she blinked, how many muscles she could feel rebelling against the forced relaxation. It was not an easy task to pose for a man who worked hours at a time without a word. The endless hours of silence at St. Bride's had not been useless after all, she mused.

After a while, when Juliet had begun to feel completely numb, Robert entered the room, quietly crossing over to where Juliet could see him. He flashed her a full grin, which she attempted to return with her eyes. With exaggerated gestures he waved and pointed to the artist, then walked out of her sight so that he might scrutinize the incomplete work. Jason Blackmoor continued his labors, seemingly oblivious of another's presence in the room. Robert watched with admiration as the man chose his colors and dabbed repeatedly at the canvas, angrily, thoughtfully, timidly. It was exciting to observe an artist at work, with each stroke breathing life into his painting, but Robert's eyes drifted toward the even more fascinating subject, now unmindful of his close inspection. Indeed, she was the perfect subject for a painting, he thought with a good measure of pride, though he did not approve of her chosen attire. It seemed enough to him that no one ever forgot her bright smile or golden eyes; Robert saw no need for flaunting her more private attractions. But he had to remember that Juliet was a woman now—that was obvious—and he was fairly certain that his advice would be no more welcome than Rachel's.

Two brief raps at the half-opened door caught Robert's attention, and he turned just as Malcolm, the butler, entered and announced a guest in his deep voice, lowered so as not to disturb the artist. "Master Robert, you instructed me to show Mr. Farrell in directly on his arrival." With a short bow, Malcolm left the room.

Before Malcolm had even announced it, Juliet had felt Alec's presence, and it became impossible at once to maintain her elegant pose, her impassive expression. Her breaths became shallow and shaky, her throat so dry and tight that she was forced to swallow several times in succession. How provoking that he should come here like this! To her own home! Invading her privacy! And blast Robert for his part in this! Why, if she didn't know better, she'd swear he was trying to play matchmaker. Well, Juliet Hampton did not need anyone's help in finding a man. She had done perfectly well all by herself!

The conversation that ensued was hushed, but the sounds drifted throughout the otherwise silent room.

"I got your note, Alec. Is there more news from Boston?"

"No, but I plan to leave for Virginia at dawn, day after tomorrow, and I did want to see you before I left New York. How are things with your father?"

Robert sighed his despair. "I feel very much like I have been trying to talk the sun out of rising."

"I understand exactly what you mean. Perhaps by the time I return you'll have made some progress."

"It's no use, Alec. I'm afraid he's even more stubborn than I!"

Alec chuckled softly at that. "My own father was every bit the same. Give it some time before you come to any decision, Robert. You have nothing to lose and everything to gain."

His quiet words were directed at her brother, yet Juliet felt his black eyes fall on her bared flesh as surely as she felt the sunlight. The blush in her cheeks deepened and grew hot, and to her utter mortification, she began to tremble.

"Please! Miss Hampton!" the artist snapped irritably. "You could not possibly be cold! You must be still!"

Her temper just barely held in check, Juliet took a deep breath and clenched her teeth tightly together, concentrating with all her might.

Robert noted with satisfaction where his friend's eyes were drawn time and again during their conversation. There was something between them, he was sure, something more than the animosity apparent on the surface. It was probably only that Juliet refused to admit that she liked Alec, and liked him quite a bit.

Robert gazed thoughtfully at Alec. Why couldn't she see that he was a good deal like her? A man whose pride and spirit matched her own. Fully aware of the disturbance they were creating, Robert resumed the conversation. Another confrontation between the two could do no harm, he reasoned.

"When do you plan to return?"

"In a month, perhaps a bit longer. I have quite a few things to settle at home myself. Do your best to work things out while I'm away, and we'll see how they stand when I return. Your father may yet see the light."

Though the conversation ended there, Alec made no move to leave, for he was completely captivated by a living, breathing work of art on display in the far corner of the room. His eyes roamed hungrily over the thick, radiant curls, bewitching honey-colored eyes, soft, full mouth, and gracefully tapering neck, and finally rested on the rounded contours of ivory skin generously visible above the low neckline. Juliet Hampton was enough to drive any man to distraction. Forgetting Robert for the moment, he strolled toward the artist to briefly examine the work, then continued casually on until he faced Juliet. Her eyes narrowed and brightened as they met his, and for a long moment the room remained so quiet that every brush stroke on the canvas could be heard. All at once the silence was shattered with a slash, and the artist flew at his painting, ruining what it had taken long, exhausting hours to create. The little man tossed his brush to the floor, where it landed with a precipitate snap.

"I am an artist!" he shouted furiously, raising clenched fists high into the air. "I must have quiet, and I do not work with an audience!" He turned an accusing eye on Alec, who stood a full head taller, before he began to gather his tools. He retrieved the discarded brush and packed it and everything meticulously away, ignoring Juliet's attempts to placate him.

"I am sorry for the interruption, Mr. Blackmoor, but if I heard correctly, Mr. Farrell was just about to leave." She flashed Alec a wrathful glare. "Can't we please continue?"

"Absolutely not! My inspiration is gone! I work without interruption, or I work not at all!" he declared dramatically.

Within minutes he had finished cleaning his brushes and arranging his colors just so.

"Tomorrow?" Juliet ventured timidly.

"Perhaps," came the curt reply. He turned back one last time before marching out of the room, to add in a voice that shook with emotion, "But no interruptions!"

Juliet grimaced and drew a lengthy breath, raising her hand to the back of her neck and massaging the muscles that had grown stiff and uncomfortable during the long session. When she looked up, her eyes locked with Alec's, and her face quickly changed to reflect every bit of the resentment she felt. He was totally to blame for the artist's fit of temper! How she hated him!

Though she was suddenly very tired, she haughtily lifted her chin and sauntered toward the door. He was not even worth talking to, she told herself. As she passed by him, Alec took hold of her hand, and the tingling warmth she felt at his touch kindled such rage that only Robert's presence prevented her from tearing those black devil's eyes from his face.

"I came to say good-bye," he said easily, briefly touching her hand to his lips.

"And now you have done so," she snapped with arrogant finality.

Ignoring her haughty anger, he let his eyes fall boldly to her breast and continued, "I should like to see more of you when I return."

"That will be impossible. I believe I informed you that I intend to be married in the autumn."

"Ah, yes! Harold," he answered with a smile.

"Lord Harold," she corrected pointedly.

"I shall return long before he arrives," he assured her, "and I look forward to seeing your finished portrait."

Thanks to you it may never even be finished, she thought,

but she bit back her retort, realizing that it would have no effect, and directed her iciest stare to the hand that Alec still held in his long, dark fingers. Reluctantly he released it, and she walked from the room without a backward glance.

Alec observed the enticing swirls of blue and silver until they had disappeared, then waited until the last faint footfall had sounded in the main hall. He was jarred back to consciousnes when Robert noisily cleared his throat and raised his brows in a quizzical expression, obviously demanding an explanation for what had just occurred.

Alec's mouth fell into any easy smile as he understated dryly, "I don't believe your sister is very fond of me."

"On the contrary," Robert was quick to return, "she likes you very much! She just doesn't want to admit it yet."

"And how does one go about making her admit it?" he queried, his interest aroused.

"It just takes a little time, that's all."

"Precisely what Harold intends to prevent her from having."

"I know," Robert agreed. A long, troubled sigh removed all levity from his tone. "I believe she's trying to prove something by marrying him, though I cannot figure out exactly what it is . . . unless she wants to prove she can make herself miserable. She usually manages to do an excellent job of that!" Robert sighed again and thoughtfully rubbed his chin, wishing that he could do something to change the course of his sister's life.

The two men shared a warm handshake and repeated their farewells as Robert walked with Alec through the corridor to the main door.

Rachel was waiting to help her out of the fragile silk gown when Juliet returned to her bedroom. She efficiently chose and laid out her mistress's proper dinner attire before leaving Juliet to herself. Clad only in a thin chemise, Juliet tossed and turned on her featherbed, unable to ease the tension in muscles held so long taut. The better part of an hour passed, and she rose and paced aimlessly about her room, still finding no peace for her troubled mind. She returned to her bed, rolling over onto her stomach and resting her chin on her hands, one atop the other. As she contemplated her slightly distorted reflection in the highly polished wooden headboard, a troubled frown drew her brows together, and her eyes began to fill with tears. It had been years since she had cried, but now it was a real struggle to hold back a flood of emotion, to retain any composure at all in the face of this sudden despondency.

Somewhere she had made a very bad mistake, but she was not ready to recognize what that mistake was. She only knew that in spite of all her careful planning, something was gravely wrong. The feeling was not an unfamiliar one. There had been countless occasions in the past when she had confronted the same confusion and discouragement, had felt that no matter what she did, her life was ill-fated.

"Face it," she advised her blurred reflection. "There is something very wrong with you. When you fancy yourself a temptress, you are caught in your own trap by your emotions. When you fancy yourself a lady, you have trouble holding your temper, and you despise working the simplest bit of stitchery. And Harold . . ." She gave a short, mirthless laugh. "The only thing you've ever done that Father seems to approve of. But it is not the same pride he feels for Robert, and no matter what you do it will never be the same."

She laid her cheek on her hand, wishing that somehow everything in her life would magically fall into place. Each day only brought more disturbing questions, and no easy answers. A few short weeks earlier, the thought of being Harold's wife had not been at all troubling—even "that part" of marriage she had seen as something a woman must learn to accept. She had been so sure that Margaret had lied about the excitement a kiss could hold, the passion a touch could evoke. Had she never met Alec and briefly tasted these things for herself, she would never have doubted her ability to give herself to Harold. But now, each time the image of herself sharing his bed came to mind, she swiftly chased it away. Even more frightening was a vision of another sort, of a wild and purely wondrous rapture bursting inside her, which always included a pair of lean muscled arms and dark, penetrating eyes.

Juliet rose with a reluctant sigh when Rachel entered her room to help her dress for dinner. She shook her head and smoothed out the furrows in her brow, trying to dispel the thoughts that tormented her. Everything will work itself out when Harold arrives, she told herself over and over again. I only have to wait until then.

Later that evening Juliet wrote a brief note to Frances, accepting her invitation to tea for Sunday afternoon. Alec would be leaving New York at dawn, Mr. Blackmoor never painted on Sundays, and there was no further need to make excuses. She felt relieved when she had finished and sealed the note, and for the first night in many she found it easy to fall asleep, assured in the knowledge that she would not be confronted by Alec for the next few weeks.

Chapter 6

Sundays began early for the Hampton family, with a light breakfast at eight o'clock followed by preparations for the Sunday worship at Trinity Church. For as long as Juliet could remember, Lawrence Hampton had attended Sunday services in his designated pew at the front of the church. Though he was not a religious man, he had always felt that regular attendance at church was a necessary part of the favorable image essential to a successful businessman.

Sunday's obligation complete, the Hamptons returned home for the midday meal. The usual steady flow of conversation was absent as Juliet, Robert, and their father took their dinner this Sunday. Robert seemed anxious to be off somewhere and spent only minutes at the table, doing little justice to the carefully prepared eggs, smoked meats, and muffins. When he excused himself and left, Juliet found that she, too, had little appetite. She thoughtfully toyed with what food remained on the fine china plate, while her father ate with his usual enthusiasm, reading a newspaper and taking little note of anyone else at the table. He had finished his meal and was preparing a cup of tea when he folded the newspaper and put it aside.

"Well, Juliet," he said, as if he only now recognized her presence. "It is good to have you home."

"I have been home for almost two months now, Father," she reminded him, rather surprised by his comment. "And in another few months I suppose that I will be leaving again."

"Yes, of course," he agreed wistfully. "Both my children

want to leave the home I've made for them here." He paused and sighed. "I assume you know that Robert wants to leave and join the fighting." He watched her carefully for a reaction. If he was to win her to his side of the argument, he had to proceed with caution, for he was well aware of her attachment to her brother.

"Yes. It has been almost impossible not to overhear your arguments, Father."

Pain was evident in his voice when he spoke again. "I suppose it has. I am sorry, Juliet. You have returned home at a rather inopportune time. Selfishly, I am happy to have you here because I need you. You are a great comfort to me. But a part of me is happier knowing you will soon be back in England, safely away from this dangerous nonsense. Have you had any correspondence from Lord Harold?"

"No, but he promised to write as soon as his traveling arrangements were finalized, so I should be hearing from him any day now."

Juliet smiled warmly at her father, happier than she had been in months. This was as it should be, as she had dreamed it might be. Her father sharing a conversation with her alone! He had said that he needed her, that he was happy to have her home!

He returned her smile for a moment, then let it fade. Juliet's smile also disappeared, and her heart went out to this man, obviously torn apart by the knowledge that soon his children would leave him all alone.

"Your brother has caused me so much worry of late, Juliet. I cannot understand why he would want to be so foolish! If only he would listen to me! These past few weeks he has actually tried to convince me to pledge my money and my ships for the rebellion! Everything I have ever worked for, he wants to throw away on a hopeless cause! But worst of all, he wants to throw his own life away!" His brow was heavily creased with sadness, his voice low yet emotional. "Why would he do this, after everything I have given him?"

Juliet's eyes filled with tears, and she timidly laid a hand on her father's arm. She wanted so much to comfort him, but what could she say to ease his troubles? She swallowed hard and shook her head.

"It's not you, Father. Alec said that Robert believes in

something beyond money, something I really do not understand, either," she admitted.

Her father's blue eyes became cold at once, and something about his voice frightened her. "Alec?"

She quickly withdrew her hand from his arm, and her face grew quite red as she stared down at her lap. "Alexander Farrell. You . . . you met him. He came to lunch one day a few weeks ago."

"I know the man to whom you refer. However, I had no idea that you were on such friendly terms with him."

Juliet faced her father directly with her denial. "I'm not. . . I . . . It's only that . . . he is Frances's cousin and also a friend of Robert's . . ." Her voice trailed off lamely.

"He is no friend of your brother! Make no mistake about that! The man is a radical, a born troublemaker. He left Virginia and came here for the sole purpose of stirring up dissension, and he will not be satisfied until he has seen bloodshed. The one and only reason he was ever permitted in this house is his relationship to the Church family. He is welcome here no more. And Edgar Church, if he comes to his senses, will refuse to receive him also, blood or not."

Juliet swallowed a very large lump in her throat. Obviously her father did not know of Alec's visit two days before. She would be very careful not to mention that to him, or how things were going with her portrait. There was a long silence before her father resumed the conversation, his voice again composed.

"You are going to tea this afternoon at the Church home?"

Juliet's eyes were wide with surprise. Her father rarely took note of her comings and goings, and she was certain that she had not mentioned her plans for the afternoon to him.

"Why, yes, but . . . Frances told me . . . that Mr. Farrell has already left New York." Juliet avoided her father's eyes and scarcely took a breath for fear he might already know more about her feelings for Alec than she had ever dreamed of admitting. It seemed everything she said only announced her guilt, though she could not understand why she felt so guilty when she was telling the truth about hating him.

She relaxed a bit when her father rose, draining the last bit of tea from his cup.

"Give my regards to Elizabeth and Frances, will you?"

He dabbed twice at his mouth with a linen napkin and was almost out of the room when Juliet stopped him.

"Father?"

"Yes?" He turned back to face her.

"How did you know about tea today with Frances?"

"Oh," he smiled, "I believe Rachel mentioned it to me."

At three o'clock in the afternoon the carriage pulled to a stop before the Church home. Though there were no rolling grounds and shady trees framing the white-columned house, there was something serene about its graceful line, a peaceful welcome that was missing from the Hamptons' stately red brick.

Juliet was met promptly at the door by the family's butler and led to the small parlor, where Frances and Mary Church sat chatting on the settee and Elizabeth rested in a high-backed brocade chair. When Juliet was announced Elizabeth immediately rose and came to greet her.

Mistress Church was a woman of average height with soft silver-blonde hair mixed with hardly noticeable streaks of gray. Nearly everyone who met her said that she was a beauty, for all her forty-odd years, though few realized that her regular features were a very small part of her loveliness. Elizabeth Church exuded a warmth that was unmistakable and that made her more than the perfect hostess, it made her a dear friend. Her smile and brief embrace affected Juliet in the usual way, making her happy that she had decided to visit. Frances rose and copied her mother's example, and though Juliet returned her cordial greeting, she felt no affection for the woman who had captured her brother's heart.

At age seventeen Frances was a slight, frail creature, with very little color in her cheeks or small cupid's-bow mouth, or even in her wide, innocent blue eyes. She looked very much like a child and had always reminded Juliet of the cherubs whose sweet, angelic faces adorned paintings of the saints. Frances lived in her mother's shadow. She was naive and shy and otherwise totally frivolous—or so thought Juliet.

Mary timidly extended a hand to grasp Juliet's, her smile quivering a bit and her eyes meeting Juliet's only for a moment before dropping to the floor. In spite of her resolution to feel no jealousy for the woman, Juliet's injured pride could not help but wonder again at Allan's choice.

Conversation flowed rather well, with Juliet and Elizabeth carrying it for the most part. Nothing more serious than the ordinary "woman talk" was brought up: who had married recently, who had given birth, who had moved away, what this or that woman was wearing, and the newest ideas on fixing the high, elaborate hairdos so popular in Europe. It was not long before Elizabeth brought up the subject of Juliet's fiancé.

"We were all very excited at the news, Juliet! Do tell us how you met him."

Juliet smiled at the three attentive faces so anxious to have firsthand information about her intended.

"Harold's sister is a dear friend of mine from school, and she invited me to her home several times. That is how we met."

Her answer was hardly satisfactory for Elizabeth, who wanted more intimate details, not just basic facts. "Well? Tell us about him, Juliet!" she demanded. "Is he handsome? I'm sure he is! What is he like, for heaven's sake? What was it about him that stole your heart?"

Juliet paused a moment before answering, trying very hard to imagine herself hopelessly in love with Harold.

"He is only a trifle taller than I, and he has wonderful blue eyes and a pleasant voice, and he is extremely considerate." Particularly of his mother, she added to herself.

"As for what made me fall in love with him . . ." The lie felt bitter in her mouth, but she forced herself to continue. ". . . I cannot truly say what that was. We do not choose to love someone, it just happens." Her last words died on her lips as her eyes were drawn to a handsome dark figure lounging in the doorway. She blinked several times, unable to believe he was there. Surely she was imagining him! He was supposed to have left at dawn!

Elizabeth rose, setting her cup on the table, and took a few steps toward her nephew. "Alec!" she said, the surprise evident in her voice. "Why, I thought you'd left hours ago! Don't tell me the horses you've been breeding in Virginia are that fast!"

Alec smiled. "You're right, Aunt Elizabeth. I did leave hours ago, but Cheval lost a shoe, and I had to walk him for miles before I could have it replaced. It was very careless of me. By the time I was ready to ride again it was so late that I came back here to spend the night . . . and begin again tomorrow. I hope that I am still welcome?"

His aunt's smile dispelled any doubts. "Of course! You are well aware that you are my favorite nephew."

"I am your *only* nephew," he corrected.

"The two are completely unrelated, if you will excuse the play on words! You are probably starving, Alec. We have plenty of those silly little cakes here—the type you men despise. But they ought to hold you until dinner." She had taken him by the hand and drawn him into the room, offering him an almost untouched plate of petits fours.

"I really wouldn't want to intrude," he protested feebly, accepting the platter from his aunt.

"Nonsense! The one thing every room full of women needs is a man, and a handsome one at that! And you will not be interrupting at all. We are all family here." She flashed Juliet a winning smile, which was answered with a rather wan grin.

"Girls, Alec's horse lost a shoe," she announced as if they had not heard his explanation for themselves, "and he had to come back."

"How very unfortunate!" Juliet said, her cold stare leaving Alec no doubt as to the meaning of her remark.

"You have met Miss Hampton, haven't you, Alec? Of course you have!" Elizabeth returned to her seat while Alec strode to the mantel, propping an elbow on its ledge to study the cakes.

"Juliet was just telling us about her fiancé, Lord Harold Medford. Do go on, Juliet."

"Yes, do go on, Juliet," Alec repeated innocently.

Elizabeth's brows rose sharply as Alec called Juliet by her first name, but no one else seemed to notice the slip, and Juliet continued serenely, keeping her eyes carefully averted.

"There is very little left to say. We plan to marry here in the autumn, and then, of course, we will live in England on his country estate."

"Oh, I do hope the fighting doesn't disturb your plans! But even if there are problems I am certain that you two young people will overcome them." Elizabeth spoke with confidence. "I think that love is wonderful, but I thank God that I am past all that! I can recall so well how Mr. Church turned my whole world upside down! I thought of no one else day and night for weeks after I met him. Every time I closed my eyes I saw him, and every time I opened them—well, he was never very far away. I believe that love is something like fate. We may as well give in to it, because it's going to catch us one way or another! My poor mother certainly could have saved herself some pain by letting things happen as they would. Although now, with children of my own, I understand how difficult it was for her with me and Mr. Church—and with Jerome and your mother, Alec."

Focusing her attention on her nephew as she included him in her last remark, Elizabeth was taken by surprise by the way his black eyes boldly touched Juliet with an intimate look she instantly recognized—the look of a man in love. To her complete astonishment Juliet met his gaze with a fiery one of her own—somehow angry, somehow frightened, a look of intense and clashing emotions. Elizabeth politely turned her attention to her cup of tea and gave no sign that she had been witness to the obvious show of private feelings. Clearing her throat a trifle nervously, she tactfully changed the subject.

"Tell us how Robert is, Juliet. He visits here so seldom anymore. Where has the boy been keeping himself?"

Juliet saw that Frances nearly sprang from her seat at the mention of Robert's name.

"He's doing well, but he and Father have had quite a few disagreements lately about the war and politics. I'm afraid my brother has been influenced by some rather radical persons who would like nothing better than to see bloodshed over a silly tax on tea." Her eyes flicked over Alec suggestively.

"You must think very little of your brother's ability to decide right from wrong, Miss Hampton," Alec remarked.

"Not at all, Mr. Farrell. Robert is intelligent, but he is also noble. There are those who would take advantage of his nobility."

To her surprise it was Frances who responded to her remark, her soft voice strong with conviction. "Robert has always been committed to what is right and honest and good. And as you say, Juliet, he is intelligent, so that we must respect his decision whether or not we agree with it."

"I was born in Virginia, and things are very different here in New York," Elizabeth said. "But I am accustomed to men taking rather radical stands against taxation. When I was a young girl the men spoke of practically nothing else! Perhaps it was one of the things I found attractive in Mr. Church. He has very little interest in politics. The situation here disturbs him a great deal. It is all so strange! To have the British troops driven out of the city, to have guns passed out to everyone, not knowing who is running the government, and wondering what terrible thing might happen next! Mr. Church wants to leave New York, to travel on the Continent until all this has passed and things are more settled. It might be a wise precaution."

"You are thinking of leaving the city?" Juliet asked, astonished.

"Mr. Church has spoken of it. But, of course, things may settle themselves, and it may never come to pass."

Elizabeth's words did little in the way of reassuring Juliet, who had seen the resigned sadness in Frances's eyes when the subject was broached. Apparently this was not the first time the idea had been discussed.

"More tea, Juliet?" Elizabeth offered, to break the troubled silence that had settled on the room.

"Yes, please. I do so love real tea! I cannot accustom myself to the strange stuff served as a substitute. It seems ridiculous to make everyone suffer so that a few insurgents can prove a point." She let her eyes touch Alec in a subtle accusation.

"You seem to be under a misguided assumption, Miss Hampton. The fighting is over unjust taxation, not tea. If only it were so simple!"

"Since when is Britain's taxation of her colonies unjust, Mr. Farrell?" Juliet demanded.

"All taxation is unjust unless levied by duly elected representatives of those to be taxed. Governments exist to serve the governed, not themselves."

Juliet allowed her lips to curve into an indulgent smile. "My, my, Mr. Farrell! You Virginians certainly do have an original view of politics. Absurd, but original."

"Would that Virginians could lay claim to the formulation of such an idea!" he returned, quite unaffected by her arrogance. "But we cannot accept credit where it is not due. The idea of the natural right of people to change a government when it no longer serves to protect their basic rights of life, liberty, and property belongs to an Englishman by the name of John Locke."

Juliet's smile faded in the face of his cool response. "I suppose that there aren't enough malcontents here in the colonies! Did you search him out in England while you were there?"

It was Alec's turn to smile indulgently at her ignorance. "I'm afraid that I never had the pleasure of meeting Mr. Locke. You see, he wrote his *Essay Concerning Human Understanding* before the beginning of this century."

She had been momentarily bested by her lack of knowledge, but Juliet was not ready to concede. Her father had said that Alec was a bloodthirsty radical, and it should not be so difficult to expose him for what he was. If only she knew more about the subject! Why hadn't she taken closer note of Robert's letters?

"What else did Mr. Locke say in this essay?" she inquired, hoping to find a flaw in his argument and pounce on it.

"He said that man's ideas are learned, not naturally present at birth; that one must search for knowledge not only from books and teachers, but from feeling, hearing, touching, seeing. He said that God gave us natural laws to live by, but enforcement of these laws is up to us. Government is the natural evolution of the mutual agreement of man to enforce the natural rights of life, liberty, and property. Therefore, absolute government defies the natural law of God."

"It seems to me, Mr. Farrell, that the *Essay Concerning Human Understanding* is a misnomer. Mr. Locke obviously had no understanding of accepting one's station in life. Surely you don't believe that servants are born equal to nobility! Mr. Locke would have us believe that a king is born to serve a peasant! What a ridiculous thought!" Juliet's smile prematurely touted her victory, for Alec was far from admitting defeat.

"There are a great many perceptive people who find the idea intriguing, Miss Hampton—people who have nothing to fear concerning their own intelligence, that is. But it can be quite an unsettling concept for someone unsure of his own worth, and particularly for someone who expects recognition solely on the merits of a prestigious birth."

"Well, I must admit it is an interesting topic for conversation," interrupted Elizabeth, nervous at the hostility growing heavy in the room. "Would you care for tea, Alec?"

"No, thank you, Aunt Elizabeth. Forgive me for going on like this. I am not accustomed to the trivialities of a ladies' tea, but I am sure your conversation is usually far less intense."

"Dear Alec! You remind me so much of my father, your namesake. He, too, was a man who knew his mind and followed it—until he met your grandmother, that is; then he followed his heart."

Alec lifted the platter of tiny cakes and strolled over to where his aunt sat. He leaned over and placed the plate on the serving table, then bent to kiss his aunt's cheek.

"I believe I will excuse myself, Aunt Elizabeth. It has been a long day, despite the fact that not much has been accomplished."

"Nonsense, Alec! You have been charming! But I understand that you must be tired. Go along now, and I won't make you feel guilty about leaving us."

With a terse nod to each of the other three ladies in the room, Alec was gone. Only Elizabeth noticed the look of regret that entered Juliet's arrogant eyes for an instant, and then disappeared.

Chapter 7

The day was so dark and gray that it was difficult to tell exactly when dawn separated itself from night. Overcast skies shrouded a relentless sun but did little to alleviate the premature moist summer heat that had penetrated everything, day and night, for nearly a week. Each day the air was heavy with the promise of rain, yet each night saw that promise unfulfilled.

Juliet awoke to the same gray skies, the same uncomfortable humidity, the same angry voices that had awakened her for several days. She slipped out of her rumpled bed and lifted the heavy braid from her neck to frown out on the dull June morning. Then came a knock on the door, and Rachel entered. A satisfied smile on her tired face, she ceremoniously offered Juliet a sealed parchment envelope.

"It be from Lord Medford, to be sure. It's not to be so long before we see you married and back off to England where you belong." Rachel had never bothered to hide the fact that she was anxious for Juliet to marry, and she had told her in no uncertain terms that leaving a man might well mean losing him. But Juliet knew her own mind, and unsolicited advice had never been very effective where she was concerned. Rachel's smile faded as Juliet's pleased expression changed to a disappointed frown.

"Well?" She waited a moment for information that was not forthcoming, then pressed Juliet again. "Well? When be Lord Medford arriving?"

Juliet drew a deep breath and stared blankly at the parchment she had dropped in her lap. "Harold's mother is ill, and he is afraid to leave her side. He's made no arrangements to come here."

Rachel's frustration at learning the wedding would not take place as planned was reflected in her angry tone. "Be that all he says?"

"He says that he knows I will understand, and that if I cannot return to England before then, he hopes to sail in the spring."

"In the spring?" she repeated in disbelief. "In the spring! Well, then, we be packing your things immediately. You can yet be married in the autumn—in England."

"No," Juliet said quietly.

"No? Think, girl! The man says he *may* be here in the spring, which implies that he may not! Men do get lonely, you know, and a warm companion is never very difficult for a rich, important man to find."

"No," Juliet repeated in a distant voice.

"You can come home any time after you be married."

Rachel's badgering hacked away at Juliet's forced control. "I will not be married without my father and my brother and everyone else who is important to me! Harold agreed to that before I left, and he is the one who broke that agreement—not I!"

"And if he should find someone else? You be taking a terrible chance that you will lose him."

"No!" Juliet shouted, rising from her bed. "If I must live with his mother the rest of my life, then he must at least come here and give me the wedding he promised!"

Rachel bit back the words that flew to her mind as Juliet bitterly crumpled the neat white parchment in her hands and threw it angrily across the room. Then the younger woman turned abruptly to her wardrobe and searched out her brown riding habit. She went about dressing herself, disregarding Rachel's protests and refusing to wear more than a thin chemise beneath her garments in this blistering heat. Tossing aside the heavy brown velvet jacket, Juliet donned a white linen shirt with a small frill of lace at the throat, and a long skirt, realizing that Rachel was absolutely scandalized by her scanty attire.

"I am going for a ride, not visiting, Rachel! And I shall return to the house well before noon."

She unfastened her braided hair and impatiently combed her fingers through the long, dark strands, finally pulling them back again into a simple knot, which she secured hurriedly at the nape of her neck. Rachel remained silent, though she glared her disapproval at the younger woman, who was already pulling on her riding gloves. It had been a long time since she had seen Juliet's temper surface to such an extent, and she was not anxious to cross her when she was in such a mood. As Juliet made a move to leave, Rachel picked up the jacket and offered it to her one last time. "Even in the day's full heat, no lady would go riding half dressed."

Juliet snatched the jacket from Rachel's hand and threw it soundly back on the bed, then fixed an icy stare on her maid that dared her to say anything more. Rachel met the look but did not speak, and Juliet spun about and quickly left the room.

The day was hardly perfect for a ride, Juliet was thinking as she neared the stables, for it was far too hot and humid. But if she did not get away, she would tear out her hair! A hard ride, the wind against her face, the concentrated physical effort would help relieve the tension that was wound so tightly inside her. She entered the stables and took a brief look around but did not see Meggy, the mare she had been riding of late. Hearing a shuffling movement at the far end of the stables, she approached to find Jay, the longtime servant in charge of the family's horses, patiently cleaning out a stall. He gave no sign of hearing her, but when she questioned him about the mare, he slowly straightened up and leaned against the side of the stall. A hand pressed to the small of his back, and a grimace of pain crossed his wizened features.

"Meggy be at the 'smith's gettin' herself shod, but she be back by noon, Miss Juliet," he said, noting the agitation in her face.

Juliet stamped her foot impatiently and turned sharply to leave, then stopped short as her eyes fell on Robert's great black stallion, Ebony. She gazed at him thoughtfully for a long moment, then turned to face Jay once more. "Saddle Ebony for me, Jay," she ordered.

Jay stroked his stubbled beard and chewed his bottom lip. "Ebony aren't no mount for a young lady," he ventured timidly. "He be real easy to spook in a storm, and never had no sidesaddle on him I know of. Maybe we better be askin' Master Robert if he be—"

"He won't need him before noon, and I'll be back before then. If you won't saddle him for me, I'll do it myself!" she said firmly, and with that she turned to get her saddle. Jay ran after her protesting.

"I be only thinkin' of yer welfare, Miss Juliet! It looks like rain, ye know, and me back's been painin' me somethin' fiercely this mornin'—that always means we be in fer a storm."

He was slowly saddling Ebony now, stalling for time while he tried to dissuade her, watching intently for some reaction to his advice. But the only thing his concern seemed to evoke in Juliet was further irritation. She folded her arms across her chest impatiently.

"If you cannot saddle him any faster than that, Jay, I'll ride him bareback!"

Jay, who could well remember Juliet doing just that when she was younger, quickly finished preparing the stallion and helped her mount.

She took off as if she were fleeing some great disaster, heading north, out to the meadows where she and Robert had often ridden in the early weeks of spring. The air was hot and sticky, and much of the dew still clung to the grass and leaves, but as she neared a wooded section it became noticeably cooler. She brought her horse slowly to a halt to catch her own breath and to allow Ebony to nibble at the grass that grew so thickly in the shade. Idly she surveyed the landscape, noting the grove of willow trees and the rushing of a nearby brook. The scene reminded her of the day she and Robert and Alec had spent riding, and she blushed hotly, recalling what had taken place when Robert had left them alone. She had thought about Alec so many times since then, and even now the strange feeling of yearning that had begun in his arms was clear in her mind. At the memory of her all too eager response to his passion, she angrily jerked up Ebony's head and urged him off in another gallop, far away from the willow grove. As she flew across a long stretch of meadow, Juliet abruptly recognized the horse's determination to have his own way. He fought at the bit, and in her struggle to keep control she was well reminded that she rode no gentle mare. With concentrated effort she managed to slow the stallion to a moderate pace, scolding herself for her sorry lack of patience. My temper will get the best of me, she thought with a sigh. Turning him around, she headed for home, her anger dispelled by the exertion and the tinge of uncertainty she felt with this spirited stallion.

She had just crossed the first broad expanse of meadow when a bolt of lightning cut jaggedly through the southern sky. A squall rolled quickly in her direction, and she urged Ebony to an even brisker gait, realizing that she had little choice but to ride into the storm. The light was swiftly fading as black clouds thickened the sky, and turbulent winds whipped through the grass until it resembled the waves on a choppy sea. Juliet felt herself tensing, knowing that far more was at stake than just being caught in the rain. She could feel her horse fighting for his head, his muscles straining with apprehension as the flashes of lightning increased in number and brilliance and the echoing thunder rumbled ever louder. She was suddenly frightened, and the fear caused a sickening tightness in her stomach as she faced the thought of being thrown where she might not be found for days. As she mouthed a prayer for some kind of help, she caught sight of another rider also crossing the storm-torn meadow.

Her cries were silenced by the deafening thunder, her hands ached from the desperate hold she kept on the reins, and time and again she shifted her weight in order to maintain her seat. When the thick raindrops began to pelt him, Ebony reared repeatedly, tossing Juliet furiously about, and she knew that her only chance was the rider she had seen. She had almost despaired, thinking that she had gone unnoticed and would surely be lost in the storm, when a firm hand took hold of the rearing horse's bridle and strength far superior to her own helped fight for control of the stallion.

Even as relief flooded her, her elation was considerably subdued when she recognized that handsome dark face.

Alec pulled the skittish stallion to the nearest shelter, a rocky mound with several large trees surrounding it at the meadow's edge. Jumping down, he tethered his own horse and Juliet's in the meager shelter, then quickly pulled her from her seat and led her to a spot where the placement of rocks and trees offered a small patch of protection from the rain. It was coming down hard, large drops being hurled in every direction at once by the violent wind. With the danger passed, Juliet's relief turned to sudden anger at being caught in such a compromising circumstance with a man she so totally despised. There was precious little space for movement, and the only real protection from the rain came by pressing intimately against the man who had just saved her life. She stiffened, turned, and stubbornly inched away from any contact with him, but she found it quite impossible to keep from getting wet and also keep from touching him. Well, she was not about to compromise her pride any more than she already had, and besides, a little water never hurt anyone! She pretended not to notice the monotonous rhythm of the rain as it splattered on her slender, straight nose, her lightly flushed cheeks, her mouth set with tenacious resolve.

Alec folded his arms across his chest and observed her stubbornness with a wide grin. "It's dry back here," he remarked pleasantly.

"It is also crowded!" she retorted, raising her chin a notch.

Alec watched for a time as the rain ran in tiny rivulets down her face and dropped on the crisp linen blouse, magically molding it to the contour of her breast. Reaching out, he grasped her firmly, pulling her around to face him in the cramped shelter. She gasped at the suddenness of his move and instinctively pulled back her hand, but his own caught it long before she could strike him and twisted it sharply behind her back. He pulled her close until she was flush against his chest. Juliet swallowed hard, afraid of the anger in those dark eyes, but she met them steadily, matching every bit of his indignant stare.

"I don't suppose you might want to thank me for saving your life."

His voice was very soft, but it held an undercurrent of hostility that terrified her. She tried hard to keep her breathing steady and to mask her fear with a haughty reply. "I am perfectly capable of handling myself on horseback, Mr. Farrell, and I do not recall having asked for your help."

His eyes blazed with a wild fury that made her fear for her very life. Then a smile touched his lips as he regarded her well-acted bravery, as he felt the growing tautness of her flesh against his own and patiently waited for her facade of control to crack.

Juliet swallowed a very large lump in her throat and gulped in a deep breath of air. Her eyes began to burn, and as she squeezed them shut, a single tear escaped and slid down her cheek. Try as she might, she could not stop her lips from trembling, and the tremor seemed to echo throughout her entire body.

Alec's smile disappeared, and he relaxed his savage hold on her, lifting lean brown fingers to caress her damp cheek and trace lightly over her lips. Juliet felt helpless when his fingers touched her skin, dangerously weak so near his strength. He toyed with a strand of hair that had blown across her cheek, then his hand freed the rest of her long chestnut hair and lingered there to stroke the downy softness at the back of her neck. In utter confusion she lifted wide golden eyes to meet his gaze.

His mouth bent to take hers gently, then with increasing passion, deliberately coaxing a sweet response. Her mind counseled her the folly of such surrender, but she was powerless to still the sudden desire he stirred within her, as his tongue, thrusting deep within her mouth, awakened a need that would not be denied. He drew back, still holding her close against himself, and she rested breathlessly against his shirt, moist and matted to the hard muscles beneath. There was something very right about this moment, as the fragrant rain slowed to a drizzle and the air turned cool and fresh; Juliet felt a sense of belonging in the warmth of his body, the shelter of his arms.

When the last drop of rain had fallen, she drew a long breath and timidly raised her eyes to his. A small smile trembled on her lips as she raised her hand to smooth a drop of rain that poised, quivering, on the tip of his nose. Then at once her smile faded, and anxiously her mouth sought his.

Her head fell backward, her knees grew weak as his lips moved to her throat and lower, scorching the delicate swelling through the thin fabric of her blouse. His fingers nimbly worked the fastenings at her neck and found the full curves of her bosom concealed only by the dainty lace of her chemise. His mouth grazed hungrily over her bare, warm flesh, bringing on an amazing surge of passion, an intense shiver that reached to her very fingertips. Juliet gasped as the tidal wave of passion swept cleanly over her senses, and she pulled his head in ecstasy against her breasts. His mouth traced over the ripe, satiny curves, then he slipped the blouse from her shoulders and his lips tasted eagerly the soft pink crests, lingering until they hardened against his tongue.

Immediately Juliet cried out, aghast at his abandon. Her eyes flew open in shocked embarrassment, and she wondered in horror at the foreign warmth he had kindled between her thighs. What lunacy had taken hold for her to yield to such an insane craving? What in heaven's name was she doing? She pulled away from him in alarm and turned in haste to shield herself from his devouring gaze, her shaking fingers making several futile attempts before finally securing the tiny buttons of her blouse. At length her control returned in the guise of anger, and she turned back to face Alec with fists clenched tightly at her sides.

"I hate you!"

Alec folded his arms across his chest and raised his brows in an unspoken question. His cool demeanor rankled her even further. He was not affected at all by what happened, she thought in panic. He aroused me to the point of swooning, and he feels nothing—nothing!

She could not know that the very opposite was true, for Alec's face gave no sign of his inner battle. He wanted very much to take Juliet Hampton, and had the circumstances been even slightly more favorable, he might have forced things to their natural end. He had had his fill of women who did their best to drag him to the altar, who eagerly offered their warm, silken flesh as a calculated ploy to have their own way. Juliet was not one of those. He recognized a desperate need in her, a need to be touched and kissed, a need to be treated like a woman, and it stirred a longing deep inside him to answer that need, to savor the sweetness of mutual desire, to possess her as a wife. He grinned at the thought, for marriage was the furthest thing from Juliet's mind at this moment—marriage to him, anyway —so he let his passions cool while he casually observed her tantrum.

"I hate you!" she repeated, stamping her foot to vent her frustration and managing only to splash a stream of mud up and down her skirt. Her ravings still had no effect on Alec, who now seemed almost amused at her declaration.

"You . . . you make me . . ." She wanted to accuse him of something, but somehow the right words refused to come.

Taking advantage of her hesitation, Alec strolled toward her like a barrister intent on questioning an important witness. "I make you what?" he asked. "Do I possibly make you want a bit more from life than Harold?"

Every trace of confusion and shakiness fled, and an all-consuming anger burned at his conceited suggestion. Her eyes scattered vicious golden sparks, her words were hard and cold.

"That is hardly what I intended to say, Mr. Farrell! Nauseous is nearer to what you make me feel!"

"I'm sure I do!" he returned with ease. "It must be terribly distressing for you whenever anyone gets too close to that wall you've built around yourself, and I'm sure it makes you quite ill to know that I can see right through it."

"You don't know what you're talking about!"

"Don't I? You certainly put a lot of time and effort into making yourself miserable! And you never even consider the people you hurt along the way."

"Like whom?" she demanded, a rising curiosity mixing with her anger.

"Like Frances, for one."

Juliet's lips curled in contempt. "Oh. Dear little Frances."

"And Mary? She would love to have you as a friend, especially with her family so far away." At Juliet's skeptical expression, he continued, "Unless, of course, you are still jealous that she has Allan and you don't."

"I have not cared for Allan in a long, long time!"

"I must say, I do believe that," he hurried to agree with her. "You haven't cared for anyone in a long, long time! Poor, unloved little Juliet. You don't care about anyone, and you won't let anyone care about you! You think you are so much better than all of us."

"I *am* better than you, Alexander Farrell!" she sneered, her head held high and her eyes narrowed. "You're nothing but a bloodthirsty radical, a seditious fool! It will serve you right when they hang you for treason! And I shall watch them do it with pleasure!"

"Will you?" His voice was slow and dangerously quiet, but the silken rage in his tone managed to penetrate Juliet's bravado.

In a flash his hands were on her shoulders, pulling her roughly against him once more. There was no gentleness in the hand that forced back her head or in the demanding mouth that covered hers. She clawed and pushed at him blindly, but in spite of the hatred that raged in her mind, a crazy, exquisite excitement coursed through her, effectively destroying her desire for further argument. Her fury metamorphosed into a passionate hunger, her muffled protests were magically quelled, and the savage kiss that continued was one of mutual urgency. When their lips finally parted, Juliet could not bring herself to meet his eyes. How could he make her feel so helpless, so confused? How could she even hope to fight the overwhelming longing to remain in his arms?

Frightened, she pulled away from him and hurried to her horse, but to her further humiliation she found that she could not mount him alone. Alec could scarcely suppress a chuckle as he observed her futile attempts to heave herself into the saddle, and finally he came to assist her, well-aware that his help was not exactly welcome. Still staring resolutely away from him, she slapped the reins on the steed's neck, scattering mud in every direction when the horse lurched forward to obey her command. She maintained a furious gallop all the way home, in spite of the slippery ground to be traveled.

At Hampton House, Jay paced the length of the stables, nervously kicking at the small hoofprint-shaped puddles made by the heavy shower of rain. He scanned the landscape time and again, then watched the house for some sign of Robert or, worse, Master Lawrence, before hopefully searching for Juliet once more. He finally let out a long sigh of relief when he caught sight of the great black stallion returning home. His sharp eyes widened considerably when he took in the disheveled rider—hair unbound, hemline soaked in mud, once-crisp linen blouse a mass of revealing wrinkles. Jumping down with very little help, Juliet ignored his inquiring look and without a word strode purposefully toward the house.

Chapter 8

At dinner that evening, Juliet idly poked at her food, pondering over how best to tell her father that there would be no wedding in the fall. Should she act angry, upset? Or should she be casual, self-assured, nonchalant?

Her father had nearly finished a hearty helping of beef and potatoes when he took note of his daughter's disinterest in the meal. He observed her closely for a few moments, watched her move her food about the plate with a heavy silver fork, staring into it as if she expected some strange revelation to appear. He cleared his throat, but still her attention was riveted on the food growing cold on her plate.

"I was told you were caught in the storm today."

With a start Juliet let her fork clank loudly on the china plate, and her eyes blinked wide with surprise.

"Um . . . yes, I was," she stammered, trying her best to sound casual and adding a weak smile in an attempt to hide her guilt. She said nothing further, silently waiting for the harsh reprimand she was sure to receive for taking Robert's horse, but to her surprise he continued on a completely new course.

"You received a letter from your intended today?"

"Yes . . . yes, I did," she answered, caught off guard by the question. She had expected to inform her father in her own way and in her own good time, but now it was obvious that he had already been informed.

"And?"

Noting Robert's sudden interest in the conversation, she let the truth spill out.

"And he will not be sailing as he had planned. He hopes instead to sail . . . perhaps . . . sometime in the spring. . . ."

"Hopes?" her father repeated. "Perhaps? Sometime? Are you quite sure he plans to come at all?"

Juliet's face fell at her father's cross-examination. He seemed unconvinced of Harold's devotion for her, and in the wake of her fiancé's cancelled plans she could not assure him otherwise.

"Why did he postpone his voyage, Juliet? Surely he must have given you some reason why he isn't coming," Robert encouraged her.

"His mother is ill, and he says he is afraid to leave her side," she answered quietly, flashing a brief, grateful look at her brother.

"Have you considered a wedding in England then?" her father asked.

At his words, all traces of quiet docility disappeared, and a determined young lady fearlessly faced her father. "I do not intend to return to England unless Lord Harold comes here first. We had an agreement, and he has broken it. I certainly do not intend to do as Rachel suggests and throw myself at him if he has changed his mind. He said that he will come as soon as he is able, and I intend to wait. No matter what you think, Father, Harold is very anxious to marry me, and it is extremely doubtful that he has changed his mind. He is not the type of man to make rash promises, nor would he make false excuses had he decided that his promise needs to be broken."

Her eyes burned with such intensity that even Lawrence Hampton thought it best to back off. He realized that his daughter was an attractive woman and had never doubted her ability to win a husband, but he saw her headstrong temperament as a definite liability and felt it best for her to be married as soon as possible. A title in the family could do no harm, after all, even if the man had little else to offer, and he had no desire to anger her further and run the risk of changing her mind altogether. He was completely blind to the hurt in his daughter, to the part of her that wondered why her father was so easily convinced that Harold had forgotten her. It stung her to realize that her father approved of her going to England, that he would see her swallow her pride to extract a marriage from a titled man. He never once considered the possibility that Harold was not good enough for her.

"Well, Juliet, it is your decision, of course," he said in a low, patronizing tone. "We will let the air settle a bit and see how you feel about things in a week or two. But a long, cold winter here could prove very lonely for you."

Juliet sighed her frustration. How could she tell him that the long months would be just as lonely for her with Harold as without him? She was suddenly very tired of listening to well-meaning advice from someone who understood nothing of how she really felt. Excusing herself, she hurried off to her room. Though it was early she undressed immediately and dismissed Rachel for the night. In a plain cotton night rail she nervously paced the room, unable to settle the turbulence in her head as one frustration piled upon another.

Why, why, why? Why did Harold have to postpone his plans? Why did there have to be constant bickering between Robert and Father? And why did she run into Alec no matter how carefully she planned not to? At this last thought, a voice struck a chord in her memory. "I can recall so well how he turned my whole world upside down! . . . Every time I closed my eyes I saw him, and every time I opened them—well, he was never very far away. . . ." Juliet struggled to relieve herself of the thought. It could not be! No, it simply could not! Love is the very last thing I feel for him, she assured herself. It is, as Rachel said, his devil's eyes that somehow keep me from acting rationally. Oh, Harold! How could you do this to me? How could you leave me here when he gives me no peace? Even when I sleep, my dreams betray the desires I try so hard not to have!

Suddenly fearful that she was losing the battle to exile the devil from her thoughts, Juliet crossed herself and did her best to pray. The sisters at St. Bride's had spoken about the evil desires of the body and the endless struggle of man, but at the time such lectures had seemed inappropriate. They were for women like Lady Margaret who needed them. But today, even in her anger she had barely overcome the longing to hold Alec, to feel the splendor of his lean muscles hard against her, to satisfy a yearning that spread like the plague.

A sharp rap on the door suddenly intruded. "Who is it?" she called, making her voice sound heavy with sleep. She had no desire for further discussion of her plans with her father, at least not this evening.

A hoarse whisper came from the hall. "It's Robert. If you're tired, I promise I will only be a moment."

She had opened the door before he finished, a bright smile on her lips. It had been years since Robert had visited her in her room. He entered and shot her a reproving glance.

"You obviously were not asleep."

Juliet tried to look repentant, but a smile tugged at the corners of her mouth as she closed the door behind him.

"No. But I really am too tired for a lecture," she replied, unable to keep her smile from widening. It was like old times, with Robert here. Oh, for the playful conspiracies they had once shared!

"Juliet . . . I . . ." He began timidly, then stopped as if reconsidering what he wanted to say. Something in his face was different, frightening. Juliet's smile vanished, and dismay and uncertainty clouded the eyes that had laughed only moments before.

He took a deep breath and hurried with the words, as if by saying them quickly they might be less painful. "I came here to say good-bye. I'm leaving in the morning."

It was like a sharp razor cutting her deep—she knew that she had been wounded, but shock dulled the pain.

"Where are you going?" she managed.

"North. I need to get away for a time. Father and I haven't been getting along, and . . ." He stopped and shook his head, fastening his eyes directly on hers. "I cannot lie to you, Juliet. Anyone but you. Even when we were children I could never lie to you."

"What is it, Robert?"

"I am leaving to join the fighting. It is the right thing for me to do. I cannot stay here and wait for a confrontation with Father that might make me back down."

"I don't understand! You don't have to leave!"

"But I do! How can I explain it to you? I cannot just let things happen as they will. I have to be a part of it. I have to try—"

"But what about Frances?" she broke in desperately. For

once she was grateful for his devotion to the frail creature. "You aren't going to leave her?"

Robert's mouth curved into a sad half-smile. "I won't be the only man leaving his lady love. Many will be leaving wives and children as well."

"But, Robert, you cannot! I won't let you!" she burst out, shaking her head.

Robert took firm hold of her shoulders. "I leave tomorrow at dawn with Alec. He's back from Virginia."

"Yes, I know," Juliet let slip. On seeing her brother's puzzled expression she began to fling accusations. "This is all his idea, isn't it? Father said that he was a troublemaker, and he was right! Don't listen to him, Robert! He can't make you do anything!"

Robert gave a short laugh. "You have been listening to Father, Juliet. I'm doing what I want to do, what I must do. It has nothing to do with Alec, or anyone else besides myself. For God's sake, Juliet, didn't you read any of my letters? I've been committed to the cause for a long, long time."

Their eyes locked, a pair of golden ones pleading, a blue pair resolutely holding fast. Finally Juliet looked away, unable to face the reality of being left here all alone.

"Please, Juliet," he quietly requested, "please, let's not fight. I didn't come here looking for another argument. I've had enough of that from Father."

"Why *did* you come?" Her voice was breaking with the tears she just barely managed to contain.

"Several reasons." Robert assumed a businesslike tone. "First, I wanted to ask you to take care of Frances for me. She needs someone strong like you. I was hoping that you might become good friends."

Juliet's eyes dropped to the thick carpet to hide the jealousy suddenly erupting inside.

"Promise me," Robert urged her.

"I promise," she answered dully.

"Next, I want you to promise that you will not marry Lord Harold until I come back and give my approval. I don't intend to give you away to just anyone, you know."

At his words, Juliet could no longer hold back her tears, and she flung her arms about his neck. She held him tightly and let the tears fall until her whole body convulsed with sobs.

"I cannot stand it if you leave . . ." she said brokenly.

"Juliet," he whispered, cradling her gently. "You're still a mixed-up, hurt little girl, aren't you?" He sighed. "Do you remember how you used to do everything anyone said you couldn't do? I was the only one who believed in you then. I believed you could run faster, and ride better, and now I believe that you can do whatever needs to be done, no matter what this war brings. That is why I want you to take care of Frances for me. I don't trust anyone else to do it."

She took a difficult breath and mouthed the words against his shirt. "I . . . promise . . ."

He held her still, stroking the hair back from her tear-stained face. "Now then. I want you also to promise never to do anything as stupid as taking Ebony out in a storm."

Juliet froze. Had Alec told him of their meeting? What exactly did he know? "I . . . I . . ."

"No excuses," he cut in. "If Father ever found out, he'd send you packing off to England again, and I, for one, don't like that idea very much. I don't know how you ever got that horse and yourself back here in one piece, but then, you always managed to get the best from the wildest of the lot."

Juliet let out a sigh of relief. Jay must have told him. Thank God it had been Robert and not Father!

Reluctantly, Robert released his hold on her and forced a brave smile. "It's late, and I have much to do before tomorrow morning."

"Can I help with anything?" she offered hopefully.

"You already have. I know I can depend on you. Just don't let that temper of yours make any more rash decisions till I get back."

He planted a kiss on her forehead, then turned away and was gone.

Juliet stared at the door for several moments, then went to open the latticework window that faced south, with its imposing view of the city. The night was clear and the stars bright, and below, the city's whale-oil lamps flickered in front of every seventh house. Somehow it all looked as one, as if the earth and sky blended easily together, one large ebony backdrop sprinkled with thousands of twinkling stars. Yet tomorrow the earth and sky would separate again; the clogged city streets would contrast with the bright blue expanse of sky. She left the window and went to her bureau, rummaging hastily through two drawers before locating a small brass box. Prying open its lid, she looked long and hard at its contents—a heavy solid-gold charm dangling from a thick gold chain. She lifted it from the box, fingering the cool metal, which was pounded cleverly into the shape of three ancient women. It had been years since she had looked at it, or even thought of it, but now the sight of it stirred her strength anew. "I always believed you could . . ." Juliet remembered with a determined smile. She would not let Robert down.

The dawn had barely begun to lighten the black sky when Juliet woke to the muffled clops of a rider galloping up the front drive. She sprang from her bed and quickly wrapped a loose robe around her night rail before checking to be sure that the hallway was clear and quietly closing the door behind her. Straining to hear the hushed voices on the first floor, she crept cautiously in the direction of the sound. A rectangular shaft of light poured from the half-opened parlor door, while the remainder of the house lay quiet and still in the muted light of dawn.

Alexander Farrell thoughtfully paced the parlor, studying the various objects that cluttered the room, while Robert sat at the desk that had been his mother's, gnawing at his lip and forcing the appropriate words to appear on the short farewell note to his father. Finally he finished, then glanced around the room, fixing its contents affectionately in his mind. It would be a long time before he would return, perhaps he would never do so. He began to check over his belongings, compactly folding and squeezing what he could into a bundle fit for travel.

"Has there been any news from Boston?" he asked, rousing his friend's attention from his steady contemplation of his mother's portrait. "Any more fighting?"

"As a matter of fact, the news is not from Boston. I heard quite a story about a giant oaf of a backwoodsman by the name of Ethan Allen. Have you heard about him yet?"

Robert shook his head.

"It's an unusual tale to say the least," Alec continued.

"This Allen and a group of hard-drinking rascals—who prefer to call themselves militia, though they have received no commission from the state of New Hampshire or anyone else—managed to take Fort Ticonderoga. A fellow named Arnold had just accepted a commission from the Massachusetts Committee of Public Safety to take the fort, and he was very upset to learn that some renegades from Vermont territory had decided on the same target. So off he went, without the men he had begun to organize for the task, mind you, to prevent Allen from stealing what he felt ought to be his victory." He gave a short chuckle. "According to the story, Allen and Arnold decided on a joint command, much to the dismay of the commander of the fort, a Captain Delaplace, who was extremely anxious to surrender and be done with it, but didn't quite know who to surrender to!"

"But the patriots took the fort?" Robert asked, pleased with the news.

"Yes, but it was hardly a great military feat, Robert. The fort was poorly kept and even more inadequately staffed. Allen has been boasting about 'storming' the place, though not a drop of blood was spilled on either side, in the name of the Great Jehovah and the Continental Congress! An overstatement, I would say, for someone leading a group of drunkards the Congress had not the slightest notion of sanctioning. Regardless, Fort Ti and also Crown Point just a few miles to the north are now in patriot hands."

"That *is* good news! No matter who is responsible."

"Yes," Alec agreed. "The heavy cannon that was taken there could definitely prove useful . . . provided the Congress in Philadelphia can be persuaded not to store it away until it can be returned to the British."

"Returned to the British?" Robert repeated incredulously. "You must be joking!"

"I'm afraid I'm not. It seems that there are men in the Continental Congress who yet believe this struggle can be dealt with defensively and like gentlemen. They will have to change their minds soon enough, for we are fast being pushed into taking a firm stand."

"I am ready to fight, and there are others who feel the same. I only hope the fighting will be brief. The victories that have already been won are very encouraging."

"I don't mean to dash your hopes, Robert, but your father is right in one instance. It is doubtful that a war with Britain could end quickly or easily. Ticonderoga was hardly prepared for an attack. Delaplace might have surrendered to you and me, had we pointed a primed musket in the right direction." He smiled. "Any real fighting we might have encountered would have been with Arnold and Allen over the laurels of victory."

Robert had finished his packing, and a neat bundle now lay on the desk. He approached Alec, whose eyes had again found the painting. Robert knew instinctively that Alec supposed the woman in the portrait to be Juliet, a mistake that occurred whenever someone saw it for the first time. Instead of advising his friend of his error, he bided his time and waited for him to comment.

"The painting is already finished?" he asked Robert after a bit, his eyes reluctantly leaving it.

"Yes," Robert answered noncommittally, joining Alec in his perusal.

"She's wearing a different dress."

"Yes, she is. What do you think? Do you like it?"

There was a brief moment of consideration before Alec answered bluntly, "No. I don't like it at all."

"Oh?" Robert sounded surprised. "Is it because of the dress?"

Alec tossed Robert a wry glance. "No, it's not that." His eyes returned to a serious study of the face. "There's something missing. I can't explain exactly . . ." His eyes narrowed, and he spent a long moment considering. "Her eyes," he said finally. "Your sister's eyes have fire and life, never that empty, hollow look." He shook his head. "It doesn't even look like her."

Robert smiled in admiration of his friend's perception. "It is, in fact, a portrait of my mother, to whom Juliet obviously bears a striking resemblance. You're the first person I can ever recall who knew it was not her."

Robert took a final look at the portrait, then quickly scanned the familiar surroundings one last time. It was difficult to face the thought that this house would no longer be home. Though he tried to conceal the pain he felt at leaving, a stinging in his eyes blurred his vision as he set himself to gathering up his bag and following Alec out of the room.

Juliet stood in the shadows and watched in silence as the two departed. Her breast ached, though she forced herself to breathe steadily, holding back the emotions that smoldered painfully inside her. Her brother was gone; her fiancé would not be coming until spring. These things she understood and was capable of accepting. But the strange loss she felt as Alec walked away was something beyond her comprehension. She was deeply touched that he had recognized that the woman in the parlor portrait was not her. "Full of fire and life," he had said, "never empty or hollow." Why, then, did she sometimes feel so empty? How could it be that he was able to see the part of her she kept so well hidden from everyone else?

As if in a daze, she forced her feet up the stairs and wandered to her room, wondering why she felt that aching emptiness so acutely now that he had gone.

Chapter 9

On the fifteenth day of June, Alec and Robert approached the outskirts of Boston, where volunteer militiamen from everywhere in New England had been collecting for two months, since the events at Lexington and Concord. The American camps were buzzing with the news of the arrival of British reinforcements for the waiting General Gage, including six thousand soldiers and three major generals: Howe, Clinton, and Burgoyne. After the April incidents, Gage had patiently marked time in anticipation that the rebellion would show signs of quieting, but the news from everywhere was discouraging for him.

The great majority of the colonists still hoped to be reconciled with the motherland, but they were prepared to fight in order to secure a guarantee for their rights as English subjects. As evening fell, the hills around Boston were aglow with the fires of militiamen, most of whom had never before seen battle. They were anxious for action, for a chance to prove their courage, for a share in a glorious and honorable fight. Even before his arrival Robert had been caught up in the zeal of the men who hungrily anticipated doing battle. Only a few were not so eager, for they realized that what they were about to begin would involve much more than a splendid and easy victory. Alec, quiet and apprehensive, realistically appraised the "army" ready to face the seasoned professionals. There were thousands of men, undisciplined, for the most part without uniforms, armed with muskets they had previously used only in hunting game. Poorly housed in tents or crude huts, they had no adequate medical care, not even a central chain of command—not to mention a regular government.

On the evening following their arrival, General Israel Putnam directed twelve hundred men in the construction of a redoubt, a low stronghold, at Breed's Hill, located on the strategically important heights just to the north and east of the city of Boston. His move was in response to word that General Howe planned an attack for the following day. In addition to the makeshift protection thrown up in haste on Breed's Hill, similar defenses were built to the left and right and on Bunker Hill, closer to the mainland, should it be necessary for the front-line soldiers to fall back. Robert and Alec were among those who labored on the Breed's Hill redoubt, stacking rocks until a waist high barricade marked the crest of the hill, which looked out over the sea. With the morning's first light, Howe sighted the barricade and made his final decision to attack.

Both Breed's Hill and Bunker Hill were located on a peninsula, a curved finger of land jutting far out into the bay and nearly joining itself to the British-held city of Boston, which was on a similar peninsula to the south. Despite the precautions the men had taken to prevent a rear attack, the natural geography made it a relatively simple task to cut off the slender thread of land from the mainland. It was the Americans' good fortune that General Howe chose not to do so. He desired a victory that would prove the invincibility of the British once and for all, so he opted for a frontal assault.

The men in the redoubt on Breed's Hill were organized into three ranks, each to take a turn at firing, then reloading as the ranks behind took aim and fired. They were ordered to hoard their limited supply of ammunition, to wait until the last minute before firing so that every shot might be an accurate one, a deadly one.

The sun's full brightness fell on an awesome sight, those brilliant red and white figures marching in resplendent formation toward the redoubt like so many neat rows of freshly painted tin soldiers. Robert knelt at the low wall, his fingers cramped and tight around his musket, his breath coming in short, nervous pants. Closer and closer they came, thousands of feet falling with each beat of the drum, the identical toy soldiers changing quickly into men: old men, young men, men with faces and shapes and names . . . Robert's index finger twitched above the trigger, fear taking hold as the hated redcoats came well within range.

"Fire!"

Several hundred cracks of gunfire fused into a single, horrible roar, and in a magical instant a perfect row of red-coated soldiers crumpled and fell to the ground. The thick, heavy smoke stung Robert's eyes, while a weird cacophony of discharging muskets and dying men's screams echoed in his brain. He froze, watching in horrible fascination as the veterans of battle trampled over their dead comrades as easily as they might have a few worthless blades of grass. They were men! Flesh and blood! Could no one else see what he saw?

"Reload! Reload!"

A large tanned hand on his shoulder jerked him aside as Alec knelt, took aim, and fired. Mindlessly Robert lifted his powder horn, then rammed a tiny ball of lead deep in the long barrel of his musket, deaf to the joyous cries which rose from the redoubt when the British ranks fell back.

Accustomed to heavy losses in his front lines, Howe had planned to take the redoubt before the rebels had a chance to reload. He was truly shocked at the spectacle before him of ill-trained militia causing row after row of his seasoned troops to fall, and he immediately launched a second assault. Again the militia held their ground, forcing back the redcoats with their deadly accurate close-range musket fire. Unwilling to accept a defeat, Howe regrouped his men and once again gave the order to take the hill.

Oblivious to the premature cheers of victory, Robert fixed his eyes on the terrible sight of human carnage and wondered how he had ever thought to feel elation at killing the enemy. He was vaguely aware that the redcoats were once again marching toward him and that he, like most of the others in the redoubt, had but a single last shot.

"Fire!"

The muskets roared in unison, and the front lines of red-coats fell at the sound, but the hundreds more behind them marched relentlessly up the hill. Realizing the futility of defending the redoubt with empty guns, the Americans began to retreat. Alec literally dragged Robert from the hill, while the younger man clutched at his empty gun in a catatonic stupor. A few courageous men made a valiant last attempt to defend their ground, facing a sea of gleaming bayonets with rocks, fists, and unmatched bravery. As the British took the hill, those who scrambled to get away too late became easy targets in the area between the two hills, while those who still refused to run were savagely hacked apart. From the safety of the redoubt on Bunker Hill, Alec watched helplessly as men who had labored and laughed beside him screamed their agony and breathed their last.

General Howe had his victory; the British had taken Breed's Hill. But in surveying the dead and wounded who lay at its foot, Howe could feel little elation at his conquest. The Americans had retreated, but not without exacting great cost, and the general would never again underestimate his American enemy.

The remainder of the day was spent in the gruesome task of retrieving the dead and the wounded who lay in the questionable stretch between the two armies. As the night fell peacefully and the weary sought their pallets, Robert and Alec took their rest on the cool ground. But for them and for most of the others, sleep was long in coming. Several hours into the darkness, when most of the exhausted had finally succumbed to slumber, Robert bolted upright, uttering a frightening gasp. His breathing was deep and rapid, his eyes wide with fear, darting from one sleeping soldier to another. Trembling visibly, his hands clamped tightly over his ears, though the only sounds to be heard were muffled movements of sleeping men and the loud crackling of green wood in the campfire. Rolling on his side, Alec looked on, his brow furrowed deeply with sympathy. He rose and went to Robert's side, and with a firm grasp on his wrists, he pried the shaking hands from his ears. Then he took Robert's face in both his hands.

"It's over, Robert. It's over." His words were firm and calm, and he repeated them several times.

The terrified gleam finally left Robert's eyes as Alec continued to reassure him, though in its stead came a terrible look of despondency.

"Do you want to talk?"

Robert shook his head slowly and kept his eyes averted. With a deep sigh, Alec returned to his blanket, though his concern remained with the other. At length Robert spoke in a strange and distant voice, as if he spoke to himself rather than anyone else.

"I do not think I will ever be a soldier."

"Nor will I," Alec agreed. "It is not a pleasant thing to see death."

Robert doubtfully turned to Alec and studied his dark eyes. He would stand no pity, and he had not thought to expect understanding, yet that is what he found.

"Do you think you are alone in what you feel?" Alec gave a brief, mirthless laugh. "I would think much less of you, Robert, had you enjoyed the fighting as much as you had thought to. When we came here, we did not know what we know now. But the question remains, are we to submit to tyranny or are we ready to fight for what we believe, knowing more exactly the cost?"

Robert looked away and spoke to the night. "To see someone's lifeblood spurt from an open wound, to hear someone crying out when he knows he is about to die, to see the mutilated corpses littering the landscape—it sickens me!" His voice broke with emotion, and it was a long time before he could continue. "And what difference then if he wears a red coat or no uniform at all? What difference if the battle be lost or won? What difference if we hold one worthless hill near Boston? What of the dead, Alec? What of those who died?"

Alec took a deep breath and weighed his words carefully. "Every man must decide that for himself, Robert. It is not an easy decision, especially when we've seen what we did today. Those who expected to win easily know now that such a thing will not be. And as for those who died . . ." He paused to find the right words. "Had I died today, I would hope that the others would continue my fight, remembering for what it was I died."

Robert made no reply, but Alec's words seemed to offer him

97

some measure of comfort, and soon he relaxed, a short time later giving himself up to sleep.

When the sun was still but a half-circle on the horizon, a youth of fifteen or so came to rouse Alec from his hard earth bed.

"General Ward be wantin' to see Alexander Farrell. Ye be he?" His voice was clipped, and his manner spoke of strict military discipline, in spite of his youthful appearance.

Alec nodded and stifled a yawn. "Where is the general?" he asked in a heavy voice, blinking to free his eyes from sleep.

"Follow me," answered the youth, and without a moment's hesitation he turned and strode through the maze of sleeping soldiers to a simple canvas tent. He paused only long enough for Alec to catch up, then directed him with a jerk of his head to enter.

A deep voice barked at him long before Alec's eyes adjusted to the darkness. "You are Alexander Farrell—from Virginia?"

"Yes, sir," came the reply. He straightened his casual stance in response to the authority in the other's voice.

"You have ridden for some time for the Committees of Correspondence, is that correct?"

"Yes, sir. For nearly three years."

"Then you have contacts in Philadelphia and New York."

"Yes, sir."

"Know the roads well? Lesser ones as well as main ones?"

"Yes, sir."

"Good. Then you will deliver this parcel to the Continental Congress in Philadelphia for me—to John Adams, personally." He handed over to Alec a small packet of paperwork, all the while appraising the younger man, who stood a full head taller and wore no uniform. "You are related to the Lees of Virginia?" he asked.

"Yes, sir. They are distant cousins."

"All Virginians I've ever laid eyes on admit to being cousins in one way or another." He let out a deep, throaty chuckle that made Alec relax a bit. "Do you realize, boy, that the Congress has not decided yet whether or not to take credit for what is happening here?" He patted the parcel that Alec held firmly in his hand. "They will, boy, they will! Ride swiftly and God's speed."

Thus dismissed, Alec placed the package safely inside his shirt, and with an unpracticed but passable salute to the general, left the tent.

Chapter 10

"Captain Barkley! It is so good to see you again!" smiled Juliet, intercepting the familiar seafarer on his way to her father's study.

Barkley was a man of less than average height, of solid limb and large girth, which he carried extraordinarily well. The captain sported a large, unshapely nose and matching mouth, which were seldom noticed when one's eyes were caught by the generous growth of bright red beard, now threaded liberally with silver.

Captain Barkley's visits to Hampton House had always been happy occasions for Robert and Juliet as children, much to their mother's dismay. Safely out of sight, he would bounce them both on a generously muscled leg, and with tiny, dark eyes aglow would tell them stories about his great adventures at sea. The children could have spent a lifetime listening to that gruff voice relating the most amazing stories. For Juliet, a little girl struggling for recognition, Captain Barkley was a very special man who treated her in the same warm, off-handed manner as her brother, never once making her feel inferior or out of place because she was a girl. But Claire Hampton had hardly been pleased to observe her young daughter's adoration for an ordinary sea captain, albeit her husband's own business partner.

Now his expressive dark eyes crinkled up as he loudly returned her warm greeting.

"Little Juliet! It always be good to see ye!" He lowered his voice to a conspiratorial whisper. "What mischief have ye gotten yeself into o' late?" he teased her playfully.

"None at all," she assured him with a slight lift of her chin, though her smile let him know that she remained unperturbed at his reminder of her childhood indiscretions.

A thick hand patted her arm, and brown eyes twinkled as he consoled her in good humor. "Not to worry, m'dear girl. Ye'll think o' somethin' soon—ye always do!"

"Captain Barkley!" she scolded him lightly. "You should not give a lady such improper ideas!"

"Right ye be 'bout that, little Juliet!" he responded quickly. "The ladies I know have enough improper ideas o' their own!"

Juliet made a feeble attempt at an expression of reproof but hardly managed to suppress a smile before sending the captain on to her father's study.

Lawrence Hampton sat comfortably behind his desk in a large leather chair, hands folded patiently. He neither rose nor greeted his expected guest, who let himself in and closed the door. In silent irritation Hampton observed the captain shuffling across the room and helping himself to a glass of Madeira, which he quickly drained. With an expressive smack of his lips, Barkley eagerly refilled his glass. Hampton waited until the captain had settled himself in the chair directly opposite, by this time having seen half the second glass of wine disappear in much the same manner as the first. Only Hampton's hands, which crossed and uncrossed several times in the interim, hinted at his agitation.

"Well?" he asked at length, his tone casually demanding.

"Good wine," the captain remarked, secretly relishing the irritation he had aroused in the other. "Ye could always pick a good wine, Larry, I say that for ye."

With an almost imperceptible sigh of exasperation, Hampton rose and carefully measured out a glass of wine for himself before he returned the bottle to his desk and generously placed it within reach of his guest. Savoring a slow sip of his wine, he allowed Barkley to fill his glass once more before asking another question more to the point.

"Did you get the information?"

"Don't I always?" Barkley returned, squarely facing the man who yet managed an undisturbed demeanor. Cool steel-blue eyes met Barkley's tiny brown ones, and a mirthless grin twisted Lawrence Hampton's thin mouth.

"Yes," he agreed softly. "You are very good at what you do."

Barkley snorted loudly in response. "All I do is follow ye orders, and well ye know it."

"All the same," Hampton insisted, "you follow them well."

Barkley turned unhappily away from the half-compliment to reach deep inside his fine linen shirt, which was never properly buttoned. He produced a roll of papers and handed them over to his employer. There was no hesitation as Hampton took the proffered item and eagerly read its contents. It was several moments before his attention returned to his guest. When he spoke again, a satisfied smile touched his lips.

"It's so much more than I'd ever dared to hope! Are you certain that this information is accurate?"

The captain nodded. "Checked most of it out meself," he said, "and paid well 'nough to get the truth 'bout the rest."

"Well, well, well," Hampton smiled happily. "It seems that Juliet has made quite a choice for herself, does it not? I assume you offered the young lord my daughter's warmest regards?"

The seaman nodded, and Hampton continued thoughtfully, again looking over the papers, "It seems that the family money has been wisely invested. The poor return noted in several of these entries is no doubt due to poor management."

The captain nodded again. "Lord Harold—the young un's father—was a natural-born businessman. He made money hand over fist, and his bereaved widow be still reapin' what he sowed. She be leavin' the runnin' o' things t' her brother, though, and a less likely prospect I never laid eyes on—except maybe for Harold hisself."

"Oh, yes. How is the dear woman? Her illness prevented her son from sailing off. Is it as serious as all that?"

"More serious, I'd be sayin'," Barkley commented with a mysterious grin, ". . . for Juliet, that is." The twinkle in his eye caused Hampton's brow to darken.

"What exactly do you mean by that?"

"I be meanin' that whoever be marryin' Lord Harold be havin' t' contend with his 'sick' mother—her only illness bein' that she be none too pleased to have another daughter. Not that I blame her, ye understand. Lady Margaret is a shrew if ever I met one! Takes after her mother in that respect and goes her one better, to be sure! Lord Harold be walkin' around like a scared little pup with his tail between his legs, just waitin' t' be told what to do! And ye better believe, the two women in that family be quick enough to tell him! Never saw a man so cowardly afore a set o' females in me life!" He chuckled softly and downed another glass of wine before giving Hampton a sidelong glance and adding, "Got it bad for little Juliet, though. He be wantin' t' marry her, all right! And he made sure I be knowin' it well afore I took me leave." He shook his head. "Don't know what that pretty lass be seein' in such a simperin' blue blood as he!"

Hampton ignored Barkley's last comment, pleased with the reassurance of Harold's devotion. "You feel certain that he will come here, then—in the spring?"

"He'll come. It may be later 'n spring, though, with all the trouble there be news of. But the spring or the summer or the next spring—he'll come," he said without a trace of a doubt. Then he raised his brow. "But will little Juliet wait?"

The pleased look disappeared completely from Hampton's face, and his eyes narrowed as he answered. "You may be sure that she will, Adam. I intend to see to that myself."

He turned his attention back to the papers, taking quill in hand to make various notations here and there, but the captain remained seated, ignoring the unspoken dismissal and toying thoughtfully with his empty glass. Noting that it was not his intention to leave, Hampton lowered his pen.

"Was there something else?"

"As a matter o' fact, there be somethin' else, Larry. Somethin' I be needin' t' speak t' ye about." The captain paused while the other man replaced the quill and leaned back in his chair, again folding his fine long fingers and resting them on his chest.

"I be wantin' t' take me ship and join the fightin', Larry. I hear they be beggin' for privateers, and it kinda suits me fancy t' be fightin' with the youngbloods for what be right."

For a long moment, Hampton's carefully controlled countenance reacted visibly to this shocking revelation. Then he gave a short snort, which passed for a laugh.

"You've developed quite a sense of humor of late, Adam."

The captain pursed his lips, but no trace of levity was in his tone. "I always be ready t' make light o' what be funny, Larry, but I not be makin' light this time."

"You . . . you couldn't possibly be such a fool! Look at yourself! You're a wealthy man! Do you intend to waste it all—your entire life's work—on a stupid cause? Do you actually mean to sail your ship in a ludicrous attempt to single-handedly stop the imperial navy? I do believe you may be growing senile in your old age!"

"I not be seein' many more years than ye, Larry." The rejoinder came as an unwelcome reminder, and Captain Barkley smiled knowingly at the other's frown. "Yea, I be a wealthy man," he agreed, "but I also be an old one. An' I be havin' no wife or children t' be thinkin' of, only meself. If I be wantin' t' waste me money, I be doin' jus' that. I never noticed that ye give me advice when I went about wastin' me life."

"Are you blaming me for your never having settled down? Never having a family?"

"I not be sayin' that," the gruff voice returned. His tiny brown eyes took on a wistful, faraway look as he continued. "I be married once—ye never knew it, though. It be a long time ago in England. A pretty young thing she be! A bit skinny . . . didn't ha' much shape t' her at all 'at I recall to. But she had a smile that could dazzle the sun, me Molly did! Weren't a soul who noticed 'nother thing 'bout her 'sides her smile. I made up me mind to marry her as soon as I laid me eyes on her.

"She be a young girl, maybe fifteen, maybe not, but she promised she be waitin' for me, and I promised t' come back. When I finally put in t' port, long time past, she be disappeared, and it be takin' me days t' find her. And when I did, I be wishin' I had not. She be joined up with some flashy gentleman fellow who be havin' more money 'n I ever dreamed o' havin' then, and she weren't about t' come back t' me wi' me half-empty pockets. I would o' killed her with me bare hands if it hadn't o' been for the babe. Me own little girl child, just like little Juliet—she tol' me was me own, anyway. I thought t' take me child away wi' me, but then I be thinkin' the better o' it. What kind o' life be a girl child havin' wi' a seafarin' man her only kin? So I be leavin' them both behind and tryin' t' forget.

"The next time I be puttin' in at New York, here ye be, offerin' me a captaincy and a fine ship o' me own. I never be one t' enjoy the stealin' and burnin'—whether it be Spanish or Frenchies or Dutch or whoever. But I be carryin' a heavy load o' hate in me heart, an' I be feelin' that the world owed me somethin' for that . . . I just be takin' it in me own way." He regretfully shook his head.

"That is a very poignant story, Adam," Hampton commented dryly, "and one that would better be forgotten."

"That be the point!" the captain returned in a forceful bellow. "Too much be forgotten!" He continued then in a softer tone, "Twas ye that sent me t' Manchester, t' check out this Lord Harold. I be on me way one mornin' t' see a certain gentleman 'bout the matter when I be hearin' a strange voice callin' out me name. I turns meself 'round an' sees nobody I be recognizin'. But there be some scrawny ol' laundry woman carryin' a bulky bundle an' hurryin' towards me. So I be thinkin' she mistakes me for some other man, an' I begins again on me way, when she calls out 'Adam! Adam Barkley!' So I stops meself dead in me tracks, an' I be facin' her squarely—an' a uglier woman I never did see! Her skin be all parched an' wi' the deep marks o' the pox, an' her body be a poorly bound sack o' bones. 'Don't ye remember?' she says t' me. 'It's Molly!' An' then she smiles.

"Well, a good westerly right 'bout then would o' blown me over, sure! Not me Molly! I be sayin' t' myself, there be a mistake! This toothless hag, half rotted away—this not be me Molly! But even when I be denyin' it, I be knowin' it to be the truth. An' I be comin' t' know that me girl child be dead—died o' the pox, Molly says . . ."

He sighed long and deeply and looked at the empty glass as if he wished there were more wine. "All the years I be spendin' t' make me revenge, all the hate I be plantin' in all that time, an' now I be findin' that the Lord be taken' care o' revenge in His own way. All those years be wasted . . . all for nothin'."

"So now you intend to throw your money away on a hopeless cause. That ought to straighten things right away!" Hampton commented with heavy sarcasm.

"Ye be makin' yer investments, an' I be makin' me own. I not be askin' ye t' understand, Larry. Once I thought ye a

106

fine, hard-workin' lad, jus' needin' a bit o' guidin'. But after all these years, I'd sooner spend me time tryin' t' talk the tide from comin' in than tryin' t' change the way ye think. Ye got ye a little girl child and a fine young boy, both, and everything ye touches be turnin' t' gold. But I heard 'bout a king once who be doin' the same, and his end not be so happy as ye might like t' think."

"Forego the parables, Adam, and do what you please. Make a fool of yourself before you die if you must, but do not blame me for the way things are. Money has always bought everything that's ever been important, and it always will."

Without even saying good-bye, Hampton turned his full attention to his papers and again began making careful notations in the margins. Barkley rose and made to leave the room, stopping when Hampton called what would be his final words to the man.

"Do not expect a loan from me when this thing is finished, Barkley. It has never been my policy to forgive and forget."

Chapter 11

Just a little over a week after Robert and Alec had left the City of New York, droves of enthusiastic Whigs had turned out to cheer General George Washington, recently named by the Second Continental Congress as commander-in-chief of the newly formed Continental Army. The very same day, an eager assemblage of Tories applauded the return of Royal Governor Tryon from England. Only a bit of tactful timing prevented the two from meeting, but a great many citizens became uneasy about remaining in a city so obviously divided by politics. The long hot days of summer passed slowly, winding a monotonous thread of tension around New York, a tension that threatened to erupt in violence. At summer's end, the royal governor gave up trying to squelch the countless local disturbances and moved himself to a safer and more peaceful location, a warship in New York Harbor.

Everyone's eyes were on Boston, where General Washington had taken on the difficult task of transforming a spirited group of militiamen into an army capable of facing an all-out war with Britain. By this time, despite low pay and total lack of compensation to the soldier or his next of kin for his injury or death, about six thousand men had enlisted in the Continental Army for a term of one year, and the state assemblies had pledged the general seven thousand more short-term militiamen. This was far short of the twenty thousand the Congress had hoped for, but the men stood ready and willing to fight. There would be no turning back.

On the island of Manhattan, a premature winter chill persisted for several days, and the darkness fell ever earlier in the last days of October. Juliet watched from the large front-parlor window as the fancy coach and four rattled up the long half-circle drive to the main entrance of Hampton House. She crossed to the door when she heard Frances enter, wondering why the girl had written her such an urgent note requesting to see her this very evening.

Malcolm took Frances's cloak and nodded at Juliet's order for tea, leaving the two women to retire to the parlor alone. A cheery fire brightened the deep colors in the room and lessened the discomfort of the damp evening air. Offering Frances the chair nearest the fire, Juliet pulled another chair close, and after a comment on the early frost, inquired about the reason for the other's visit. Frances rose and nervously gnawed at her bottom lip, while Juliet took note of her obvious agitation, having never before seen her so upset. Gripped by a sudden fear, Juliet also rose from her seat and grasped her visitor's arm, cutting short her pacing and forcing the fairer woman to face her.

"Robert! Have you heard from Robert? Is he well?"

"No, no," Frances answered, quickly allaying Juliet's worst fears. "It's not that. I haven't heard from him—not a word. I'm sorry, Juliet. Of course you must have thought . . . I *am* sorry."

Flooded with relief, Juliet seated herself once more and waited patiently for Frances to explain her visit. The slim blonde finally took a long, deep breath and began in a surprisingly calm voice.

"Papa has decided to leave New York. As you know, he has spoken of leaving the city all summer, but it still comes as something of a shock." She began to pace again, slowly and thoughtfully, as she continued. "Mama and he will go to England. Papa has an uncle there he is very close to, and business connections if his stay is extended. They intend to close the house, to let most of the servants go . . ." Her voice trailed off, and her eyes seemed far away and misty.

"What can I do to help, Frances?" Juliet offered, remembering well her promise to her brother.

The quiet composure left Frances's voice, and her wide blue eyes gave evidence of her distress. "Oh, Juliet! I cannot leave

New York! Mama and Papa may never come back here at all! I might never see Robert again!" At this last remark, her eyes flooded with tears, and her voice broke with emotion.

"Of course you'll see Robert again!" Juliet reassured her. "You cannot think for a moment that he would forget you as easily as that!"

"But if I leave . . . leave for England . . . he might think . . ." She raised her chin with determination. "I cannot go! I will not! I promised Robert that I would wait for him, and I will!"

Juliet cocked her head and raised her brows, genuinely surprised at the courageous resolve quiet little Frances was demonstrating.

"But Frances, you can't stay in New York all alone! You said that they plan to close the house—"

"Oh, Juliet," she broke in, "I had hoped that I might . . . that is, that you might . . ."

Frances faced her with wide blue eyes, apologetic and at the same time imploring. A silence fell as Juliet realized what Frances was pleading.

"You want to stay . . . here?" she asked finally, trying to hide her shock.

"I promise I shan't be a bother! I could be a help, really I could!"

"Oh, it's not that, Frances," Juliet managed convincingly. "It's only . . . well, what about Allan and Mary? You seem to get on so well with Mary!"

"Yes, I do. But . . ." Frances gave a quick look around and lowered her voice considerably. "I know that this will go no further, Juliet. Allan is in a rather . . . questionable financial situation at the moment. He has made some unfortunate investments in business and in land north of town, and Papa's had to help him out more than once. If I go to Allan, he would not turn me away, of course, but it might be a sacrifice for him to keep another person in his home. Besides, Papa might be very angry with him for taking me in. I couldn't have them fighting on my account." She frowned, having received no encouragement from Juliet. "I suppose your father might object to me staying here," she suggested, tactfully offering Juliet a gracious refusal.

"No," Juliet answered, then repeated it more confidently.

"No. It will be perfectly all right for you to stay here. I shall talk with Father. Don't worry." Juliet forced herself to smile, and with her next words made certain that Frances knew the invitation was legitimate. "Why don't you pack the things you will need for the next few days and come back? You can send for the rest later. You're welcome to spend the night if you wish. It's nearly dark now."

"Oh, I couldn't leave without talking to Mama! She . . . she will understand that this is what I have to do! I know she will!" she said firmly, then frowned and added hopefully, "I think she will . . ."

With a flighty whirl, Frances turned to leave, startling a stout maid heavily laden with a steaming tray of hot tea. As if the near collision had jarred her into reconsidering her freshly made plans, she rushed back again to Juliet.

"Are you certain your father won't object to my staying here?" she asked, taking hold of Juliet's hand.

"Of course I am certain. Don't worry, Frances. I shall take care of everything." Almost before Juliet had finished her words of reassurance, the impulsive blonde was climbing into her coach, her cloak entirely forgotten in her rush to leave. Juliet's mouth twisted into a strange grimace as she considered the repercussions of her reluctantly generous invitation. She began to pace the parlor, so deeply involved in her pondering that she nearly jumped a foot when the maid, still supporting the heavy silver tea service, asked if her mistress would be wanting tea. Juliet sighed as she dismissed the woman, reluctantly returning to her thoughts.

She certainly did not look forward to having Frances living here, but a promise was a promise, and if Robert was ever informed that she had refused to take Frances in . . . well, it would certainly be easier to put up with the girl for a few weeks than to face Robert later with a lame explanation of why she had not. As for Father, he might prove a problem. She would have to convince him that it was best for Frances to stay here. It should not be so difficult, she thought wryly, since he had always encouraged their friendship and had remarked many times that Juliet should try to be more like her. True, that had been many years ago, but Juliet remembered it well.

Gathering her confidence, she marched to her father's

study and knocked on the door. She heard her father's discontented muttering, a loud ruffling of papers, and finally a bellow bidding her enter.

"Are you very busy, Father?" she asked docilely.

He cleared his throat loudly and haphazardly continued to shuffle papers into three neat stacks on the top of his desk.

"Just finishing up for the day, actually," he answered, though his annoyed frown belied his casual acceptance of the interruption. "What is it, Juliet?"

Juliet decided that the best attack would be a direct one, if for no other reason than to save her father's valuable time. He had never reacted favorably to a show of timidity, but she could recall once or twice when he had slyly sidestepped her determination, particularly when she was angry.

"Father, Frances Church was just here. She wants to come and stay with us while her parents are in England."

"Frances Church wants to stay here—with us? While her parents are in England?" he repeated in surprise. "What does Edgar have to say about that?" he asked, an odd expression crossing his features, as if the idea amused him to some extent.

"I don't really know," Juliet admitted in a small voice, then, in a stronger one, "but Frances is determined not to go with them, Father, and she will obviously need some place to stay. I should think Mr. Church would be grateful to know that she was somewhere safe," she reasoned.

"Somewhere safe?" he barked back. "That is precisely the point, Juliet!" he said, banging his fist on the cluttered desk. "New York is not safe! Why else would the Churches and half a dozen other of my business associates be leaving their homes? Do you think it is a coincidence?" he demanded.

Juliet was hurt by his condescending tone. He had never given her credit for having any amount of intelligence, and apparently her years away at school had not altered his opinion.

"I know very well why Mr. Church is leaving New York, Father, though you never choose to discuss such things with me, nor do you allow me to read about such things on my own."

She referred to an incident a few weeks before, when Rachel had informed him about Juliet's purchase of the *Liberty*

Tree, a radical newspaper, during a shopping trip in town. Such papers were available on nearly every street corner, and Juliet had meant to look for some news about the fighting, and perhaps about Robert. But after a stern lecture on the danger of supporting open rebellion against the King, her father had taken the paper in question and thrown it into the fire, watching with smug satisfaction until a curling stack of thin glowing embers was all that remained.

"Relatively safe is what I meant," she corrected herself. "Safer than anywhere else she might stay here in the city, and more comfortable, too."

Lawrence Hampton put a thoughtful finger to his lips and tapped them several times. "What about her brother? Is he leaving, too? Why doesn't she stay with him?"

Still angered by his patronizing attitude, Juliet avoided answering the question. If he was going to be difficult about this, so was she! "Frances is my friend, and I want her to stay here with me," she stated simply.

Her father's eyes narrowed skeptically. "I had no idea that the two of you were so close."

She felt uneasy under her father's close inspection; he seemed to know that she was skirting the issue, but she felt compelled to forge ahead—she had promised Robert, and now Frances.

"We were never that close," she admitted carefully, then raised her chin and continued crisply, "but at least she would be someone to talk to! Robert is gone, Harold will not be here until spring, and there hasn't been a grand party in months! Is it too much to ask that I have someone my own age to talk to?"

Once again he tapped a finger to his lips and considered. It was much easier for him to understand a selfish motive for taking in Frances than a charitable one. When he finally agreed to her stay, Juliet realized that her professed motive of self-interest had convinced him, and she filed the information carefully in the back of her mind.

It was nearly a week before Frances actually moved into Hampton House, into the room closest to Juliet's on the second floor. For the first few weeks, Juliet was careful to avoid any unnecessary confrontations with her, hoping to mask her dislike as long as possible. They saw each other at mealtimes, where conversation was limited to stilted smiles and inconsequential talk about the weather and such, and short periods of awkward silence. When they encountered each other elsewhere during the day, Juliet would force a smile and continue about her business. Though she did her best to hide it, the cold, hard glint in her eyes and the distasteful frown that lurked close behind her forced smile let Frances know that Juliet considered her an intruder, though she was treated as politely as any visitor might be.

The Continental Army's siege of Boston had reached an impasse. Having penned in the British in the city proper, General Washington could not proceed without the heavy artillery necessary to drive the redcoats to the sea. He was forced to hold his position and hope for something of a miracle. The one that took shape came in the form of a Boston bookseller by the name of Henry Knox, whom Washington appointed chief of artillery—a strange phenomenon in an army almost totally devoid of heavy guns! Undaunted by the unfavorable situation he encountered on accepting the position, Knox almost immediately formulated a plan to bring the cannon captured earlier at Fort Ticonderoga to Boston, where it could be put to good use. Possibly because there was no other solution in sight, Washington agreed to the daring plan, which would mean the actual dragging of the guns through mountains and thick woods for more than two hundred miles. Moreover, the scheme was to be set in motion in mid-November, stacking the odds even higher against its completion, for the men would also be facing the harsh cold of winter. Among those valiants who had volunteered for the task was a young New Yorker who had come to Boston just prior to the Battle of Breed's Hill—Robert Lawrence Hampton.

As Christmas approached, Juliet threw herself into the tasks of shopping for the household, planning an elaborate Christmas Day meal, and decorating the house as it had never been decorated before. She was overflowing with energy and excitement for this project, for she knew in her heart that Robert would be coming home. At Frances's suggestion the Christmas dinner would include Allan and Mary and little Edgar, who were also invited to stay for the gay festivities planned afterward. Juliet bought gifts for everyone with her father's approval, and even the unwelcome help Frances offered at every turn failed to dim her spirits. There had been no more news of fighting; the British troops had been held at Boston. And, of course, no one expected any more fighting until spring. Surely Robert would come home!

The fine Christmas goose was served and eaten heartily by all but Frances and Juliet, the gifts were opened, the holiday spirits were raised in numerous toasts to a better New Year, and even a few hesitant flakes of snow danced in the blustering wind as darkness fell. Still Robert did not come.

Later, when the guests had gone and the house had quieted, Juliet wandered aimlessly about her room, returning hopefully every few minutes to scrape the frost from the windowpane and look out on the empty night. He has not even written! she thought in despair. When I was away, he always sent a special letter at Christmas, along with something he had picked out weeks before, something I could treasure. Her eyes burned with tears, though she somehow managed not to cry. Even the beautiful palomino mare her father had surprised her with had done little to raise her spirits, though indeed she was a fine horse, spirited, every bit of sixteen hands, the color of a newly polished gold coin, with a tail and mane of silver white.

Juliet opened the top drawer of the tall chest of drawers and withdrew a small brass box. Lifting its lid, she removed a long neck chain from which hung a heavy circle of gold engraved in fine detail. She studied the faces of the three old women depicted there. One held a spindle on which the thread of life was spun, another held straws that measured the amount of good or bad luck one would have and the last held scissors with which to cut the slender thread of life. Clotho, Lachesis, and Atropos: the Fates. At another low point in her life, the Christmas spent at school after learning that Allan had married, Robert had sent her the neck chain along with a letter Juliet would never forget:

. . . I am sending this to remind you that the Fates are yours to hold. The straws of fortune are dealt out to you, and they must be grasped without hesitation, but you can strive to realize any dream, if only you have will enough to do so . . . Never let Fate lead your life, Juliet, never give up your freedom, for freedom is the very reason for living. . . ."

Robert had known his sister well. He had offered her a challenge to go on with life, to overcome the pain of a lost love, knowing Juliet could never say no to a challenge.

The night was black and silent, but sleep was elusive, and there seemed eternities between each striking of the clock. Several times Juliet got out of bed to peer through the frosty window, watching large snowflakes drifting lazily to the ground in the quiet of the night. Sighing, she pulled a quilt about her shoulders and left her room, deciding that a bit of her father's brandy might help her find the sleep that so obstinately refused to come. The house was a mass of vaguely familiar shadows in the darkness as she hurried across the cold marble floor, gratefully wriggling her toes in the plush warmth of an oriental carpet when she reached the main parlor. The fire there had died to a few bright orange coals, and a chill was spreading throughout the room that had been so warm and cheery just a few hours before. Juliet shivered as she touched the cool glass decanter, and with a sudden burst of decision, she seized the entire bottle and headed for her room. Hiding it carefully beneath the quilt, she crossed her arms around it and cradled it to her breast as she padded up the stairs.

Taking a secure grip on the bottle with one hand, Juliet was gingerly reaching for her doorlatch with the other when a soft voice broke the heavy silence. She jumped and very nearly dropped the decanter.

"Juliet, are you all right?" Frances asked, walking over to her.

Closing her eyes, Juliet let out a sigh that was both relief and annoyance. "Frances," she whispered.

"Here—let me help you," she said, tugging at Juliet's sleeve. "Are you well?"

Juliet put a finger to her lips and glanced quickly about the dark hallway. Then she jerked her head toward the door, and Frances nodded agreement. Lifting the latch, she allowed them both entry before shutting it again with quiet precision.

"What's wrong, Juliet?" she whispered, eyeing her companion with obvious concern as Juliet unwrapped the brandy decanter and placed it on her vanity.

"I couldn't sleep so I went downstairs to get a glass of brandy," she replied, amused at the other's solicitous stare at seeing the bottle. "Do you want some?" she offered, her voice holding a hint of a challenge.

To Juliet's further amusement, Frances could not keep from cringing at the thought. "No! . . . No, thank you, I mean. Are you certain . . . I mean, well . . . that looks like a whole bottle! I mean . . . a whole bottle of brandy!"

Juliet chuckled at her wide-eyed disbelief. Frances actually thought she intended to drink the whole bottle! Well, maybe she would!

"You wouldn't . . . you don't intend to . . . become inebriated, do you?" she stammered timidly.

"What if I do?" Juliet returned, defiantly raising the bottle to her lips.

Frances gulped, and though it seemed impossible, her pale blue eyes grew even larger. Juliet made quite a show of taking a good long swallow, but almost immediately felt regret as she choked on the burning liquid until her eyes watered. It was a long time before she could draw a steady breath, and when she finally recovered, she found that Frances no longer wore a worried expression, but unsuccessfully hid a smile behind a small white hand. Though she could not explain why, Juliet returned her smile, and then, suddenly, they both began to laugh. Peals of merriment filled the room until they were actually weak from laughter. Juliet plopped herself on the bed and wiped the tears from her eyes. She could not remember having so good a laugh since she and Robert were children and had gotten away with some outlandishly mischievous prank. Frances leaned against the tall bedpost, her softer laughter dying away long before Juliet's, though a gay smile remained in her eyes and on her lips. Juliet rolled over and patted a spot on her bed, where Frances took a graceful perch beside her.

"What are you doing up so late?" Juliet asked in a voice that resumed her former quiet caution.

"I . . . I couldn't sleep either," she answered softly. "I . . . I was hoping that Robert would . . ." She quickly lowered her eyes to hide the despair.

Juliet suddenly realized that she was not alone in her disappointment this Christmas. Stretching a comforting hand toward the small white fingers clutched nervously together, her voice was a soothing balm. "I know. I had hoped that he would come home, too."

"Juliet, you worked so hard on this Christmas! The dinner was wonderful, and I did so enjoy seeing little Edgar open his gifts. It was very generous of you and your father." There was a brief silence before Frances broke it timidly.. "I . . . I . . ."

"You what, Frances?" Juliet asked in a kind voice she very seldom used.

"I have a gift for you," she managed to say, immediately adding an apology. "It's not anything expensive or elegant; it's only something I worked on especially for you . . . and it did turn out rather well."

"Well, what is it?" Juliet asked, her curiosity well aroused.

"It's in my bedroom—I'll be right back."

She was out and back in a flash, holding a flat, square package, which Juliet excitedly unwrapped to find a fine piece of stitchery depicting a proud dark brown horse's head. Juliet smiled down at the gift, genuinely touched by the effort that had gone into its making. For a long while she stared at the work, fumbling for an appropriate way to express her appreciation, but none came to mind.

"Robert said you love horses, and he told me that a horse named Ginger was very special to you, so I tried to make it look like her . . . though I don't really remember her very well. All horses look pretty much the same to me."

"It's beautiful, Frances. All that work . . ." Her voice was weak, and it was difficult to continue. "All that work." She swallowed hard and started again. "You have such patience, Frances! How I envy that!"

"You envy me?" Frances repeated in disbelief. "It is I who envy you, Juliet."

Unable to hide her own amazement, the obvious question burst from her lips. "Why should you envy me? I can hardly do anything properly! I cannot hold my temper; I cannot sit still long enough to take one decent stitch—much less do anything nearly as perfect as this!" She looked again at her gift with admiration before adding the deepest reason for her envy. "And Robert loves you . . ."

As Frances eagerly argued with Juliet's low self-assessment, a fond smile softened her words. "Juliet, you are so lucky to be the way you are! You are so strong and full of fire! Oh, how I wish I could be more daring! I'm afraid to death of horses; I think I always have been! And it's so hard for me to speak my mind, even when I feel things very strongly! And Robert loves you, too—just the way you are! I only wish that I could be more like you."

It was a revelation for Juliet. All these years, even the past few weeks living together, Frances had remained a total stranger, a hateful image, a fair girl who did everything easily and perfectly and who had stolen her brother's love. Suddenly Robert's last visit to this very room flitted through her mind. "I was hoping you and Frances might become good friends . . ." She squarely faced Frances, whose pale blue eyes met hers.

"It took a great deal of courage to stay here with us when your parents left for England, and it took even more to come here and ask for a place to stay," she reminded her.

"Yes," Frances agreed cautiously. "And I did stay here because of Robert, but . . ." She pursed her lips and carefully measured her words. "I have a confession to make, Juliet. I was afraid to go on that ship. I was only on a ship once in my entire life." Her eyes grew large and frightened at the memory. "We went to visit Aunt Colette and Uncle Jerome in Virginia, and I was deathly ill from the moment my feet left solid ground!"

Juliet stifled a smile. "What you think is courage in me is really a bad temper, I'm afraid. No one is brave unless he really has to be. When the time came, you made a decision to stay here and wait for Robert, which is brave no matter what other things might have motivated you! And I haven't seen you walking about with a sour face, asking why he left you here all alone. You've been cheerful and patient, and that's more courageous than anything I can ever recall doing."

Juliet's kind words prompted a pair of dimples to appear in Frances's cheeks and her eyes to dance excitedly. "Thank you, Juliet," she said as the two embraced each other for a long, warm moment.

Frances turned to leave the room and was almost out the door when Juliet called out to her.

"Frances?"

"Yes?"

"I'm very happy you decided to stay here."

"So am I!"

The door clicked securely closed, and Juliet fell asleep almost instantly, thinking that perhaps Robert had picked out a special gift for her this Christmas after all.

Chapter 12

Though the days of the New Year passed more quickly due to her newfound friendship with Frances, Juliet still spent long, anxious hours thinking of Robert, from whom there had been no word. The winter had been the most bitter of recent years. Great chunks of ice bobbed on the surfaces of the Hudson and East Rivers, and the North River froze completely over. The population of Manhattan went about the business of keeping warm and waiting for spring.

The arrival of February brought the first units of the Continental Army to New York under General Charles Lee. There was an immediate panic as droves of people hurriedly packed whatever they could, jamming the roads leading north and out of the city, while others sought refuge in New Jersey, crossing the Hudson in spite of the danger and bitter cold. By month's end, the City of New York was virtually deserted by most of its citizens and left in the hands of a few stalwart residents and the rebel army, who began to work at developing defenses against a British attack. During the weeks that followed, just north of the city proper, a string of fortifications was built from shoreline to shoreline, from the Hudson to the East River. Cannons were placed at strategic positions on high ground and at intervals along the coast. Some of the soldiers worked feverishly digging deep trenches, while others errected crude barricades of logs and dirt.

From the vantage point of her second-floor window, Juliet watched the great throngs of people clogging the roads leading out of the city. Even Allan and Mary had fled, with little

Edgar bundled against the harsh cold and a wagon piled high with their most valuable possessions. Mary's family lived near Boston, but with General Washington still holding the British at bay in that city, it offered no more safety than did New York. So they ran, as many of the panic-stricken townspeople did, into the bitter cold of winter with no destination, leaving themselves at the mercy of strangers who often exacted a high price for hospitality.

Day after day Juliet watched as friends and acquaintances left and troops continued to pour into the city. Although nearly everyone she knew had taken flight, Juliet's father refused to be "intimidated by the radicals, even if they have uniforms and refer to themselves as an army." Juliet could not have been happier with his decision, though she hid her feelings when he offered both Frances and her an opportunity to leave the city. If he had the courage to stay, she had stated simply, she would remain here also.

This morning in February, Juliet frowned as she saw her father leaving the house as he had several mornings during the past weeks. There was little or no business, she was sure, with the town filled only with rebel soldiers and Tories afraid to stray far from home. Yet he always insisted he was leaving the house on business, and he was certainly not the type of man to go for a pleasure drive—especially not in the middle of a frozen February. She puzzled over his departure for a moment, then glanced over her shoulder as Frances joined her at the window. Each day they shared a growing hope that Robert might soon be here, that he could be just a short distance away.

"Father just left," she announced without expression.

"Where in the world does he go every day?" Frances mused aloud. "Business couldn't be that good, unless he's secretly supporting the Continental Army." She chuckled at the absurdity, but Juliet did not share her humor.

"Mmmm," she agreed halfheartedly. Her mind was no longer on her father. "Frances," she began in a slow, reflective voice, "do you suppose that Robert could be here already . . . and be under the assumption that we left the city with everyone else?"

Frances considered for a moment, then slowly shook her head. "When Robert left, I promised I would wait for him here. He knows that I would never break that promise. He'll come back as soon as he can," she finished confidently.

"But if he tried to see you—I mean, if he is here, and if he went to your house, he would find no one there. He would have to assume that you'd left."

Frances's brows drew together in a worried frown. "But then he would come here, of course," she argued. "This is his home."

"You forget that he and Father did nothing but fight before he left. He may think it unwise to come here wearing a uniform." She looked out on the troops and amended, "If he has a uniform, that is."

"Then he would send a message to us," Frances insisted.

"Not if he thought we had gone," Juliet pointed out. "How could he know we're still here? Father has practically kept us under house arrest since the soldiers started coming. Even if Robert found out that Father had stayed, he might not know that we did."

"Now, Juliet, you know that your father is only trying to do what is best. Besides, since all the servants have left, there's plenty of work to keep us occupied."

Juliet had to agree with that. In spite of her father's exasperation, servant after servant—over thirty in all—had taken flight with the other townspeople. Juliet could never remember her father showing such anger as the morning when Malcolm had given notice. It was the first and only time he had disobeyed an order in over twenty years of service. Her father had offered money, pleaded, threatened, and sworn, but to no avail. Malcolm and the others had gone. Only Rachel and Jay remained behind, and Juliet and Frances found themselves doing things that were normally considered far below their station. But Rachel could hardly manage to do alone what it had taken over a score of well-trained servants to accomplish. The two younger women learned to enjoy the time they spent together, helping each other to dress and undress, making their own tea and helping with the cooking, and doing the lighter tasks of straightening and dusting and such. Rachel, with some help from Jay, pumped the water and did the heavy cleaning and kept the necessary fires lit so that the house did not absorb the winter's chill. Rachel left the house every so often, whenever it was necessary to secure provisions that were not available in the well-stocked storage cellar.

Juliet heard Rachel clanging about in the kitchen, then recognized the sound of the back door of Hampton House slamming shut. From the window, Juliet watched the gray-haired figure stride from the house, a large wicker basket slung in the crook of her arm. Juliet's eyes turned again to the soldiers scurrying here and there in their labors. From so far away it was impossible to recognize a single face. She could not help but voice her frustration.

"He could be here now—right here! And we would never even know!" she said with a bang of her fist on the windowsill. With a sudden burst of decision, she whirled and marched to her wardrobe. Flinging it wide, she snatched a pale yellow chintz dress, which she tossed on the bed. Frances's eyes grew round with fear as she watched Juliet gather her clothing and begin to dress.

"Help me, Frances," she urged her companion, who had frozen in horror at the thought of what Juliet might be planning.

"You're not going to—"

"Oh, yes I am!" she cut in boldly. "I will only be gone an hour or so. I'll be back long before Rachel returns—or Father. Now button me up," she ordered.

"But Juliet," Frances appealed as she reluctantly followed instructions. "It's dangerous, and you know it! We're Tories—at least our families are. And your father says they tar and feather Tories!"

"Father hasn't been tarred and feathered now, has he? And he's left the house nearly every day!"

"No," Frances admitted sheepishly, "but I've heard they do it, all the same. Besides, your father goes out of his way to avoid confronting them, Juliet. You are talking about going out unescorted for a face-to-face confrontation with an army of men! You could be . . ." Frances paled visibly and could not complete her sentence. A hand flew to her quivering mouth.

Juliet's voice softened as she considered her friend's good intentions, but her purpose did not falter.

"I cannot stay here and wait! It's been months, Frances! Months! Even if Robert isn't here, perhaps someone will know something; perhaps they can tell us why he hasn't even written to us."

Neither of the two had ever admitted the possibility that Robert might be dead.

Frances looked away, not wanting to be convinced but unable to offer a strong enough argument to deter her headstrong friend.

"Listen to me, Frances," Juliet pleaded. "I'll be careful. Nothing will happen. I . . . I'll take Father's gun. I know how to use it, and I'll be fine!"

It was a half-truth. She knew where her father kept his pistol, primed and ready for firing, and had secretly observed when he taught Robert to shoot. But that had been many years before, and she had never actually held a gun, much less shot at anyone or anything.

"It will only take maybe fifteen minutes or so to walk to where the men are working, so I ought to be back in an hour. Don't worry!"

Juliet carefully removed the key from its hiding place behind the thick leather-bound copy of the *Iliad* on the shelf of books in her father's study. She opened the drawer of his desk and cautiously removed the pistol, easily accessible though discreetly kept at the rear of the deep drawer under several papers. It was much heavier than she had expected it to be, and it was difficult to hold. It seemed somehow weighted at the long barrel, and only with both hands and a great deal of effort could she level it at a target. She aimed with utmost concentration on several objects in the room, acquainting herself with the awkward feel and realizing that perhaps she had not watched her father as closely as she had thought. She locked the drawer and replaced the key, hugging the pistol tightly to herself under the folds of her cape.

The stinging wind whipped Juliet's thick hooded cloak in every direction, making it nearly impossible to walk a straight line. She pulled its billowing folds tightly around herself and clenched her teeth to keep them from chattering. The bright sunlight was cruelly deceptive, offering no warmth in the strong, biting wind. Everywhere she looked there were soldiers of every age and description. The "uniforms" proved as many and varied as the faces of the men wearing them, for though a good many had assumed the buff and blue of the Continental Army, a good many others sported blue, red and blue, blue and white, or no uniform at all but an attire closely akin to frontiersman's garb. Scanning the sea of unfamiliar faces, Juliet began to question the wisdom of coming here alone. The pistol made her feel far less secure than she had hoped, and she saw unhappily that she had managed to attract a trifle more attention than she had intended. Encountering no one she perceived to be safe to question concerning her brother, she began to retrace her steps home. She remembered Frances's warning and the stories she had heard about beatings, running Tories out of town on a rail, and such, and did her best to ignore the alarm she felt when a few churlish men lost interest in their work and approached her. Much too quickly they caught up with her, and five or six of the unsavory characters surrounded her, preventing her from passing. Their hungry eyes roamed over her slender form, though much was hidden by her heavy cape.

"Well, if it not be a female!" one remarked, eyeing the fine features and delicate skin flushed deeply from the cold.

"Let's hope she not be the enemy!" said another.

"Ye wouldn't be the enemy, would ye?" the tallest and broadest of the group demanded, leering at her in a way that made her skin crawl. "Ye look friendly enough to me."

She ignored the man's suggestive remark and raised her chin, addressing him as she might have a gentleman.

"I am looking for my brother, Robert Hampton," she explained. "He's a member of your army."

They all laughed at her remark, and one finally let her in on the joke. "He not be a member of 'our army,' ma'am, lest he be from Vermont. Who he be with? Who he be fightin' under?"

Juliet frowned in despair. She had no idea who her brother was with; she knew only that he had left to join the fighting one day last summer and she had not heard from him since. There were so many soldiers! Why, even if she knew a hundred rebel soldiers, she might walk for hours without seeing a familiar face. With the utter hopelessness that engulfed her at this realization, a twinge of fear also began to grow as she glanced at the hostile group that had gathered around her. She shivered and clutched her cloak tightly as she forced the fear from her face and voice, levelly asking the men to let her pass. But they had had enough of digging ditches and stacking rocks for one day, and had no intention of letting such a pleasant diversion slip through their fingers.

"Would ye know the password?" one of the men questioned, clueing in his would-be cohorts with a broad wink. The others were quick to follow his lead.

"We got to protect ourselves, ye know. The enemy's everywhere!"

Another nodded and agreed. "New York's full o' Tories, t' be sure!"

"If ye doesn't know the password, we might be forced t' search ye . . . to be sure ye not be a spy, ye understand."

Juliet swallowed hard and tried to keep panic from clouding all reason as the largest of the group stepped closer, a malicious grin curving his lips. There must be a way out of this if I just keep my head, she rationalized. Surely these half-dozen ruffians would not risk hurting her in plain sight of many onlookers. But as her eyes searched the faces of the soldiers, she knew that she was wrong, for if her pleading look was answered at all, it was with a lustful gleam or a dispassionate stare. Nearly suffocating from the closeness of the overly bold soldiers, she began to shiver uncontrollably, as much from fear as from the cold. She gripped the pistol in her hands underneath her cloak, knowing full well it might protect her from one or two of them, but never five or six. Unable to endure it a moment longer, she summoned every ounce of her strength and tried to break through the circle of men that imprisoned her. So unexpected was her move that she almost succeeded, but her cloak was far too long and heavy to allow her such an easy escape.

As one of the men grabbed hold of her arm, the pistol clanged to the frozen ground. Her cloak billowed open in the harsh wind, and Juliet gasped at the chill that penetrated her instantly to the bone. She struggled to wrench free from the iron grasp in an effort to dive for the gun, but already it was being retrieved by one of the soldiers, who wore a surprised smile on his face.

"The little Tory had herself a gun!" he announced in amusement.

"She be a Tory, all right! This be proof enough for me!"

The tallest member of the group approached her slowly, hitching up his breeches and eyeing her like a vulture, relishing each step as he closed in on a trapped animal. In desperation, she swung her foot until it struck sharply against his shin, then jerked with such force against the man who held her arm that she quite nearly won her freedom. She sank her teeth deep in his fleshy hand when he snatched her back against himself, but he only tightened his hold and twisted her arm cruelly behind her back. As she cried out in pain, the largest of the group smiled wide, displaying an uneven row of brownish teeth, and moved to take hold of her shoulders.

"Ye want t' fight, Tory? I be glad t' fight wi' ye."

The repulsive grin faded when a calm masculine voice shattered his momentary bravado.

"I am sorry, gentlemen," came the silky words laced heavily with sarcasm, "but I must disagree with your verdict. The lady in question is no Tory. She happens to be my . . . sister."

The soldiers scrambled to release their captive, jaws dropping as they caught sight of the deadly end of two pistols leveled coolly at them by a man with coal-black eyes. Alec looked very much like Satan himself at this moment, and none of the soldiers seemed anxious to question his authority. Though her knees were quaking and her head was spinning, Juliet defiantly stretched out a shaking hand to the man who had confiscated her father's pistol. Eyeing Alec and then the girl, he begrudgingly relinquished the firearm and muttered a low curse before stomping off, followed quickly by the others. Tucking one of his guns securely in his belt, Alec bundled Juliet's cape firmly about her, offered her a strong muscled arm, and propelled her away to a place of safety.

A short time later, as she slowly regained her senses, she realized that she sat on a simple cot in a tiny room and that a friendly fire crackled in one corner. Alec knelt before her, rubbing her hands and wrists briskly until they stung with pain as feeling rushed back into them. He lifted her feet into his lap and removed her impractical embroidered slippers, and his lean brown fingers massaged every trace of cold from her feet, working their way casually over her slim calves. Her eyes gradually adjusted to the light, and she began to feel much better, though still a bit numb and shaky. So often in her dreams she had been taunted by that pair of dark, haunting eyes, that surely this was a dream also, she thought as she stared into their depths, though they were softer and kinder than she had ever before imagined them.

Without a word he rose and went to a far corner, where he rummaged through a leather sack and returned with a small metal flask and tin cup. He poured a bit of liquid into the cup and handed it to her. She took it in both hands and raised it, trembling, to her lips, taking a deep swallow. It was as if she had tasted liquid fire! She choked until her face was red and she was completely out of breath, and still her throat burned so badly that her eyes watered. It was several long moments before the violent reaction was quelled and the burning sensation became a warm glow; then every trace of tenseness left her and she felt odd and drowsy. She watched wide-eyed as Alec drained the cup and set it aside, then crouched before her and crossed his arms. A hint of a smile crept into his tone as he teased her softly.

"I know that you can handle yourself and that you did not ask for my help, so I don't expect you to thank me. But I would appreciate an explanation—what are you doing here? It's hardly a day for a stroll . . . though I've noticed you've a penchant for inclement weather. I would think, however, that you'd have the good sense not to parade yourself in front of an unorganized army of women-hungry men."

Juliet's large golden eyes stared at him without blinking. His deep, rich voice was more than calming, it was hypnotic, and his words did not at first penetrate the mellow glow that had taken hold. Alec studied her as she sat there motionless, and his smile deepened until dimples creased his cheeks.

"If I didn't know any better," he said lightly, taking her hand and giving it a pat, "I'd think you'd had one too many! Come, Juliet, it's not quite that strong."

She blinked and gave her head a shake, realizing with a jolt just where she was and with whom. It had been months since she'd seen him; she had never really thought to see him again, though his handsome image had occupied her mind during these last months far more than she would ever admit. She felt a renewed shakiness simply because he was so near her, and as her eyes locked with his, an uneasy tension made it difficult to form words of explanation he demanded.

"I . . . I was looking for Robert," she blurted out finally, finding that the words came more easily once she had begun.

"Do you know where he is, Alec? Have you seen him? Is he well?"

Alec frowned for a moment before he answered. "I've not seen Robert in several weeks, but then I'm not in one place very long. General Ward commissioned me to deliver correspondence for the army, so I've been riding back and forth between New York and Boston for some time now. The last I saw of Robert he was in Boston, and it is very possible that he's still there, especially if he hasn't been home to see you. But tell me, what are you still doing here in New York? I thought everyone but a few die-hard politicians had left this place. The roads were so crowded with people a few weeks back, I'd never have imagined you'd stayed on."

"Father refused to run away," she answered with considerable pride. "He said that he would not give up our home to the rebels, that he would stay here and fight for it if he had to. Almost all of the servants are gone, though. There's only Rachel and Jay now, and Frances and I—"

"Frances?" Alec asked in surprise. "Do you mean my cousin Frances?"

She nodded. "The Churches left before Christmas, but Frances stayed here in New York because she was afraid that if she left, she might never see Robert again." She lowered her eyes. "And now it's been months, and we haven't seen or even heard . . ." Her voice rose and broke off painfully. She closed her eyes and bit her bottom lip.

"He's well, Julie," Alec reassured her, giving her hands a squeeze. "There's been no fighting to speak of these last few months, and I saw him myself not so very long ago. Don't worry."

Impulsively, Juliet leaned forward until her head lay against his shoulder, and his arms went around her in comforting embrace that effectively banished every trace of fear. He was so warm, so strong, so sure of himself, she thought enviously. How she wished she could be more like him! A moment later came a small voice, muffled against his shirt.

"Thank you, Alec."

He pulled gently away from her to admire her face in the firelight. Golds and coppers flickered from her hair and eyes, and her skin glowed the color of warmed honey. He touched his lips affectionately to her forehead, her cheek, her mouth, briefly, gently, forcing down a burning desire for so much more. He was fully aware of her vulnerability at this moment, but he resolved not to take advantage of it. Someday she would respond to his kiss for a different reason, and in anticipation of that day, Alec would bide his time.

Suddenly fearful and uneasy, Juliet looked away, hoping that he did not see the hunger he had awakened in her, that he was not aware of the frantic beating of her heart. He had never kissed her that way before, as softly and tenderly as a devoted husband might kiss his loving wife, and the warmth and longing she felt at such a kiss was as frightening to her as anything else she could name.

Alec rose reluctantly and spoke again in his teasing tone. "If you vow never again to leave your house unescorted, I will be happy to see you safely home. I assume that no one knew of your intention to . . . inspect the troops?"

"Only Frances."

"I'll wager she took a bit of convincing before letting you go," he said with a wry smile. "We had better be off then, before you're missed."

He picked up her shoes and slid them over the thin stockings that covered her feet, then held out a hand to help her up and pulled her cape tightly about her. He donned his heavy leather jacket and tricorn hat, put both his pistols in his belt, and paused to toss Juliet a reproving glance as he took her father's pistol in hand.

As they walked through the streets, Juliet questioned him about the great projects that were under way all about them. Up close the island was beginning to look as if it were covered by giant molehills, particularly near the water.

"Why are they doing all this? It looks even worse up close. They are making an absolute mess of this island!"

"They are indeed!" he laughingly agreed with her. "General Lee is in charge of fortifying Manhattan against a British attack. That means trenches and barricades, and I'm afraid, as you say, a mess!"

"There must be a million soldiers here, Alec."

He chuckled at her exaggerated estimate. "Not quite a million, Julie. I wish there were!"

"Half of them don't even have uniforms, and the other half

don't match. Why does General Lee think that the British will attack here?"

"I'm afraid it's inevitable, Julie. With the finest natural harbor on the coast, it's the logical place."

"Well, I haven't seen any fighting yet, and I don't think there will be any here," she hoped aloud, trying to sound confident. Then she smiled, deciding once and for all that she liked it when Alec called her Julie.

"Oh, there will be fighting here, all right," he said. "It's only a matter of time. Howe has had about enough of Boston; he could not get a foothold there because most of the people are patriots. But here in New York it's a different story. The population of this city is basically loyal to the King."

"This population doesn't look very much like the King's men to me" she commented wryly, looking pointedly at a group of soldiers they were passing. "The loyal population to which you refer is basically all gone."

"Yes, but they'll return when the fighting is over. Besides, Howe is fairly certain he can take New York because it's an island, and their navy will make it nearly impossible for us to hold it."

Juliet stopped short and looked at him incredulously.

"Are you saying that after all this, you will not be able to hold off a British attack? You honestly plan to lose New York? Then why, in God's name, are you here?"

Alec stared down at her face and smiled in spite of himself. She stood defiantly awaiting an answer, even though the wind whipped at her cloak and burned her cheeks.

"Despite what your father may have told you, Julie, this war was not entirely my idea, nor do I decide how it is fought. The army is here because we have no choice. Strategically, we must at least try to hold this city, or the British will effectively divide the northern colonies from the south."

"But Alec," she argued, "if you really think to lose . . ." She could not finish, for she was afraid to draw a conclusion.

"As someone told me once, this entire war is impossible. But here we are, ready to fight, because we feel we have no other choice. The stakes are far too high to simply throw in our cards, and there is always the chance that we could hold New York as we did Boston. Most of the soldiers here are depending on it."

"Why not you?" Juliet studied his face intently, unable to understand why a man would fight against such odds. Her father would never risk everything he owned in such an unlikely game—he was far too clever. And yet, Juliet respected Alec all the more for fighting for what he believed in, though by her father's definition it made him a fool.

"Because I know a bit more than most of them, I suppose." He saw her worried frown deepening, and the fear that began to fill her eyes. "The British own the sea, and in spite of all our elaborate preparations, they will soon own this island. I am not saying that to frighten you, Julie, I am only saying it because it is the truth, and I think you need someone to be honest with you . . . for a change."

He began to walk with his hand at her back, urging her to keep up with his brisk gait. They did not speak again until they had reached the start of the long drive in front of Hampton House, standing close to the stone wall to escape the brunt of the heavy winds. Alec's fingers lightly brushed Juliet's cheek, chapped a deep pink from the cold, and he smiled at the frown on her face.

"I ride out tomorrow at dawn, but hopefully I'll be back within a fortnight or so. I can't promise you anything, but I shall try to see Robert and let him know that you've stayed in the city and that you are well."

As relief and hope flooded her face, she flung her arms about his neck, standing on tiptoe to kiss his cheek. "Oh, thank you! Thank you, Alec!"

"I cannot promise," he repeated sternly, disengaging her arms, "but I'll try. Now you had better go in and thaw out before you turn so pink that everyone will know you've been half-frozen. And put this back where you found it!" He placed the gun firmly in her hand.

"Thank you," she said again, smiling into his austere expression.

Gasping as a sudden gust pulled at her cloak, she turned, lifted her skirts, and ran almost the entire way to the house. Remembering Alec's words just as she reached the main entrance, she passed by the door and circled around the back of the house to the stables. Rachel had surely returned by now, and she needed time to gather her wits and think of a plausible tale to tell concerning her absence. She threw open the

135

door and rushed inside, the wind blowing the door shut behind her with a resounding whack. Totally out of breath, she stopped for a rest, leaning against the first rough-beamed stall. Without any warning, a low, hoarse voice came out of the darkness.

"Ye be all right, Miss Juliet?"

She squinted, trying to make her eyes adjust to the inadequate light, though she recognized the voice long before she could make out his gaunt features.

"Jay," she said, relieved, though still quite out of breath. "I . . . I . . . yes. I am well." In her haste to explain her presence, she said the first thing that came to her mind. "I was just . . . going to check the horses."

Her vision was returning, though there were still a few spots of white that were slow to fade after the long walk with Alec in the bright sun. She bit her lip, hoping Jay would not question her further.

The thin man's brows met in a troubled frown, and he thoughtfully scratched his meager growth of graying hair.

"What did ye think would be amiss wi' them?"

"Nothing! Nothing . . ." she answered too quickly. "Just checking." She squeezed the cold metal of the pistol to her chest and nervously took a few steps forward, looking up and down the various stalls with feigned curiosity.

"Well," she said, turning a bright smile back at Jay, who stood staring after her, a puzzled frown on his face. "I see everything is fine here."

"Miss Juliet?" he called as she turned to leave. She stopped short and dared not turn back to face him, so sure was she that her guilt was evident in her face.

She swallowed hard and did her utmost to sound casual. "Yes?"

"Be ye wantin' t' warm ye by me fire afore ye go t' the big house?"

She smiled and sighed her relief, turning round to follow him into his small room, where a cheery fire warmed the dirt floor and stone walls. Juliet stood very near the fire, her cape opened to catch its radiant warmth. When she looked about, she smiled gratefully at the old man, who sat on a less than comfortable looking pallet. How little this man had, she thought, her eyes scanning the room and its sparse furnishings, yet how loyal he had always been to her family.

"Jay," she said, slowly rubbing her palms together, the gun held close against her in the crook of her arm. "Do you have any family?"

"Ye be me family," he answered simply. "Robert most of all be me family, but ye all be like family t' me."

She was touched by his answer, and she could not bring herself to lie to him; she felt she owed him the truth. But how could she explain that she had come here because she had gone out strictly against her father's orders, that she could not go inside half-frozen or someone would surely find her out. She noticed that his interest was caught by the arm that cradled the gun, partly visible under her opened cape.

"Jay," she began, "I . . . I . . ." Her brow knit in confusion as she tried to find the right words of explanation. She was afraid to be totally honest with him; he might inform Rachel or, worse, her father. Jay watched her struggle for a few moments, stroking his stubbly beard.

"If ye be havin' trouble ye can tell me 'bout it. Robert made me promise t' see after ye afore he left, an' ye needn't worry 'bout me tellin' Master Lawrence."

His statement took Juliet completely by surprise. Robert had asked Jay to take care of her!

Before either could say another word, a loud whack echoed again through the barn. Juliet barely had a chance to flash a pleading look at Jay, who jumped up and headed for the door. He had not stepped more than three paces out of his room before encountering a highly irritated Rachel.

"Did Juliet go out riding?" she asked bluntly.

Her voice was only slightly raised, but Juliet recognized the fury that was concealed in her tone and timidly stepped out of Jay's small room. The older woman's face contorted strangely, and she seemed far angrier at having found Juliet here than she had been a moment before. Though her voice became soft and respectful, anger sparked in her cold blue eyes.

"Where have you been?" An accusation weighed heavily in her question.

Before Juliet had a chance to reply, Jay's hoarse voice responded calmly and normally to the angry query.

"Juliet be wi' me this mornin'. It be a long while since we talked 'bout the ol' times, and I reckon it be an easy way t' lose track o' the hour."

Rachel took in Jay's face, and her eyes narrowed in suspicion, though the old man's small gray ones gave no sign of his guilt. She turned then to Juliet, who raised her chin a notch in an arrogant gesture intended to remind Rachel of her place. It was quite effective, and after a terse "Your father is expected home any moment" and a single last accusing look at Jay, the woman whirled about and strode from the stables.

Juliet waited until she heard the reassuring slam of the heavy stable door, then rushed over to Jay and gave him a quick hug.

"Ye better be goin'," he said, blushing in embarrassment at her sudden show of affection. "There be plenty o' time for explainin' t' me, but not much time t' be gettin' in before Master Lawrence be askin' questions."

Juliet left the warmth of the stables and ran to the house, anxious to tell Frances the bit of news about Robert that had nearly been so costly.

Chapter 13

The month of February ran its course, and soon March winds blew in milder and warmer breezes, and with them the promise of spring. With the break in the weather, Juliet found herself becoming less content with staying indoors and performing the household tasks that had kept her busy during the short, cold days of winter. She longed to breathe in the fresh outdoor air and used every available excuse to spend her time in the garden, where the first sprigs of green were forcing their way through the moist brown earth. Nature was awakening, and like a child she was caught up in its miraculous rebirth. Often Frances would join Juliet in the garden, and she would talk and laugh and share memories of what springtime had meant to her in years gone by. With wistful blue eyes, Frances recalled the grand parties that her mother had always planned when the weather grew warm, the long walks along the breezy shoreline beaches, spectacular fireworks that lit up the sky, and exotic animal exhibits that had drawn people from far and wide.

Juliet listened politely to Frances's tales of springtimes past, desperately missing the freedom she had enjoyed the year before. As the days grew brighter, she dreamed of riding on her fine new mare, whom she knew could run like the wind itself. Jay exercized Amber, as Juliet had named the proud golden horse, in the confines of a fenced riding ring by the stables, and except for a half-dozen or so short jaunts in the cold beginning of January, Juliet had not ridden her at all. She could hardly be satisfied to celebrate the arrival of spring with a quiet walk in the garden and a bit of reminiscing! She wanted to be a part of it all—to ride her mare through an open meadow, to run barefoot on the new sprouts of grass, to wade in the water of a rushing stream that would still be chilled with the memory of winter. Her long years of schooling seemed dim in her mind, and the adventurous spirit of her childhood had returned. Had she not experienced such a close brush with disaster the day she had gone in search of Robert, she would surely have taken leave of the house by now on some capricious pursuit in honor of the newly arrived season.

It was strange, she mused as she flicked a feather duster here and there in the small parlor, that while at school those long years she had seldom felt such rebellious urges; yet now, when she was home again . . . There was something about this place, Manhattan, something magically alive in the hills to the north of the city, and, indeed, in the city itself. It was so unlike the quiet sameness of the English countryside! Everything was here: the proper and improper, the rural and urban; most of all, Manhattan was an island dynamic and ever-changing. Juliet thought of the unsightly trenches and barricades that scarred the once beautiful shoreline. When the soldiers left and the townspeople returned, there would certainly be a lot of work to be done. But New Yorkers were a hardy lot, and no doubt they would rise to the task.

A series of sharp raps at the main door jarred Juliet from her thoughts, and without hesitation she ran to get her father's pistol. Just a few days before, he had taken her aside and shown her where he kept it hidden, giving her a solemn if brief lesson in its handling. He never actually expected Juliet to hit whatever it was she might be aiming at, but he hoped she would get off a shot that would bring Jay, who was also armed and seldom missed his mark.

Juliet grasped the pistol in trembling hands and ran to the window, hoping to recognize a horse tethered at the post. There was none. She cocked the gun and cautiously made her way to the front hall, passing a terrified Frances, who stood halfway up the stairs, a trembling hand clutched to her mouth.

"Wait, Juliet," she said in a frightened whisper. "Let me go. You stand back and . . ." She closed her eyes and did not finish. She came down the stairs, leaning heavily on the banister, and walked bravely toward the carved double doors, which vibrated ominously as a heavy fist knocked from the opposite side. She took a deep breath.

"Who is there?"

She nearly fainted with relief when she recognized the voice that broke the silence.

"Frances? Is that you? It's Alec."

"Alec!" she gasped. "It's Alec!"

She unbolted the door with a single motion and threw her arms around her cousin, while her happy laughter spilled about the room. Alec smiled wide at her fluttery excitement, then frowned as he caught sight of the dangerous end of a fully cocked pistol, which Juliet still held tightly in both her hands. He disengaged himself from Frances and held out an open, expectant hand, into which Juliet placed the gun without protest.

"Tell me, Miss Hampton," he said, eyeing her with a disapproving glare as he carefully released the gun's hammer from its firing position. "Exactly how many men have fallen prey to your marksmanship since I saw you last?"

Juliet raised her chin a notch and answered him with a cold smile, though she was deeply glad to see him.

"None. But then, you are the first uninvited visitor we have had."

Frances's blue eyes widened in surprise at Juliet's less than cordial welcome, but Alec ignored the slight with a grin that managed to dispel all hostilities.

"Indeed, Miss Hampton, I am not to be considered a guest. I come merely as a humble servant,"—he gave a short bow of servitude—"a messenger from your dear brother."

Thrilled at the news, both women immediately assailed him with excited questions about Robert, and he was forced to retreat a step and hold up his hand in order to answer them. Reaching inside his coat, he withdrew a sealed letter and handed it over to Frances, to whom it was addressed. She stared for a moment at her name written neatly in Robert's own hand, then her worried eyes searched Alec's face.

"Is he . . . Does he still . . . ?" Her voice broke off, and she swallowed with difficulty.

"He is in good health," Alec answered, taking her small

white hand and closing it on the letter. "And he sends you his love," he added with a smile.

She held the letter as if it were something very fragile and carefully plucked at the seal, then stopped and looked at Alec and Juliet apologetically. She did not wish to read his words aloud; after all this time she wanted to be alone and undisturbed in reading whatever he had taken the time to write to her. But it would not be polite or proper to read it to herself while they looked on in awkward silence. As if he knew her thoughts, Alec suggested she retire to her room and read her letter privately, and offered to return a reply if she had one prepared when he took his leave.

"Yes, Frances," Juliet agreed, forcing herself to be happy for Frances, though she was disappointed and more than a little envious. "You can tell me later what he said, and besides, you will want to answer him right away."

"When I make my return to Boston, I will see that your reply finds its way safely to Robert, be it one week or several," Alec promised. "But you'd better be about it quickly. I leave again tomorrow dawn, but I cannot stop here then, as I might well encounter a guard far less willing to be disarmed than the one on duty today."

Frances whirled on her heel and flew happily up the stairs. When she had disappeared from view, Alec faced Juliet with a pleased, expectant smile.

"How did you know Father would be away?" Juliet inquired.

"He is gone a good deal of the time, or so I've been informed. And I asked the groom if the coast was clear."

"Jay?"

He nodded. "Robert suggested it when he gave me the letter."

As he spoke, his dark eyes gave her a complete going over, which deepened the color in her cheeks and caused her to look away in embarrassment. Her attire, a plain cotton gown, was hardly a proper one for entertaining, but it served the purpose of cleaning and gardening far better than most of her other clothing. Her thick, dark hair was tied back with a drab kerchief, and there was even a smudge of dirt on one side of her nose.

"As I told you, we did not expect guests," she said, fingering the dark fabric with regret. "I'm afraid I must resemble a chambermaid."

"The prettiest chambermaid I have ever seen," he answered honestly. Then, with his finger he lightly touched the smudge of dirt on her nose and added with a sly grin, "Clothing never did a woman make."

Juliet touched the spot on her face, then wrinkled her nose at the dirt that readily transferred itself to her finger. Rubbing the remaining dirt from her nose, she ruefully stole a peak at herself in the looking glass in the hallway and drew the kerchief from her head. He always seems to have me at a disadvantage, she thought uneasily. She was never really prepared for what he said or did, and heaven only knew what he was thinking behind that handsome smile of his, or what those black eyes really saw.

"Could I offer you some tea, or perhaps something to eat?" she asked politely as she led him into the small parlor. She could not explain why she chose that room, which was not normally used for entertaining. It had once been known as Mistress Hampton's study, and Claire, who had considered the family portraits private items to be preserved for future family members and never for public display, had insisted on their placement in this room.

"I believe I'll pass on the tea, thank you. Tea seems to make me very argumentative for some reason. But a glass of wine would please me greatly." He eyed the crystal decanter and glasses on a table in the corner of the room.

Juliet obliged his request and took a seat in her mother's chair, while Alec made himself comfortable in another chair a proper distance away, yet well in range of quiet conversation. He lifted the glass to the light and studied the wine's clarity, then paused to sniff its bouquet before taking a sip and savoring its warmth and flavor.

"I have finally discovered something on which your father and I agree. He does know how to choose a fine wine." He twisted the glass in his hand and noted the way the light shimmered on its surface with the movement. "I am certain that he would not welcome my approval, however." His eyes smiled as he raised the glass again to his lips. "Particularly when his wine was served to me by his lovely daughter in his private parlor . . . alone."

Juliet dismissed the implication in his words in a sober voice. "As you know, Frances is close by. And you make it sound as if I am intentionally entertaining you behind my father's back."

Alec raised a brow at her words, knowing full well that for all her denial she was doing exactly that. She matched his stare with an accusation.

"You hate my father, don't you?"

"Not at all," he returned, totally undisturbed. "It is only that we disagree on everything—except wine, that is."

"Politics do not necessarily mean everything. Your Uncle Edgar does not agree with you about the war, yet you seem to get on well with him."

"Oh, I do," he agreed pleasantly. "What you fail to realize, Julie, is that two people might act in the same way for completely diverse reasons. You have to observe someone closely to learn what he really feels, regardless of what he might tell you he feels. Actions speak quite a bit louder than words, but only if you are watching closely enough."

"That does not explain why you find fault with my father for his feelings about the war and not with your uncle. They are both opposed to rebellion against the King, and I personally find loyalty a trait to be admired. Moreover, my father has bravely chosen to remain here, while your uncle left for England. I'm proud of his courage."

Alec's eyes bore into hers from across the room, then he took a deep breath and attempted to explain his assessments of two very different men.

"My Uncle Edgar is a very successful banker. He loans capital when the odds of a fair return are in his favor, and when he perceives it otherwise, he neatly and tactfully manages to decline. That is the nature of his success. Friendship to him is something totally separate, as it must be in his profession. He would give a friend a gift of money if that friend were in need, but he would not lend it to him for what he feels would be a bad investment. He is a generous man, but he is not a gambler. When the trouble broke out here, it was perfectly natural for him to leave the colonies, not because of loyalty to the King, mind you, but in the interest of his own safety, both physical and financial. He saw the odds as closely stacked, and he was not about to wager on the outcome one way or another."

Alec sipped at his wine and assured himself that Juliet was listening to him attentively. "Your father, on the other hand, sees the rebellion as a losing proposition. Therefore, he proclaims loudly that his loyalty rests with the King. As far as his courage in remaining here . . . I suppose I must give him that, though his bravery is rooted in his attachment to the wealth he has acquired, and not in anything so admirable as allegiance to a monarch, for all his swearing to the contrary.

"Your father is a gambler and an excellent one. He knows when and how to mislead the unwary, when to make a temporary concession, and when to call a bluff. He plays a game using people as pawns, and he does not lose very often. When he does, as with Robert, it is not so much for lack of skill, but rather because he has underestimated his 'opponent.' A hypocrite often finds it impossible to believe sincerity in anyone."

"And do you think I am a hypocrite, also?" Juliet ventured softly.

For a long moment, Alec regarded her with steady contemplation. "I do believe you try to be, but you just aren't very good at it!"

The hint of a smile left his eyes, and he again spoke seriously.

"There are countless ships that sail the sea, and no two are exactly alike. Each was built with a specific purpose in mind to which it is best suited. The heavily armed warships and the great cargo vessels—one can easily recognize their purpose and name their value. But if the vessel be a sleek and spirited schooner, longing to let the wind fill her sails and to challenge the roughest seas, her worth cannot be proved with an ill-suited and cumbersome cargo. She is in need of a captain to guide her with a gentle, knowledgeable hand, one unafraid to unleash her speed and power to its fullest length, trusting the stuff of which she is made.

"It would be a mistake to keep such a ship anchored in a safe port, to be admired for her beauty but never tried, to grow weathered and useless without the character of one that has faced the sea. It would also be folly to load her overmuch, until she rests precariously low in the water and there is difficulty and danger in keeping her on course. Should the sea become rough, the cargo would be tossed overboard no matter what its value, to save the vessel itself."

He paused to taste his wine. "You would have yourself married to a boring gentleman with a great deal of money, spend your days buying gowns and ordering servants about, your evenings giving lavish parties and showing all of your dull new friends just how happy you are and what a success you have made of yourself. Yet, when all have admired you, when you possess the wealth that you think you desire, you will long to throw it into the sea, to be free of the heavy anchor that has taken your freedom, your chance to prove your real worth."

His analogy was so painfully accurate that Juliet could think of no words to strike it down. Not daring to meet his eyes, she rose, turned her back to him, and strode toward the window. She idly fingered the soft curtain fabric and gazed thoughtfully out on the bright spring day. Her eyes became troubled, and her brows drew together in a worried frown.

"How could you know anything of what you say?" she whispered. "Why do you make me feel like I am failing so miserably at everything I am trying to do?"

Her eyes blinked painfully, and her breast suddenly ached, but she bit her lip and traced the squared casing of the windowpane, trying to get a hold on her emotions. She heard Alec rise and come to her side, and she could hardly breathe at all when she turned and met those dark eyes. His voice came low and gentle, completely void of the chiding that usually underscored his words.

"I know you, Julie, because I am so much like you. At the barest hint of a challenge I feel forced to prove myself, and I never stop to think that only I really doubt who I am, what I am." He paused and held her face between his hands, his thumbs passing like a caress over her now damp cheeks. "You are a beautiful woman, Julie, whether dressed in homespun or satin. You are filled with life and potential, whether you choose to suppress it or channel it to the use intended. You are warm, and you want very much to love and to be loved, though you do your best to deny it, to act as if it does not matter to you."

His arms closed about her, and his mouth met hers lightly, then with mounting pressure and intimacy. "It does matter,

Julie," he whispered hoarsely against her cheek. "It matters so very much. . . ." His lips made their way to hers once more, and his tongue hungrily took her mouth. The rush of emotions that poured into her consciousness was far more intoxicating than the taste of wine that flavored his kiss, and she felt at once weak and dazed. Taking her chin in his hand, he gently tilted her head back again, forcing her golden eyes to open and meet his. Then he waited for something, seemed to search for something in her face.

"Oh, Alec," she murmured helplessly. "You are right. I am not happy doing all the proper things with the proper people. I'm so different from Frances, though I try so hard to be like her. What am I to do?"

"Break your engagement," he answered firmly.

She felt as if someone had doused her with a pail of cold water. She broke away from his embrace and shook her head vehemently.

"I cannot do that!"

"Why not?" he demanded, following her as she slowly backed away.

"Because . . . because . . ." she stammered. Her eyes darted about in careful avoidance of his accusing glare. "I cannot do it, Alec!" she insisted. "Father is so pleased with my plans! What could I tell him? That you convinced me that it was the wrong thing to do?"

"Why not tell him the truth? That you've decided you will not be happy married to Harold. Why do you have to tell him anything at all?"

She turned on him in hot protest. "I owe my father something! He . . . he loves me," she blurted out lamely.

"If he loves you so much, why would he want you to be unhappy? Your first duty is to yourself, Julie, can't you see that?"

She gave him no answer, but her eyes grew visibly harder. Alec's anger flared as he recognized the familiar determination. He knew nothing he could say now would change her mind, but he continued to speak to vent his own frustration.

"So! It's your father you want most to impress with your title and your money." The sarcasm grew bold in his tone. "But Julie, you've made such a sorry bargain! Surely your father, who so loves his profit, must realize that! You could certainly attract someone more prestigious than a mere lord! A[n] earl at the very least, or a duke . . . Why, even George himsel[f] might show some interest and grant your father a title of hi[s] very own! It would take a bit of doing, but then, you are a de[-] termined young woman, and the talk is that he prefers hi[s] whores young—"

Juliet gasped at the insult, and her hand flew across hi[s] face. The vicious, ringing slap left a vivid impression of crim[-] son on his tanned skin, but she was far from satisfied an[d] drew back to strike him again. Her hand was caught in[-] stantly in an iron grip, and Alec drew her with a savage jer[k] against his lean muscled body.

"You had better never slap me again, Juliet Hampton," h[e] warned in a dangerously soft voice, "or I might be tempted t[o] teach you a lesson I am certain you would never forget."

Though his black eyes and threatening words terrified her[,] she straightened her spine and refused to back down.

"I am not afraid of you," she spat. "There is nothing tha[t] you could do to make me cower at your feet!" Her voice gre[w] stronger, and her eyes narrowed. "You are jealous of my fa[-] ther, of his success and his money and of my loyalty to him[.] You may have convinced Robert to turn against him, but yo[u] will never convince me!"

Their eyes locked, each stubbornly refusing to yield an[y] ground. Juliet's heart pounded furiously in her breast, a[s] much from fear as from anger. She well realized that she wa[s] tempting fate by returning the menacing gleam in his eyes[.] To her surprise, he broke the stalemate by relaxing his hol[d] on her and curving his lips in a reckless smile, which man[-] aged to unnerve her far more effectively than anything h[e] might have said.

"Does it not occur to you that my very presence here is evi[-] dence of your defiance of your father?"

He sauntered to the table where he had left his glass o[f] wine, leisurely lifting it to drain its contents. Then he casu[-] ally reached inside his coat and removed a letter identical to the one he had given to Frances a short time before. Juliet'[s] eyes widened in sudden distress as he strode to the fireplace[,] took flint and tinder in hand, and proceeded to kindle a thi[n] orange flame. Realizing his intent, she rushed to stop him[,] groping vainly for the letter while he held it just out of her reach and alarmingly near the fire.

"Please, Alec," she pleaded frantically. "Please let me have it! Please! I . . . I am sorry for what I said—really I am!" she conceded. "Please?" Her voice was much humbled, and her eyes meekly begged the favor. To her relief, he moved as if to hand it over, then halted his movement and reconsidered.

"But it is in direct defiance of your father, Julie," he needled her.

"O-o-oh!" she sighed in exasperation. "Give it to me!" she ordered sharply, then snatched it abruptly from his hand. Once the letter was in her possession, she showed none of the polite patience Frances had shown. She tore at the seal and read without pause what her brother had written, not giving Alec another thought.

Dear Juliet,

It was strictly by chance that Alec managed to find me here, as I had not seen him since the last weeks of summer. I was surprised to learn that you and Frances remain on Manhattan and even more surprised to hear how you contacted Alec. I hope that your experience convinced you to be more cautious in the future. I cannot write much about military matters, but I can tell you this much. I have seen fighting, and it is far worse than anything I had anticipated or even imagined. How could anyone envision the horror of men screaming and dying for the sake of holding a piece of ground? At that moment, nothing in this world seems to be worth such great cost; yet a soldier must continue the fight and do his best to remember why. I have decided it would be for the best if I did not come back to New York, and have requested to remain here as long as I can be of service. Father was right when he said that I did not realize what I was getting into. Perhaps if I had known fully, I would never have been able to leave home at all. If I come back to you and Frances, and everything I love most in the world, it might prove too great a temptation for me. I do not think I could leave you all a second time. I know that you will understand and never tell Frances it was my decision not to come home now. Time is so short—Alec must leave soon. Take care and thank you for keeping your promise to me. I never once doubted that you would.

Robert

On finishing the letter, Juliet heaved a painful sigh and frowned deeply, turning wide, troubled eyes on Alec. He had helped himself to a second glass of wine and stood silently studying her, leaning forward and resting an arm on the high back of her mother's chair.

"Why did he wait so long to write, Alec?" Her voice was quiet but strained.

Alec traced a finger around the rim of his glass.

"He volunteered for a difficult campaign that took nearly two months."

Juliet was anything but appeased by his answer. "He could have let us know that he was well! At least that!" she flung back, letting her bitter hurt come to the surface. "How can he do this?" she demanded, waving the letter angrily in front of Alec's nose.

"Do what?" Alec asked, puzzled at her outburst.

"He has requested to stay in Boston."

"Does he say why?"

"He is afraid that he would not be able to leave home again, after the things he has come to know. Didn't you read this letter?"

Alec ignored her last comment, lowering his eyes and contemplating what remained of his wine.

"It was not easy for your brother, Julie. I was very concerned about him after the battle at Breed's Hill. We were close enough to see everything that was happening . . . to see the blood . . . the bodies littering the landscape . . ." Alec closed his eyes tightly to shut out the gruesome memory.

"It is difficult to learn to put yourself in another place and time, to separate your feelings from what you are doing, or to simply refrain from thinking at all. But that is what a soldier is expected to do. I have heard that men lose their minds on the battlefield, that there are those who can never seem to drive the ghastly spectacle from their thoughts, and I don't doubt it at all. Thank God that Robert has at least held on to his sanity."

Juliet's eyes flooded with tears.

"But he doesn't want to come home, Alec!" she choked out.

In a single moment Alec closed the space between them and wrapped Juliet in his arms.

"He will come back, Julie," he crooned softly, stroking her tousled hair. "It will all be over someday, and Robert will come home."

Juliet pulled back to look him squarely in the eye. "You didn't read my letter?"

Alec's jaw fell open in a look of surprise that was closely followed by an angry scowl along with a booming protest.

"Miss Hampton! Generals of the Continental Army, not to mention delegates to the Continental Congress, trust me daily with their vital correspondence. I have spent years carrying letters to every colony and Canada, and in all that time I have never once read a single missive that was not properly addressed to me!" He paused to take a much needed breath. "Might I also remind you that the seal on your letter was broken by no other hand than your own? Why would you accuse me of doing such a thing?"

His tirade of denial was not totally convincing to Juliet, who gave good reason for her accusation.

"Perhaps the years have affected a change then, Alec, for if you will recall, you saw nothing wrong with reading my letter to Allan. And I know for a fact it was not 'properly addressed to you.'"

A glint of recognition slowly dawned in his eye, and close on its heels were a flash of white teeth and a hearty chuckle.

"I had forgotten all about your letter to Allan," he grinned. Juliet's eyes flashed in justified anger, and noting her reaction, Alec did his best to assume a sober expression. "I'm sorry, Julie," he managed, though his voice was not exactly apologetic. "I have a confession to make. I never read any letter you wrote to Allan, or anyone else."

She raised a brow and stared at him skeptically.

"It's true," he went on, his voice becoming a trifle more convincing. "I knew that you were taken with Allan—at the Churches' Christmas party that year so long ago it was written all over your innocent little girl's face. You do not remember meeting me then, but well I remember you!

"When I met you with Robert in town that day, you were so condescending and intent on putting me in my place that I thought you needed someone to put you in yours! I guessed about your having written to Allan. It was a fairly safe wager. You were young and in love, and he was far away—what else would one expect? Your reaction left me no doubt at all! You should have seen your face! I certainly wish I *had* read whatever it was that made you blush so!"

He made no attempt to suppress the smile that crinkled the corners of his dark eyes, though Juliet's fury burst forth like an angry snarl.

"You are the crudest, most ill-mannered, disgusting, repugnant—"

Her string of angry expletives was cut short by a rap on the half-opened parlor door.

"I do hope I'm not interrupting anything," Frances called in timidly before she entered. "I've finished my letter, and I was afraid you might be impatient to leave, Alec."

"Not at all, though it is nearing noon," he remarked with a glance at the small mantel timepiece. "Jay informed me that Rachel often returns home by noontime, and that she would not exactly be overjoyed to see me here."

"If you have yet a moment, Alec, perhaps you can tell us what news there is of late. What is happening in Boston?"

Alec briefed Frances on the latest events of the war. He told her that Robert had volunteered in November to follow Henry Knox on the heroic expedition that brought the heavy guns from Fort Ti to Dorchester Heights, just south of Boston. It was only a matter of time now until the British would make their withdrawal.

Other news was not so encouraging. The short-term enlistments in the Continental Army were proving to be a great worry for its leaders. In Canada, after overcoming an unbelievable series of obstacles in a daring march through the wilds of Maine, Colonel Benedict Arnold had led his force, joined by General Richard Montgomery, who had marched via Lake Champlain and Montreal, in a foolhardy attempt to storm the reinforced city of Quebec. The decision to attack had been one of desperation, for the greater part of the army that had shown such valor in undertaking a winter campaign in Canada had informed their leaders of their intent to leave for home when their enlistments expired—the very next day.

The result had been catastrophic: General Montgomery had been killed, Captain Daniel Morgan captured, and Benedict Arnold seriously wounded. General Washington had begun to plead with the Congress for longer periods of enlistment, but changes were slow in coming. Most men still preferred to join the local militia, for it meant a shorter period of tour and better pay. But the consensus among those knowledgeable in warfare was that militia could not hope to win a war; there had to be a regular army of trained, experienced, and disciplined professionals.

Juliet half listened to Alec's briefing on the war while dashing off a response to Robert at her mother's desk. She folded the letter and entrusted it to Alec begrudgingly, making sure by her expression that he knew he was not yet forgiven. He accepted it good-naturedly and with a quick salute took his leave. He had taken but a dozen strides when he halted and hurriedly retraced his steps, pulling a well-worn pamphlet from the pocket of his leather coat and offering it to Juliet with a humble bow.

"I think you will find this interesting reading, Miss Hampton, as you once expressed a certain fascination for the principles of John Locke. I will warn you, however, that you may find it dangerously seditious . . . and I fear your father would not approve."

His manner was so formal and polite that Juliet could hardly subdue a wry smile of admiration. She watched as he retrieved his horse from the stables and urged him to a respectable gait, fading quickly into the spring day. Then she turned her attention to the obviously well-read pamphlet entitled simply *Common Sense*.

Chapter 14

It was Sunday morning, already a clear day with dazzling sunlight, when Juliet rose and made preparations for attending services at Trinity Church. It was the one social function that had continued as usual even after the mass exodus of townspeople, though the congregation, like the city itself, had dwindled to a meager number of stalwarts. The reverend continued in his ritual of offering prayers for George III, Defender of the Faith, even in the face of numerous threats to his person. A few weeks prior, a most upsetting incident had occurred when a carousing band of patriots had marched on the church during Sunday services. With drum and fife creating a noisy disruption and causing most of the women in attendance to faint dead away, the reverend had uttered a polite invitation for the rebels to leave the premises, which, to the relief of all present, had been peacefully done. For the most part, the same members of the congregation had returned the very next Sunday to be served the usual fare of fire and brimstone, which Juliet found ever more disturbing, for the smaller congregation meant that the reverend's accusing eye fell upon her far more often.

It had been nearly a fortnight since Alec's visit to her home. Juliet's anger had swiftly dissipated and was replaced just as quickly by a restless yearning for his return. Whenever she felt listless or melancholy she would anticipate his encouraging smile, the challenging lift of his brow, the brief warmth and comfort she had known in his arms. When she brushed out her hair before the looking glass and secured it neatly atop her head, a smile curved her lips, and her thoughts took their natural digression of late, to a handsome pair of dark eyes that carefully noted every strand of shiny chestnut. She cast aside her drab work clothing and chose gowns that flattered her coloring and followed the firm contours of her slender form. The days passed by, and Juliet found her anticipation growing as quickly as the daffodils and tulips that stretched their brightly crowned stems in yearning for the sun's warmth.

She had read with absolute fascination the pamphlet *Common Sense.* It had been simply and effectively written, and she found herself the victim of the propaganda, with feelings that surely had to be termed treasonous. She was hardly alone in her reaction, for the writing had created a furor since its first publication in January and had directed many minds toward a previously unmentionable idea—the complete and total separation of the colonies from Britain. But the pamphlet had been something more to Juliet, for it meant that Alec recognized that she had a mind of her own and that she could formulate an opinion, and that he wanted that opinion to coincide with his own.

This morning, after church, she gathered some flowers from the garden and brought them to Frances, who was tidying and airing out the bedchambers, which she had taken to doing every other day.

Juliet watched as her friend fluffed the pillows and shook out the linens and blankets. No matter what the task, Frances went about it with a certain grace that was pleasant to observe. Her movements resembled the skillful ease and elegance of a dancer, even when she performed the duties of a chambermaid. A playful smile on her face, Juliet skipped to Frances's side, presenting her with the bunch of freshly cut flowers with an exaggerated curtsy. The smile was returned, and at Juliet's suggestion, Frances followed her back out to the garden for a break in her tiring duties, as well as a friendly chat.

As she finished showing off her well-tended flowers, Juliet eyed the soft purple lilac buds just beginning to spring forth from the woody stalks like delicate lace.

"Lilacs are favorites of mine," Frances said fondly. "They remind me of my Aunt Colette. When I was a little girl, she let me help her make pomanders, and even now I remember that lovely essence in her room. It was delightful, even in the cold, stuffy winter months. She used to say that spiced fragrances were appropriate for the rest of the house, but a lady's room should emanate only what is sweet and soft. And she gave me a pomander to bring home for my very own room, too. I wanted to stay with her then. I had no desire to come home. It's sad that she never had a daughter of her own. There are so many things that she would have been able to teach her."

"But your mother taught you everything, Frances," Juliet protested gently. "Certainly there was nothing lacking in your tutelage. Just look at yourself—you are a perfect lady!"

Frances shrugged off the compliment with a quick smile, then tried to explain. "There are things that my mother never taught me, perhaps she had no way of doing so. I love my mother, and I am proud of her accomplishments. She knows how to give the most wonderful parties and how to make people feel happy and important. But Aunt Colette . . ." She paused to touch the tiny buds, and her smile deepened with tenderness. "Aunt Colette is different. She is a great lady and a strong person. I remember thinking that she could do anything she wanted to do, no matter what it might be. And she had an almost uncanny understanding of how I felt about almost everything, before I even said a word. Of course, I was a child then, but still, she left a deep impression on me." Frances perched on the stone bench nearby and admired the peaceful harmony of nature as she remembered another garden, long ago and far away.

"Did she ever visit you here?" Juliet asked, resting her back on the bark of a tree.

Frances shook her head. "Not that I recall. I believe that she and Uncle Jerome visited Mama and Papa here before Allan and I were born, or perhaps when we were just infants. They wrote each other faithfully, though, right up until the time Mama left for England." Frances's eyes lit up as she added, "But Alec and Justin used to visit quite a lot when they were at college. They were always such fun! Allan and I used to tag along with them; we thought everything they did was absolutely wonderful!"

"Justin?"

Frances's eyes lost their playful glow, and a frown creased her brow. "He was Alec's older brother. He . . . he passed away several years ago." An awkward silence settled for a moment before she went on. "Alec was very close to Justin. The two of them attended Princeton together. His death was very difficult for Alec, I think. Though I've never actually heard him speak of it," she added thoughtfully. She smiled. "But then, Alec is not one to wear his feelings on his sleeve."

Juliet smiled as well. "No. He's certainly not."

Frances lifted her eyes to the spotless white clouds that hung in the sky, resembling great puffs of cotton. The sun was nearly overhead, and there was still a good deal of work to be done. With a reluctant sigh, she took her leave of Juliet and returned to finish her chores in the house.

Chapter 15

Juliet was in the kitchen busily preparing loaves of bread, kneading the dough on a lightly floured table. It was a task that she did not mind, for the end result was seen so soon after its undertaking. It was not like a tapestry, which took months of daily concentration and showed such little progress in exchange for so much toil. With the long latticed windows opened to release the heat of the freshly stoked oven, Juliet divided the dough, flattened each piece into a rectangle, and folded the sides carefully toward the center until a neat loaf took shape. All the while she hummed a melody she remembered from the last party she had attended at the Church home—the dance she had shared with Alec. Swaying in time to the tune as she worked, she paused in her labors to stare dreamily into space, remembering that romantic occasion when Alec had entertained her with an easy boyish charm, yet still had left her breathless with his masculine assertiveness. He had danced with no one else, yet she had to admit he had flirted outrageously with several others.

Juliet's eyes hardened, and a wave of jealousy swept over her as she vividly recalled that buxom redhead. As the hated visage came to mind, she struck a fist none too gently into the mass of dough, sending several geyserlike puffs of flour from the wooden surface. Then she remembered the woman's brazen smile, which Alec had acknowledged with his own roguish grin. Juliet vented her growing wrath on the dough, squeezing until long, sticky lengths of it stubbornly attached themselves to her fingers. At that moment Alec appeared at the opened window, where the sill was low enough to allow him an excellent view of her toils. He observed with amusement her spiteful expression when she shook the dough loose, landing it with a plop on the table and sending a generous cloud of flour about the kitchen.

"I heard once that bread, like a woman, responds more favorably to a gentle touch."

His voice startled her so that she let out a gasp, and a hand, covered with the white muck, flew to her breast to still her racing heart. Her eyes immediately narrowed, and her temper flared at the taunting smile he flashed at her.

"I know perfectly well how to handle a loaf, Mr. Farrell," she returned haughtily, noticing with satisfaction that he scowled at her cold greeting, ". . . and furthermore, I have much cause to doubt your success," she paused to amend boldly, "nay, even your experience with either bread or women."

Alec sighed his vexation as Juliet patched up the loaf and purposely ignored his presence. Though she was acutely conscious of his careful scrutiny, she finished her labors with studied disinterest, placing the pans in the oven with one graceful sweep. She pumped enough water to wet her hands thoroughly and loosen what dough remained clinging to her fingers before drying them on her apron. Then she discarded the soiled apron and scarf in the distasteful fashion of a princess casting away a dress that no longer pleased her and turned a condescending stare on Alec, who patiently supported his head in his hand, an elbow propped nonchalantly on the sill.

"What is it you desire, sir?" she questioned curtly, hoping to convince him by her tone that she had no interest in his presence.

Alec' eyes dropped to her breast, where an obvious glob of dough clung to the otherwise fashionable chintz.

"A beautiful woman should never ask that question of a gentleman, Julie. My original purpose for coming here is to deliver a missive from your brother to my cousin, as I believe you may recall. But since your question was to know of my desire . . ." His eyes rose leisurely to meet her golden glower, ignoring the import of the same. "I must confess that it runs in a less gallant and more . . . shall we say . . . intimate vein."

Juliet's eyes flashed at the bold suggestion, though she knew a vaguely familiar excitement in her breast. There was something very attractive about this man who knew her well and desired her for that same knowledge, and Alec's dark eyes at this moment spoke undeniably of desire, setting her heart to flutter. She began to tingle at the memories that came to mind, memories of being held and kissed and wanted, and she was suddenly very grateful for the knowledge of Frances's presence, for she was not of a mood to battle such shameless thoughts.

"Oh, yes," she managed with hard-won calm, "a letter for Frances."

She politely invited Alec inside and directed him to the parlor before setting out to find Frances, who was performing her systematic labors on the second floor. When her calls at the foot of the stairs were not answered, Juliet hurried up the stairs to make a search. She opened at least a dozen doors, and still there was no response to her calls. Finally her eyes were caught by the unbolted door leading to the unfinished third story of the house. Seldom did anyone go up to the attic, which was used only for storage; even Juliet had not been up there since she was a child. To an inquiring call at the bottom of the stairs there came a timid reply, and a moment later Frances appeared on the landing that broke the stairway at mid-point, sporting a guilty countenance.

Frances was relieved to find that Juliet alone had discovered her intrusion. Her guilt turned to mischief, as she excitedly beckoned the other to join her.

"Come quickly, Juliet! Look what I've found!"

Her curiosity much aroused, Juliet forgot Alec for the moment as she turned to discover the source of Frances's excitement.

The eaves of the house dipped at severe angles on either side of the long room, so that only the middle offered a thin, lengthy pathway one could follow without stooping. A thousand diverse objects were stored along the walls, but Frances hurried past most of them to a place where a staggering amount of clothing had been carefully packed away in rows of neatly tied bundles. She had opened several of the packages and lovingly removed certain articles.

"Look!" she exclaimed fondly as she lifted a tiny lace garment. "It's difficult to believe that Robert was ever so tiny and helpless! But look . . ." She fished about the small pile of disruption she had created and found a square of parchment. "It says: 'Christening, Robert Lawrence Hampton, September, 1756."

Juliet shared a brief smile with Frances over the idea of such an incredibly dainty garment ever fitting her older brother, but her eyes were caught and held far longer by a white cotton shirt and heavy cotton breeches, similar to what she remembered Robert wearing before she'd been sent off to school in England. She lifted them out from the others and could hardly resist the temptation that entered her mind. What fun it had been to dress as a boy—romping and playing and riding without worry of criticism. Holding the shirt to her breast and the pants at her hips, she checked the near perfect fit, for Robert had been a trim youth. She sighed and gnawed at her bottom lip, considering, wishing that somehow an excuse to don the garments would present itself, but none came to mind. When Frances noted Juliet's sudden preoccupation, her brows rose sharply in realization of her train of thought.

"You wouldn't . . ." Frances stopped short of offering Juliet a challenge, knowing full well that it would only serve to make the temptation irresistible. She did her best to hide her dismay, to sound calm and reasonable. "It is quite silly for us to be here, rummaging about. I was curious as to what was up here, though, and when my cleaning was finished I decided to have a look. I hope you are not angry," she went on, wishing that the strange gleam in Juliet's eyes would disappear. She knew the look well, and it usually meant trouble.

"No, no," Juliet answered thoughtfully, still much engrossed in the possibilities such garments brought to mind.

"If you should like some help with the bread," Frances offered, hurriedly folding away the christening gown and the other scattered items, "I would be happy to give it." She cast a hopeful glance in Juliet's direction, only to encounter the

162

same ominous sparkle that had been there before. Gathering her resolve, Frances snatched up the shirt and breeches from Juliet's hands, avoiding her surprised face. She quickly smoothed and folded them away in a fashion similar to the others. Juliet could barely suppress a grin at the fear she read in Frances's countenance, even though the blue eyes remained carefully averted.

"The bread is in the oven," Juliet said. "I came to find you because Alec is—" Suddenly Juliet realized she had left Alec waiting. Gathering her skirts high, she flew down the attic stairs, taking them two at a time. Then on past the tidied bedchambers, much as she had raced as a child, fleeing her brother in a forbidden game of tag. She rounded the corner to the main stairway with something akin to a flying leap, but with high-heeled slippers, cumbersome petticoats, and a long lack of practice, she little resembled the girl who had landed on the fourth stair with a graceful spring. Just as she had committed herself to the foolhardy vault came the realization that a dangerous flight of stairs lay threatening before her. Yet she could not have timed her daring stunt closer to perfection, for Alec, who had grown weary, then angry, then concerned with her lengthy disappearance, had just ascended every step but the top one, so that Juliet plunged headlong at his chest. Caught off balance, he instinctively forced all of his weight against the opposing force, spilling Juliet back and onto the floor with a thud and landing a good deal of himself on top of her. He had not a second to break the impact of the fall, but he thanked his stars for the plush carpet that cushioned their landing. Juliet was rendered completely motionless. Alec anxiously repeated her name, observing her pale cheeks and ragged breathing, then heaved a long, worried sigh when her eyes finally fluttered open.

"Are you hurt?"

She shook her head, becoming quite embarrassed as her panic began to fade.

"Is Frances all right?"

Juliet took a deep breath and nodded. Greatly relieved by her replies, Alec could hardly help the dawning realization that through some strange quirk of fate, he had literally fallen into a most advantageous position. He became pleasurably conscious of Juliet's heaving breast softly rising beneath him, and their thighs rested in a tangle, enjoying more than a little intimate contact. Neither was he alone in the awareness, for when his eyes locked with a pair of bright golden ones, Juliet gave a short gasp at the impact on her senses.

"I forgot you were waiting . . ." she lamely attempted to explain, her voice soft and trembling.

In quick response came a hoarse, eager whisper. "If you find it so easy to forget me, Julie, then I ought to give you a reason to remember."

Alec's mouth lowered to hers with deliberate slowness, relishing her undenied anticipation, her passion-filled eyes, her softly parted lips. His fingers touched the slender column of her throat, and he felt her pulse quicken under his touch, then race when his lips sought to follow the caress. Her arms crept timidly about his neck, then a mad feeling of abandon took hold, and she ran her fingers greedily through his thick black hair. When he lifted his eyes to meet hers again, she almost gasped at what she saw. For he was no longer laughing at her, no longer taunting; his dark eyes were filled with a joy and a longing that seemed to match her own. She only knew that she wanted him to kiss her, that the feel of his arms and his thighs and his mouth had brought her to the threshold of paradise. She drew his head toward her opened mouth, and while her tongue moved to meet his, her hands smoothed over the entire length of his back. Her defenses lay about her in total devastation; she yielded, indeed, welcomed his touch; her limbs began to tremble with eagerness. While her senses reeled in ecstasy, her spirit soared like a swallow on the first day of spring. The man whose black eyes saw her deepest secrets, who possessed an intimate knowledge of the woman she truly was, wanted her. His eyes were blazing with desire. It was frightening! It was heavenly!

An incongruous feeling of intrusion broke rudely into Alec's passion, and his gaze migrated reluctantly to a pair of wide blue eyes and a mouth agape with surprise. With hard-won poise, he hastily broke the embrace, offering a supportive hand to Juliet. But she was not aware of the reason for his hasty withdraw and was disinclined to shatter such an exquisite moment of magic. Her hesitation brought a quick remedy of the situation from Alec, who pointedly made note of his cousin's presence.

"Frances! Juliet . . . tripped and . . . fell . . ." He cleared his throat and aided Juliet as she scrambled to her feet.

She was quite thankful for the arm that steadied her. Her vision wavered and darkened as she stood upright, and she was forced to sway heavily against Alec. Frances uttered a gasp and rushed to Juliet's side in obvious distress. In spite of her protests, Alec lifted Juliet into his arms and followed Frances to her room, where he deposited her with utmost care on her bed. Frances grasped her hand and patted it while she whispered her name in a tight, nervous voice. As Juliet timidly opened her eyes on the anxious faces, her embarrassment grew even more acute.

"Are you all right?" Frances asked, with blue eyes frightfully large. "Can I get you something?"

Juliet nodded mutely to the first question, then stole a glance at Alec as she weakly requested a cup of tea. Frances jumped up to comply and left the room in a rush, not even realizing that she had once again left the two of them alone. Juliet let out a long sigh and turned to Alec, whose face had lost all trace of concern and, indeed, sported a self-satisfied grin. She squirmed beneath his regard, highly irritated that he found the situation humorous.

"I would like to know what you find so amusing?" she demanded, pressing her hand to her temple where her words seemed to echo with a dull throb. "Frances must think . . . well, I don't know what she must think! Just how long was she standing there anyway?"

"I assure you I don't know, Julie. The moment I saw her, I made every attempt to redeem your reputation."

Juliet bit her lip and looked away. "How am I going to explain this to her? Frances will never understand."

"Oh, I think she might," he countered easily. "After all, she is quite fond of your brother, and I am sure they have shared a chaste kiss or two."

"Chaste kiss!" she protested. "You could hardly term what she witnessed that! Divine Providence! What am I going to say to her? What can I say, Alec?"

"Why not tell her the truth?"

She narrowed her eyes at him suspiciously. "What truth?"

"That you find me utterly irresistible, that when we collided at the top of the stairs, it seemed perfectly natural for you to kiss me, and—"

"I kissed you?" she objected indignantly. "You must be joking! I never . . ." Her voice grew sharp, and her chin jutted disdainfully. "You conceited fool! You know perfectly well that I am engaged to be married to a titled gentleman! How dare you suggest that I threw myself at you!"

"It seems to me, Julie, that you did exactly that." He ignored the rage that flooded her face and added with a lazy smile, "There are far easier, and less painful, methods of finding your way into my embrace." He casually ran a finger up her arm.

She snatched away from his touch, aghast to find that her longing to hold him was revived in an instant. "Are you suggesting that I . . ." The appropriate words refused to come, and she looked away from the object of her vexation.

"Methinks the lady doth protest overmuch," he quipped.

Fiery golden eyes flew back to meet his teasing countenance. "Exactly what do you mean by that?" she snapped.

He took a seat on the bed, bracing his arms on either side of her and leaning near. He smiled down at her slowly, until a row of even white teeth gleamed in contrast to his darkened skin. "I mean that you are not so upset about what Frances might think, but rather, by what you feel and are unable to explain to yourself, much less anyone else."

She felt uneasy about his closeness, and the flesh on the back of her neck began to prickle pleasurably. She summoned the last of her anger to give a derisive snort. "And just what is it that you think I feel?"

His face softened to a different kind of smile, and no hint of mockery marred his words. "The very same thing I feel myself . . . a magic . . . a closeness that I have never known before . . . a compelling desire to be one with you in every way."

Her anger was spent as amazed tawny eyes searched darker ones for truth. She ought to have denied that she had ever felt any such thing, to make light of his declaration, but she found herself instead wanting it to be true.

He lifted her hand and touched it to his lips, and she vividly recalled the feeling of those lips on her mouth.

"It is time we put an end to games and reconciled ourselves

with our feelings. I love you, Julie. I love your spirit and your courage and your determination—and I'm even learning to love your temper because it is a part of you. Fate has brought us together time and again, until it is impossible to deny that something, some very special bond, exists between us, yet it is just as impossible to explain it."

Juliet turned away from his words and tried to withdraw her hand, but he was everywhere—in her mind and in her longings—and his voice fell soft and sensuous on her ears.

"An hour seldom passes that I do not think of you, and my nights are filled with dreams of what life will be when you are mine." He placed a finger to the side of her face and forced her to look at him squarely as he continued. "You are a part of me, Julie. You pull all the pieces of my life together and give my existence a reason, a future."

His face drew closer until his lips brushed lightly upon hers, and she was grateful when, on hearing Frances's footfalls in the hallway, he abruptly drew back to a proper distance. He rose and went to help his cousin as she backed through the partially opened door, and she smiled in relief when he lifted the heavy tray.

"I'm sorry to be so long, but I waited a few minutes to take the bread from the oven. If you hadn't asked for tea, Juliet, it would have been burned to a crisp!"

Frances prepared tea for Juliet and Alec, oblivious of the eyes locked in silent, intense communication. She kept up her nervous chattering all the while, until she noticed Juliet's preoccupation, and then she quickly apologized.

"I *am* sorry, Juliet! I'm afraid I've been rambling on like a rain-swollen brook! You do look a bit flushed. Perhaps if I left you alone to rest—that is, if we left you alone," she amended, suddenly aware of the odd looks passing between the two.

"No, no," Juliet assured her. "I want to know if there is news from Robert."

Frances nearly bounded from her chair at the mention of his name. "Of course! How on earth could I have forgotten? It must have been the shock of seeing you on the floor with Alec—that is, the excitement . . ."

Alec rescued his cousin from any further verbal blunder by interrupting her before she could explain. "I did see Robert, and he is well. He sends you both his love and"—he paused to retrieve two letters from him shirt—"these."

He had scarcely placed the sealed missives in the proper hands before everyone jumped at the sound of the main door slamming shut. Frances gasped, and as blue eyes met gold, two voices breathed the name in unison.

"Rachel!"

Frances froze, biting her lip and wringing her hands, but Juliet forgot her headache to take immediate charge. "Quickly, Frances! Go downstairs and keep her occupied for as long as you are able. I know a way out if you can keep her downstairs and away from the west wing."

"I shall do my best. But how can you . . . ?"

Juliet put an arm around her shoulder and gave her an encouraging hug. "Do what it takes," she whispered. "Faint, scream, drop a vase—I don't care what you do, but give us as long as you possibly can!"

Juliet peered through the partially opened door and watched Frances make her way down the long hallway. She strained to hear the faint footfalls on the stairs, then the light patter on the marble floor in the downstairs hall. She pressed a forefinger to her lips, then motioned for Alec to follow her as she tiptoed gingerly through the hall toward the west wing. Consisting of more than a dozen comfortable guest suites that were seldom used even when the house was fully staffed, this wing of Hampton House had been closed off for months. Juliet proceeded to the last room on the left, swung open the massive door, then closed it behind them again.

She drew back one section of heavy velvet drape and fastened it with a quick knot in a gold braided cord. Sunlight flooded in, enlarging the beautifully furnished suite.

Juliet opened one of the windows and leaned out, taking note of the location of various branches and doing her best to recall exactly how escape had been managed by two mischievous children a decade before. She turned her back to the window and perched on its sill, leaning out and back to study the branches overhead. Ah! There it was! A good bit higher than she remembered, but it was still a sturdy limb and would provide a good first hold. Yes, it would do very well!

As she swung herself back inside, the room grew dim and

blurry, and she groped for the closest object at hand to steady herself. That happened to be Alec. When she leaned against him, waiting for the dizziness to pass, his arms went about her, and he lifted her easily from the floor. She felt small and helpless nestled so near his broad, muscular chest, though for all her vulnerability at this moment her feelings were far from unpleasant. What was it that made her so reluctant to leave the comforting closeness of his arms? She could name no feeling in the past that matched the one she felt now. Alec made her conscious of every aspect of herself—the hurt little girl, the spirited young maid, the thwarted tomboy, the warm, yielding woman. She sighed and relaxed her cheek against his chest, wrapping her arms loosely about his neck. Somehow they seemed to belong there, as she seemed to belong in his arms, as his mouth seemed to belong on her own. He lowered his lips to her hair and whispered softly against it. "Are you still dizzy from the fall?"

She nodded.

"I had hoped that I might have something to do with your lightheadedness."

A precipitate crash prevented her from answering. It sounded almost as if someone had dropped a vase! She stirred against him. "Frances! Quick! Let me go!"

"Frances can take care of herself," he returned easily, resisting her struggles to be free. She abruptly ceased her wriggling about and firmly demanded that he release her.

"I fully intend to, but not before I say a proper good-bye."

She lifted her eyes to his in curiosity, but he gave her no time to determine his intentions. His lips slanted across hers in a kiss that sent the world swimming, with all thoughts of Rachel and Frances and the rest of the universe suddenly drowned in a sea of passion. Her arms tightened about his neck, and she wished that this splendor could go on forever.

"I love you, Julie."

She could hardly even draw a breath, but the words came softly tumbling from her lips. "I love you, Alec."

Her mouth sought his then with an even stronger yearning, brilliant and powerful and beautiful in its honesty, sealing a covenant of two hearts joined in love. With a heavy sigh and deep reluctance, Alec forced himself to end that kiss, drawing back from her and turning away to survey his means of escape. When his eyes fell hungrily on the linen-draped bed, he steeled himself against the temptation that threatened his best made plans. Juliet followed his gaze and gulped. She had absolutely no resolve to fend off his advances at this moment, for her own thoughts were brazen to the point of making her blush. Her cheeks grew hot, and she clenched her hands in tight fists at her sides, but as her eyes ventured timidly to his, his wide boyish grin left her absolutely limp. She bit her lip and looked away. Get hold of yourself, she thought, Frances needs you!

Clearing her throat and avoiding his gaze, she moved closer to the window and pointed out the branch overhead.

"That is the closest one strong enough to hold you. Once you reach it, work your way to the trunk. The best climbing branches are on the other side."

As she brushed against him to indicate the opposite side, she hoped that he did not notice the tremor in her voice when she continued. "It's a relatively simple way down. I climbed this tree myself when I was seven. Only have a care when you first swing out. Be certain that you get a firm hold."

Alec seemed much amused by her careful instruction.

"My dear Miss Hampton, you have already admitted to doubting my experience with women and bread. Have you also such doubts as to my ability to climb a tree that you would see the need to inform me of how it is done?"

She raised her chin and met his challenging smile. "It would certainly seem so!" She poked a finger at his chest. "Now get thee gone!"

She watched Alec's agile movements as he swung to the branch above, then quickly moved from one hold to another until he was out of sight in the new green foliage. Juliet shut the window, smiling at the latch that had been bent apart for so many years and never repaired. She pulled the knot from the gold cord and held the curtain open just a bit until she saw Alec drop safely to the ground. He made an excellent landing for the first time, she thought with a proud grin, and her smile deepened as she noted his brisk, firm strides to the stables. But when she let the drapes fall back into place, she quickly assumed a sober expression and left the west wing.

Back in her bedroom, Juliet rushed about, concealing any incriminating evidence. Robert's letter was tucked under the feather tick; the bed was smoothed. She picked up the tea service, then set it down again. There was no way to take it safely to the kitchen unnoticed. Better to leave it and admit that she and Frances had taken early tea in her room. But the third cup! How could she explain that? And all of them nearly full!

As a knock sounded at her door, she forced down one large gulp and placed the cup under her bed. Then she plopped herself down and tried to sound sleepy as she called permission to enter. Through half-closed eyes, Juliet noted Rachel's walk—an angry, direct stride—and wondered what in the world Frances could have broken to incur such wrath.

Rachel stopped at the side of Juliet's bed, hands planted firmly on her hips, brows raised expectantly as she surveyed the girl, then the tea tray, then returned to Juliet again. Juliet was not new at this game, however out of practice she may have been. If no one asked a question, she was certainly not one to volunteer an answer. Ignoring the dark countenance that demanded a response of some kind, she pretended to drift off to sleep, provoking Rachel even further. With an impatient sigh, the older woman spoke, the control in her voice managed only with tremendous effort.

"What have you been doing?"

Juliet's eyes fluttered weakly open, and her voice was pure innocence. "What do you mean, Rachel?" She took a long, deep breath and pressed her trembling hand to her forehead. "I . . . fell," she whimpered. "And I am not . . . feeling well. I . . . shall do my share of the housework as soon as I feel"—she winced as if in pain—". . . better."

Rachel clenched her jaw as she watched the well-acted performance. She always knew when the girl was lying, though it was nearly impossible to catch her at it. She leaned over to feel her forehead, for she had to admit the girl's face was flushed, but as she did so, her foot touched something under the bed that made a soft clank. She drew back immediately to investigate and missed the pained expression on Juliet's face, which was definitely not acting. While Rachel was retrieving the cup from its hiding place,

Frances, who had hurriedly cleaned up the vase she had so carelessly knocked over, joined them in Juliet's room.

"Is everything all right?" she called in timidly.

Rachel stood up slowly, studying the third cup openly, then looking suspiciously from one girl to the other. Frances gulped and paled visibly under the intense gaze, and Rachel, sensing at once the weak link in the chain, approached her steadily.

"We had hoped that you might join us for early tea," Frances blurted out, "so we fixed a cup for you . . ." She took a step backward.

Rachel nodded and smirked.

"And drank it for me, too? In Juliet's bedroom?"

"No. I mean, yes. I mean . . ." Frances threw Juliet a helpless glance and looked very close to tears.

Juliet quickly came to the rescue.

"Frances and I planned to have tea in the parlor," she said calmly and rationally. "I ran up here to get"—she paused half a second—". . . a book of poetry. I don't know how it happened, but I tripped and fell. Frances was kind enough to bring the tray up to me. I suppose that she was so upset that she made three cups instead of two."

"Yes!" Frances agreed. "That's it! I was so upset, I made three cups rather than two!"

Rachel's stare never moved from Frances. It was obvious that she was a poor liar. "And you put one of them under the bed?"

Frances's smile faded, and she swallowed hard.

"She put it on the floor by the bed, Rachel. You kicked it under the bed yourself; I heard you do it."

Frances nodded gratefully, but her eyes remained fearfully wide.

"But why on the floor, Frances? I never saw you place a cup anywhere but on the tray before—"

"My Lord, Rachel!" Juliet was sitting up now, almost exploding with the heat of her anger. "Frances is a guest in my home! She is not on trial for misplacing a silly teacup! Remember yourself!"

Rachel's gray eyes bore into Frances's soft blue ones until the girl actually trembled. Juliet had had enough. With a clipped, curt tone, she ordered Rachel to leave her room as she might have ordered an unimportant kitchen maid from the dining room. Although the older woman said nothing and complied with the order, her behavior declared a stalemate rather than a victory for either woman. Rachel would not be forgetting the incident, that was a certainty.

Chapter 16

It was late the same evening when Lawrence Hampton invited Juliet to his study to discuss a matter of importance. Juliet did her best to calm the clashing emotions rising inside her. She knew that her father had noticed the sudden change in Frances at dinner. It had been painfully obvious. Every other evening she had chattered incessantly about trivialities such as the latest fashion or who had said what at a party over a year before. Juliet's father usually smiled indulgently but did not really listen. This evening, however, the table had been strangely void of conversation, and Frances had seemed unduly concerned with avoiding eye contact with anyone as she moved her dinner aimlessly about her plate. Juliet made an attempt to fill the silence, then abandoned it, deciding to have a long talk with Frances later and settle things then. Her father had made the first move, though, and now, sitting in his study, she felt very much like a dog caught in the smokehouse.

With studied poise, she answered his casual questions about what had happened that afternoon, thankful that he had chosen to question her and not Frances.

"Really, Father," she added. "Rachel was quite rude to Frances. I was terribly embarrassed for her, and tonight at dinner—well, it was obvious that she was very upset."

Lawrence Hampton studied his daughter cautiously.

"You get along well with Frances, don't you?"

"Yes," Juliet answered honestly. "I didn't know what a comfort she would be to me. She has become dearer than I ever imagined. It has been so boring of late, and I have been so lonely—"

"I know that you have," he interrupted, "and I wish to speak with you about that now."

Juliet waited for the ax to fall.

"You have often questioned me about where I go when I leave here. You are my daughter, and I expect honesty from you. Therefore, I have decided to be totally honest with you."

He took a seat in his leather chair and folded his hands on his chest as he leaned back. "I have been meeting with men who share my political convictions, brave men who refuse to let the outcome of the rebellion settle their loyalties for them. We are loyal to the King, and we intend to prove that loyalty beyond a doubt. We have plans to put an end to this 'war,' and we hope that no fighting need ever take place on this island. I and many other loyal Tories intend to do all we can to see that the rebellion is crushed." He paused and considered his next words carefully. "My part, unfortunately, will be small. I have reason to believe that I will be arrested within the week."

Juliet gasped, and a trembling hand flew to her mouth. She shook her head in disbelief.

"I'm afraid it's true." His voice was bitter and resentful. "There is a committee of traitors, men who have set themselves up in judgment of anyone who is loyal to the King. They have devised an oath to be sworn—an oath of treason! I shall never take such an oath!"

"But they would arrest you? They cannot do it!" she protested, her eyes filling with tears.

Her father rose from his chair and poured himself a glass of wine. "It will be only for a short time. The British have just evacuated Boston, and they will be here soon enough. It matters not if our plans are thwarted; they will easily have this island, despite what the rebels have done to it."

"But how . . . can you crush the rebellion? Before the British come here?" she choked out. "How are you so sure that—"

"Juliet," he answered her with a patronizing tone, "I cannot discuss these technical matters with you. I have told you these things for one reason." He took his seat and faced his distraught daughter once again. "I will be incarcerated for a time, but it will serve my purpose. No one will question my loyalty when all this is finished. Do you understand why I must do this? Why I must buy a reputation with unjust long hours in a jail?"

Juliet shook her head.

"It is for you, Juliet. For your future, for your life with Harold. Robert has cast a blemish on this family. He is a traitor. I shall redeem our family name because your happiness is much more important than any sacrifice I am making."

Juliet swallowed hard and dared not raise her eyes. She had not thought seriously about Harold for a long, long time. She had carefully pushed the troubling image from her mind. And only a few hours before she had come to realize why: she was deeply in love with another man. She stared down at her fingers and began to speak in a very small, very tight voice. "Father, I have not even heard from Harold in well over six months, not a single word—"

"Of course not! You know that mail from England has been tampered with by these seditionists!"

"But he promised to come in the spring—and it is spring! He is not here! I . . . I do not know for certain that he will ever come."

Hampton rose from his seat once more and approached his daughter, putting an arm about her shoulders. "He will come for you, Juliet. I am certain that he will. What difference a month or two? Since you have been home, I have come to realize what a fine young woman you are. All the years I spent with Robert, while you were so far away . . . Only now do I come to realize that you are truly my daughter—not only a Farmington, but a Hampton."

"But I . . . I shall have to go away. We shall be separated again. . . ." She squeezed her eyes closed as they overflowed with painful tears.

"I shall come to visit you every year. I promise. And we shall be closer than we have ever been before."

He waited for her to face him, but she did not. His arm about her felt strangely cold and uncomfortable, and she wished that he would take it away. As he did so, he wielded his final and most deadly blow.

"When you marry Lord Harold, it will be by far the proudest moment of my life. The pain Robert has caused me, the time I spend in prison, everything will be worth those precious moments of happiness. Thank you, Juliet."

He pressed a kiss to her forehead, displaying more affection for her in the past few moments than he had done in her entire life. When she did not respond, he thought of her mother, who had likewise never responded to affection. Yet Claire had never cried, never raised her voice or lost her temper. What a strange mixture this child was! Perhaps he ought to have kept her closer to home all these years, for he could not comprehend her moods, could not judge her next move with any amount of accuracy. Rachel had told him that she did not trust the girl. She was untamed, she had told him, and she had hinted that Juliet was an excellent liar, though she had little proof. If only he had forced her to go to England and marry Harold the year before! But at the time he had envisioned the gentleman she had chosen to marry an opportunist, a man seeking the Hampton money in return for his title. He had not known then exactly what Harold Medford would bring to the family.

Hampton finished his wine as he watched his daughter plod slowly from the study. Something told him that all was not as smooth and easy as it seemed on the surface. Hopefully the marriage would not be delayed much longer.

Juliet readied herself for bed, not wanting anyone to witness the tears that continued to fall long after she had left the study. So her plan had worked. Her marriage to Harold would indeed win her father's heart—and break her own. She looked out on the night, on the campfires that had replaced the neat rows of whale oil lanterns in front of every seventh house. Alec was out there somewhere. But Alec was the one man her father would never accept, much less welcome as a son-in-law.

Her sobs continued until her chest ached and she was so tired that she hardly had strength to move. She did not even hear Frances knocking lightly or entering her room, and was surprised when she drew close to put an arm around her dearest friend, her eyes misting in sympathy.

"What did he say? Was he terribly angry?"

Juliet shook her head. "No, no. He doesn't know anything about today. It's only that . . . Frances, he's going to be arrested!"

"Arrested? Whatever for?"

"He is going to refuse to take an oath against the King, and he says that he will be jailed because of it."

"Oh, Juliet, I'm so sorry," Frances murmured. "But at least there is some good news," she added brightly.

"What good news?"

"The British have evacuated Boston!"

"I know. Father told me. But why is that—?"

"You mean you haven't read your letter from Robert?"

Juliet made her way to her bed and fished about under the mattress until she found the letter. She quickly scanned the brief note, which was scarcely a full written page, and was forced to smile under her tears. The last of the American troops were leaving Boston, and Robert would be coming home. She closed her eyes and breathed a silent prayer of thanks.

Frances made no move to retire. She seemed strangely preoccupied as she paced about the room, and Juliet noticed that she nervously avoided looking in her direction.

"Is something bothering you, Frances?"

"Oh, Juliet! I am at such a loss! You are my best friend in all the world, and you are like a sister to me! I . . ." She broke off and shook her head, unable to continue.

"What is it, Frances? Is it about what happened earlier today?" Juliet referred to Rachel's inquisition, not to the scene Frances had witnessed at the top of the stairs, which she had momentarily forgotten.

The words rushed forth like water through a dam that had just sprung a leak.

"Oh, yes! I know that you're lonely, Juliet, lonely for Harold—I feel the same loneliness for Robert, even though we've been separated a much shorter time. And I also know that Alec is handsome and charming and that he can be very sweet, but . . ."

"But what, Frances?"

"Oh, Juliet! Alec is a . . . a womanizer! Whenever he visited our home, there were always women dropping by on silly, lame excuses. Mama even got angry about it once; I heard her come right out and tell a particularly brazen young woman, 'Stop making a fool of yourself. There is a girl in Virginia, and Alec is definitely spoken for!' And you know that Mama hardly ever loses her temper."

"And what your mother said . . . is it true?" Juliet steeled herself for the answer, keeping her voice carefully void of all expression.

Frances nodded solemnly before she attempted a smile. "I do like Alec, and he has always been like a brother to me, but . . ." She let out a sigh. "I know there have been women in his life, but he never really cared for any of them. I never even thought to mention it until now. I hope that he did not . . . take advantage of your loneliness for Harold." She paused and continued with her last bit of courage. "He has traveled a good deal, and I have heard Mama speak about how things are different—more relaxed, well, you know what I mean—in France and in Europe in general. Certain things that are considered scandalous here are easily accepted there. I am not making excuses for Alec, you understand. He ought to know well enough that you were not brought up that way, even if you were educated in England. You are Robert's sister and my dearest friend, and I intend to tell him exactly that the very next time I see him!"

Juliet almost laughed at that, but she was too despondent to have any laughter left inside her. In the few short hours since she had admitted her love for Alec, she had been bitterly reacquainted with the painful feelings she once known for Frances's brother, Allan. She had vowed not to make the same mistake again; she ought to have known better this time. Why had she made it so easy for him to find his way into her heart?

Her voice sounded calm when she finally spoke. "You needn't bother talking with him, Frances. What you saw today did not mean anything, to either of us. It was something that happened, though I couldn't explain how or why. But believe me, it didn't mean anything."

Frances heard the listlessness in Juliet's voice and noted the absence of the usual animation and expression in her face. She wanted to believe what Juliet told her, but she simply could not dismiss what she had seen as something meaningless, something that had happened only to be quickly forgotten. Juliet cared more for Alec than she admitted, Frances was sure of it. If only Alec truly cared for her in return! But Frances had seen far too many of his one-sided romances in the past to hope that this was something different, and there was the matter of the girl in Virginia. . . . They were both committed to other people, she resolved sensibly, and it was all for the best this way.

Frances bid Juliet a fond good night and quietly left her to her own thoughts. But there was very little thinking to be done; it was clear now to Juliet that the decision had already been made.

She went to her bureau and removed the golden charm that pictured the three old women who worked their wills on others without a second thought. Robert had been mistaken, she thought bitterly. Lachesis had withdrawn every straw but one far beyond her reach.

Chapter 17

The month of March expired quietly in the gentle winds of spring, giving birth to the benign rains of April that cleanly washed away the final traces of winter. It was a time of rapid growth for all things, urged on by ample rainfall and an ever stronger sunlight.

On Manhattan, a special committee of six well-known patriots had been in control of municipal affairs for some time, but they now confined their duties to summoning any man of place who had not fled the island to take an oath of loyalty for or against the monarch. Of those who remained loyal to the King, some were tarred, feathered, and run out of town, others were shipped unceremoniously out of state and left to fend for themselves; those who pledged themselves to the rebellion were put on probation and watched carefully to determine if their sworn loyalty was in fact their true one. Each day's sun brought new rumors of spies, plots, and intrigue running rampant, for the patriots felt certain that the Tories were up to something; they nervously waited to find out exactly what that something was.

The last ranks of the Continental Army and its commander-in-chief left Boston and arrived in Manhattan in early April. As General Washington explained in a letter to the Congress, New York was of utmost importance, for if lost to the British it meant an end to ". . . the intercourse between the northern and southern colonies, upon which depends the safety of America."

General William Howe, who had taken full charge of the

British forces in the colonies, teamed up with his brother, Admiral Richard Howe, and now commanded both a fine army and navy, far exceeding the best the rebels had managed to assemble. Still smarting from his defeat at Boston, however, the general proceeded slowly and cautiously, unwilling to go directly to New York to face another possibly similar confrontation. Instead he made his move to Halifax, Nova Scotia, where he safely delivered the loyalists and their families who had fled Boston and replenished his troops before sailing for New York. So it was that General Washington was given time to supervise even more extensive defense construction, particularly on the upper end of Manhattan, including Fort Washington and Fort George.

The month proceeded slowly for Juliet, though she and Frances had been very enthusiastic when General Washington arrived on April thirteenth, nearly two weeks after her father's arrest. Since then, Rachel had spent three mornings each week away from the house: the first, as before, to go marketing, and on Sunday and Wednesday to deliver a generous basket of provisions to Hampton at the jail. The jailers were not adverse to accepting some tasty morsel as an innocent bribe, insuring that Hampton was well cared for. Each time they were careful to check every item in the basket, however, and any conversation was always monitored by a guard—and usually by several other prisoners as well, for the jail was dreadfully overcrowded.

Juliet and Frances had been strictly ordered to keep close to the house, a mandate they obeyed as much from fear as from docility, for the army literally surrounded the house now that the work had begun on forts to the north as well as the south.

The golden sunshine, the pleasant breeze, the crisp new greenery that had sprung from the earth, the wondrous perfection of spring—Juliet found joy in none of it. If she could have erased the past year of her life, if she could have scattered the memories of that handsome pair of ebony eyes, the warmth of his body against her own, then perhaps she could have appreciated the beauty of spring. Yet it seemed to her that she could sooner learn to forget her own name than to forget the man who haunted her dreams.

These past weeks had seen a change in Juliet that worried

Frances to distraction. The bright golden eyes had dimmed, and though Juliet did more than her share of the work, she undertook the tasks without her driving desire to accomplish what she had set out to do. Frances watched her in the garden one day, patiently pulling at the weeds that plagued the various plants and herbs. Yet it was not exactly patience, she thought to herself. It was more like indifference. Juliet seemd so detached, so aloof, so uncommunicative, that Frances actually longed to see that old mischievous gleam in her eye. Nothing seemed to rouse her; she had simply ceased to care about everything—except perhaps Robert's homecoming. Frances did her best to cheer Juliet, but she failed miserably at it, and finally she simply hoped that Robert would not be much longer in coming home.

Early one morning as Juliet plucked at the withered leaves of a barren rose bush, a familiar voice close behind her startled her from her labors. She jerked about, her hand scratched deeply by several of the thorns. She did not even notice. Standing but a few steps from her was a handsome, dashing young figure in a uniform of buff and blue. She felt numb. She was certain that she was dreaming as her eyes scanned him fully and clouded over with tears.

"Robert!" she whispered.

Then she ran to him, flinging her arms about his neck. He was thin, yet his lean flesh was well-muscled and firm. His face had bronzed, and the soft skin of adolescence had been weathered to a more manly texture. Even his eyes had changed. They were not so clear and sure as she remembered; they seemed older, kinder, gentler. But Robert was here and he was safe, and that was all that mattered as she held him close.

"Oh, Robert!" she whispered as she sniffed back her tears. She tried to laugh and made her voice sound strong. "You look beautiful!"

She did her best to smile when he returned the compliment, but the uniform was a sad reminder that he was not home for good. She let her eyes feast on him, and she noticed that he was staring at her, too. How she had missed him these past months!

"Frances?" he asked, his brows raised hopefully.

"Oh, she's in the parlor . . . dusting, I think. I'll get her."

Juliet took a step toward the house, but Robert caught her arm and drew her back. "I have a better idea," he said with a wide grin. "I'll surprise her myself."

With that, Robert took off in the direction of the house, his hand smoothing his hair neatly into place and brushing at any dust that might have dimmed the bright blue of his coat or marred the dull yellow of his breeches. Juliet watched him walk eagerly away from her, needlessly fussing with his appearance for the woman he so obviously loved. Tears of envy coursed down her cheeks. She loved Frances, too, but it was difficult to drown the jealousy, especially now, when she was doing her best to scale a mountain of her own broken dreams.

Suddenly an odd feeling came over her, an eerie sensation of being watched. She whirled about and there stood Alec, calmly observing her pain. She briefly noted the warm understanding in his dark eyes, then forced herself to turn away. No! She could not allow herself to enjoy the momentary comfort of his arms only to face the brutal thrust of loneliness when he was gone. He meant nothing to her anymore. It had all been a foolish diversion, and now it was finished. She wiped the tears from her cheeks and turned back to the rose shrubs, where she began again to deliberately pluck at the browning leaves. When her chore was completed, she moved on to the rows of newly planted herbs and pulled at the weeds that grew so quickly, silently hoping that he would leave her in peace. Several moments passed. The silence became heavy. Finally Alec approached her. He squatted down opposite her, and his face was dangerously close to hers. She concentrated on the task at hand, carefully keeping her eyes on the ground.

"Julie?" he whispered softly, his rich voice a gentle caress that made her feel weak. She knew she must get away from him. She steeled herself as best she could, rose, and headed for the house. A restraining hand caught at her, and she swallowed hard as his fingers came in contact with her bare arm. Blood rushed to her cheeks until they were hot and pink, and she dared not raise her eyes.

"Julie? What is it?" he asked gently.

She twisted the kindness she heard in his tone. It was only deception, she told herself. He was making a fool of her with his feigned doting concern! Well, she would not let him do it!

A gust of anger filled her sails as she bravely raised her eyes to his.

"They've arrested my father!" she answered in a voice as hard and as cold as tempered metal.

"So I heard."

"They've arrested him!" she repeated. "Jailed him like some common criminal because he refused to sanction your stupid rebellion! Because he is loyal to his king!"

Alec took a deep breath. He was not really prepared to handle this side of Juliet. He had seen her temper flare numerous times in the past, but this was somehow different.

"You probably will not like what I tell you, but I shall be perfectly honest. Your father is better off in jail—" At his words, she jerked angrily at the hold he had on her arm, but still he held fast, his fingers biting deep. "Let me finish! The Tories in this city are up to no good. Sooner or later, something will happen for which they will be held accountable, justly or no. If your father is in jail, he will be safe at least from hanging. Be happy for that much."

He abruptly released his hold on her, and she pointedly strode in the opposite direction. But as she neared the house, she suddenly realized that it offered her no easy escape. She had no desire to interrupt Frances and Robert, and certainly none to entertain Alec privately in the house, so she quickly sought out another chore in the garden and set herself to it.

Alec frowned as he studied her actions, puzzled by the change in her manner. She was not trying to be arrogant or condescending as she had been before. The festering anger he saw ran deeper, having its source in something he could not name. He advanced on her again, determined to know what was on her mind.

His voice, though gentle, was nonetheless a command. "Tell me what's bothering you."

She ignored him. Alec waited for a sufficiently long space of time, then his patience abruptly snapped and he jerked her to her feet. Juliet's breath caught in her throat as she was pulled tightly against his chest, but her eyes glowed almost red with her fury.

"How dare you!"

He scoffed at her anger and proceeded to hurl his own accusations. "Do you realize, my dear Juliet, that your 'warm welcomes' rival the North Sea in an ice storm? Pardon me if I appear confused, but I seem to recall that the woman I left was as warm and willing as any woman I have ever known. Pray tell me, what has caused this sudden frost? I believe you owe me some explanation."

It frightened Juliet when Alec lost his temper, and though she carefully hid her fear, her heart thudded so against him that she knew he must feel it, too. She struggled to be free, but his arms were like bands of iron. Facing the fact that she was trapped, she met his eyes again with a loathing that startled him.

"You are sadly mistaken, sir. You place far too much store on a casual flirtation!"

"You know very well it is more than that!" he returned hotly.

"I happen to know, Alec," she sneered, "that you are 'definitely spoken for' by a woman in Virginia!"

Relief and recognition dawned in his dark eyes. Frances must have mentioned his intended, and this was all a simple misunderstanding. Juliet was actually jealous!

"I am no more spoken for than you, Julie," he replied, the familiar mocking tone creeping back into his voice. "Or have you forgotten about Harold?"

"Indeed I have not!"

Alec heaved a long sigh. Why did she have to be so difficult?

"Julie, my engagement to Cassandra was arranged by my father. It was none of my doing, and I do not intend to be held to it. Do you think me completely without honor? Do you really believe that I would use you and then . . ."

Juliet's resolve began to crumble. "Frances said . . ."

"I can imagine what Frances said!" he answered wryly. "I do not claim to have been a monk all these years while waiting for you to grow up. Neither have I been the lecher that many accuse me of being. There have been . . ." He paused to look at her. She looked so very much like a hurt little girl. He did not like to see her hurt, and he wanted to choose his words carefully so that he would not add to her pain. "There have been times when I needed someone soft and warm, and a woman presented herself to fill that fleeting purpose. But I have never made false promises to anyone, including Cassandra, and I never claimed to love any other. That honor is yours, Julie, for I have already pledged my devotion to you, and I intend to have you for my wife."

Her heart leaped at his declaration, yet she pulled her eyes away from his handsome features and recalled that she had more to consider than the veracity of his words. If she consented to be Alec's wife, it would destroy her father, who at this very moment suffered for her sake. She could not, would not turn her back on him now. She swallowed hard and gathered her courage.

"I am going to marry Harold," she said quietly.

Alec's patience waned, and he muttered a low curse.

"Juliet Hampton, you are a fool!"

He took advantage of her proximity, pressing intimately against her and kissing her in a most thorough manner. But she held her breath, forcing down the tide of passion that rose within her in spite of herself. When Alec drew back, she turned abruptly away and calmly repeated her statement.

"I am going to marry Harold."

It was too much for Alec. He took hold of her shoulders and shook her until her teeth rattled.

"Look at me!"

He continued to shake her until she obeyed him. She blinked back painful tears and faced his dark eyes, where even through her blurred vision she saw something she had never seen before. She vaguely realized that what she saw was hurt, that he truly loved her, but she could not afford to dwell on that now. She had made a promise to her father, and that had to come first.

"You said you loved me."

His voice sounded odd, she thought. Words had always come so easily to him, and a smile had always been close on their heels. These words came hard, and they seemed to draw blood on his pride. But she must not think about that . . .

"I did not mean it."

"Julie, listen to me. I love you. I want you. I want to marry you, to have children, to make you happy as I know you can be. I want you more than I have ever wanted anything—" Something made him stop. She realized it was his pride. He searched her face, which was curiously void of all expression, and her eyes, which looked at him blankly as if they did not see him at all. "If you tell me to go, I shall do so," he said quietly.

Juliet hesitated, at war with herself. "Then go," she murmured.

He released her and took a difficult breath. "If I go, I shall not come back, Julie." His brow darkened as he waited for her to change her mind, then his nostrils flared as she stared stonily at the flowers and the trees, as if he had already gone.

How beautiful the flowers are, she was thinking, and how sadly out of place. It felt to her like winter. Everything seemed so cold and dead.

"Good-bye, Alec," she choked out through a tight throat, not daring to look at his face.

Moments later, when she heard the urgent gallop of a horse leaving the stables, she had no tears. She felt only a strange emptiness that ached to be filled. She had been rudely awakened from a dream that was never meant to be. But her father had told her a long time ago that only fools believe in dreams.

Chapter 18

Rachel kept her eyes properly lowered as befitted a servant as she offered the guard a freshly baked loaf and several slices of smoked pork. She was always careful not to betray her condescending attitude toward the rebels, for she realized that on her visits here, she, a Tory, walked on thin ice. This morning it proved a difficult task to be patient while the guard searched through her basket and carefully looked her over. She had important news and was most anxious to inform her employer. As she sat waiting for Hampton to be brought into the tiny room, little more than a cell itself, she cast furtive glances about, wondering just how closely the guards, and the other prisoners for that matter, would be listening to what she had to say. She would have to be very cautious. She wanted no slur cast on Master Lawrence, no scandal to disgrace the family name. However, he had to be told immediately what had taken place, for she needed his guidance in handling the situation.

Hampton was escorted to his seat, accepting the basket from the guard without appreciation, while Rachel waited until she was certain that she had his full attention.

"We have had visitors at Hampton House, sir."

"Visitors?" he asked casually, his voice betraying only idle curiosity.

"Master Robert, sir. He's here on the island and in uniform. He comes and goes as he pleases, sir, and even joins Miss Juliet and Miss Frances for dinner."

She saw that his jaw tightened and his eyes grew hard and cold, but his voice remained as it had been, disinterested.

"You said visitors. Was someone with him?"

"Aye, sir." She swallowed hard before she continued. "Mr. Farrell came with him, too, though only once. I heard it said that he rides correspondence for the army and has left the island for a time. He don't wear a uniform, sir, but I heard Robert call him a captain, all the same." She paused. "What I wanted to know is, what shall I do if he be coming back again? Shall I . . . ?" She looked meaningfully toward the guard.

"Of course," he answered silkily. "Make everyone comfortable, Rachel. I want no trouble in my home while I am away. Be careful that there is none."

With that he rose, in effect dismissing her. She opened her mouth to protest. She had so much more to tell him! Yet he obviously meant to be patient for the time being, as he was in no position to wield his usual power. And besides, she did not wish to announce to so many ears what she had seen in the garden that day. She had always known that Juliet was no good, though she had carefully hidden her true feelings from her father. He seemed to have such great plans for her. He would not like being told that those plans had gone awry. Rachel watched Hampton being led back to the crowded cell and drew a heavy sigh. If he wanted her to bide her time, then she would certainly do so.

Alec pressed Cheval to pick up his pace, for the dark stallion had grown accustomed to a far too leisurely gait these past weeks. As the horse tossed his head and reluctantly responded to the command, clods of mud were sent flying behind them, and Alec winced at the painful jarring of his arm. It was only a flesh wound, and a clean one at that, but it had been bothersome enough to slow him down quite a bit as he worked his way back to New York.

The news he carried was from the south, his first trip there in nearly a year. General Charles Lee had taken charge of the southern army, but his own brand of eccentric stubbornness and an unyielding belief in his personal military expertise had already posed a myriad of problems. In South Carolina, Lee immediately had found fault with the construction of Fort Sullivan and had termed it useless, doing his best to force abandonment of the project. His tactless handling of the situation had made him many enemies and had divided the army into two, each going about business with total disregard for the other.

It had been easy enough for Alec to forget caution while riding on the deceptively quiet country lanes. Indeed, it had been difficult to remember that the colonies were at war, though he had seen things on this trip that made the war a frightening reality. The lovely city of Norfolk had been heavily bombarded from the harbor on New Year's Day by Lord Dunmore, who had acted in retaliation for the British ships lost to American privateers. By essentially destroying the city, he had caused the privateers little pain, while the women and children rendered homeless in the cold of winter were left to bear the brunt of Dunmore's justice.

It had not been the sights of destruction marring the landscape, however, that had brought on Alec's careless actions and led to the painful reminder in his upper arm. He had been leaving the crude "comfort" of a small roadside inn the hour before dawn when a sniper's bullet caught him just as he was mounting Cheval. The bullet might have meant his death had not the early morning mists aided him in his escape, or had his mount been a less disciplined one. But he had known better than to stop in that small village beforehand, particularly when he was close to home and following paths where he might well be recognized. There were nests of Tories everywhere, and the needless destruction of wartime spawned bitter reactions in everyone. A lone patriot recognized as such could easily find himself feeling the bite of such bitterness. Someone at the inn might only have guessed at his mission. Regardless, someone had tried to stop him, and had come very close to succeeding.

The trip had been different for other reasons as well. Alec was accustomed to spending long hours in the saddle, but he could not dispel the drudgery that seemed to travel with him on this route. Even when he rode at breakneck speed, every mile had seemed as endless as the mile before, the roads and paths seeming to be part of a menacing maze that rambled on and on and led him nowhere. His usual energy was absent; sleep brought little in the way of relief for his troubled mind.

Even his easy rapport with Cheval was absent, and his patience with the steed wore thin.

In his state of distraction, Alec took the longer route back to New York, riding north before crossing over to Manhattan, rather than ferrying across the Hudson. As he neared the familiar crossing at Kingsbridge, he reluctantly admitted to himself what he had been denying for days. He would be a long time forgetting Juliet Hampton. She had dealt his pride a painful blow and laid him low with her repeated denials of what he knew she felt. He chided himself, for obviously he knew less about her than he had supposed. Perhaps she really was like the woman who waited for him in Virginia, though the idea rankled him and caused a surge of disclaimers to flood his consciousness. Cassandra Collins's blatant flirtations had come close to embarrassing him, and he was not one to embarrass easily. The girl simply had no pride. Vanity, arrogance, yes. But not a shred of real pride. He sighed his frustration as he admitted that the easy comparison did not work. If there was one quality that Juliet Hampton possessed, it was pride, perhaps in too great a degree. She took on life with her chin held high, fighting all the way, and for that he loved her. If only he could have turned her in the proper direction! If he could have made her see that their combined strengths could tackle the world no matter what problems were posed. . . . The debating in his mind refused to be stilled. Rebuttal followed rebuttal in an aimless succession that left him worn and tired and, more, defeated. He shook his head, realizing that Cheval had once again abandoned his leaping strides and taken to a sluggish jog.

He reached the northern part of Manhattan and idly noted that the construction of Fort Washington had proceeded admirably in his absence. Then he finally traversed the familiar road to the southern portion of the island and found he was on the brink of total exhaustion. There was none of his usual exhilaration at having completed the final leg of his journey. He only wanted to take his rest.

Having delivered the papers he had carried these many miles, he was directed to a tent. The army had experienced a transition of sorts these past weeks, for the most part giving up private homes for canvas tents. The island was covered with them, as Washington's army had swelled to nearly twenty thousand. Alec had scarcely noticed the change as he rode by.

He tethered Cheval a short distance from his tent, removed the saddle, and began to rub him down. It had been a long journey for the stallion, too, and Alec always saw to the animal's comfort before he sought the same for himself. He went deliberately about his task and took no notice when Robert eagerly approached his side.

"Good to see you back, stranger—that is, Captain Stranger, sir," Robert amended with a grin. "You never did mention how you worked the promotion."

Alec snorted and continued his work.

"General Lee happened to like me, and he feels that anyone even remotely related to him ought to be given 'suitable rank,' as he calls it. He saw to it before anyone had a chance to object. Of course, I must agree that most Virginians are destined for greatness . . ." he added with a halfhearted grin.

"Well, Captain Greatness," quipped Robert, comically mimicking a salute, "could I interest you in a dinner invitation for this evening?"

Alec paused in his work, then took up a stiff brush in his right hand and moved to brush Cheval's mane. He raised his arm, then sucked in his breath and winced as a stabbing pain ripped through his injured limb. He muttered a curse, having lost his good humor of a few moments before. He took up the brush in his left hand and struggled to proceed, but Robert interrupted his uncoordinated endeavor, taking up the brush and, in painful contrast to Alec, effortlessly completing what he had begun. He turned to Alec with an expectant smile.

"Well?"

Alec sighed and caught the brush that Robert tossed playfully to him without returning his smile.

"It was a long ride, Robert, and I'm tired. Some other time, perhaps."

"Tomorrow?" Robert pressed. His smile reminded Alec of a fox when he added, "Juliet will be there."

He eyed Robert's grin for a long moment, his black eyes showing no emotion.

"In that case, Robert, the answer is quite simply, no, thank you."

He turned and lifted the flap of his tent, then entered,

scowling at the less than comfortable looking cot that was its only furnishing. Robert followed, not one to give up so easily.

"Did you quarrel with Juliet?" he queried bluntly.

Alec threw his belongings on the cot, ignoring the invasion of his privacy. With a quick tug of a heavy cord, he unrolled the blanket to make his bed.

"Did you?" Robert persisted.

"Why don't you ask her?" was the only reply Alec gave, and without another word he took to his bed.

Robert had been going to the house whenever the opportunity presented itself, usually several times a week thanks to the lax discipline that had taken hold of the army while the British kept their distance. With each visit, a striking contrast between the two young women who dined with him became more evident. While Frances glowed with a fresh, natural beauty, Juliet was silent and remote, and the last remnants of her sparkle seemed to die before his eyes.

Tonight would be different, he vowed as he tossed Jay his reins along with a friendly greeting. He would get a rise out of his sister tonight if he had to turn her over his knee. It was just like Juliet to make herself miserable—as he well knew she was doing.

The dinner proceeded as usual, with Frances rambling gaily and her giggles filtering about the dining room. While Robert added quips of dry humor, Juliet poked at her plate with disinterest, forcing a smile now and then. As she was pouring the hot tea they enjoyed at meal's end—despite Robert's habitual comments about feeling unpatriotic drinking the stuff—he made his move.

"I saw Alec today. He just got back."

He watched carefully, noting that her hands trembled a trifle at the mention of his name. He waited until she had filled the cups and had once again taken her seat.

"He was gone over a month, and apparently ran into quite a bit of trouble." He caught Juliet's eye for barely a moment before she turned away, swallowing hard and averting her attention to sugaring her tea. "He was shot—"

Robert was stopped before he could say another word as Frances let out a gasp and Juliet spilled the entire contents of her cup directly into her lap. She clutched the top layers of steaming fabric away from her skin, threw a single bewildered look at Robert, and ran from the dining room.

While Frances seemed flustered by what had just taken place, Robert was oddly pensive and seemed oblivious to the exclamations and questions she heaped upon him, leaving him absolutely no time to answer. When she noticed his preoccupation, she broke off in mid-sentence, completely perplexed.

Robert rose and poured himself a glass of brandy, pacing slowly and thoughtfully as he enjoyed its warmth and settling effect. All the while Frances observed, her eyes troubled and her brow softly furrowed. She felt like an outsider, as if she had seen what had just happened, but at the same time had not seen it; as if what she had heard meant little, while what had been left unsaid told the story.

Time passed. She meekly awaited Robert's explanation. He returned to the table and pulled a chair close, so that their conversation might be a private affair. "Frances, have you noticed that Juliet has been . . . different? Quieter? Not like herself since I have been home?"

Frances gave a slow, solemn nod. "But it began long before you came home from Boston, Robert. It began when your father was arrested . . . or rather when he told Juliet that he was going to be arrested. I remember it clearly because it was the same day that I saw Juliet and Alec on the—" She halted abruptly, and a blush rushed to her cheeks, reddening her skin from her neck to the roots of her hair. She made several attempts at clearing her throat, none of which proved effective, and she could not for the life of her manage a square look at Robert.

Observing her painful embarrassment, his own thoughts proceeded in an uncomfortable direction. What exactly had Frances seen? He briefly considered the sorry ramifications if Alec had compromised his sister in his absence. Had Alec been any less of a friend, Robert might not have deemed any further investigation necessary before calling him out. But Robert knew Alec to be a man of honor, and therefore he pressed Frances for the necessary answers.

"What exactly did you see, Frances?"

Though it seemed impossible, her face became an even darker shade of crimson. She swallowed hard several times before she could answer, her eyes riveted firmly on the wringing hands in her lap.

"Well," she began in a tight voice, "we were in the attic, Juliet and I. That is, I was, and Juliet joined me. I didn't like the way she was looking at some of your old clothing, Robert. It frightened me!" She glanced about nervously to assure herself no one else was listening. "I was afraid she might actually try on a pair of breeches!" she whispered, wide-eyed. "So I took them from her and was tidying up everything when she said something about forgetting Alec was here. She took off like a flash! I would swear that her feet failed to touch half of the steep stairs that lead to the attic!

"I didn't want Rachel to be angry with me for being curious—it's so dreadful when Rachel gets angry!—so I finished packing everything neatly away, just as it had been, before I came down the stairs." She paused to gather her courage, clearing her throat again before she could go on. "I walked through the hallway toward the main stairs, and there they were, on the floor at the top of the stairs! Alec said that Juliet fell, but . . ." She sought his eyes, her own a startling blue against her red skin. "But I saw him kiss her, Robert, and it didn't look like any accident to me!

"I am so afraid that he led Juliet on, Robert. Mama always said that Alec was something of a lady's man, and I've noticed that women look at him . . . that way, you know what I mean. But I never thought to warn Juliet about him before that day. I mean, Juliet is engaged to marry another man, and I naturally assumed . . ." She sighed.

"It's all right though, Robert. I spoke with her that same night, and she told me"—she frowned and did her best to recall Juliet's exact words—"that it was just something that happened, that it did not mean anything to either of them, it was something one cannot explain." She sighed again. "I believed her then, maybe because I wanted to. I felt guilty because Alec is my cousin, and Juliet had no reason to be wary of him. But I think that maybe Alec really did hurt her, even though she would probably never admit it."

"What exactly did you tell Juliet about Alec?"

"Only the truth," vowed Frances. "I told her about a girl in Virginia to whom he is engaged and has been for years. And I mentioned that he has always been something of a romancer, that he does not take most women very seriously. . . ." Her blue eyes became suddenly large and fearful. "Robert, do you think it was wrong of me to say something? I was only trying to prevent her from being hurt."

Robert wrapped a comforting arm about her shoulders. "Everything will work out for the best, Frances," he assured her. "But I do believe it's time I had a heart-to-heart chat with my little sister."

He kissed Frances's forehead, the tip of her nose, her small cupid's-bow mouth. Then he rose from his seat, and, with a quick pat on her head, he left the dining room.

By the time Juliet had managed to strip off her clothing, the tea stain had penetrated every layer through to her skin. It is just as well, she thought. She had no real desire to return to Robert and Frances. She donned a cotton night rail and took a seat at her favorite window, looking out over southern Manhattan. Dusk was falling. The first of scores of campfires that would flicker in the night sent their telltale gray coils swirling toward the sky. The first star twinkled prematurely in the charcoal-colored heavens, unnoticed until the brilliant streaks of pink and red that stretched out from the western sunset had died away.

Juliet lifted her feet to the sill, drawing up her knees and hugging them to her chest as she caught sight of the star blinking its weak light long before others dared. She sighed and propped her chin on her knees. The first star, the bravest star, the magic star that granted wishes to all who observed its lonely struggle.

"Please let Alec be all right," she whispered. "I ask nothing more than that he be safe."

Fearful thoughts raced through her mind. Shot, Robert had said. Had he lost an arm? A leg? Or had his chest been penetrated by some tiny ball of evil that would fester and destroy his life? She shook her head to dispel the gruesome thoughts. He was safe, she told herself. Robert had been casual in mentioning his injury, so certainly it could not be a serious one.

When a knock at her door interrupted her musings, she kept her precarious perch and called out permission to enter. She was mildly surprised to see that it was Robert, and she flashed him a quick acknowledging smile before she turned her attention back to the star, which had been joined by half a dozen others in the rapidly darkening sky. Robert opened the window adjacent to the one where Juliet sat and also took a seat on the sill. The silence grew heavy between them, and Juliet felt uneasy, although she had never before felt uneasy with Robert.

"Where is Frances?" she finally asked him.

"Downstairs. Helping Rachel with the dishes, I believe."

"Oh."

Again there was silence.

She found it impossible to bear the uncertainty. "Is Alec hurt—was it serious?"

"A minor injury. A flesh wound in his arm."

Juliet sighed her relief. "Thank God," she murmured.

"I asked Alec to come to dinner tomorrow."

Juliet's eyes widened with distress before she turned away. "You should not have."

There was a brief pause.

"Is he coming?" she asked in a tiny voice.

"What do you think?"

She sighed. "I think not."

"Why not?"

There was no reply.

Robert retreated a bit, then attacked from another direction. "The first day I was home from Boston, Alec came here with me. But by the time I got back to camp, he'd already gone south. He'd planned to leave the next morning anyway, but he left that same afternoon . . . right after he saw you. Now why do you suppose he would do that?"

Again there was no answer, but Robert was not one to give up easily.

"Did you quarrel?"

"It doesn't matter, Robert. It doesn't make any difference anymore." Juliet's voice was totally without expression.

Her lack of response began to annoy him. He came to his feet and paced the short distance to the bed before returning to her at the window. "Do you know that I am very worried about you, Juliet? Do you know that you have changed so much that I feel as if I don't know you anymore? What's happened to you? How can I reach you? What's wrong with you?"

Juliet lowered her eyes, which were quickly flooding with tears despite the effort she made to hold them back. With them came the agonizing pain that she had denied these past weeks, and the need to spill her troubles on an understanding ear.

"Oh, Robert! Everything is wrong! Everything!"

"Tell me what happened with Alec."

"Nothing happened . . . and everything happened. Please don't ask about Alec, Robert. I am trying so hard to forget—"

"Why would you want to do that? Doesn't he care for you?"

"He loves me, he wants to marry me," she cried. "But I cannot! I cannot!" She sniffed as she took a shaky breath. "Father is depending on me, Robert. He's been different these past months since you've been gone. He talks about my wedding often, and of visiting me in England after I'm married. He even showed me how to use his pistol—just like he showed you. He's proud of me, Robert. Of *me!*"

Her voice grew small and distant. "I've always wanted him to be proud of me, but no matter what I did, it was never good enough. He is proud now, though. He said that my wedding will be the proudest moment of his life. He said that it will make up for all the hurt that you . . ."

"That I caused him?" Robert supplied.

She nodded.

He snorted, and his voice was filled with disgust and disbelief. "You're going to throw away what you feel for Alec and wait another year for a man you don't love?"

Juliet looked away. "I have no choice," she said quietly.

Robert closed the distance between them and roughly brought her to her feet. His voice was firm and filled with authority. "You do have a choice! You do! Do you understand me?"

He paced before her as he spoke his mind. "I've been away almost a year, though it seems more like ten, and in that time I have done a great deal of thinking. Everything seems so different when one stands a few paces back and takes another look—a different perspective, one might say. What I thought about most was Father. At first I felt guilty about leaving, and when I saw fighting and how terrible it really was, I . . ." His voice broke with the painful memory. "I didn't want to come home at all. I didn't want anyone to know that I had made a mistake, that I wasn't so sure about anything anymore. I thought when I left that it would be so simple and easy." A frown furrowed his brow, aging him far beyond his years. "Every single man who joins our army does so of his own free will, knowing that we might fail. And every one of us has someone who is waiting for him to come home, someone who suffers the loneliness, the uncertainty. Yet we go, in spite of the pain we leave behind.

"I thought often of Frances, of the trials she has faced this past year, the separation from her own family. But she has never once complained, Juliet, because she realizes that it is something I must do.

"But Father? His 'love' for me is based on something else, on an extension of his own pride. Do you realize that up until the time I left, I had never made a single important decision? He does not even know who I am! And neither does he know you!"

Juliet opened her mouth to defend her father, but Robert forged ahead, giving her no chance. "If he knew anything at all about you, he'd know that you feel nothing for Harold. But he doesn't see that, does he? He doesn't care that you'll spend your next twenty years as miserable as you've spent the first!"

He drew a breath to calm himself before continuing. "Look at yourself, Juliet. You're on the verge of becoming the type of woman our mother was, cold and uncaring. I believe that her spirit was dead a long time before we were even born. Thank God that we had each other to love when we were children!"

Juliet lowered her eyes, and her voice was low and shallow. "And now you have Frances."

"And you have Alec."

She shook her head and took a step away from his penetrating glare. It was only then that Robert really lost his temper.

"Juliet Hampton, do you know how long I've prayed that something like this would happen? Ever since you stepped off that ship with your silly nose so high in the air! Alec is a fine man, and if you're going to consider Father's feelings, you might as well be fair about it and consider Alec's as well. Do you think it impossible that he might need you, too?"

Juliet lifted doubtful eyes to his, then sighed sadly and shook her head. "Alec is strong and sure of himself."

"And he's proud and arrogant and spirited and stubborn. In short, my dear sister, he reminds me very much of you." Robert smiled kindly down at her troubled frown, knowing that she wanted very much to be convinced that her love for Alec was right. "Juliet, the most difficult part of loving someone is in learning to accept him as he is, not as you would have him be. If Father cannot accept you for what you are, then he deserves to lose you. But does Alec?"

She pondered over all that Robert had said. She had never even considered the idea that Alec might need her as she needed him. But Alec had told her once that he was like her, and then there had been that look in his eyes when she had asked him to leave. . . .

As for Father, would he ever learn to understand? Would he ever forgive her for not going through with the marriage he so heartily endorsed? Yet, as Robert said, loving someone meant accepting him as he was. . . .

"Alec is engaged to a girl in Virginia," she said thoughtfully, after several long moments of silence. "And he is very angry with me, Robert. He refused to come to dinner tomorrow."

Robert could hardly suppress a smile of relief. "He did at that," he responded lightly.

As he made his way to the door, she followed, protesting all the while. "What shall I do, Robert? How could I ever begin to explain things I said to him? He'll never listen to me! I know he won't! His temper is every bit as bad as mine!"

Robert's mouth curved into a very familiar kind of grin. "You aren't afraid of a challenge, are you, Juliet?"

Chapter 19

The moment Robert left her room, Juliet began to pace. She paced and paced and paced, and still she had no thought of retiring for the night. Listlessness and fatigue had fled, and with them, the desire to sleep. Her heart felt light with the thought of seeing Alec again, of holding him, of explaining away all the hurt she had caused him. But how could she see him if he refused to come here? She would write him a letter! Yes, that was it! She would explain everything to him in a letter.

She ran to her desk and took up the quill, only to find that the words of explanation would not come. She bit her lip and tossed the quill aside. She would have to see him. If he would only hear her out, then everything could be settled. She scribbled a note to him, asking that he come to see her, adding that it was urgent. She folded and sealed it, happily thinking that everything was neatly resolved. She would give the letter to Robert, and Robert would convince him to come. She closed her eyes and smiled briefly, then frowned. Robert had already left Hampton House for the night, she had seen him go. She could not even ask him to deliver her note until tomorrow. What if Alec left Manhattan before receiving it? It might be weeks, even months before she saw him again, and she could scarcely bare the thought of waiting through one more day! No. She needed to act now and leave nothing to chance. Besides, she thought with a cocky grin, she'd been looking for an excuse to try on those old clothes of Robert's ever since that day in the attic.

The moon was low and just beginning to wane when a thin young lad on a golden horse galloped from the stables behind Hampton House. A slightly oversized tricorn covered thick, dark hair tied back in a too-long queue, while a white cotton shirt billowed sadly over narrow shoulders, and heavy cotton breeches were an equally poor fit—tight through the buttocks while bagging at thigh and waist. A nicely tailored brown jacket camouflaged many of the flaws in shirt and breeches, but it, too, had quite obviously been made for a broader set of shoulders and more muscular arms. There was no fault to be found with the mare, however, who took to the road with an easy confidence.

The lad slowed the golden horse to a walk whenever he approached a campfire, passing the rows and rows of tents and sleeping men with careful scrutiny. Sentries took little notice of the youth. His frame was hardly one to instill fear in anyone, and the soft-skinned face was anything but menacing as he rode among the thousands of soldiers camped on the island. An hour of fruitless searching passed, and the smoky haze of dawn was just beginning to lighten the eastern horizon. The lad's face reflected his frustration, yet on he rode, watching, searching. Finally he saw it! Tethered close by a tent a short distance from any others was a stallion he would have recognized anywhere. He picked up his speed, cantering gingerly through the rows of canvas housing until he reached the familiar steed. Slipping from the saddle with a surprising mixture of grace and agility, it was his extreme misfortune to attract the attention of a groggy middle-aged lieutenant, who was relieving himself nearby.

Suffering a good deal from the prior evening of overindulgence, Lieutenant Dregs was in the mood for an argument, and the lad's untimely clip-clopping followed by the thud of his dismount echoing painfully in his head seemed valid enough reason for one.

"Hey, you, boy!" he growled.

The youth stopped dead in his tracks and hoped against hope that the gruff call was meant for someone else.

"You, boy!" again came the menacing bark. "Turn around here and face me when I talk at ye."

Sheepishly, with shoulders hunched and head bowed, the lad complied. He was just a few steps short of his destination, but he dared not cause a disturbance that might very well cost him the entire trip.

"What ye be up to there, boy?" the lieutenant boomed, taking a firm stance with feet braced well apart and hands at his hips. He noticed that the lad was reluctant to answer, and that he kicked nervously at the dusty ground with the toe of a heavy boot. Those seemed like mighty fine boots for a boy to be wearing, and the clothes were fancier than any Dregs had ever owned, despite the ill fit.

"I said, what ye be up to?" he demanded again. "Look up at me, boy! What ye got t' be afeared of? Seems t' me only reason ye'd be afeared o' somethin' is if ye up t' no good!"

Cautiously, a pair of rather startling gold-colored eyes lifted to meet the lieutenant's narrowed bloodshot ones. The boy had noted a slur in the man's speech and a slight rocking to and fro of his heavy frame, though his feet remained solidly planted. He readily recognized that the man was looking for trouble, and the boy had no desire to be on the receiving end. He hesitated only because he feared that his voice would betray him. He was not sure if he could give a passable imitation of a young man's voice, but it seemed he would soon be forced to find out.

"Boy!" Dregs bellowed furiously.

He cleared his throat, and his voice came tight and hoarse. "Yes, sir."

"That's better!" nodded the lieutenant. "Now. For the last time, I asked ye what ye be up to."

The lad cleared his throat again and answered with obvious difficulty. "I have a message, sir . . . for Captain Alexander Farrell. I was only going to deliver it to him . . ."

As the watery red eyes narrowed suspiciously on him, the golden eyes lowered self-consciously and shoulders hunched forward, preventing the soldier from getting a good look at his face.

"Well," the heavy man considered, rubbing a hand over a stubbly growth of beard. "Cap'n Farrell be takin' his rest, ye see, an' I think he'd not be wantin' t' be disturbed by the likes o' ye." He scanned the boy's appearance, and his eyes drifted momentarily to the mare. This lad was certainly a strange mixture of finery and rubble. Something was wrong here, he felt sure of it.

"That's a fine piece o' horse flesh ye got there, boy. Where'd a fella' like ye come across such a filly?" As he spoke, he circled slowly about the boy, eyeing him up and down from every angle.

The gold eyes met his almost immediately, flashing for a moment with undisguised contempt. "She's mine!" snapped the lad, his bravado coming as a mild surprise to the soldier. Lieutenant Dregs discarded his immediate impulse to strike the lad, tossing a glance at the nearby tent. He had no desire to rile Captain Farrell, but this boy needed to be taught some manners.

"I'll deliver my message and be on my way," the boy said.

Captain Farrell was a dangerous man, Dregs thought; it was hardly worth risking his life to get the best of this smart-mouthed little ruffian. The boy just could mean something special to the captain, yet Dregs was not about to concede totally to the skinny stripling. With two long strides, he blocked the entrance to Alec's tent, arms folded across his chest as he lorded his advantage in size and age over the boy. "I be takin' the letter, boy," he bellowed. "I be seein' t' it bein' delivered . . . meself!"

The boy's eyes once again scattered angry sparks, and the smoothly curving chin stuck out in defiance as he gave his head a determined shake.

"Now listen here, boy! I be seein' t' it, I tell ye, or it not be seen to at all!" the soldier pledged with a snarl.

For a fleeting moment the lad matched the rage the officer had turned on him, with eyes narrowed to dangerous slits and lip curled in scorn. Though it was a painful blow to his pride to do so, he was inevitably forced to admit his defeat. He spit at the ground, then angrily kicked at the spot, sending a waft of soft brown dust several feet in the air. Turning on a heel, he made for his horse, his strides landing with heavy thumps as he marched away. He threw a final loathing glare at the man who had hindered his plans, then began to loosen the knot that held the reins. The soldier had followed the boy to the horse and now stood a few paces from the entrance to the tent. As the boy's eyes drew longingly to the site of that tent, his youthful daring made an unexpected rebound. He toyed a moment with the reins, leaving the slip knot secure enough to hold, then, without any warning, he made a mad dash for the tent.

The lieutenant, for all his excessive weight, was quick on his feet as he lunged at the boy, catching at his leg and managing to land both of them flat on the ground, half in and half out of Captain Farrell's tent.

With the onslaught of unexpected commotion, Alec bolted upright from a dead sleep, clutching the pistol it was his habit to keep nearby, wherever he made his bed. His black eyes grew wide with amazement, and he did his best to keep from blinking so as not to miss a moment of the bizarre struggle taking place before him. A feisty little scrap of a boy was holding his own against an adversary more than double his size, kicking, scratching, biting his defense against the various holds the soldier attempted to secure. Each time the meaty arms banded around the slender youth, a squirm and a well placed foot or elbow managed to fend off the confinement.

Amazement changed swiftly to amusement, and Alec lowered the pistol to await the outcome of the fight. He winced as the lad tossed a handful of dirt in the other's face, then firmly wielded a heavy boot at the man's shin, sending him hooting and hopping about on his remaining good limb. It was at that moment that the boy's eyes sought Alec's, and recognition stunned him absolutely senseless. He sat there dazed. When the struggle continued, it became apparent that the lieutenant was out for blood. He doubled a thick fist and swung at the youth with all his might. Fortunately the lad ducked at the proper moment and avoided a crushing blow to his face. The soldier, red-faced and determined, attempted a quick succession of blows at the boy, who backed away in sudden terror. Belatedly, Alec found his tongue.

"That's enough, Lieutenant!" he barked in a voice that left no room for argument.

The soldier heaved his fury in deep, lengthy snorts, walking a dangerous tightrope as he considered throwing one final—and, he would make certain, accurate—punch. But the deadly click of a pistol being cocked managed to divert his attention just long enough for the boy to slip from the far corner of the tent to the safety of the captain's side.

"I said that was enough, Lieutenant," Alec repeated in a voice that seemed overly smooth and calm.

The heavy man's lips tightened until they were white, but he finally spouted his protest in a near-proper tone. "This . . . this ragamuffin here claims t' have business w' ye," he blubbered. "I offered t' help him, when he picks a fight w' me! The lad don't know respect for his betters, sir! But I've a mind t' teach him a bit o' it, right now!"

He lifted his doubled fist again and took one long stride toward the boy, only to find the cold, dark barrel of the pistol leveled at him at point-blank range. He jerked to a halt, voicing his suspicions with an indecisive mixture of fear and anger.

"Them be pretty nice boots for a simple lad t' be sportin', Cap'n, an' he rode himself in here on a filly fittin' fer a king."

Alec's voice coiled gracefully around Dregs like a snake around its prey. "I appreciate your concern, not to mention your tactful handling of the situation up to this point. However, I believe that I will take care of things from here on. The . . . boy is an acquaintance of mine, and I will see to it that he causes no further trouble."

"But Cap'n . . ." the soldier objected, rubbing a finger over the deep impression of teeth marks on his wrist.

"I said I will handle it. You are dismissed."

The silky restraint in Alec's voice discouraged the soldier from any further protests, and Dregs made his retreat.

Alec waited patiently for his angry shuffling to fade away before carefully releasing the hammer of the pistol and repositioning it on the ground at the side of his cot. Only then did he make a long and thorough inspection of the boy who stood beside him. He took in those heavy-lashed golden eyes peering doubtfully out at him from the small-featured face, and he was ready to question his own sanity, already questioning hers.

He was hardly amused at the situation as it stood. It had been another near-sleepless night, and when he'd finally managed to doze off, here she was, back to haunt him in the flesh—as if her place in his dreams were not torture enough! He sighed his impatience. He fluffed the leather bag wrapped in a blanket that served as a pillow of sorts and stretched out on the cot, as if he were anxious to return to his rest. Wincing, he folded his hands behind his head, then sternly turned an expectant eye on the one responsible for so rude an interruption.

"Well?" he demanded tersely.

Juliet took a deep breath, trying to bolster her courage. If she had hoped for a warm welcome, she was sadly disillusioned. He was going to be difficult about this, that much was painfully obvious. The words of explanation she had envisioned flowing glibly from her lips refused to come to her. It almost seemed as if he had forgotten her already, and fear took a tormenting hold of her at the thought.

Alec turned away from her continued silence, frowning darkly at the peak of canvas over his head. He was hardly in a state to receive a visitor. The shirt he wore had lost its crisp freshness long before he had reached New York, his arm was cramped and aching, and he was in sore need of a shave, not to mention a bath. But then, he countered irritably, she doesn't exactly resemble a lady gone calling in those silly boy's breeches! She has no room to complain about my appearance, he thought angrily. It's certainly not as if I invited her here.

Juliet sensed his growing impatience and knew that she must say something and quickly, so she forced herself to begin.

"I . . . I missed you, Alec."

She gnawed at her lip and waited for his reaction, but he only continued to stare at the patch of canvas overhead. Sorely conscious of her own disheveled appearance, Juliet found her confidence ebbing away. She brushed back the strands of hair that had been pulled from the dark strip of leather at the back of her neck. Tears stung her eyes as she realized that she was covered with dust from her recent scuffle. She retrieved her tricorn from the dirt and turned it slowly around in her hands, trying not to cry.

"I . . . Robert said that he invited you for dinner. I . . . I'd like you to come."

Alec closed his eyes, and his mouth tightened ominously. Just what did she think she was trying to do? If she expected him to provide—what had she called it?—a casual flirtation while she waited for her Lord Harold to come and marry her, well, she'd better think again!

"If you came here to ask me to dinner, you could have saved

yourself the trouble," he said brusquely, without even opening his eyes. "The answer is no."

"Will you visit for at least a little while before you go?" she pressed in a small voice. "I have missed you so these past weeks, Alec."

With a brief grimace of pain, he uncrossed the hands from behind his head and kneaded at his troubled brow. He resolved to resist the temptation that stood before him. He wanted much more from her than an abbreviated encounter, however sweet that might be. And he would not be at her beck and call all the while she awaited another man! "Miss Hampton," he said curtly, shielding his eyes with a forearm, "I am very tired."

Anger flared in Juliet, fending off the despair that threatened to make her give up the fight. He would not even look at her, she thought indignantly. Why, she ought to turn her back on him and forget the whole thing! But she had tried to do just that this past month and had found it quite impossible. He had said that he loved her, that he wanted her more than anything else. If he had spoken the truth, then he could not possibly have forgotten his devotion in so brief a space of time! Though it pricked at her pride to do so, she was forced to admit that the greater part of this situation was her own fault. She had hurt him and given him good reason to be indifferent. Still, if he really loved her, there must be some way to reach him. . . . Juliet put aside a good deal of her pride as she courageously played her final trump card.

"Can I at least"—she swallowed hard and winced at the boldness of the request she was about to make—"kiss you good-bye?"

Alec could not believe it! How could he hope to withstand such torture? It seemed as if the woman had lost all reason! He opened his eyes to face her as she took a precarious seat beside him on the too-narrow cot. Her hands planted gingerly against his opened shirt, she braced herself as she leaned forward until her lips touched his. When he made no move, she worked her tongue between his lips and explored his mouth with an eagerness and hunger that was as shocking to herself as it was to him. A delicious tingling flowed at every point of contact as her hands moved to his broad shoulders and neck, and finally she lay full against him on the canvas frame bed.

212

Her lips were soft, warm, teasing to his cool mouth, and he soon reacted with demands of his own. At length, she reluctantly lifted her head, and Alec met an uncertain pair of golden eyes.

"Julie," he scolded in a hoarse whisper, "that did not feel like good-bye."

A half-smile tugged at her lips, and her eyes were bright with mischief. "Shall I try again?"

Alec turned away from her, trying to hide the urges that were becoming too much for him to bear. How could he resist this flagrant attempt at seduction, particularly when he was hopelessly in love with the temptress?

"Damn but you're difficult, Captain Farrell!"

He blinked his amazement, and his attention returned to her in short order. Her eyes softened then, and became almost shy as she spoke in a low, gentle voice.

"I love you, Alec. I know that I hurt you and gave you good reason to hate me, but . . ." She swallowed hard, and her forefinger timidly traced the line of his mouth. "I need you so, Alec! I . . . I was hoping that you might forgive me for the things I said." She kissed him lightly and sighed. "How can I tell you that my life is empty without you? How can I take back the words I spoke in haste?"

With a hand behind her head, Alec pulled her close and kissed her long and hard. His hand slipped beneath her shirt and grazed the swell of her breast, spurring a shudder of pleasure that shook her slender form. He was easily convinced by the passion she returned, had he not been by her tender words.

It was with tremendous effort that he again turned away from her, forcing himself to remember that she was inexperienced, for all her eager response. He wanted her badly, but he could already see the burn on her soft skin from his unshaven face, and he had no desire to have her here, on this sorry excuse for a bed, with the risk of interruption grating heavily on his mind. She gasped when he gave her derriere a sharp whack and ordered her to get up. With a good deal of discomfort, he followed suit. He took hold of her shoulders, and his voice was strong, almost stern.

"Are you sure about everything you just said to me?"

She nodded eagerly and leaned forward to kiss him, but he held her at arm's length.

"You won't change your mind again?"

She shook her head. "Never."

"And will you marry me?"

Her grin was wide as she flung her arms about his neck. crying out her answer again and again, while Alec's expression remained solemn, his words firm.

"I am not the fool that Harold is, Julie, and I will not be content with idle promises, only to see you slip away. If you are to be my wife, the vows shall be spoken here and now. I know of a chaplain who will be willing to say the words; I have only to fetch him."

Juliet's eyes widened like saucers as she drew back to face him. "You want me to marry you here and now?" she repeated in disbelief. "Just look at me, Alec! I look like a lad!"

"I have looked at you, Miss Hampton, and I can assure you that you have seldom looked more lovely than at this moment."

"But, Alec," she protested, "I had thought at least to wear a gown!"

"And I had thought to shave," he countered, "and also to invite my mother. However, the situation seems to call for none of our well-thought-out plans. Before I leave New York tomorrow at dawn, I intend to have made you my wife." Juliet blushed deeply at his words, and he tilted back her chin to smile into her eyes. "I shall make you this promise, my love. When I take you to Beau Rêve, my home in Virginia, we shall be married a second time in a fine church, with all the pomp and trimmings you could ever want. But for now I should be content to simply be made one before God."

He kissed the palm of her hand and waited for her answer. She sighed away her misgivings and nodded her agreement. Alec took his leave in haste to find the preacher.

Reverend Jonas Jones was a slight, excitable man of about forty. He preached an excellent sermon in a voice strong and well-suited to dramatization. Yet, as those who obligingly attended his services soon discovered, he delivered but one sermon, written over and over with only minor rephrasing, so that attentive members of his flock could have, after a month's passing, delivered it as well as he.

As Alec strode deliberately toward the preacher's tent, he recalled a portion of the man's sermon, reminding the soldiers of the "sanctity of the union of the flesh between man and woman. . . ." He had thought, after hearing it for the third time, that perhaps the Reverend Jones preached the same sermon again and again because he saw the same thing day after day. An army always attracted a fair number of prostitutes, and this one was no exception. Business for them, no doubt, was good. Alec knew he would have no trouble rousing the man to perform a nuptial service, but the reverend might well voice some objection to blessing the union of a man to what appeared to be a young boy. He decided that it would be best to say nothing until Jones met the bride, then he and Juliet would work together to convince the man of the truth.

Though roused suddenly from a sound sleep, the preacher eagerly agreed to perform the ceremony as soon as he had readied himself. Reverend Jones promised to meet Alec at his tent in less than a quarter hour, then sent the prospective bridegroom in search of a pair of sober witnesses, preferably ones who could pen their names. Though the hour was early, there was a gradually increasing stir of activity, and Alec had little trouble securing two likely prospects. They were a pair of familiar faces, though he had never been properly introduced to either before he interrupted their halfhearted wrestling match and requested the favor. He had thought to seek out Robert as a witness at first, then changed his mind. He had no way of seeing Juliet safely to his home in Virginia and no way of offering her proper protection until his duties with the army were completed. He had very little to offer a bride, he knew, and though he was normally a patient man, he could not bring himself to wait for a more opportune time and place before marrying the woman he loved.

His haste grew out of several motives. He wanted her, but more important, he wanted to free her from her self-imposed obligations to her father. If Juliet had made up her mind to love him, to forsake all others, Alec had no doubt that she would do so. And when this war was finished, whatever the outcome, she would stand beside him and make the best of their life together. In the interim, he would be leaving her to the "care" of her father; at least he could be certain that whichever way the cards fell, Juliet would be safe—as long as Lawrence Hampton knew nothing of their marriage. He would have to caution Juliet against telling anyone, including Frances. Especially Frances, he amended thoughtfully, for while she had all the best intentions, she usually managed to say the wrong thing at the worst time.

The two wrestlers, members of Knowlton's Rangers of Connecticut, were happy to do a fellow soldier a favor. When asked if they were able to sign their names, the younger of the two, a tall, skinny seventeen-year-old with bright carrot-colored hair and an overabundance of freckles, was quick to assure Alec that they could.

"This here be a teacher!" he smiled proudly as he slapped the other heartily on the back. "Taught me and me brother t' read an' write proper, so we taught him t' wrestle," he explained. "He still haven't got the hang o' it though."

The second, a captain also, though his years numbered only twenty-four, flashed a perturbed set of blue eyes on the younger man. "If the truth be known, sir, there is very little—including wrestling—that the Durkin brothers knew before I was kind enough to teach them. They prefer to consider themselves expert fighters, when actually they are very slow to learn that, like all teachers, I allow a pupil a victory now and then. Keeps them interested, you understand."

Jacob Durkin shook a threatening fist before the handsome captain's face, but Alec was quick to put a stop to the good-natured banter. "I would very much appreciate your help in this matter, gentlemen, as the young lady in question awaits us in my tent at this very moment," he said earnestly.

They were almost to the site when Alec offered what he hoped was a plausible explanation for Juliet's attire, and one not too distantly related to the truth. "I must explain that the lady's father is very much opposed to the union, and the marriage will necessarily be kept a secret, at least until the war is finished."

The two nodded their understanding.

"Therefore," Alec went on, "her attire is not exactly . . . that is, she came here in . . ."

Private Durkin smiled away Alec's explanation, and a gangling arm landed a solid blow on his back, forcing the breath from him. "We be real good at keepin' secrets," he assured

Alec confidently, "and the captain here has got himself a reputation for volunteerin' for almost anything!" There was no time for further discussion as they reached Alec's tent, where the Reverend Jones now stood beaming, a thick well-worn book tucked under one arm. Alec lifted the flap of the tent and the four men were soon cramped inside, while the preacher's eyes flicked over a lad sitting on the cot and rose expectantly to Alec. "Well!" he remarked pleasantly. "Everyone seems to be here . . . except . . . the bride."

Juliet hopped off the cot, placed her small hand in his larger one and warmed him with her smile. The minister's eyes widened, and he gasped at the situation before him.

"Sir, I must protest! This cannot be your bride! Why, he is . . . that is . . ." he sputtered, unable to say exactly what the person was.

The young redhead grinned from ear to ear and jabbed an elbow at the other witness's rib, as if clueing him in on some private joke. The preacher, however, was not smiling. It was just like these soldiers, he was thinking, to devise a practical joke such as this! Marriage to a lad—indeed!

"Sir," came a soft, almost shy voice from the lad, whose golden eyes pleaded innocently before dark lashes fluttered coyly over them. "Perhaps my intended did not explain my circumstance to you, in which case I can certainly understand your distress. I was forced to don this wretched set of breeches," she went on in a tortured voice, "for safety's sake. I can assure you that it is not my chosen attire, and I beg your kind indulgence in overlooking it, in the interest of seeing Captain Farrell and myself properly wed."

Her voice was cultured, refined, and utterly feminine, and the preacher could hardly help but be impressed. Captain Farrell's regard for the lad—er, girl—whatever—was certainly obvious, and under normal circumstances, the minister would have proceeded in haste. But he had borne the brunt of more than one practical joke and was not quite convinced. . . . He eyed the soft-skinned face, the small nose, the gentle curve of the chin. Perhaps he had been hasty, after all. He knew that Captain Farrell was from a fine old Virginia family, and that he had influential connections. Not the usual prankster type, to be sure! The two young witnesses, now they were the ones he could not trust. He sighed, in a quandary, for if these two had concocted the scheme, it would spread through the ranks before nightfall that Reverend Jones had sanctioned the marriage of a certain captain to a lad! His ministry would be finished!

"Could you at least remove your hat?" the uncertain minister requested in a pained voice.

Juliet quickly doffed the tricorn, and Alec did her one better, pulling at the strip of leather that bound her hair until it fell about her shoulders. Reverend Jones sighed his relief. It was a woman Farrell wished to be wed with, there was no mistaking that now. He opened his thick book and happily progressed with the service, though he could scarcely disguise his grimace of distaste whenever his eyes fell on the girl's dirty clothing.

The ceremony ended and was sealed with a proper show of affection; the papers were signed and witnessed; and the two young witnesses sought payment for their services, which, they said, entailed kissing the bride. Durkin sheepishly pressed a kiss to Juliet's cheek, all the while blushing so profusely that his freckles actually disappeared. The captain, however, made a great show of pulling her close and kissing her soundly on the mouth. Luckily, his eyes caught sight of Alec's, and he broke off just in time to save himself from a fit of the new husband's jealousy.

Alec thanked them both for their help, the older man a bit less cordially than the younger, and they departed. The minister presented Alec with the completed documents and gratefully accepted a reward for his services. Wishing the couple happiness and many children, he left the odd pair to themselves.

Once back in his own tent, Alec pulled Juliet into an intimate embrace and kissed her deeply, lingeringly, as if trying to remove every trace of another's touch from her lips and mind. She sighed her contentment against him and toyed with the too-large gold band that had recently found its way from his smallest finger to the third one on her left hand.

"Well, Mistress Farrell," he began, noting her smile as he tried out her new name. "The time has come for me to exercise one of my rights as a husband, and the time has come for you to perform your most important duty as a wife."

Juliet's smile faded, and her eyes flickered nervously over to the cot. It had not exactly been the wedding day she had dreamed of up to this point, but she had accepted a short, informal service in a tent in place of an ostentatious ceremony in a great church because being Alec's wife was all that really mattered to her. Now she felt a sudden and bitter disappointment as she considered the inadequate surroundings, for she had dreamed of this moment for longer than she would ever admit. But not like this—in a hot, cramped tent with sounds of every kind filtering right through the canvas to any number of persons who might be standing about. And certainly not while her hair still held the dust of her fight with Lieutenant Dregs. And certainly not while she stood dressed as a boy, and poorly dressed at that! Her eyes fell and remained on the dirt floor, unable to admit to Alec that these things were important to her, yet unable to convince herself that they were not.

Alec noted her downcast expression, and had seen her eyes fall on the cot, so he knew well the trouble that furrowed her brow. He tilted her chin back until he met her eyes.

"You will ride back home immediately and get out of these clothes, and you will not mention our marriage to anyone, including Frances," he ordered gently. "I will have someone accompany you, and hopefully, as the hour is early, you will not have been missed as yet."

"And you?" she asked, surprised at his command.

"I intend to get some much needed rest. I am to leave tomorrow at dawn, and I will need to catch up on all the sleepless nights I have spent lately—thanks to you," he added with a wry grin. "Remember, Julie, that your most important duty as a wife is obedience, and I will expect it from you always."

She smiled at him, relieved that he did not expect anything more from her now, happy at his kind consideration of her feelings. Then the frown returned just as quickly, as she wondered why Alec did not seem anxious to consummate their vows. She did not in truth know what consummation involved, but she knew from Lady Margaret's lectures that there was a bit more to it than kissing. Perhaps Alec had no taste for it, she worried, for according to Margaret, while most men found making love extremely pleasurable, there were a few who would just as soon do without. Could Alec possibly be one of those? Or perhaps he was, like her, confused about what exactly went on between married persons. She stole a doubtful glance at him and found his black eyes regarding her closely.

"Alec," she began, then swallowed nervously and cleared her throat. "Do you intend . . . I mean, there is more to marriage than . . . that is . . ." How on earth could she say this? She could feel her cheeks growing hot and red as she spilled out her worries in a rush, keeping her eyes carefully averted. "I have been told that the most important duty of a husband involves something more than . . . instructing his wife in obedience."

Alec forced himself to hide his smile and feigned astonishment at her remark. "Something more, you say? Whatever do you mean, Juliet?" He paused, finding her acute embarrassment highly amusing. "Would you care to explain my husbandly duties to me, my love? The information would be at least as useful as your instructions for climbing a certain tree."

Juliet's eyes widened when the impact of his statement hit home, and he laughed when he saw the anger sparking in those fiery golden eyes. "Mistress Farrell," he scolded, "I am in sore need of a shave and a bath, not to mention a few hours of sleep. If I may be so bold as to say so, you also strike me as one in need of a cake of soap and a tub of hot water—and, perhaps, a change of clothing?" he teased. He smiled as he took her face between his hands. "This much I promise you, Julie. I shall not leave Manhattan tomorrow before I have performed the husbandly duty to which you refer. So ready yourself, my love, for this night will belong to us alone."

Alec released her and called to a young private he knew well, requesting that he see the lad, whose hair had once again been bound and partially hidden by an oversized tricorn, safely home to Hampton House.

Chapter 20

Juliet stood before the glass, brushing the dust from her hair, having shed her boyish apparel for a simple blue chintz dress. She had slipped safely into the house without being noticed, and she hummed a song while she reflected on her extreme good fortune. A moment later, Frances burst into her room and barraged her with questions until she was quite out of breath.

"Where were you? My goodness! Rachel asked about you, and I had to tell her you were still sleeping! I was frightened to death that she would come up to see for herself! She always seems to know when I am not telling the truth! Thank goodness that you're safe! But wherever were you? I've been looking everywhere!"

"I went for a ride," Juliet answered simply, "and I forgot the time. I'll hurry and do what needs to be done before Rachel gets back and makes trouble for both of us. Let's finish our chores early, and maybe Jay will fetch a hot tub for us. Wouldn't that be heavenly?"

Frances nodded doubtfully. This was only Wednesday, and Jay usually hauled the heavy loads of water to the tub on Saturday. The comforts of a hot bath meant a good bit of extra work for him, as well as for Rachel. But Juliet was smiling, and she had not smiled so brightly in a long, long time. Frances had no intention of ruining her good mood by disagreeing with her about anything.

The day dragged on. Though she kept herself busy until an

hour before dinner, Juliet found the waiting endless, her patience sorely lacking. When she announced her plans to have a bath, Rachel made a comment about her father not approving of her sleeping late and about causing extra work when there was already enough to be worrying about. But Juliet had not asked her for an opinion, she told her, and as usual, paid it no heed.

The warm water was a soothing balm for her tired, tense muscles, and the delicate perfume of an expensive cake of soap relaxed her to the point of drowsiness. Excitement and nervousness ebbed away as she vaguely recalled that she had not slept a wink the night before, nor rested a bit throughout the day. As Rachel combed the tangles from her long, damp hair, Juliet could scarcely hold her head up, and she informed her maid with a yawn that she was simply too tired to even think about dinner with Robert and Frances. Rachel had helped her into a simple cotton night rail when Juliet dismissed her, saying that she would be going directly to bed.

The moment Rachel left the room, Juliet threw off the simple gown and replaced it with a special one, which Lady Margaret had given her before she left England, saying with a sly wink that it was "not necessarily for Harold." It was also of cotton, but it was softer, thinner, with narrow straps of white woven in and out with a light blue satin ribbon. The same ribbon was tied below her breasts, gathering the folds of the garment close against her waist and hips. A good measure of her bosom was visible above, and what was covered left little to the imagination, but Juliet did not feel any surge of excitement when she put on her daring sleeping attire. She felt nothing but tired, and as she lay down on her bed, she fell instantly asleep.

The moon was high when Alec reached Hampton House, tethering Cheval a good distance away. The groom had been helpful in the past, but his courtesies were done for Robert, and Alec was not one to ask favors for himself when he could not return them. He climbed the tree easily, without a thought to his injured arm, which seemed to have mended considerably now that he had gotten his much needed rest. He made his way gingerly down the darkened hallway toward Juliet's room, listening intently for sounds of anyone stirring. There were none. He stepped into the room, where the moonlight sent great shafts of silver spilling through the latticed windows. He saw her then, curled up asleep like a child in the center of the bed, the rich gold and brown of her hair scattered all about her. As she stirred and nestled a cheek closer to the comforter on which she slept, a strap slipped from her creamy shoulder, and her breasts rose pale and soft above her gown. His admiring eyes fell on her flesh, and the desire to have her rose strong in him, warming his blood. Yet he was reluctant to wake her, sleeping so peacefully there in the moonlight.

Perhaps he would not be proving his manhood this night, after all, he thought with a fond smile. But spend this night with his wife he would, if he had to make do with holding her close as she slept. He doffed his jacket and shirt, then boots and breeches, discarding them on a nearby chair. He lifted her slowly and cautiously, settling her head against his chest, then, still holding her, he eased himself into the bed and pulled the comforter over them both. Her breath fell soft and even against him, and he could not resist a brief caress of her bared shoulder. At length she stirred against him, and her heavy lids fluttered open, then closed again as she nestled contentedly closer, then open again as she realized that she was no longer dreaming. She met his eyes with a sleepy smile.

"I dreamed that you held me as I slept," she sighed, "and my dream appears to have come true."

"I, too, had a dream that you welcomed me warmly into your bed, and my dream also seems to have come true."

"Oh, Alec, I do love you so!" she whispered against his throat. "There could never be anyone else, Alec. Never could I love another man as I love you!"

He lifted her chin, and his eyes looked deeply into hers for a long moment, seeing them wide and warm and expectant. His lips began to play a teasing game about her mouth, sweeping over it, sampling it lazily, heightening her desire to be kissed more thoroughly. His lips parted to satisfy his own growing hunger, his tongue gently prodded, inspiring Juliet to a like response. The last traces of drowsiness vanished in a crazy, whirling gush of emotion, and her lips parted anxiously. Her

223

arms encircled his neck and forced his mouth to answer her newly awakened demands.

While his tongue stirred a tantalizing giddiness in her head, his fingers drifted over her throat, then cleverly moved on to slip the narrow straps of her gown from her shoulders. He drew a shaky breath as his fingers grazed the satiny mounds of flesh, heaving, trembling beneath his touch. His mouth leisurely followed, tracing the line of her throat, the upper curve of her breast, the depression between. Then hungrily he lingered at the soft pink tips until the sheer pleasure of it was almost more than she could endure.

He tugged at the ribbon at her waist and rid her of the garment, sighing as he savored the feel of smooth skin against his own. His hands roamed deliberately over every curve of downy flesh, magically stirring up a wild and turbulent deluge of passion. Filled with an urgent longing, Juliet's golden eyes grew dark and liquid, her full breasts rose and fell in swift excitement, her heart pounded furiously in her ears. His touch was a heavenly sort of torture that only served to sharpen Juliet's yearning and left her aching for something more.

A muffled cry of pleasure escaped her lips as his hand came to rest on her upper thigh, drifting boldly upward to the private center of her passion. His touch was sweet and tender, smoothing, fondling, exploring until she was hot and moist and pulsing. She pressed hard against him, and a shower of burning sparks scattered to the very tips of her fingers and toes. Her response swept Alec closer to an already raging fire, stretching his careful restraint to its breaking point. His senses were bursting with the yearning to have her, his mind soaring crazily with the knowledge that his waiting was near an end. He lifted himself above her, and something else was between her thighs, something smooth and warm and hard. His hand beneath her urged her eager response, until the unyielding probe of his manhood plunged deep inside her flesh.

The pain exploded with astonishing suddenness. Her body went rigid, her eyes flew open, her face tightened with the burning anguish that destroyed her awesome rapture. A confused pair of amber eyes met darker, apologetic ones, and she shrank away from him, recalling at once that many women did not enjoy their duties in bed. Painful tears of disappointment refused to be held back, though she buried her face in Alec's throat in a futile attempt to hide them from him.

Alec held her and waited, desiring mutual fulfillment far more than a quick easing of his lust. As the time passed, Juliet quieted and relaxed once more beneath him, and he kissed away her tears while his fingers entwined gently in her hair. She smiled up at him, at the understanding in his dark eyes, at the gentle way his lips smoothed over her face. She sighed as she gave herself up to his kiss and was amazed when her passions leaped skyward once more. She became suddenly aware of a new, wild throbbing inside her, growing more and more powerful with every beat of her heart. As she drew him close, Alec's lips met hers with an unrestrained hunger, demanding, insistent, unrelenting. He began to move inside her, slowly, then with ever growing haste, until she, too, was caught up in a frenzied search for something just beyond her grasp, an elusive spark of sunlight in a world of total darkness. Again and again she arched to meet his driving thrusts, instinctively struggling toward that unknown, unreachable height of pleasure. It was a mindless, animal sort of craving, a crazy, uncontrollable need that welcomed his hard, savage propulsions and responded recklessly, erratically, desperately. All at once the spark of passion burst forth like a glorious sunrise in the darkest winter night, in them and between them, flinging them into momentary paradise.

In her wildest dreams she had never imagined it so, this incomparable feeling of utter fulfillment, this ultimate triumph of her physical being. Everything she felt for Alec seemed to be captured in that single exquisite moment of perfect union. The breathless euphoria faded swiftly, giving way to a warm closeness and intimacy that was even more precious because it was lasting. She clung to him possessively, never wanting to let go of this moment. "Is it always like this?" she whispered sleepily as she settled her cheek against his chest.

He laughed softly, a low, purring laugh that sent a pleasant tingle through her. "It will be for us," he pledged softly.

Her lips formed a smile as her eyelids grew heavy. "I could

want for nothing more, Alec," she murmured, "for I am completely happy. . . ." Her voice trailed off in a yawn, and a moment later she was asleep in his arms.

Alec smiled and pressed a kiss to her forehead. He had never thought to treasure a woman in such a way as he did at this moment. In the past such contentment had eluded him; his pleasures had been but a quieting of a need. But the beauty of becoming a part of his wife, of joining her in flesh as well as mind and heart, had changed Alec in a way he had not thought possible. He was no longer alone, no longer empty, no longer in search of a reason for his existence.

Juliet woke a few hours later, when the moon had dwindled to a pale, soft shadow in the sky. She raised her eyes to Alec, who watched her as she slept, still wondering at the natural serenity he found in having her near. She blushed under his warm regard and ran a hand over his chest.

"Aren't you going to sleep at all?"

"I did sleep a bit," he replied, "but I find that holding you close does not exactly encourage slumber."

"Mmm." She smiled, rolling on top of him and propping an elbow against his chest to support her head. "Do you realize, Alec, that I know very little about you? We ought to remedy that now that we are married, don't you agree?" She ignored his frown and continued, "Tell me about your home."

His hand crept slowly up her arm and over her shoulder, brushing away a long strand of hair as he answered distantly, "It's in Virginia."

He leaned forward to press his mouth to her throat, then tasted the smooth skin of her shoulder. Juliet's breath quickened, and she became conscious of Alec's rising desire, but she was not satisfied with his vague reply.

"But where exactly in Virginia? What is it like?"

Her voice sounded odd and shaky, and it trembled when his finger traced the swell of her breast. Their eyes met and held fast, and Juliet melted against him, her thoughts suddenly running in the same direction as his.

"Ask Frances," he whispered as he pulled her beneath him, effectively putting an end to every thought but one.

When Juliet woke again, she found that Alec was already dressed for his departure and sat beside her on the bed. She sat up also, clutching the comforter to her breast and trying to smile a warm good-bye, though she found herself very close to tears. She had known all along that he had to leave at dawn, and yet it was so much more difficult than she had expected it to be. She bit her lip to keep back the words she knew she must not say. He could not stay; she must not ask it. It would only make it harder for him to leave.

"We have things to discuss, Julie, and so little time. . . ." Alec sighed at the black sky, already beginning to gray in the east. Juliet nodded bravely but did not dare speak for fear her voice would betray the tears welling up inside. "First, I want you to promise that our marriage will remain a secret—from everyone, including Frances." Her eyes questioned this order until he went on to explain. "I cannot offer you protection or even the most meager of comforts until my service with the army is finished. My enlistment ends in December. If I knew for certain what will happen here . . . But I do not. As long as your father knows nothing of our marriage, I know that you will have a home and the necessities of life. How I wish that I could send you home to my mother!"

Juliet looked away in sudden panic. She had no desire to be sent to a woman she had never even met, for all Frances's comments about wonderful Aunt Colette. A mother to Juliet was someone who disapproved heartily of everything she was and did, and she could imagine being introduced as Alec's bride, while another woman—whom Alec's mother no doubt favored—had waited faithfully for him all these years. It was certainly not a scene she looked forward to.

"I could not leave Frances," she mumbled nervously.

"The overland trip is long and dangerous, and I would not ask it of you, my love. And the waters are not safe enough for me to entrust you to them, either. So it seems that I will owe your father a favor, should the island be taken by the British."

"Do you think it will?"

"My thinking has not changed on the matter, in spite of the twenty thousand soldiers here now. Many of them are not so much dedicated to the cause of freedom as they are interested in instant glory. When it comes time for the actual fighting, I fear that the greatest talkers will make the poorest soldiers."

He put a hand to the back of her neck and pulled her close for a farewell kiss.

"I do not expect to learn of any masquerades played while I am away. Stay close to the house, and if there is any fighting, get Jay and Frances and lock yourself in the cellar and wait." He kissed her again, lingeringly, reluctantly noting the first tinge of gold that shaded the sky. "I love you, Julie. Remember that while I am away. And I will come back for you. If I have to battle Fate every step of the way, I will come back."

"Wait, Alec!" she said suddenly. "I have something for you."

She fished about under the comforter for her nightgown and slipped it quickly over her head, unaccustomed to his eyes upon her bared skin. She ran to her bureau and removed the small brass box, returning at once to the bed and extending it to Alec. He took it from her with a puzzled frown, pried open the top, and withdrew the golden chain.

"The Fates?"

She nodded. "The most important gift I ever received from anyone. I was away at school and so unhappy, and certain that there was nothing left to live for, when Robert sent me this, along with a letter that said, 'You can strive to realize any dream, if only you have will enough to do so. . . .'"

She took the chain from him and worked the clasp at the back of his neck. It had always been too long for her, but it fit Alec perfectly. She smiled. Somehow knowing that he would wear it made the parting easier. He would be back, and there would be time for their life together.

Chapter 21

As the pleasant days of spring turned into the longer days of summer, the American troops on Manhattan played a tedious game of waiting for Howe to make his move. The month of June had passed by almost without incident, two notable exceptions being the discovery of a plot to assassinate General Washington and the favorable news for the patriots from Charleston, South Carolina. After overhearing a certain conversation in a tavern one evening, a patriotic steward had lost no time in spilling the Tory plan to poison General Washington and several other generals as well. When the plot was revealed, many Tories were arrested, and Thomas Hickey, one of Washington's own bodyguards, was hanged. From South Carolina came the news that a fort constructed of palmetto logs and dirt—which General Lee had termed useless—had held off an attack by Admiral Peter Parker for ten hours, at which time the British had withdrawn.

On the ninth of July, the Declaration of Independence, approved by the Congress in Philadelphia five days earlier, was read to the soldiers camped on Manhattan. In the hours of celebration that followed, alcohol flowed freely, and a certain group of tents just north of the city, housing prostitutes and gamblers, experienced a surge of business. To cap off the festivities, one particularly rowdy group made their way to Bowling Green, to the gilded statue of King George III dedicated only a few years prior, after the repeal of the hated Stamp Act. The statue was literally hacked apart, the soft lead carried off and melted down into bullets for the army, and the head stuck on a pike for display.

In years to come, Juliet would remember little of the great moments in history that occurred that summer. She would remember only the long days of waiting for Alec, the nights spent dreaming of his return, and those secret, stolen moments of rapture shared with him as his wife. But their brief moments together became a fool's paradise when General Howe sailed into the lower bay with over one hundred ships on the second to last day of June. In July Admiral Howe and his troops joined his brother on Staten Island, increasing their ranks until their powerful force included nearly five hundred ships and thirty-two thousand soldiers. There were rumors that nine thousand German mercenary soldiers (nicknamed Hessians by the Americans, who feared and hated them) roamed the island freely, drank excessively, and ravished any women who struck their fancy. Juliet shuddered at the thought.

Then, in early August, Alec returned, and Robert with him. Alec had given up his simple leather and buckskin for a splendid new uniform copied from General Washington's. With war officially declared, the Congress had announced that buff and blue were the colors of the Continental Army, though securing a uniform was left up to the individual, and the militia from the various states still wore nearly every color in the rainbow.

When he came to her room late that night, Alec found Juliet pacing restlessly, and it was several moments before he could coax her to tell him what was on her mind.

"It's your uniform," she told him finally. "It makes everything seem so different, Alec."

"Only in your mind," he smiled. "The only real difference is that now I would not be shot as a spy if I were captured."

Juliet gasped and shook her head. "Don't say that, Alec!"

"Julie," he said gently, taking her into his arms, "this is something we have lived with for a long time now."

"But when I looked at you, Alec, I could forget everything else except the love I feel for you. And now, when I see you in that uniform, you are a soldier, not just a messenger for the army. It's as though the war has finally come between us. How can I forget when it's a part of you?"

Alec held her close and stroked her hair, not really understanding why she found a simple change in clothing so threatening.

"I'm so afraid, Alec!" she cried suddenly.

"So am I, Julie." He sighed and nodded while Juliet searched his face. "Yes, I am afraid. Only a fool could see that forest of English masts out there in the bay and not be afraid. It will not be so easy a victory for us here as it was in Boston. England aims to keep her colonies, and she's ready to wage quite a fight to do it."

"And must you be a part of it? Is it so important to you?"

His black eyes contemplated her steadily before he gave an answer, measuring his words with care. "A few years ago, the cause was merely something for me to believe in, an honorable fight for the sake of the future, when my past seemed aimless and futile. Now I have you, Julie, and you are what I live for, what makes my life worthwhile. I find that the fight is more important to me now than it was when I began. Important to us, Julie. I want children with you, and I won't have them denied the rights that our fathers came here to establish. I shall not see my home subject to a whim of Parliament. As a man of honor I cannot accept these things. A dream is never purchased without cost, and I have seldom witnessed a more deserving investment than this one."

"Is it more important to you, then, than I?" she challenged, hating the selfishness inside her that forced her to pose the question.

"If it were a question of choosing, then I would do so. But it is a question of who and what I am, not what is the most important thing." He sighed, knowing that he had no adequate words of explanation, until he remembered something. "Are you familiar with a poet by the name of Richard Lovelace?"

She shook her head.

"Lovelace lived over a hundred years ago; he was a Cavalier who also left behind the woman he loved." He chuckled. "All Virginia gentlemen fancy themselves Cavaliers, don't you know? Descendants of the faithful followers of the king who emigrated during the years of the Commonwealth. Now that the throne has been restored, the descendants of that same loyal faction are fighting to be free of George's tyranny! An irony, you must admit. And ironic as well that a Cavalier's words should be so fitting to voice my own feelings at leaving your arms.

> "Tell me not, sweet, I am unkind
> That from the nunnery
> Of thy chaste breast and quiet mind
> To war and arms I fly.
> True, a new mistress now I chase:
> The first foe in the field;
> And with a stronger faith embrace
> A sword, a horse, a shield.
> Yet this inconstancy is such
> As you too shall adore;
> I could not love thee, dear, so much
> Loved I not honor more."

Juliet attempted a smile, but her voice broke painfully, and she could no longer hold back her tears. "I am jealous of Honour, Alec."

She felt his arms about her, and as she held him fast, the familiar warm solace once again assuaged her fears. She felt stronger because of his strength, surer because of his honesty, made whole because of his need. Her tears were mingled magically with a sea of wondrous passion, and totally trusting in his strength, she fell deeply asleep in his arms.

In the earliest hours of the morning, Alec turned to find her wide awake, her eyes riveted to a point on the ceiling, her mind a million miles away. He brought her about with a playful tap on her nose.

"Do I awaken to find my bride thinking of another man so soon?"

"In truth, Alec, it *was* another man I was considering." She sighed and looked away. "I cannot help but feel guilty about deceiving my father."

"I can understand that easily enough. My own father and I disagreed on a great many matters, and when I finally left home I began to realize that he was not at fault for all of them." He hesitated, unable to discuss her father to any extent, for he considered Lawrence Hampton one of the lowest characters he had ever met.

"He was so proud of my plans to marry Harold, Alec! He's in prison now because of me."

"He's in prison because of his own convictions, Julie, not yours."

She nodded slowly. "Yes, but also for my sake. For my future. How will I tell him about you, Alec? How can I ever explain how much I love you?"

"You will tell him nothing," he ordered sternly, but his voice softened and became comforting when he continued. "In all truth, Julie, deception does not come naturally to me, and I know you feel the same. Still, I could not take the chance that he would turn you out and leave you without protection while I am still unable to care for you. When this year is finished and I return to you, I intend to face your father with the truth. And if he can accept the fact of our marriage, then perhaps our relationship can be turned into an amicable one. It will be his decision."

With a quick smile, she found herself in his arms.

"Tell me about your father, Alec. What did you quarrel about?"

She felt him tense at the question.

"The past is best forgotten, Julie." He paused but a moment before changing the subject. "I ought to have delayed our marriage until I could properly assume my responsibilities as your husband. Yet I am hard pressed to admit my error, for the time we have spent together has meant more to me than any other in my life."

Juliet nestled closer to him. He had a way about him, a way that made her feel almost invincible, as if their love could conquer any obstacle thrown in its path. He pressed his lips to her temple, where he could feel the gentle throbbing of her heart. He let his fingers glide over her silky skin, lingering at her breasts before moving on to her waist and resting casually on her thigh.

"Julie," he whispered as he planted brief, countless kisses on her mouth and neck. "Have I managed to scatter all thoughts of your father?"

Her eyes grew soft and warm like honey, and her words were oddly broken by her quick, deepened breathing. "My thoughts are definitely not those of a daughter, but those of a wife."

She drew his mouth to hers for a kiss of fiery intensity that left her shaking with desire. Feeling every inch a woman, she moved against him, answering his need as she fulfilled her own, until one final magnificent thrust brought an explosion of stinging tension, then fused into a rich, mellow warmth that spread to every fiber of her being. In utter contentment she held him close, drifting at once into a velvety slumber.

Late in August, the British landed fifteen thousand soldiers and five thousand Hessian reinforcements on the Brooklyn shore. For two days Washington ferried across to Long Island from Manhattan to observe the British troops and to make a decision on how to prevent them from taking the island. Splitting his army to leave about five thousand men on Manhattan, Washington moved the rest to Long Island, manning the redoubts that had been built on high ground during the past months. In addition, he sent riflemen out to cover the main roads, hoping to pick off the enemy in their rigid marching formation while taking cover in the heavy woods. But Howe had been at Bunker Hill, too, and would never again launch a frontal attack against a fortified American stronghold on high ground. Instead, part of his army found its way through a poorly guarded pass and attacked the Continental riflemen from the rear.

Though a rifle was initially a more accurate weapon than a musket, it took even longer to reload, and its length made it virtually impossible to attach a bayonet. So it was that the soldiers who had prided themselves so greatly on their marksmanship found themselves defenseless against an onslaught of Hessian bayonets after firing a single shot. Many fled, many more attempted to do so but were savagely run through as a bloody slaughter ensued. Helplessly Washington watched from the entrenchments on the heights, waiting for Howe to attack. He did not.

Howe's hesitation gave Washington time to make another decision. Trapped between the British army and the East River, he knew that his position was hopeless unless the British launched a frontal attack. But they were already unloading artillery to shell from a distance, and only the wind kept the warships from coming into position and sealing the fate of the Continental Army. Hours passed; rain began to fall; daylight waned. The weather had forced an undeclared truce. The next morning, after dispatching word to the Congress, Washington began to organize his retreat. When dusk fell, a shroud of fog dropped about them, making possible an amazingly organized and successful retreat that so shocked the British it earned the general the nickname the "Old Fox." Colonel John Glover and his band of New England fishermen worked their way back and forth across the river tirelessly through the night, until nothing but a few useless pieces of artillery remained behind. But the Battle of Long Island had been costly to the patriots, with over a thousand killed, wounded, or captured—more than three times the British losses.

Robert had been among those left behind to defend Manhattan, but he was quickly informed of the events on Long Island. When he finally came to the house for dinner one evening in early September, it was evident that the outcome of the battle had affected his mood. He was quiet and sullen, and he could not bring himself to relate the gruesome stories he had heard, nor could he get them out of his mind. The defeat had taken its toll on the entire army, with a sudden rash of desertions numbering in the thousands. The cocky, blustering volunteers who had thirsted for British blood suddenly found that they no longer faced an army of easy targets. Only those truly dedicated remained, watching the army literally dwindle before their eyes. Though Juliet and Frances knew the cause of Robert's despair, they could do nothing but wait and hope, which was exactly what Washington was forced to do.

The second week of September there was a real hope that the war might be over. The Continental Congress sent three men, John Adams, Edward Rutledge, and Benjamin Franklin, to meet with General Howe in a stone mansion on Staten Island. But when the elegant dinner was finished, the sad truth remained. The situation with England had passed the point of peaceful reconciliation; there would be no turning back.

That same week Alec managed to get to New York. When he came with Robert to Hampton House, the dinner they shared was solemn, and attempts at levity fell far short of their mark. He bid Juliet a formal farewell and took his leave with Robert, but his eyes had found hers longing, pleading for him to come to her.

Later, in her room, Juliet waited for him, perched on the windowsill to enjoy the refreshing coolness of the night air, but she found it difficult to keep a leash on the feelings churning inside her. There was no question that there would be a battle here; it was only a matter of time—time that was running out. And Alec in that uniform . . . It made him so much more a part of this war, it made him a soldier. Tears stung her eyes until they overflowed and ran down her cheeks, though she told herself repeatedly that Alec and Robert were safe.

Unknown to her, Alec had slipped silently into the room and watched her cry those useless tears, staring out over this island that would all too soon be a battleground. How could he comfort her? he wondered. It was not his way to make empty promises that would be impossible to keep. When he went to her it was with no words of comfort, only a warm embrace, a gentle kiss, a shared understanding of the cruel inevitability of war. From a fear that there would be no tomorrow sprang a fierce, naked need to draw one to another. Each kiss, each touch seemed to reflect the frustration, the helplessness, even the anger, until they lay spent and breathless.

When it was time for Alec to leave, Juliet found her resolve to be brave sorely lacking, because she knew that this time he would not be coming back to her in a matter of days, or even weeks. She raised her eyes to take a long, hard look at the face she loved so well—the perfectly shaped mouth, the straight nose, the black eyes that saw into her soul. She flung her arms about his neck, unable to let him go. He held her tightly for a time, feeling the sobs that shook her, then gently loosened her arms and lifted her chin.

"I will come back to you, Julie. I promised you that before, and I promise you that now. If you remember that I love you more than anything else, that knowledge will make you strong."

He kissed her deeply, longingly.

"I am not strong, Alec! I'm not!" she choked out.

"Yes, you are!" he said firmly. "You must be! You are a Farrell now, and a Farrell laughs at disaster, scoffs at impossibilities. It's why I married you, Julie. Because I know that you can do whatever you really want to do, even if you have to fight Fate every step of the way. We are a pair of gamblers, you and I, wagering everything on a most unlikely prize, on freedom."

He pressed his lips to hers a single last time.

"Wait for me, Julie. Remember that I love you, and that I always will."

Chapter 22

It was a hot September Sunday, over two weeks after the Battle of Long Island, when Howe chose to attack Manhattan. It began just before noon, when his warships moved up the East River and poured a steady stream of fire on the Americans defending the central coastline. When the firing ceased and the smoke cleared, the militia caught sight of the landing British troops, a solid mass of bright red coats and glimmering bayonets. What a fearful sight it was to the militia, untrained in battle! They immediately gave up ground and ran, while Washington made a futile attempt to rally their courage, galloping among the fleeing soldiers and striking anyone within his reach with the broadside of his sword. Though he screamed commands at them, they scarcely fired a shot. Many fled hysterically, leaving weapons and provisions behind while the British advanced.

Howe pushed on until he had taken all the ground he had planned for that day, stopping at the house of Robert Murray for refreshments in the exhausting heat. The American army fell back, finally stopping at the Hollow Way. The Continentals in the city to the south were almost completely cut off, and only by racing along a little-known path on the western edge of the island did they manage to join the bulk of the army. The men had been saved, but the equipment they were forced to leave behind was indeed a heavy loss. In a single day the City of New York had been lost. The British made ready for an extended stay.

On Tuesday, September seventeenth, Lawrence Hampton

was released from prison and accompanied to his home by nine British officers and several of their aides. Hampton House now lay within British territory and would provide comfortable lodging for the men. The aides would perform servants' duties for a time, until the city was returned to normal and Hampton could restaff his home.

It was a homecoming of mixed emotions for Juliet, for she had not missed her father as much as she had anticipated, and his presence meant she would once again be playing a role to please him. The brief, cool embrace they shared left her empty and thinking of another's arms that had warmed her considerably more.

Rachel, in charge of half a dozen young soldiers and who would serve the entire entourage suitable meals, proved herself equal to the task. The rest of the aides were set in motion stripping the linen from the furniture in the guest rooms until the entire west wing was bustling as it never had before. Dinner that first evening was a stiff and formal affair that contrasted sharply to those casual and intimate meals Juliet and Frances had shared with Alec and Robert. Dressed in a beautiful gown of yellow silk, Juliet was introduced to the officers by her father, who announced in the same breath that her intended was a titled gentleman from England. All the same, there was a good deal of interest shown her as well as Frances. Hampton saw that while Juliet was polite and cordial to the men, her manner was subtly discouraging toward any who wished individual attention. He would not have to worry overmuch about his daughter with the soldiers, he thought with pride. She seemed able to handle things quite well herself.

It was very late that same evening when Rachel, who had been up since dawn, came to Hampton's study. He was getting ready to retire and had extinguished all the lamps but his desk light; he took his seat once again because Rachel's expression told him that the matter was urgent.

"Sir," she began reluctantly, "what I have to say will be distressing to you, and it's been a long and difficult day. I know what you've been through, sir, but the truth will out, and time won't be changing it none."

"Go ahead," he instructed.

"I told you that Mr. Farrell been coming about here in your

absence, and at the jail, with no chance o' sayin' anything that would get passed the guard and the rest o' them, I thought it best to keep things to myself. But the truth be known, sir . . ." She faltered, groping for the right words while Hampton waited patiently. She drew a deep breath and began anew.

"A few weeks back, I woke early and thought I heard someone stirrin' about the house. I kept myself quiet, and I saw him—Alexander Farrell—leaving her—your daughter's—room."

Hampton showed no outward sign of emotion, though he rose and poured two glasses of his finest wine, offering one to Rachel. She took it, but placed it on the desk without ever touching it to her lips.

"Are you absolutely certain about this?"

"Quite certain, sir. It was him I saw that mornin', and it not be the first time he been there, either. He went out through a window in the west wing, knew the way like he be livin' here all his life, and let himself down that old oak tree easy as if it be a flight o' stairs, I tell you."

Hampton sipped at his wine for a time, then put it on the desk and folded his hands on his chest. His eyes were cold and distant, as if he were deep in thought. Rachel fingered the glass of wine he had poured for her, somewhat in awe of the gesture from a man so powerful to her, a mere servant. But if her information thus far had brought about such a show of gratitude, then how much more urgent to tell him the rest of the tale.

"That not be all, sir," she broke in hesitantly.

The steel-blue eyes flew to her face, immediately attentive.

"A few days ago, before we heard that awful shellin' and took to the cellar, I was takin' some linens and things upstairs. I thought at the time that Juliet be in the garden, so I let myself into her room without knockin'. There she be, all alone in her room, lookin' strangely at somethin'—until she be seein' me. Then she folds up this paper and stuffs it in a drawer, and I pretend not to have an interest in it. But I be goin' back t' her room the very next day when she be truly in the garden, and I sure enough found what it be she be hidin'."

She produced a small brass box and placed it on the desk before him. Hampton stared at it. Something about it was vaguely familiar, yet if he had ever seen it, it had been a very long time before. He pried off the lid and removed a piece of badly creased parchment, worn so that it was no longer crisp. When he unfolded and examined the document, his face went absolutely livid with rage. Even in the dim light, Rachel saw the change and drew back. It was a long, tense time for her until Hampton slowly regained his composure and carefully refolded the parchment. He saw, as soon as he replaced the paper, that a plain gold band lay also in the box, and he examined it briefly before pushing the lid tightly into place. He ran a finger thoughtfully over the box, over the raised relief decorations on the sides and lid. He was still absorbed in his considerations of it when he began to speak.

"Rachel, I have seen this box before. Where did it come from?"

"I not be knowin', sir. She brought it with her from England." After a moment she added, "It used t' have a gold neckchain in it, with a round pendant. A strange sort o' charm it be, with three old women on it. Never saw her wear it, though, and it looked to be a might large. . . ."

"Three old women," he repeated pensively, then a smile of recognition began to curve his lips. "The Fates."

He paused a moment, remembering the Christmas gift that Robert had sent to his sister so many years before. Hampton had given him the money for that neckchain, and it had cost a fair penny. Moreover, it had been made long enough to fit a man and would not have fit Juliet correctly unless some of the links were removed. Nevertheless, Robert had insisted on buying it and sending it with Captain Barkley immediately, in order that she receive it by Christmas.

"Rachel, where is that charm now?"

"I haven't seen it, sir." She frowned at him, puzzled at his sudden interest in the piece.

"If you do see it, I want you to tell me immediately, do you understand?"

She nodded.

"Good. Now, I want you to return this to its proper place." He handed her the box. "I don't want Juliet to know that it was gone, and I don't want anyone to know anything about this conversation."

"Yes, sir."

Even after Rachel had left him to himself, there was little overt expression of the burning hatred that raged within Lawrence Hampton. He had not expected this sort of deception from Juliet; he had underestimated her, and Alexander Farrell's persuasive powers as well, for a second time. But he was not beaten. He was more intent at this moment than ever before on acquiring the Medford holdings. It would be a bit more difficult now, he knew, as he sipped at his wine. But he would find a way to have his empire . . . and to exact his revenge at the same time.

Chapter 23

On the Friday night after her father's return home, Juliet woke to the sounds of excited shouting outside Hampton House. She ran to her window to see what the commotion was about. Soldiers were galloping at breakneck speed down the long, curved drive and off toward town. Even in the total darkness, Juliet could not miss the angry streak of red that slashed the southeastern sky. She watched for a time before returning to bed, not wanting to wake Rachel or anyone else to help her dress and unable to leave her room in her present state of attire for fear some of the soldiers had remained behind. The next morning she rose early to find that the heavy smell of fire had blown northward, and a gigantic dark pillow of smoke hung low in the sky. Opening her door a crack she called for Rachel, and as she dressed, she listened to what limited information the maid could offer.

"A young soldier rode here last night from town and said that every able-bodied man be needed t' fight the fire. It started at Whitehall Slip, he says, and be spreadin' fierce and quick. Arson, he says. The rebels said they'd be burnin' the town before they'd give it up."

Juliet took one final look from her window before going down to breakfast. The cloud had mushroomed over the city, and she could even see a few tongues of orange flame leaping hungrily toward the sky. The old wooden structures would be just like tinderboxes in a blaze such as this, and even the fine brick houses would not stand a chance in a fire raging completely out of control.

The house was quiet, the dining room deserted. Juliet helped herself to the last bit of warm tea in the pot on the table and noted from the dishes not yet cleared away that her father had already eaten. She wondered for a moment if he had gone to help with the fire. On an impulse she carried her tea to his study, and there she found him, intent on his paperwork. When she gave the door a timid rap, he immediately looked up and bid her enter, shuffling aside the business that had interested him a few moments before.

"Juliet! I trust you slept well. I am happy that you came here now, while the house is fairly quiet. I have been waiting for a chance to speak with you alone."

"The fire seems still to be burning out of control. Do you think it will do a terrible amount of damage?" she asked, taking a seat.

"It will to the people whose houses are burning. I imagine there will be quite a few surprised faces when the townspeople return to their homes, only to find them gone." His offhanded tone came as a mild shock to her, and she could not help but feel sorry for those people. He misread her worried expression.

"Don't be concerned, Juliet. This house is far enough from the city to be safe even if the southern half of the island goes up in smoke. I did not wish to discuss the fire with you, however. What I want to speak with you about is your pending marriage."

Juliet fixed a carefully blank expression on her face and began a speech she had mentally rehearsed several times. "Father, I have not heard from Harold in a very long time, and I am no longer certain—"

"That is why what I have to say will not only relieve the doubts you feel, but will also cheer your heart."

He opened the drawer of his desk and removed a paper, which he handed over to his daughter. She set her cup on his desk and stretched out a hand to retrieve it, flashing her father a puzzled look, which he answered with a smile.

"Well, go on. Read the letter."

While doing her best to still her trembling hands, Juliet broke the seal and read the missive. After a few moments she raised her eyes to her father. "Where did you get this?"

"Early this morning a Lieutenant Colonel Peterson made a

point of seeing it safely into my hands. It seems that Harold went to quite a bit of trouble to get it to you. I would certainly like to know what he has to say."

Juliet obediently handed the letter back to her father. It said very little, actually. Only that Harold planned to make arrangements to sail as soon as word reached England that New York was once again safely in British hands. As her father scanned the note Juliet looked away. She had planned to write Harold quietly, to break the engagement without her father's knowledge. Father would have believed after all this time that Harold had lost interest or found someone else. But this letter changed all that.

"Father," she began slowly, staring down at her hand, "I am not sure that I still love Harold. I mean, it has been so long since I have seen him, and so much has happened since then. . . ."

"Absence seems to have made Harold's heart grow even fonder."

"But what about my heart?" she returned. "I cannot even remember what I feel for him anymore! And I am not sure if"—she swallowed with difficulty—"if I want to be Harold's wife."

Her father's eyes narrowed on her, and he drew a deep breath, letting it out very slowly. Then he folded his hands and rested them comfortably on his chest. "You are so very young, Juliet, and I forget that sometimes. So young and impressionable. Perhaps I expect too much of you. . . ."

Juliet felt anger at his patronizing tone, and though she kept her eyes lowered, he was at once aware of the slightest flaring of her nostrils, the barest tightening of her mouth. He promptly retreated and proceeded with care along a different course. He needed to arouse her trust, not her anger.

"I am sure that this long separation has been difficult for you, as well as for Harold, and I ask you not to make a mistake now that you will regret the rest of your life, merely because you have had to delay your wedding. Harold seems to be an honorable man, and he is obviously very much in love with you. You are a lucky girl, Juliet, to have found him. And you have made your father very proud." He sighed deeply and let a tired frown crease his brow. "These past months in prison were certainly difficult ones for me. I felt bitter whenever I thought of my own son, fighting right alongside the men who had put me there. But then I would remember my daughter, bravely waiting here for my return. I would think of how proud I would be, giving her in marriage to a fine young man."

Juliet felt a burning tightness in her throat.

"And if I did not marry Harold . . . if I decided that I would not be happy with him . . . would you think that I had betrayed you, too?"

Hampton rose from his seat and paced the floor thoughtfully, as if giving her question his utmost concern. He must tread carefully; he must not force too much too soon.

"Juliet, you are my daughter, my own flesh and blood. The most important thing to me has always been your happiness. When you were much younger, I knew that you did not want to go away to school, and I did not want to send you. But your mother convinced me that it was for the best, and now I find that my little girl is a fine young lady. So perhaps, at the beginning, we don't always see what will make us happy in the end, what is really the right thing to do. Marriage is a very important step in your life—the most important, certainly, up until this point. I would hope that my good judgment would be taken into consideration before you make any decision of such import."

"But a person must learn to make his own decisions someday, whether right or wrong," she argued, remembering what Robert had said to her.

"I agree. And I suppose that is one of the reasons I am here, to help my children if and when they make mistakes. Someday Robert will be coming back here. It should be obvious by now that this revolt will be crushed, but knowing your brother, he will be one of the last to admit it. And he may never admit to me that it was all a stupid mistake. But he will be back, and he will be penniless, and I will have to help him make something of himself in spite of what hurt he has caused me."

"And you will be able to forgive him?" she asked in surprise.

"Did you doubt that I would? I admit that it will be difficult, but he is my son, after all." He paused only a moment. "As you are my daughter. My children are everything I have in the world that really means anything to me. You know that, don't you, Juliet?"

She could not force herself to meet his questioning look, but she finally managed a brief nod.

"Good," he said, patting her hand lightly. "Then off with you. I have a good deal of work to catch up on. I shall see you at luncheon. The fire should have blown itself out by then."

Juliet rose and stared out the window.

"It's been burning all night, Father. There must be a great deal of damage done. I wonder if I could be of some help—"

"The most helpful thing you can do is to stay away from trouble. People panic when there's a fire, and I don't want you endangering yourself. The soldiers will take care of it. Besides, you would only be in the way."

His stern admonishment wounded her pride, but she nodded in mute agreement. Though her eyes stayed on the great dark cloud that covered much of the sky, she was thinking not of the fire, but of what her father had just said. What had happened to her since she walked into this room just a few short minutes before? She had been so sure of herself, so convinced that marrying Alec had been the right thing to do. But now she was suddenly a little girl again, feeling that she had somehow done the right thing and the wrong thing at exactly the same time. If only her father did not hate Alec so! If she had married anyone else, she knew that she could trust her father to accept him for her sake. But Alec was the one person her father would never accept. She sighed deeply, and a troubled frown pulled at her brow. At length she glanced about to meet her father's deliberate scrutiny, and realizing that he had dismissed her several moments before, she made haste to leave the study. She did not see, therefore, that as he sat back down at his desk, a slight but knowing smile came to his thin lips.

Chapter 24

The second week of December arrived in New York with a light, powdery blanket of snow. Juliet idly watched the snowflakes drifting to the ground, accumulating into a shimmery shroud that matched the silence of the winter morn. When Rachel entered the room, she suppressed a shiver and wondered why Juliet had not complained of the cold. She went directly to stir up the fire before helping her to dress, noticing that her mistress seemed preoccupied.

"Do you think that we will be using the sleigh instead of the carriage today? It's been so long since I've ridden in a sleigh."

It was one of the old Dutch customs still observed in New York, and Juliet had always loved the way a sleigh seemed to float through the snow-laden streets.

"That I would not know," Rachel responded, knowing full well that Juliet was forcing herself into idle conversation. "You rose early this morn. Breakfast will not be for at least another half hour."

The maid efficiently finished with her duties, and Juliet dismissed her, choosing to remain in her room until breakfast. The soldiers in residence at the house were beginning to wear on her. She was expected to be a hostess at every meal, as well as afternoon tea, and she had seen many of the same men at the parties she had attended in the past few weeks. Socially, the City of New York was well on the road to recovery, and Juliet's calendar was filling up with teas and socials and balls. The war was still not over, and though everyone spoke

251

as if there were no chance for the "Old Fox" to escape his fate, no one could tell exactly when it would come to pass.

Juliet pressed a finger to the frosty glass of the latticed windowpane, doing her best to rouse herself from the mood of depression that had come with the colder weather. How long it seemed since last summer! How long since she had watched the sunrise from this same window with a pair of strong, dark arms about her! Had it been less than a score of weeks since she had last seen him? It seemed like a score of years! It was difficult to accept the time that separated her from Alec, but even more difficult to continue her struggles alone. The events of these past months had changed her in a way that time alone could not. She had been forced to rely on herself, for Alec as well as Robert was gone; she had not confided in Frances, and she did not dare to speak with her father. So she had bitten her tongue when she wanted to scream; had held her temper and seethed inwardly, even when she felt she might burst. She thought of everything she had faced in silence since Alec had left her behind that morning. Then she walked to her bureau and searched out her most precious possessions, kept secretly in a small brass box.

She slipped the plain gold band on her finger and admired the glimmer of metal against her meticulously manicured hands. It was the only thing that assured her that it had not all been a dream—that, and a badly creased piece of parchment worn frail from being folded and unfolded. She lifted the paper carefully from the box and smoothed it gently on the top of the bureau, blinking back her tears. She thought of Alec and worried about his safety, and wondered, too, if it would all be in vain.

The American army had been driven from Manhattan long before. Even Fort Washington, on the northwestern tip of the island, had fallen to the British in mid-November. The two thousand or so men in that final stronghold had panicked and surrendered almost without a fight, while Washington, viewing through field glasses from across the Hudson the sad slaughter of those who had resisted, actually sobbed at the sight. Then, on the twentieth day of November, Cornwallis had taken Fort Lee, just across the Hudson in New Jersey. The Americans had evacuated in the nick of time, leaving behind even more guns and ammunition that they could not afford to lose. The "Old Fox" was on the run with what remained of his battered army, and Cornwallis was in hot pursuit, anxious to close in for the kill.

At the same time, Benedict Arnold had kept General Carleton from retaking Fort Ticonderoga and had forced him to retreat into Canada for the winter. But Carleton had already won control of Lake Champlain, and the invasion of upper New York State was only delayed until the spring.

How long would it go on? she wondered sadly. And what would life be like when Alec finally did return to her? Some said that everyone who had fought in the revolution was guilty of treason and ought to be hanged. Others said that only the leaders would be hanged, but that all the soldiers in the Continental Army would have to be dealt some type of punishment, for they, also, were guilty of the crime. And the prisoners of war? There were already thousands of them in the city. It was said that hanging would have been a merciful end to their suffering, for they were packed into makeshift jails with barely enough room to breathe. Neither army was known for humane treatment of the men taken captive, but in New York the situation was decidedly worse than what was considered the norm. The British had taken a great number of them in little time, and the fire had caused overcrowding of every available building. Prisoners were held in warehouses, in partially destroyed churches, in abandoned taverns, in buildings offering little or no protection from the weather. Or, worst of all, they were put on a ship that had been stripped of its fittings and left forgotten in New York Harbor. There was almost no chance of surviving the terrible conditions of the prison ships, and their counterparts in the city boasted little better.

So what was there to hope for? she thought in despair. Even if the war ended tomorrow, Alec would be branded a criminal. But at least he would be alive, and as long as he lived . . . Perhaps her father would help her if she told him everything. No, that was impossible, for even if her father offered his help, Alec was a proud man and would probably never accept it. She sighed deeply and wondered how it had all seemed so simple just a few months before. What had Alec said to her then? That a Farrell laughs at disaster, scoffs at impossibilities.

She was being asked to do just that, to hold her head up and smile as if her world were not crumbling around her.

She gathered her resolve, lifted her chin, and set her mouth with determination. Her father would be taking her and Frances to a luncheon at the Harris home today, and she would be expected to be frivolous and charming and witty. She had become very close to her father since his return from prison; he had accompanied her to all the various social engagements these past weeks, or Juliet would not have attended at all. It seemed important to him, this mingling with the elite, and to please him she forced herself to go and to make a favorable impression.

By the time the Harris luncheon was finally over, Juliet was exhausted, and not even the idea of a sleigh ride home could rally her spirits. It had been most difficult to hold her tongue and listen to all the derisive talk about the Continental Army. And one woman had actually remarked that the *Whitby,* one of the prison ships in Wallabout Bay, ought to be sunk as a humane gesture, not to the poor dying men on board, but "for the loyal citizens, who have put up with the horrid stench quite long enough."

The ride home in the sleigh was long and quiet. Bundled warmly in soft woolens and furs, Juliet reflected sadly on the somber faces staring out from shacks and tents that offered scant protection against the cold and snow. While the rich were wagging their tongues about which party would be *the* affair of the season, the families who had returned to find their homes destroyed were shivering in the cold, wondering how they would survive the winter.

Just as the sleigh was turning off the main road, Juliet's eyes caught sight of something that made her gasp in horror. Tied to the back of a wagon was a great dark brown stallion, rearing and pulling at his bit every step of the way. The young soldier who drove the wagon coaxed the lead horse onward, literally dragging the other behind. There were two other soldiers on horseback doing their best to help, smacking at the stallion's hindquarters and shouting orders angrily at him, though each man respectfully backed off when the horse began to kick. It was obvious that the steed had a mind to stay where he was, and his snorting and pawing at the ground gave the soldiers good reason to be fearful. Juliet's face paled visibly at the sight. She would have recognized that horse anywhere—it was Cheval! She pulled her eyes away and tried with all her might not to think about what this meant. But a strange numbness came over her that had nothing to do with the cold, and she suddenly was forced to face a possibility that she had refused to recognize existed—until now.

Lawrence Hampton's eyes had been fixed on his daughter's face ever since they left the Harris home. He had sensed the anger that rose in her at the continued flow of insults concerning the rebel soldiers and had been relieved when it was finally time to depart. Then he read a different feeling in her face, one of loneliness and sadness. She ought to be ready any day now to confide the secrets she had kept so carefully hidden from him. Her trust in him was growing, of that he was certain. By springtime, if everything went well, she would be marrying Lord Harold after all. In the interim, perhaps her interest in charity work would help to ease her mind. She seemed to be concerned about the poor wretches who had been burned out, and had already spent a considerable amount of time with the Reverend Helscher talking over what might be done to help them. He would have to make sure that the work did not take up too much time, however. Juliet had to remain properly social at least until Harold arrived. But he was getting ahead of himself; there were quite a few other things to be arranged first.

Hampton's eyes narrowed as his daughter's face suddenly drained of color and she bolted forward, almost standing upright in the swiftly moving sleigh. Following the direction of her glance, he saw the reason for her unexpected burst of emotion. Lawrence Hampton was also familiar with that fine piece of horseflesh fighting to be free. A satisfied gleam came into his eye as he observed Juliet trying to hide her shock. Fate was no longer on Farrell's side, Hampton thought with delight.

Chapter 25

Lieutenant Michael Alford was young, blond, and extremely handsome, with a smile that dazzled and a wit and charm that captivated. His walk was brisk and self-assured, his manner light and engaging. He called no man his enemy—and certainly no woman—for that was the most important thing his mother had ever taught him: to be a friend to everyone, but especially to influential people.

His mother, a beauty who had been an actress in a small London theater, had lived by that one rule and had achieved a good measure of success, considering where she had started. Michael's father, Lord Michael Gray, had made a comfortable life for her until her death seven years before, and though he had never recognized his bastard son officially, he had always been very generous in doing so monetarily and had lent an aristocratic hand in the boy's upbringing.

Michael had enjoyed his easy life in London until he had chanced to encounter his half brother, the young Lord Simon Gray. The cocky nobleman had made it clear from the outset that he doubted their kinship existed at all and had insulted the young lady in Michael's company, finally forcing a fight. Alford, who had long since learned to deflect the inevitable insults concerning his parentage, had easily laid low his brother with a few well-placed blows, but Lord Simon had soon revived and had challenged his brother to a duel. At that point the boys' father had intervened, purchasing a military commission for his out-of-wedlock son and sending him off to make his own way in the world.

At the age of twenty-five, Michael found himself in New York, doing what he had always done best—making friends, enjoying life. Because he was bright and personable, and most of all because he was an excellent listener, people often spilled their troubles to him. It was said that he knew more things about more people than anyone else in the entire army, and he was clever enough to use his knowledge wisely and profitably. He still received an allowance from his father, which he used to buy useful information, as often with liquor and his company as with a straightforward monetary exchange. Just recently he had taken up the task of informing certain wealthy families of the whereabouts of their rebel sons, now imprisoned in New York. It was information not too difficult to come by and not too difficult to market. It seemed to Michael that every hand in this city, no matter which side one professed one's loyalty to, was open to a bribe.

Michael enjoyed the work for the profit, surely, for he enjoyed his comforts; but he also delighted in the challenge of it, as there was little in his life that offered him a challenge. His duties with the army were made easy because he remained on good terms with the military elite; if not directly with the officers, then at least with the wives and mistresses of those same men. He had never met a woman he could not charm to distraction if he set his mind to it, though it was seldom necessary to try very hard. Women seemed to love him for exactly what he was—a cavalier, a poet, a naturally entertaining man who enjoyed life.

It was dark by the time Michael reached the warehouse where the note had instructed him to come. He noticed that the snow was turning gray and ugly on the southern streets as he trudged along the last few steps toward a solitary figure standing in the shadows, obviously waiting for him. He found the secrecy intriguing, for the note had not been signed, and the messenger had disappeared before he could be questioned as to its origin. Probably some Tory whose son was mixed up in the revolution wanting information badly enough to pay for it but not badly enough to admit his shame publicly. He smiled to himself. He would accommodate the man and, as always, he would be the soul of discretion.

He introduced himself to the figure in the snow, who stood about equal to him in height, and followed him silently into the warehouse. The man traced a path through a maze of stacked crates to an office where a single lamp glowed in the darkness. When the man removed his tricorn and greatcoat, Michael was genuinely surprised at the silver in his hair and the age of his skin, for he had moved like a man much younger than his three score years. He took a seat across from the older man, who sat behind a desk now, his alert steel-blue eyes clearly visible in the lamplight.

Lawrence Hampton introduced himself and without preamble stated his business.

"I have been told that you have proved very helpful to certain persons in obtaining information about prisoners on this island. I have also been told that you may even be able to secure information about men who are yet with the 'Old Fox.' " He briefly noted the young man's quick smile and warm blue eyes before he continued. "I wish to know the whereabouts of two men. One of these men is my son; the other is . . . a friend of his. I am willing to be extremely generous in return for whatever help you can offer me in this matter."

"I will be frank, sir, as I know your time is valuable," Michael said politely. "In return for a stipend, I have informed several families of men I found imprisoned on this island. It is a relatively simple matter to speak with prison guards about their captives, to learn the names of elite prisoners and then to go about locating their families. In one case I did manage to find a young man whose family had contacted me first, and asked that I search for him. But among so many prisioners, I was most fortunate to do so, and I could not guarantee that I could do it again, no matter how generous the offer might be. As far as locating someone yet with Washington's army, I hesitate to say that it would be impossible, but it would most certainly take a great deal of time and expense."

"But it could be done," Hampton pressed him.

Michael smiled easily. "It could be attempted, sir."

Hampton sat back in his chair. "You undoubtedly are curious about the trouble I went to to arrange this meeting in absolute secrecy. There is a good reason for my discretion, as there is a good reason for everything I do." He paused as if to emphasize his last remark. "The other man I want information about . . ." He took a deep breath and measured his words of explanation. "My daughter is a very impressionable young woman. This past summer, while I was imprisoned by the rebels who had the island, my daughter met this man, and now she fancies herself in love with him. She is already engaged to a fine young nobleman who will be coming to New York to marry her soon. I intend to see that the wedding takes place. I will not see her waiting for a common criminal while she turns down this chance for a successful marriage." He paused briefly, giving Michael a chance to ask the obvious question.

"But, sir, if your daughter is determined to wait for this man, how could finding him change her mind?"

"Her mind will be changed when you discover he is dead, Lieutenant."

Michael digested Hampton's words very carefully. He had no intention of being a partner to murder, and he wished that to be clear from the beginning.

"Sir, I have absolutely no way of locating a man if he is dead. The woods in Brooklyn are littered with bodies that have not been claimed, but I do not engage myself in that type of work. I help families locate their loved ones, and loved ones their families. Nothing more."

Michael half rose from his seat, but was halted by Hampton's words.

"You misunderstand me, Lieutenant. Please be seated and hear me out."

Michael settled himself in his seat once more and waited for Hampton to continue.

"I have good reason to believe that the man I am interested in finding is a prisoner. Only today I saw his horse being dragged south along the road that leads from Fort Washington. I have no way of knowing, of course, but I think you might be able to find that horse, for he is a magnificent creature, and he was being very difficult. The soldiers would be sure to complain loudly when they had finished the task of moving him. There were three of them, young ones, and each wore a small green feather in his cap."

"That could prove helpful in finding the horse, but not necessarily the man," Michael remarked.

"The man's name is Captain Alexander Farrell," Hampton went on, "and I believe that you will be able to find him also, for two reasons. First, I intend to provide you with adequate funds to do so. I am not unaware that nearly everything in this city is for sale at the right price. Second, the man is tall and striking, due mostly to a pair of black eyes that few people ever forget. And he had in his possession a gold neckchain with a unique charm on it, which I can describe to you in detail."

Michael smiled indulgently. "Let us say, for the sake of argument, that I was able to find this man. What difference would it make? Your daughter would still be in love with him."

"Not if you can prove to her that he is dead. He does not have to be dead, you understand. We only need convince her that he is. Time and a bit of maneuvering ought to take care of the rest, if what I hear about your prisons is true."

Michael thought for a moment. "It seems to me, sir, that you are going to a great deal of trouble needlessly. I could probably convince your daughter that the man is dead today. What difference will my searching make in the matter?"

Hampton regarded Michael shrewdly. The man had made a small point in his favor and had lost a larger one with the same comment. Hampton always appreciated someone who was interested in saving him money, but he appreciated someone who could follow orders without question much more. And he had just finished telling the man that he never did anything without good reason.

"I said that my daughter is young and impressionable, Leiutenant, but she is not a fool. She will not take anyone's word that the man is dead on faith alone. We will need that neckchain. And I want you to have a good look at the man so you can contrive an accurate description—of his death." He paused, then added, "There is one more thing. I want to know myself where he is and if he is alive. Then I can proceed in removing him permanently from her life. As for my son, I should like information about him for obvious reasons, but also to reinforce the story you are going to tell my daughter. I know that your mother was an actress, and I have been told that you are also blessed with the talent. That is why I chose to contact you and not someone else. I cannot stress how important it is to me to settle this affair neatly and quickly."

Michael nodded appreciatively. "I am impressed, sir. Your own information seems to be very complete."

"I am quite thorough in everything I do, Lieutenant. That is the reason for our meeting this evening. When I feel the time is right, I will contact you and have you to my home for a second meeting. At that time you will act as if we have never met before. You will meet my daughter, and she and I will ask for your help in finding these two men. Afterward, when it comes time to discuss your fee, I will dismiss my daughter and you can give me whatever information you have come by. Is that clear?"

"Perfectly," Michael answered. "How long do you think it will be before you send for me?"

"That depends on many things. You will wait for my summons no matter what information you accumulate in the interim. And remember that we have never met before."

Michael nodded and removed a small folded scrap of paper from his breast pocket. "Now," he said, helping himself to the quill pen on Hampton's desk. "You were going to tell me about a horse. . . ."

It was a quiet dinner for Juliet, as her father was called away suddenly on an urgent matter of business. She was grateful for his absence, since she then had no need to be on her guard, to hide the preoccupation that weighed so heavily on her mind. She heard none of the conversation that flowed about her, nor did she taste any of the small bit of food she managed to force down. One thought kept running through her mind: Alec's horse . . . British soldiers . . . It had to mean that he had been captured, or that he had been—no! She would not even consider that possibility. There must be some other explanation, she thought. Perhaps he had been thrown, or maybe Cheval had come untethered and run off. But Alec was an excellent rider; he never would have been thrown by his own horse. And it was just as inconceivable that he had been careless about keeping him tied. That left only one possibility, or rather, only one that she could face. Alec was a prisoner somewhere on the island. He must be in one of the churches, she thought, or in some makeshift shelter—he must be! Oh, dear God! He could not be on one of those dreadful prison ships! No! He was safe and well, she assured herself. All she had to do was find him.

But it would be like trying to find Robert among the thousands of soldiers on the island that day last winter. And what excuse could she use for searching the prisons? Well, that was simple enough. She would be searching for her brother. Why had she not thought of the prisoners before? she chided herself. Because she had simply not wanted to face that possibility; she had wanted to believe that Alec and Robert were safe. But all that had changed today, everything had changed. She had to face the fact that Alec was a prisoner somewhere, and she had to try to find him at once.

Robert shivered and frowned at the slushy mixture accumulating all about him on the frozen ground. Bucks County, Pennsylvania. He had never been here before, and being here now was something of a miracle. He laughed at the thought, for as he looked around him he saw very little that seemed miraculous. The army, if one could even use the term for such a sorry collection of scarecrows, had made camp on the west bank of the Delaware River. But therein lay the miracle: in the week previous, these same six thousand men had miraculously achieved a safe crossing of the river's dangerous rain-swollen current.

Four months, sixteen endless weeks of retreat, he thought tiredly. Of being part of an army running for its life . . . of leaving behind the guns and artillery that could have meant a chance at victory . . . of dragging along a dying comrade when he was already so weary he could hardly drag himself. And always with the knowledge that the enemy, vastly superior in number and supplies, was not very far behind.

The Continental Army was safe now, for the time being. The men and a dozen or so pieces of artillery were safe—until the river froze over and the Hessians could make a crossing to finish the job. Perhaps the river would not freeze until after New Year's, in which case the army would be finished by itself, even without a battle. Well over half of the men would complete their enlistments at year's end, and they would be able to leave with honor, having fulfilled the time they had sworn to serve.

God! It was so close to Christmas! Robert had hoped to be home by Christmas . . . home with Frances. He had heard that General Howe had left Trenton just a few days before to return to New York. They said he had taken a mistress there, a pretty blue-eyed blonde, and had been anxious to return to her. He had left Hessians in Trenton and more troops in Amboy, New Brunswick, and Princeton to help, if necessary, in finishing off the Americans. It did not look to be much of a struggle. Even the two thousand soldiers that General Sullivan had marched here and the thousand that General Horatio Gates had added to the total brought it to less than ten thousand, including the sick and dying. And for all the excitement and shouting that had occurred when those fresh Continentals came to join them, Robert could not see that they really made a difference now.

His mouth twisted into a sad sort of half-smile. It rankled him to think of giving up. He would rather have made a fight of it to the bitter end. He had changed so much these past months, and the better part of the change had been effected when the army was forced to flee Manhattan. The British and Hessian soldiers were no longer men to him, they were trespassers stealing his homeland, destroying not only Robert's freedom, but his pride, a part of himself. He felt a hatred now, and a desire to kill; instead, he had been forced to retreat. He was roused from his contemplation by the arrival of a cart piled high with cast-off clothing from the citizens of Philadelphia. Several men ran past him, hoping to claim whatever might give them some relief from the penetrating cold. Wearily Robert drew the heavy Dutch blanket closer about his shoulders, for he had no greatcoat to shut out the winter's chill. His boots, at least, were still in fair condition, while many of the men were barefoot.

Robert found himself wondering briefly about Alec, whom he had not seen in weeks. For Juliet's sake he hoped that Alec was well. Those last few weeks in New York, it had been obvious that his sister was very much in love with the man. This would be a difficult time for her, living with Father and without Alec. Father was so very clever, and if he wanted Juliet to marry Harold, Robert knew that he would do his best to see it done. Juliet had always tried so hard to please Father. It had been the most important thing in her life until she had fallen in love with Alec. Robert hoped with all his heart that Alec was safe, but he had to admit that the odds were not in his favor. The last he had heard, Alec had ridden to Fort Washington the day before it was taken, and no one had seen him since then. He heaved a heavy sigh. There was nothing he could do. So, like the other men around him, he waited and tried not to think.

Chapter 26

The December winds were blowing sharp and cold, and Juliet shivered as she hurried from the carriage up the front steps to her home. Once inside, she gave her heavy cloak to James, one of the new servants Father had hired, and he announced that there were guests in the main parlor. When she entered the room, a smile touched her lips despite the despair so heavy in her heart. Frances sat on the sofa chatting with Mary, while Allan relaxed nearby in a large wing chair. And running about from one end of the long room to the other was a strange mixture of angelic golden curls, bright blue eyes, and a devilish grin spreading ear to ear. How Edgar had grown!

Allan rose and was quick to greet Juliet with a touch of lips to her hand, followed by Mary's soft and timid regards.

"It's so good to see you both!" Juliet smiled. "And you, too, Edgar. Now how did you grow up so quickly?" she asked him, stooping to his level as he gallantly copied his father's greeting. "Why, you're practically old enough to escort me to a ball!"

Edgar's smile spread even wider, then disappeared as he asked in earnest, "What's a ball?"

"A ball is a grand party that men and women attend wearing their very finest clothing."

"Oh!" he replied importantly, "that sounds nice! . . . But I have to ask Mama."

Juliet rose again, having made a new friend, and turned an amused expression on the two proud parents.

"You will be staying to dinner, of course."

A pained look passed between Allan and Frances, who then faced Juliet almost apologetically. Allan cleared his throat and ran a finger about his collar before he managed to explain.

"Mary and Edgar and I have been traveling for days. When we returned we found our house destroyed, as well as Father's house. We had heard about the fire, of course, and after the soldiers left Boston, we stayed with Mary's family, but it was so crowded and uncomfortable. We were happy to be coming home, hoping for the best. Now we find that we have no place to go. We had thought that we might stay here, but Frances tells us that you have more than your share of visitors at the moment. We were wondering if you might possibly be able to help us?"

Juliet politely listened to the all too familiar story. She had known that Allan's smaller house was gone, along with the Churches' grand mansion. But she had not thought of them returning here and finding no place to go. The guest rooms in the west wing were occupied, every single one. The servant's quarters were crowded with military aides and the new help that her father had hired recently. Even Robert's room was occupied now by Colonel Reynolds—there was simply not a spare space available.

"It would be temporary, of course," Allan went on. "A few years ago, I bought some land north of the island. But I need to go there and see exactly what remains of the house that was there. I wouldn't want to take Mary and Edgar along only to find the same predicament we have encountered here."

Juliet sighed deeply and looked at Frances's wide, pleading eyes. Suddenly she knew what had to be done.

"As Frances told you, the house is crowded, so I'm afraid I can't offer you spacious accommodations. But if Frances would not mind sharing my room for a while, then I see no reason why you could not take hers. With regard to meals, we're already feeding an army; a few more will make no difference at all. In fact, I hope that you will decide to stay here, in spite of the lack of comfort," she continued graciously. "I would find your company most refreshing after so much military talk at every waking hour. You've no idea how boring it can be!"

Frances smiled gratefully, then could not keep from giving Juliet a quick, sisterly hug. She had never doubted that Juliet would find a way to help, for it seemed to her that the girl always knew exactly what to do.

Late that same evening, when the lights had been extinguished and the house was quiet, Juliet lay stiffly keeping to her side of the bed, not wanting to disturb Frances yet unable to sleep. She had never shared a bed with anyone but Alec, and that had been a very different matter. The thought of another person in her bed made her uncomfortable and uneasy. How could she ever have considered marriage to Harold? she wondered. Little did she realize that Frances, who lay still and silent beside her, felt the very same uneasiness that she did.

After what seemed like hours, Juliet carefully slipped out of bed and walked to the window. It was strange how she always came to this window when her mind was troubled. She looked out on the city, where whale-oil lamps glowed brightly in the dark winter night. Somewhere in that city a man thought of her at this very moment. If only she could find him, she thought desperately, but the provost marshall had refused her request, and each attempt she had made to see the prisoners had ended in futility. She had tried taking the men provisions, bribing the guards, even crying and spilling out her heart to the officer in charge, all to no avail. There was disease, the provost marshall had argued; the men were dangerous; and if he allowed one woman to go searching about for her brother, there would soon be hundreds of requests to do the same. He could not have that, she had to understand, as it was his duty to maintain a semblance of order and safety. She now sighed her frustration and pounded a fist on the windowsill.

"Can't you sleep?" came Frances's quiet voice in the darkness.

"No. I'm sorry if I woke you, Frances."

"That's all right, I wasn't asleep anyway."

She sat up in bed and hugged her knees to her chest. "I'm sorry, Juliet. I know that it isn't easy for you to share your room with me. It was so generous of you to help Mary and Allan. You are such a kind person, as well as a dear friend."

Juliet shrugged off the compliments. "I think sharing a room will be good for us, Frances. We haven't spent much time together lately, just the two of us, that is. And I do miss the talks we used to have when the house was empty."

"So do I," Frances sighed. "Sometimes when I remember those days last summer, I wonder if I did not dream it all. It seems so long ago, so far away."

"And today seems almost like a nightmare," Juliet murmured, taking a seat at the foot of the bed and wearily leaning her back against the post.

Frances nodded in agreement. "I remember thinking last spring of the grand parties I was missing because of the war. Now I wonder how I ever could have thought that parties were such fun. They seem so unimportant now, with Robert gone."

"Everything will be different when he comes back, Frances. You know it will."

"Yes," she agreed, then looking askance at Juliet, she timidly added, "and everything will be different for you when Alec comes back."

Juliet opened her mouth as if she meant to object, then reconsidered as she squarely met the pair of blue eyes in the meager light. Instead she got up and lit the lamp beside the bed.

"You are very fond of Alec, aren't you?"

Juliet nodded her answer.

"I thought so, even though you never talked about him to me after I told you about his fiancée in Virginia. I'm sorry about what I said that day, even though I was honestly trying to help. Robert told me that Alec really does care for you and that he would not be at all surprised if you were to marry him someday."

"What else did Robert tell you?" Juliet asked, smiling as she remembered the night she had spoken to him about Alec.

"Only that you never really cared for Lord Harold. Is that true, Juliet?"

Juliet sighed, and a frown deeply creased her forehead. "Oh, Frances! I promised Alec that I wouldn't tell you, but I'm so tired of keeping it all to myself! Sometimes I feel like

I'm about to burst! There is so much I have to remember, and so much I have to forget!" She took a seat on the bed once more, running a hand over her brow. "Frances, Alec and I are married."

Frances stared at her, wide-eyed with shock. "But that's impossible, Juliet!" she finally managed. "How could you be married to Alec?"

Juliet rose to fetch the small brass box from which she removed her secret parchment treasure and presented it to Frances.

"My goodness! You really are married to him!" she gasped. "But how? When?"

Juliet shook her head. "None of that matters now, Frances. The only thing that's important is that Alec is my husband, and at this very moment he needs my help. And there's nothing I can do to help him. God knows I've tried! These past days I've spent every waking hour thinking of how I might find him. But it's no use! The provost marshall isn't interested in my problems, and he wouldn't accept a bribe, not that I had much of one to offer. I heard a rumor that he's making quite a bit of money selling the rations, meager as they may be, that are set aside for the prisoners. They say that the men are literally starving to death! And the smell from any one of those places is horrendous! I almost choked on the air outside; if they had let me in, I probably would have fainted."

"Juliet, wait! I don't understand what you're saying! Do you think Alec might be—"

Juliet interrupted her, but her voice sounded dull and lifeless. "I am nearly certain he was captured. The day we were returning home from the Harris luncheon, just before we turned up the drive, we passed two soldiers on horseback and a third one driving a wagon with a horse tied to the back of it. Do you remember that?"

Frances frowned thoughtfully before she answered.

"I vaguely recall them passing by, and I remember that a horse was making terrible sounds as if they were hurting him. But I looked the other way. I hate to see anyone mistreat an animal."

"Frances, didn't you look at that horse? It was Cheval."

"Are you certain? I don't know how you could be sure; after

all, we only saw him for a moment. But then, all horses look alike to me."

"Well, I did see him, and I am certain. As certain as I have ever been of anything!" Juliet sighed her frustration. "Do you think I wanted to recognize him? More than anything else I wanted to be wrong! But it was Cheval, and there is no sense lying to myself about it. Alec is a prisoner somewhere, and I can't help him, I can't even find him!"

"Juliet, do you suppose that Robert is—"

"No," she answered firmly. "Robert is well and still with the army. I know he is. Anyway, if Robert were a prisoner, Father would help him to get free. And he will help him when the war is over, he told me he would. But Alec . . ." Juliet's voice cracked, and she was suddenly very close to tears.

"Your father said that he would help Robert? Even after everything that's happened?"

Juliet nodded, still unable to speak.

Frances looked away, considering. "I think that Robert was wrong about him then. He never thought that your father cared about him, not really. And he told me that your father would never forgive him for leaving, but obviously he misjudged him. Since I've been living here, it has become clear to me that your father truly loves you, Juliet, and maybe, if you explain to him about Alec—"

"You don't understand!" Juliet got up and began to pace the floor. "Father hates Alec! He could never accept the fact of our marriage. Besides, he wants so much for me to marry Harold. How do I tell him that I simply cannot?"

"Be reasonable, Juliet. You are married to Alec, and there's no way to change that. Your father will have to accept the fact sooner or later, so you may as well bring it out into the open now and beg his forgiveness and his help. I refuse to believe that he would turn you out, though he might be very angry at first. If he can forgive Robert, then he can forgive you. And I think he might help you to find out where Alec is, for your sake, because you are his only daughter and he loves you."

Juliet gnawed at her lip. She had been over this time and time again in her mind, but she had always decided that it would be best to keep things to herself. There was Frances to consider. If Juliet were to be turned out of the house, it could very well mean that Father would do the same to her. Somehow they would survive, but it would certainly be a struggle. The Churches had other friends in the city, and surely there were people who would be willing to take Frances in. Yet, with the city trying to house an army that matched the population one for one, it would be difficult to find someone able, not just willing. Allan had come here as a last resort, had he not?

Perhaps even more insurmountable was the problem of Alec's pride. If she did manage to enlist her father's help, would Alec ever forgive her for turning to him? Would he ever be able to live with the fact that Lawrence Hampton had saved his life? But what good all that pride if Alec were, at this very moment, starving to death? What difference would anything make if he were to die?

Frances was right. She had to tell her father and trust that he would help her, in spite of his disappointment, in spite of what she had done.

The lamp was extinguished, and she climbed into bed a few moments later. As soon as she found the right opportunity, she decided before falling into a troubled sleep, she would tell her father and let the cards fall where they may.

Chapter 27

With the arrival of Allan, Mary, and Edgar just a few days before Christmas, Juliet once again found a reason to put forth her best effort in making the holiday a joyous occasion. Aware that Allan was heavily burdened with financial problems, Juliet began a last minute Christmas buying spree. It was a great time for herself and Frances, anticipating the happy moments when their specially chosen gifts would be opened, particularly the ones bought for Edgar. Juliet paid outrageously to have a cream-colored satin suit made for the little boy—a copy of the one she remembered Allan wearing the night of the last party at the Church mansion. She also bought him a beautiful painted rocking horse and a small carved sailboat, as well as a finely carved and painted replica of a great sailing ship, which he would appreciate more as he grew older.

A child made Christmas seem so different; it took on a whole new meaning. The excitement in those wide blue eyes and the hug that Edgar ran to give Juliet even before he played with any of his new toys, not to mention the tearful appreciation Mary and Allan expressed when they realized what Juliet had done, more than made up for all the trouble and expense. Brushing aside everyone's insistence that she had done too much, she reveled in the brief happiness so easily bought. But she could not help thinking of Alec, spending this day in prison, going hungry while the soldiers and guests at Hampton House greedily gobbled up the two geese she had ordered prepared according to family tradition. This year

275

more than ever before, she had worked very hard to bring Christmas to as many as she possibly could. She had nearly emptied the attic, giving every piece of clothing (except for a certain outfit of boyish garb, which she hid at the bottom of a coffer filled with woolen blankets) to the Reverend Helscher for distribution to needy families. At her suggestion, her father had even given a donation to the reverend for special needs not met by the clothing and furnishings contributed by the Hamptons and other well-off citizens.

As she sipped at a glass of Christmas punch laced with spirits, her eyes rose slowly from the child at play with his new toys to meet the steel-blue eyes of her father. His lips twisted upward into a smile, and she knew that the time had come to ask him for the one Christmas gift she feared he might refuse her.

The party spirit began to fade. Edgar grew disinterested in his play, and finally everyone retired for the night except Juliet and her father. She poured herself one last glass of punch before a maid removed the great punch bowl to the kitchen, and her father, sensing that she was not ready to retire, got himself a glass of wine and took a seat near the fire. He watched her wander thoughtfully about the room, pause to look out the window, idly run a finger over the various seasonal decorations that were spread about. At length, when the house was considerably quieter and the servants had returned the large parlor to some semblance of order, Hampton moved a second chair close to the fire and invited Juliet to take it.

Seated, she nervously stared at her cup, not knowing where or how to begin her story, much less her request.

Her father's voice came warm and unhurried. "You have done a fine job these past two years, Juliet. Even without Robert, I have been able to enjoy Christmas."

"Thank you, Father, but it was you who made it all possible. And your kindness to the Reverend Helscher—you are a very generous man, Father."

He gave a short laugh. "You must remember, Juliet, that only wealthy people can afford to be generous. I have worked hard and been fortunate, and I am no miser, certainly. I am happy to help where I see a need," he said, then added to himself, and where I see it suits my purposes.

Juliet closed her eyes and concentrated on gathering every bit of her courage together before she began. There would be no turning back, and if she presented her case badly, there would be no second chance. She lifted a resolved set of golden eyes and spoke calmly.

"Father, for a long time I have wanted to tell you something, something I did that may hurt you, but that was not done for that purpose." She drew a deep breath to slow the flow of words that was rushing to her lips. "It concerns my engagement to Harold, in a way. I am going to be honest with you now, Father, as I ought to have been honest from the first. I do not love Harold, nor did I ever love him. I accepted his proposal of marriage because . . . because I wanted to come home as someone important, because I wanted to do something to make you love me. . . ." In spite of her effort, her voice broke emotionally.

Her father smiled and took her hand. "I am your father, Juliet. I have always loved you."

Juliet shook her head as the tears spilled out and ran down her cheeks. "I did not know that until now!" She drew a deep breath and attempted to calm herself, but it was no use. "You . . . you never noticed me when I was a child! You sent me away! You always took Robert to the docks or out riding, but never me! You were proud of him, but never me!"

"Juliet, I thought that a little girl belonged with her mother. I wanted to take you places, truly I did, but it wasn't proper! I thought it best to send you to a fine school, even though I missed you. I often spoke to your mother about having you come home. She wouldn't hear of it. And after she died, I was convinced that she had been right. You were such a lovely little lady then, I felt it was best that you returned and completed your education. It was out of love that I sent you away, Juliet, I thought by now you understood."

"It was not because . . . you were . . . embarrassed by me? I . . . was never like Frances, you know. I was always . . . different."

"Of course not! But Juliet, you certainly do not resent being taught proper manners and rules of propriety! There are those people who say that it does not matter what other people think. They are fools! This is a real world, and people do not exist as separate entities. One must be careful to display a favorable picture to the public. Being an outcast of society can only hurt you. You must conform to the rules, or at least appear to conform. That is the hardest thing to learn, I think, that a person is judged by what he appears to be, not what he really is."

Juliet was suddenly feeling the effects of the Christmas punch. She almost argued with her father's reasoning, which had been her own before she met Alec. But this was not the time for argument!

"What is it that you have done, Juliet? Tell me, and perhaps together we might find a solution. I want to help you."

"If you want to help me, Father, then first you must forgive me. I cannot change what I have done, and to be honest, I would not if it were possible to do so . . . except for the lies I have told." She raised her chin, and though her eyes pleaded forgiveness, she stated slowly and with a good measure of pride, "I am Alexander Farrell's wife. We were married secretly last summer. No one knows, except Frances." She paused. "I love him more than anything else in the world."

Her father rose from his seat and filled his glass of wine, trying to fix the correct approach in his mind. With his back to her, he asked, "Why didn't you tell me sooner?"

"I know how you feel about him, Father. Alec thought it best if I told no one. And at the time I agreed with him."

Hampton smiled in spite of himself. The man had done him a favor. The smile disappeared as he turned around.

"And why are you telling me now?"

"Because these past few months, I have come to realize that you truly have my welfare at heart. I should have trusted you long ago, I realize that now. And because"—she swallowed hard—"because I need your help."

"How can I help you?" he asked, resuming his seat.

Juliet's heart skipped a beat. He was still talking to her, listening to her; he really seemed to want to help! She quickly told him that she knew Alec was a prisoner, about seeing the horse on the way home from the luncheon. When she told him about her experiences with the guards and the provost marshall, he smiled indulgently.

"Juliet, you ought to have come to me sooner. It takes a man to know how to go about such things."

"Do you mean that you will help me find him?"

"I cannot say that I am pleased with your choice of husband, Juliet, for as you well know, I cannot abide the man. But if you are indeed wed to him, then I shall not see you pine away while he rots in a prison. I shall find him, and when I do he will owe me a favor. I shall expect to collect on that favor someday," he added, hoping that it made his eagerness a bit more credible. "From you, Juliet, I shall extract a promise, here and now. I want you to be honest with me from this day forward, as I have been honest with you. If I ever find that you have lied to me after this, I shall never forgive you."

Juliet nodded solemnly. "I promise I shall never lie to you again."

"It is settled then. I shall begin tomorrow, and I promise you that there will be news very soon." He toyed with the idea of telling her the news might be bad but decided against it. He would be every bit as surprised as she when Lieutenant Alford told them what he "knew." He would have to set up their preliminary meeting first thing in the morning.

She gave her father a warm hug and a quick kiss on his cheek. "Of all the Christmas gifts you have given, no one is happier with his than I am at this moment with mine. Thank you, Father!"

As she bounded up the stairs, her skirts lifted high, she remembered what Robert had said about their father. How wrong he had been! She couldn't wait to tell Frances! She knocked, then entered their room without a pause, throwing her arms about Frances.

"You told him? He's going to help?" Frances asked in wonder. "Oh, I'm so happy for you! I knew that he would!"

"I only told him because of you, Frances. You convinced me that it was the right thing to do. Thank you."

Frances shrugged off her thanks. "Tell me! What did he say? Did you ask you how you fell in love with a rebel? It's an easy thing to do, I think. What did he say?"

"He said he would help," Juliet answered, "and he didn't ask any questions about how, when, or why. He just said that he would help." A frown touched her brow as she looked back on the conversation, for her father had not seemed surprised by anything she had said. He was not one to show much emotion, still, it was not like him to accept her story so easily and without question.

Frances saw the frown and sought to relieve Juliet of her worries. "That's all that matters, isn't it?" she asked brightly. "That he's going to help?"

"Yes," Juliet agreed slowly, smiling almost hesitantly. "I suppose it is."

Chapter 28

The seventh day of 1777 was a very busy one for the Hampton household. Allan left at dawn to inspect his land north of Manhattan; Hampton was called away when someone apparently tried to break into one of the warehouses; and little Edgar threw his first temper tantrum in the house, throwing a bowl of porridge halfway across the room.

It was eleven-thirty when Lieutenant Michael Alford knocked at the main entrance of the house, arriving early for his appointment at noon. James greeted him and led him into the large parlor to wait, but after a few moments of being left alone, Michael found himself in search of some diversion. His surroundings were tasteful and luxurious, but he had never been one to take an interest in splendid furnishings. Perhaps there was a comely parlor maid wandering about somewhere, he mused. He had seen a few common women about this island who had definitely aroused his interest.

He stepped from the parlor to the hall, which was deserted, then continued to the smaller parlor in the direction of a pleasant feminine voice. He paused at the doorway to smile at the scene before him. A beautiful golden-eyed woman sat properly beside a young man on a small sofa, flirting with him until his blue eyes were wide and warm with utter infatuation. From the solemnity of her words, the divulgence of her heartfelt feelings, one would never have guessed that the young man was only four years old.

"I wanted to go with Father this morning!" he said with some urgency.

"I know you did, Edgar. It's no fun being made to stay at home. I know. When I was your age, my mother wouldn't let me go out riding at all—even though Robert was allowed to go every single day. Mother used to make me sit here, right in front of this window, and sew! And after that I had to practice on the spinet, and after that . . . Well, she never wanted me to go out and play at all! And Father never took me anywhere, either, except to boring parties. You are really very lucky, Edgar. At least you are a man. In a few years you will be able to do exactly what you want to do."

"I already know what I want to do. I want to be like Uncle Alec."

Juliet blinked her surprise. "Do you remember Uncle Alec?"

Edgar nodded. "He came to visit us twice in Boston. And he rode a 'nificent horse! He could ride faster than anybody I ever saw!" He paused, then added thoughtfully, "Papa said that you could ride faster than anybody, too! How could that be, if your mama never let you ride?"

Juliet cleared her throat and answered with care. "To be perfectly honest, I did not always listen to my mother, though I should have! Do you know what finally happened? She gave up on me, and sent me away to England for ten years!"

"Ten years?" he repeated in wonder. "That is older than me!"

"It most certainly is!"

"Did they put you in jail?" he asked in horror.

"Almost," Juliet answered, stifling a smile. "They called it a school, but it seemed like a jail to me."

"I think your mama was a mean lady, Aunt Juliet."

"No, Edgar, I simply would not listen to her, and she finally tired of trying to teach me. Mothers get tired, too—especially your mama, with all the traveling you've done. She needs you, Edgar. That's why they thought it best that you stay here while your father's away. You must try to be good while he's gone, because she misses him very, very much."

"I do, too," he whimpered, tears coming to his eyes.

"I know," she comforted him, pulling him onto her lap. "Cheer up, Edgar! He'll only be gone a few days. Maybe you could take me to town tomorrow to shop, if you aren't too busy. You could even wear your new suit of clothes."

"I'm not too busy, Aunt Juliet," he assured her, his tears stopping as suddenly as they had started. "I shall go and ask Mama right now!" he said, jumping down from her lap.

"Remember to tell her that you're sorry for throwing your porridge this morning," she called after him.

As Edgar skipped from the room, he paused momentarily to give a smiling soldier propped leisurely against the door frame a suspicious perusal. When the soldier straightened and gave the tiny lad a crisp salute, he giggled and ran off in the opposite direction. Juliet's brows raised expectantly as she also caught sight of the man.

"Could I help you, sir?" she asked, rising and making her way toward him.

"You already have," he responded smoothly, with a show of his even white teeth. "You have entertained me to the point of absolute diversion, madame!" he continued, kissing her hand gallantly. "The only further favor I request is the honor of an introduction. I am Lieutenant Michael Alford, and you are . . . ?"

"Juliet Hampton, sir. Have you business here with one of the soldiers?"

"No. I have an appointment with Lawrence Hampton, but not until noon. I'm afraid I have arrived rather early."

Juliet returned the young lieutenant's disarming smile. "I'm sorry, Lieutenant, but Father was called away on business and probably will not be back until then."

"Well!" he said, eyeing her with obvious admiration. "If you will consent to entertain me in his absence, I shall consider it my extreme good fortune to have come by early." Michael stepped into the parlor with easy familiarity, stopping below the great portrait of Juliet's mother. His eyes appraised the portrait, then the flesh-and-blood woman in the room with him, then the portrait again.

"Miss Hampton, may I say that your portrait, fascinating though that image may be, hardly compares to the dazzling beauty that now graces my presence in the flesh."

Juliet's eyes flashed her amusement. "You are overkind, sir. Yet I must confess, the woman in the portrait is not myself. It is my mother."

"Ah! Then it seems that such fine beauty has been refined even further in the embodiment of her daughter."

He strode about the parlor, examining various objects, finally remarking on the portraits flanking the mantel. "And this is . . . your father?"

Juliet nodded, taking a seat in her mother's chair, knowing that she should feel anger at this man's intrusion, but instead feeling totally the victim of his charm.

"And this is . . . ?"

"My brother, Robert."

"And where is your portrait, madame?" he questioned, turning about and taking a seat near Juliet to give his undivided attention to her reply.

"Mine, sir, was begun but never completed. The artist was interrupted by . . . several things, including the war, and he has not yet returned to the city."

"Were I an artist, nothing short of death would keep me from a subject of such perfection! Unless, of course, I felt myself incapable of doing justice to your loveliness with mere paint and canvas."

Juliet smiled indulgently at the handsome young man. She had been beset by flowery compliments before and was usually not amused. But there was something about those vivid boyish eyes that made Juliet feel that Michael Alford went about charming women as a matter of course. Instead of her normally cold reminder that she was promised to another man, Juliet challenged the lieutenant at his own game.

"If you do not claim to be an artist, Lieutenant, then do you spend all of your time turning innocent young women's heads with such extravagant adulation? Or have you some other occupation?"

"Obviously, madam, I am a soldier by profession. Beyond that, I claim to be nothing more than a poet, a minstrel of sorts, and a talented player of cards . . . not to mention a pleasant companion."

"I have no doubt of that, sir!" she commented wryly.

"I should like to engage you in a game of cards, madame. I believe the challenge would prove quite interesting—for both of us. Do you play?"

"Occasionally. I played a good deal while I was in England, but I found that most of the gentlemen players enjoyed the winning more than they enjoyed the game. They found losing somewhat intimidating, and since I played rather well, I found myself playing less and less."

His blue eyes squarely met the golden pair raised almost tauntingly. "I, too, have known a good many players who desire the laurels of victory too much. They cannot accept a loss that, if they were inclined to do so, might well improve their game. I usually cater to such opponents and allow them to win as a gesture of polite friendship. But I always win a hand or two to prove to myself that I am capable of doing so." He smiled. "I fear I may have just admitted to being one of those people who enjoys victory too much!"

"I confess that I also enjoy the winning, but only in a good contest. There is little elation in besting a poor opponent."

"Ah, madame, you speak what is in my heart! We must set up a game then, and soon. And may I say that I will very much enjoy finding out exactly how well you play."

"As I shall, sir. But I caution you, I intend to show no mercy and will expect to be dealt out the same."

His smile widened, much intrigued by this woman who wanted to be treated as an equal opponent. She was not the kind who would respond to being pampered and lied to. It would take something more to melt those beautiful golden eyes, and Michael Alford could not help but wonder exactly what that something might be. "Young and impressionable" her father had said, yet Michael's brief appraisal of Juliet Hampton already disagreed with that description. This was a woman who, much like himself, enjoyed a challenge. Yet, unlike him, she was a bit more honest in the role she played, not as interested in making or keeping friends. Michael knew a great many persons who would feel threatened by Juliet Hampton; he did not. He was confident that, like every other woman, she would eventually fall victim to his charm. But her game of romance would be well played, and he relished the thought of such a challenge.

It was nearly half an hour later when Lawrence Hampton found his way to the private parlor where his daughter was engaged in conversation with the young lieutenant. Unnoticed, he observed the arrogant tilt of his daughter's chin, though her eyes smiled her amusement as Michael related the story of his very first encounter with a horse.

"For the first time in my life, I was introduced to someone

who had absolutely no intention of becoming my friend. But my father thought it most important that I learn to ride properly, and he was watching, so . . ." He sighed, recalling the painful experience. "I gave that horse my warmest smile and got into the saddle, hoping for the best."

"Were you afraid?"

"Absolutely petrified. Even before he threw me."

"He threw you?" she repeated in amazement. "Why didn't your father choose a gentler animal for you to begin?"

"Because, my dear Miss Hampton, I had unfortunately told my father that I already knew how to ride."

"Why on earth did you do that?"

"Haven't you ever told a lie, or 'colored the truth' because you wanted so very much to please someone, to make them like you even if it was for the wrong reason?"

Juliet nodded thoughtfully. "Now that you ask, Lieutenant, I must plead guilty. But I hope less so now than when I was a child. . . ." She blinked self-consciously and turned the conversation back to her guest. "So you told your father the truth in a much more difficult and much more painful way."

"Why, no, madame! I would never admit to telling such a lie! I became so angry at that horse for rejecting my cordial offer of friendship that I hoisted myself right back into the saddle and took firm hold of the reins, just daring him to throw me again! It was not so much an act of temper, now that I think back, as it was my inability to accept defeat."

"And are you still unable to accept defeat? You said before that you did not mind losing at cards, if I recall."

Michael flashed his quick, warm smile. "I have learned a great deal about life since that time, about what is lost and what is gained. If I found a man who was my better at cards, or a woman, for that matter, I have no doubt that I should learn enough from my losing that I would soon be that one's equal. It is quite easy for me to give in on a point in question when I know that I am right, and eventually, as it is said, the truth will out. But to be bested by a mere equine? A beast ridden by men of capabilities far inferior to those I know myself to possess? No, madame! I would sooner expire than admit defeat in such a matter!"

Hampton listened carefully to this speech. Michael Alford did not impress him in the least. He was too handsome, too confident of his ability to charm; things simply came too easily to such a man to earn Hampton's respect. The young lieutenant would never amount to anything other than a well paid gigolo to some worldly middle-aged hag.

"I hope I have not kept you waiting too long, Lieutenant Alford, isn't it?"

"Yes, sir," answered Michael, rising from his seat to extend a hand to Juliet's father. "Lieutenant Michael Alford, sir, at your service. And you must be Lawrence Hampton. Your daughter has entertained me pleasantly in the interim, I can assure you."

"Good. I should prefer our meeting to take place in my study, if you don't mind. The place is more private, and we are less likely to be interrupted.

"Juliet, I told you a few days ago about a man who might be able to find your brother and his friend. This is the man of whom I spoke. You may join us in my study, if you will, for I believe you may be of some help."

Juliet's breath caught in her throat. Lieutenant Alford might be able to find Alec! For the first time in weeks she had felt a surge of real hope when her father had told her the news. She felt guilty now, reflecting on the time of frivolous conversation she had shared with the lieutenant. He could be the key to her happiness, to finding the man she loved! If only she had known!

Seated in her father's study, she could barely hold back the tide of questions that rushed to her lips, but having promised to let her father handle the arrangements, she kept her silence. He spoke of Robert first, then of Alec as his dearest friend and a close relative of guests presently residing with the Hamptons. That also had been a part of their agreement, that her marriage to Alec remain a secret until he was found, and even afterward, until they could be married in a public and proper ceremony. Juliet had happily complied with this, not wanting Alec to know that she had completely confided in her father against his wishes.

"We have reason to believe that the man was captured, as Juliet saw his horse in the possession of several British soldiers one day about a month ago. We can give you a good enough description of the animal so that you will be able to find it, I am confident of that. As far as my son is concerned, I have very little information. But I believe that he is still with the Continental Army."

Michael had taken a few quick notes as her father spoke. "Did you know, sir," he said, "that nearly four and a half thousand prisoners were counted as of the third of December last? Due to the kindness and generosity of General Howe, about fifteen hundred were released to be returned to their homes. As you may be aware, many were farmers who had been caught up in the spirit of the fight and now, having had their taste of war, wanted only to be returned to their families before the coldest days of winter. This leaves well over twenty-five hundred men who were captured and are still held as prisoners of war. Exchanges will be made for a good many of them. The reported number of prisoners taken by Washington's army at Trenton and Princeton will surely mean that an exchange will be arranged soon. I assume you know about the victory the 'Old Fox' managed to pull off the day after Christmas?"

Juliet and her father nodded. The city had buzzed for days about the surprise attack made by an army generally thought to be finished, under a general known best for his ability to retreat, against some of the best trained soldiers of Europe: the Hessians.

"What I am trying to say is that it is no small undertaking to locate one man among a thousand similar men. The fact that the man is an officer may help, as officers are generally quartered separately—but not always, especially lower ranking ones." He sighed before going on. "I would very much like to help you, and I shall do all that I can. But you must understand that there is a chance I will not find the man. There is a chance that he is not a prisoner at all."

His gaze fell on Juliet's pleading golden eyes, and his next words were for her alone. "I promise you that I shall do whatever I can to help you. But some things are out of my hands entirely, you must understand that."

Hampton was quick to answer the remark. "We do understand, Lieutenant. We will give you all the information we can, and we appreciate whatever help you can give us in return."

They spent at least another quarter of an hour listing a detailed description of both men and whatever information might be pertinent and helpful in locating them. When they had finished, Michael noted the strain in Juliet's face and impulsively reached for her hand.

"Most of the prisoners are kept decently and allotted a fair amount of food—two-thirds of what a regular soldier is dealt out, as a matter of fact. It is not quite so bad as rumors would have you think."

Juliet gratefully attempted a smile that did not reach her eyes. Thinking of Alec made her feel sad, lonely, helpless, and even Lieutenant Alford's kind words could not ease the burden of such despondency.

Hampton's mouth tightened at the gesture, while his eyes hardened to chips of cold steel. "I am certain that my daughter is most anxious for you to begin working on this," he stated coldly, rising to pour himself and the lieutenant a glass of wine. "Juliet, if you could leave us to discuss the man's fee, perhaps he could begin straight away."

It was a subtle reminder to his daughter that the man was performing a task for which he would be paid, not a favor out of the goodness of his heart. Juliet pulled her hand away and, with a brief nod to Lieutenant Alford, left the room. Hampton closed the door behind her, then returned to his desk and offered the lieutenant the wine.

"Mmm." Michael smiled his admiration. "Sir, I am impressed! By the wine"—he sipped again—"as well as by your daughter."

"I am sure that after meeting her you understand completely why I want to rid her mind of this . . . soldier. She is obviously meant for better things."

From the slow, deliberate inflection in his voice, Michael realized that Hampton's words were a reminder that he intended her to marry a nobleman, a gentle way of saying "Hands off."

"Have you come by any information?"

"As a matter of fact, sir, I have done a good deal of work, and I am certain that you will be pleased with my results." He placed his wine on the desk and withdrew a small notebook from his breast pocket. He read over his notations before he spoke.

"The green feather proved to be a very helpful clue, sir. I located the three young soldiers the very next day, and I know where the horse in question is kept. He is a great, strong creature, very particular about his master. No one can ride him, but after a drink or two someone is always willing to try, and a good bit of wagering is done on the outcome. There is a lot of talk about this stallion being the property of one man, and there are many who believe he will never be ridden by any other."

Hampton sighed almost impatiently. "I am happy to know that you have been working on this, Lieutenant, but I have no real interest in the horse, other than the fact that it might lead us to the man."

Michael tossed Hampton an undisturbed grin before returning his attention to his book. "The stallion was brought to the city from Fort Washington with considerable difficulty, as you told me, a few weeks after its capture, so I assumed that Captain Farrell was at the fort at the time it was stormed. This posed a minor problem, because many of the soldiers engaged in that fight were Hessians who do not speak English. I have a friend who speaks German, however, and with his help I was back in business.

"There were few casualties at the fort, but several hundred prisoners were taken that day and marched to the city that same night to be placed in the various jails. Captain Farrell was not placed in any one of them at first. A rather odd tale surrounds his capture. He apparently was one of the few who tried to fight, or so I surmise, for he was wounded—seriously—in the head. The wound caused him to appear quite dead for hours, and he was even tossed unceremoniously with the unfortunates who had met that fate. While the other prisoners were marched off, a few particularly ambitious Hessians were stripping the corpses of anything of value. One of them came upon a body a bit warmer than the rest, who sorely protested being relieved of his personal possessions. It took four men to subdue him, and each and every one of them swore to me that the man was not human. 'The Demon' they called him, 'with eyes like black fire,' they said. He was taken to the provost and was moved to the Sugar House jail on Liberty Street a few days ago. I saw the man myself. He seems quite well, under the circumstances, although the guard told me that he lapses into unconsciousness at odd times for no apparent reason."

Hampton drew a long, deep breath and could not suppress the smile of satisfaction already curving his lips. "Are you absolutely certain that you have the right man?"

"Quite, sir! Not only did I talk at length with the guard, but one of the Hessians came with me to identify the man at the prison a fortnight ago as the same one they had captured that night." He paused for effect before reaching into his shirt and withdrawing a small leather pouch. "The soldier who accompanied me and identified Captain Farrell sold me this."

He plunged thumb and forefinger into the pouch and retrieved a long gold chain with an unusual medallion dangling at its end. Hampton's eyes brightened.

"You have done well, Lieutenant! Very well! And I intend to pay you very well. More wine?"

He rose to refill the glasses while considering what his next move ought to be. So Captain Farrell was at the Liberty Street jail, and in good health. Well, he could not remain there, for there were quite a few people in New York who knew the man. If a single one recognized him, then Hampton's plans would be for naught. No, Alexander Farrell had to be removed, had to be put somewhere where he could not interfere with Juliet's marriage to Harold.

Hampton's eyes narrowed on the congenial young lieutenant who sat opposite. He did not like the man, he certainly did not trust him, and Michael's familiar concern for Juliet had rubbed him the wrong way. His instincts were to pay the man off and be rid of him. And yet, he had to remember that the man was a fine actor, extremely convincing. His solicitude for Juliet had seemed so sincere, yet he had possessed knowledge of Captain Farrell all the time he offered his meager words of comfort. Hampton could not afford to find a replacement who might prove inferior, and he did not want any gossip spread about his interest in Alexander Farrell that might cast suspicion on himself or his daughter. The fewer people involved, the quieter things would remain. Lieutenant Alford already knew too much, a bit more would make no difference.

Resting folded hands on his chest, Hampton carefully chose his words. "As I told you before, I shall need you to convince my daughter that the man is dead. I am certain that it will pose no problem for you to slightly alter the story you have just told me. The only problem I foresee is the man's proximity to us. That is, if he is recognized by any one of scores of people who are acquainted with him, it would, of course, ruin our plan."

"That may not pose a problem for very long, sir. He has been a model prisoner, except for the single incident of his capture, and will most probably be one of the first offered for an exchange. In that case, he will soon be gone from the city."

Hampton's eyes flashed angrily. "Freed? Do you mean to tell me the man will be set free?"

Michael gave a brief laugh. "I do not set policy for the prisoners, sir, but I can tell you what a tremendous burden these men have been to the army. I believe that General Howe is much more interested in getting back his own soldiers than he is in housing and feeding the poor unfortunates who have been captured."

A muscle near Hampton's mouth twitched as he deliberately ground out his next words. "The man must not be set free, do you understand? I want him in chains!"

Michael swallowed nervously. "I understand, sir. And perhaps I could arrange that, for a price. There are a great many men who will accept a bribe, and I know which of them can be trusted to be discreet. I am fairly certain I could 'un-arrange' his exchange, if you wish."

"That is not good enough!" Hampton insisted. Rising from his chair he began to pace the floor, his hands clenched so tightly at his sides that they actually trembled. After several moments he stopped, and when he turned to Michael his eyes held a strange gleam. "I heard something recently, something very interesting and helpful, if it is true."

Michael cocked his head, fully attentive.

"There is a story about a group of prisoners, taken in Quebec, being put on a ship bound for Africa. Have you heard that rumor?"

"Yes, sir, as a matter of fact I have. There has been a good deal of talk about it, and about the possibilities of transporting other prisoners elsewhere, as New York is so overcrowded. But I don't think it will be organized on a grand scale—there are simply too many protests to the practice."

"But it does happen," Hampton pressed.

"In a few cases . . ."

"I am interested in only one case!" he snapped back hotly.

He paused to sip his wine and calm himself. "There is a ship half-loaded in the harbor, the *Springstorm*. It will set sail for Antigua in the Indies the twelfth of January. I want Captain Farrell on that ship, and I want you, Lieutenant Alford, to put him there. I am prepared to pay you one thousand pounds, as well as whatever it costs you to bribe the necessary persons."

A thousand pounds! That was a great deal of money! Invested properly, Michael might achieve his fondest dream—returning home wealthy and self-supporting, and, eventually, purchasing a title of his own. He could ill afford to turn down such a generous offer. Moreover, Lawrence Hampton was a determined man. If Michael refused to comply after being taken into his confidence, he would have made himself a very dangerous enemy. Hampton would find someone else to do his bidding anyway, he reasoned, so it might as well be himself.

"Please continue, sir," Michael said.

Hampton nodded, his smile knowing. "First, you will make the necessary arrangements with the guards. Let them lie about what happened to him. There should not be much fuss over a single prisoner quietly being taken elsewhere. Second, you will personally see to it that he is on that ship. You should be able to handle the man alone, Lieutenant. I have heard that the jails are quite cold and overcrowded and the rations small, so that his strength ought to have suffered a good bit by this time. And he will be bound, of course. You will take him to the docks just after eight in the evening, on the eleventh of this month. I will make sure that the captain of the ship expects you. He will know what to do with Farrell from there. You have your work cut out for you, Lieutenant."

"I am certain I will be able to handle it, sir. Now about your son . . . I am sorry to say that I have little information about him. I found many a man who swore to me he could deliver a letter to someone in Washington's army, but the world is full of people who make promises and nearly empty of those who feel obligated to keep them. At any rate, I have sent off several notes of concern to your son, and I promised to pay well for any replies I receive."

Hampton nodded with detached interest. The thought of eliminating Farrell from his life was intoxicating, but still it did not satisfy him completely. As Michael gathered his papers together to leave, Hampton made one final request.

"There is something else I want you to do, Lieutenant."

Michael abruptly stopped and listened. "Yes, sir?"

"After Farrell is securely settled on board the *Springstorm,* I want you to tell him who it was that put him there. And I want you to tell him that Juliet will marry Lord Harold, after all . . . that he is due to arrive in the spring." He gave a short, mirthless laugh. "A pity the captain will miss the ceremony."

"Is that all, sir?"

Hampton drew a deep breath and arched a brow in amusement. "I'm sure that will be quite enough, Lieutenant."

Chapter 29

The eleventh day of January was a clear, crisp day. Allan had returned to Hampton House the day before, announcing that he and Mary would be gathering their possessions and moving to the house on his property near Tarrytown. It was a small house, he had said, a cottage of only four rooms. But it was in good repair and located in a pleasant setting with access to firewood and less than a day's travel from the city. In Tarrytown, Allan had found a handyman of sorts whom he had hired to chop wood and do the other heavy chores.

Juliet helped with the packing, and both she and Frances were surprised when Mary announced that she was again with child. Promising to visit as soon as the warmer weather arrived, they had bid their tearful good-byes late that morning. Juliet had a special hug for little Edgar, whose rocking horse had been tied atop the wagon. She would miss him most of all, for in a few short weeks the little boy had burrowed his way into her heart.

Later in the afternoon, Juliet began the elaborate preparations necessary for making a fair appearance at the Cotillion that evening. First a warm bath with scented soap, followed by oils to keep the skin from drying. Then Rachel arranged her hair in an elaborately fashionable coiffure to compliment a new gown made especially for the occasion. It was of antique white satin, with an overskirt of light yellow, and a neckline trimmed in delicate yellow lace, with flounces of the same lace at the end of snug-fitting half-sleeves. Frances wore a similar gown of light blue trimmed in white, and both wore tiny diamond studs in the curls piled intricately high atop their heads.

Neither was looking forward to the affair, for they had had their fill of overzealous British officers anxious to bed anything in skirts and even more anxious to brag about their conquests. It was harder for Frances, Juliet thought, for she was quiet and shy, and her parents were not here to protect her, while Lawrence Hampton repeatedly deflected unwanted suitors by pointedly mentioning Juliet's engagement to Lord Harold.

Juliet frowned now, recalling her father's insistence that no one be told of the letter she had written Harold breaking their engagement. "The man loves you, Juliet," he had said, "and when we are certain that your letter has reached him and have given him time to recover a measure of his pride, then we shall announce that the engagement has been broken. But until then, I will not have the gossips carrying the news to him before he has the chance to read your words of explanation."

He had given her letter to Captain Shelton just a few weeks before, and when the captain returned to New York in the spring and assured them that the message was safely delivered, then Juliet would finally put an end to the lie. Father was right, of course. She had no reason to hurt Harold, yet pretending to be a part of the flashy social life of New York these days was a task she would like to have seen finished. With a great many young men seeking feminine companionship an ocean away from wives and sweethearts, and the social darlings being General Howe, newly knighted, and his married mistress, Mrs. Loring, morals had declined to an alarming extent. Neither Juliet nor Frances wanted to be a part of the devil-may-care, live-for-today mentality that permeated the parties they attended.

Tonight at her window, in her splendid gown, her jewels glittering in the shrouded moonlight, Juliet watched the mists rising from the ground in the cold night air. As the clock in the hallway chimed a monotonous seven bells, an icy prickling of fear took hold of her. Her heart thudded loudly in her breast, and her hands grew cold and clammy. She knew no reason for her sudden terror; it was an eerie sensation of someone or something trying to reach her, calling her name. She made her way from her room to the parlor, where she poured herself a glass of brandy, her hands trembling so violently that she spilled a good deal of it. She hurriedly gulped it down and poured another. As the warmth spread from her throat throughout her body, she began to get hold of herself, and finally her hands stilled, her heartbeat slowed. But she could not completely shake the feeling that something terrible was about to happen, and that she was powerless to stop it.

In the thickening fog that rolled in from the sea and mingled with mists rising from the land, a young soldier nudged another man, taller and a few years older, into a small boat. In the meager light, the shadows clouded the differences between the two: the fair, healthy, blue-eyed man and the dark, thin, black-eyed one. The older took his seat with difficulty, for the fact that his hands were bound in front of him made his balance in the boat precarious. The younger lowered his pistol, which had been leveled at the other, and thrust it into his belt, his eyes quickly surveying the deserted docks before he stepped into the boat himself.

Taking his seat, he began to row, and after several moments his breath became labored. When he paused to rest, he found the fog had draped a confusing curtain of white all about him. The poor visibility worried him, but he reasoned away his fear. He did not have far to go, and if he kept in the same direction, he would surely reach the *Springstorm* safely. Nervously he began to speak, as much to himself as to the man across from him.

"Not a fine night for rowing," he remarked as he gave the oars a thrust. "Damned fog will have me going in circles if I'm not careful."

Though the other said nothing, his dark eyes glowed like two shiny pieces of coal, and the soldier saw him shiver in the damp night air.

"You ought to be more comfortable where you're going. At least it won't be so damned cold."

"Where am I going?" the prisoner asked sullenly.

"To the Indies, if I ever get to that ship."

"The Indies? Why all the trouble to take me out to this ship?"

Michael concentrated on the rowing, unaccustomed to the physical effort it took to continue. "Because, my dear fellow," he grunted as he thrust the oars through the dark waters, "someone wants you out of New York."

"Who?"

"Can't you guess?"

There was no response. The man was certainly not much of a conversationalist, he mused. He looked at the threadbare clothing and noted the man's gaunt face. He could not help but wonder what Miss Hampton saw in him.

With a grimace, Michael took hold of the oars and began again to row. "Lawrence Hampton," he said, straining to pull against the water, "said to tell you that his daughter will marry Lord Harold when he arrives in the spring."

Silence fell as heavy as the deep mist, until at length Alec snorted in disbelief and turned his face away.

"I'm afraid it's true," Michael insisted. "Hampton has everything planned, except for one small item, that is. . . ." He heaved a groan as the muscles tightened in his arms. "Once you are out of the way, Juliet may take Lord Harold for her husband, but she will most certainly take me for her lover."

Except for the incident of his capture, Captain Farrell had been docile and quiet. Michael was taken completely by surprise, therefore, when the man made a reckless dive directly for him, nearly capsizing the tiny vessel in the icy waters. In the struggle that ensued, Alec groped wildly for the pistol, but his bound hands prevented him from getting a firm hold on it. When Michael shoved against him with all his might, the gun went flying into the air, dropping a few seconds later with a plunk into the water.

"You lie!" Alec screamed. His bound hands just missed Michael's face and struck painfully on the wooden planks of the boat as he fell forward.

The man was insane, Michael thought in panic. He squirmed to the floor of the boat, trying desperately to keep it balanced. He had never been a good swimmer, and at this point he had no idea even which way to swim. In the eerie gray shroud of fog, a pair of black eyes glowed with hatred above him, making Michael fear for his life. Alec raised his bruised and bloody hands again to strike, but Michael lifted both his feet to Alec's chest, and, with all his strength, he heaved him overboard.

At the splash, Michael took a deep breath and slowly raised himself in the boat. Let the man get a taste of death, he thought, and he would learn to behave decently. Patiently he waited for the sounds of the man struggling in the cold waters. Moments passed. There was nothing except the eerie slapping of the tiny waves against the side of the boat. Michael strained his eyes, but the fog was like a dense cloud. He could see nothing.

He blew on his hands to warm them, but the cold fear that penetrated his body was not from the January sea air. Alexander Farrell was gone. Escaped. No! Not escaped, Michael assured himself. Drowned. Surely no man could find his way to shore in this fog. And with hands bound, he could not even swim. The water was like ice; it would numb and cramp a body until movement was impossible. No, Alexander Farrell would not survive. And what difference if the man be in Antigua or Hell? Either way he was gone, he rationalized. The *Springstorm* would sail on the morrow, so who would be the wiser? Michael drew a ragged breath and began to row in what he hoped was the direction of shore. He never knew that he had nearly collided with another small vessel, which had also lost direction in the fog.

Jacob Merriman was a quiet man, a Quaker, who went fishing on occasion, when his jobs as a joiner were scarce and failed to feed his wife and himself. With the high cost of firewood as well as housing, few people could afford to contract his services. The only ones with money these days were the very rich, who ordered the more fashionable furniture from England and France.

And so it was that Jacob Merriman found himself alone on that fog-draped night in New York Harbor. Alone, until he noticed a figure futilely struggling to keep afloat in the icy water.

Chapter 30

The final weeks of January and the first weeks of February, Lawrence Hampton played a difficult game of waiting. He was holding a pat hand now, and the letter that he had recently intercepted from Harold assured him that all was proceeding smoothly. Harold would be making arrangements for his voyage any day now, and Captain Shelton would not reach England for another few weeks. Harold would be gone before he could deliver Juliet's letter. Shelton was a good man, and Hampton was glad he had him now that Adam Barkley was gone. He sneered as he remembered his former business partner. Barkley would pay for his stupidity; Hampton intended to see to that.

But Juliet's marriage came first. He could hardly help but gloat at the power that would soon be his. The Medford holdings included a shipyard, of all things, though early indications were that it was in sore need of attention. Hampton would see to that, as well as to the other investments that bore infinite possibilities for profit, even if current returns were small. When he had promised several months before to visit Juliet once she was in England, he had done so with good reason, for there were many things he intended to do personally. He sighed his anticipation. Patience, patience, he counseled. It would not be much longer. And with Alexander Farrell halfway to the Indies by now, what part of his plan could possibly go awry?

Michael Alford swung off his horse and tethered him

haphazardly at the gatepost. Whistling "Yankee Doodle," that cheery tune the rebels claimed as an anthem of sorts, he skipped up the steps to the main entrance of Hampton House and rapped on the door in time to his own music. He gave the stern-faced James a smiling salute as he entered the hallway with the confidence of one who belonged there. With an almost indiscernible sigh and a slight raise of his brows, the butler formally acknowledged the visitor, leading him at once to Hampton's study. He was expected.

Inside the study Juliet paced nervously, pausing every now and then to interrupt her father's concentration on a stack of papers at his desk. "He did not tell you anything?" she asked for the third time.

Without raising his eyes, her father answered in a tone reflecting remote interest. "You read the note. You know as much as I do."

"He knows something, it said that much," she said positively. "But that was all it said," she added in disappointment.

"He will be here at any moment, Juliet. Why don't you sit down and relax." He shuffled through his papers as though searching for something in particular, but before he had found what he was looking for, James announced Lieutenant Alford's arrival.

Michael nodded a greeting to the man behind the desk, then turned his full attention on the vision of loveliness that was his daughter. She was even prettier than he remembered, with an excited flush in her cheeks and bright anticipation in her eyes. He would like to have been the cause of that animated state, he thought, and soon enough, he would be.

Michael took a seat, and Hampton put aside his business, while Juliet perched on the very edge of her chair and seemed ready to spring forth at the first mention of her husband's name.

"Do calm yourself, Juliet," her father scolded. "You look as though you are going to attack the young man rather than listen to him."

Self-consciously, Juliet settled back in her chair and tried to keep from wringing her hands, but her heart pounded so loudly that her head ached, and her breath still came as if she'd just run a mile.

"First," Michael began, opening a packet of papers on a space Hampton had cleared on his desk, "I have some encouraging news concerning your brother." He turned to Hampton briefly. "Your son. The man who brought me these"—he lifted two sheets of folded parchment—"assured me that the man who wrote them was in tolerable good health, though he was in sore need of a bath and a change of clothing."

Juliet took the proffered letters, noting by the smudges that a good many people had examined them before her. Before she asked, Michael offered her an explanation.

"Not wanting to be hanged as a spy, Miss Hampton, any correspondence I pass on is open to the scrutiny of my superior officers. I am sure you understand."

Juliet nodded as she skimmed the missive. Robert was alive and well, but she had somehow felt that he was safe all along, and this merely confirmed her feelings. The letter addressed to Juliet mentioned that he had not seen Alec in a long time. The second letter was addressed to Frances, and Juliet would not read that without permission.

"Thank you, Lieutenant. Frances will be so happy, as well as relieved."

The lieutenant flashed her a winning smile, which faded as he fingered the remainder of the papers before him. After a brief sidelong glance at Hampton, Michael's gaze leveled squarely on Juliet. "I am sorry to inform you, Miss Hampton, that the remainder of my news is rather distressing. From the information you gave me about the horse, I was able to locate the animal as well as the men who brought it that day from Fort Washington to the city." He paused and frowned, thoughtfully measuring his next words. "There were not many casualties in the fall of that fortress, and for that reason I was able to come by this information. Speaking with three Hessian soldiers—or rather," he amended, "I had a friend of mine who speaks fluent German do so—each told an identical story. The man who rode that horse was among the few who chose to fight rather than surrender."

Juliet's heart skipped a beat, and the color drained swiftly from her face. "What are you trying to say, Lieutenant?" she asked.

"Miss Hampton," Michael pleaded kindly, "you would not want me to relate the gruesome details of the incident, I am sure—"

"But I would, Lieutenant," she interrupted him to insist. "I want you to tell me exactly what you know!"

Michael nervously moistened his lips and momentarily sought guidance from Juliet's father. But the steeled countenance of the older man offered no help; it was completely up to Michael at this point. With a sigh of resignation, he lifted the first page of his notes, though he had rehearsed the tale quite enough so that it was hardly necessary for him to read them.

"As I said, he was one of the few who chose to fight. He was cut down by musket fire, but even then he would not be subdued. He fired his pistol, then tossed it aside and fought with his bare hands. Two of the Hessians took hold of him and held him fast, while a third drove a bayonet into—"

Juliet's scream of protest cut him short. "No! I don't believe you! You're wrong! He is not dead! He cannot be!" She stood before him now, violently shaking her head, her chest heaving painfully.

Hampton silently moved to get his daughter a glass of wine, still leaving Michael to convince her of the "truth."

"I am truly sorry, Miss Hampton," he said quietly.

"You have made a mistake, Lieutenant!" she accused.

"There is no mistake, Miss Hampton. I was very, very thorough in the work I did. If there were a chance—any chance at all—that the man they killed was not Captain Farrell, I certainly would not tell you that it was. But I am convinced beyond a reasonable doubt, Miss Hampton, and to allow you to exist for months, perhaps years, on false hope is, I believe, much crueler than telling the truth now, the truth that will come out in the end."

"But you cannot be sure, Lieutenant Alford!" she insisted angrily. "Who identified the body? Did you ever see the body?"

"No, I did not. But—"

"Juliet!" Hampton's voice rang out a note of unquestionable authority. "This man has no reason to lie to you! Allow him to speak his piece."

In deference to her father's order, Juliet resumed her seat

and held her tongue, but the effort of doing so brought painful tears to her eyes.

Michael drew a lengthy breath and resumed in his calm, quiet voice. "I assure you, Miss Hampton, this is not a duty I enjoy performing, but I have gone to considerable lengths to uncover the truth, and I must tell you what that truth is." He paused, seeing by the gleam in those hard golden eyes that she remained unconvinced of his story. "The three men with whom I spoke remembered the man. They described him to perfection: his height, his build, his uniform, and his eyes. 'Devil's eyes,' they called them, and there is more. One of the men told me that he took something from the body." Juliet's eyes widened with fear, and her lip trembled uncontrollably as Michael produced a leather pouch from his breast pocket, and withdrew the gold chain and medallion. "Perhaps this will mean something to you, Miss Hampton."

Every trace of defiant hope faded from Juliet's face. She had told no one of the neckchain, not even Frances. It could only mean that Lieutenant Alford spoke the truth. As the realization took hold, she sat motionless, absolutely numb. It was as if she were in another world; surely this was only a bad dream! It could not happen! Not to Alec! Not to the man she loved! She stared dumbly at the gleaming circle of gold, unaware of the tears that coursed silently down her cheeks, of the glass of wine her father had placed in her hand, which dropped to the floor. The medallion seemed to swell and waver, the room became oddly blurred before darkening completely, and she knew only a brief, sharp pain to the side of her head before her mind found peace in the comforting blackness.

After summoning a physician to be certain that the head wound she had suffered when she fainted was not serious, Lawrence Hampton saw his daughter safely tucked into bed. Then he returned to the lieutenant, who waited nervously for him in the study.

"You did very well, Lieutenant," he remarked with a smile after he had closed the door.

"Your daughter is all right?" Michael queried with some concern.

"She will recover," he answered smugly. "Broken hearts

do mend, and with my help, I can assure you, this one will mend with hardly a scar."

"I did not realize that she cared so deeply. . . ."

"Come now, Lieutenant. She's better off without him."

Michael sighed uneasily, then shook his head. "I was simply not prepared for her reaction, sir. Had I known . . ."

Hampton gave a short laugh. "Now is hardly the time for an attack of conscience, Lieutenant. You have done your job well, and the time has come to be paid." He opened the drawer of his desk and plunked down a pouch of coins. "Count it, if you wish, but you will find that it is all there. One thousand pounds."

"One thousand pounds," Michael repeated distantly, feeling far less elation in accepting payment than he had anticipated.

"Would you like to give me a tally of the other expenses you incurred along the way? At the moment, you will find my purse strings easily loosened."

Michael handed over the sheet of his expenses, and Hampton counted out the amount shown. Feeling very much like Judas as he gathered up the pieces of silver, Michael mouthed a brief and disinterested farewell and eagerly made his way from the scene of the crime.

While Hampton was chuckling at the tardy appearance of a conscience in the handsome young lieutenant, Michael was struggling with a terrible sense of guilt. He had never purposely hurt anyone before, and certainly no one he admired as much as he did Juliet Hampton. The money felt heavy in his pocket, as if he had hung a millstone about his neck. He would have to do something, somehow, to ease this awesome burden from his shoulders. He would have to make it up to her—yes, that was exactly what he would do! He would fill Juliet's life with joy and laughter until she had completely recovered from her sorrow. There was no reason why she would not fall victim to his charm, as every other woman in his life had done. But this time it would be different. He would not pursue Juliet for the mere sake of conquest; he would pay court to her for her own sake, for he felt he owed her that much. The resolution lightened his heart, and he took to the road with vigor, sure of his ability to nullify whatever harm he had done.

* * *

In a small, quiet house on the northeast corner of Manhattan, Sarah Merriman spooned warm broth into a young man's mouth, frowning her concern as convulsive shivers took hold of his lean form despite his proximity to a fire. Lines etched her normally smooth forehead, and she pursed her lips, wishing she could offer the man more comfort, or at least another warm blanket. He had been here nearly a month now, and his health had improved somewhat. But whenever he seemed on the verge of recovery, the fever and vomiting would return with a terrible suddenness, robbing him of the strength it took so long to amass. As she gently sponged the beads of perspiration from his pale brow, Sarah could not help but think what a handsome man he was. Even the deep shadows about his eyes could not take away their strange, hypnotic power, and the aristocratic line of nose and mouth spoke of fine blood, despite the heavy beard that covered the chiseled shape of his chin.

Sarah had spent long hours caring for the man these past weeks, and he had not been the first unfortunate Jacob had pulled from the harbor. She had known an attachment to every one of them. It was the way of the Quakers to offer friendship, and in doing so they had often been caught in the middle of this war. Sadly she remembered the taunts and jeers that the young soldiers had heaped on them this past summer. It was not difficult for a woman to endure such things, but the men had been sorely pricked by the insults, and as a result, some of them had turned their backs on their religion in an effort to prove themselves men. Young David Merriman had been one of these. Finding it impossible to turn the other cheek, he had followed a Rhode Islander by the name of Nathanael Greene, who had also been a Friend, and had joined in the fight for independence.

The man before her now looked nothing like her David, yet he reminded her of him as each of the others had. As he opened his eyes, a wan smile of gratitude spread over his face. Sarah set the cloth aside and wondered if the young man wanted to talk. They usually did.

"How . . . ?" The man strained against a tight, dry throat to speak, but the best he could manage was a hoarse whisper.

"My husband was out fishing and was lost in the fog. With the grace of the Almighty, he found both thee and the shore."

Alec swallowed hard and tried again to speak. "Quakers?"

"Yes, we are Friends. Please do not try to speak. Thee are very weak from the fever. Thee were a prisoner?"

Alec nodded and heaved a weary sigh.

Sarah smiled at the man. It was the first time he had remained conscious long enough to answer any of her questions. "Thee has been with us the better part of two fortnights."

Alec's eyes widened in disbelief, and she nodded at his unspoken inquiry. "Thy fever broke, then returned again and again. We prayed for thy recovery."

Alec's eyes almost filled with tears. He could not voice his appreciation now, but he silently vowed that he would someday repay his debt.

"Art thou from New York?"

Alec shook his head.

"I thought not." She frowned thoughtfully for a moment. "Thee must conserve thy strength, but if thee could tell me thy name, and where thy home is, perhaps we might get a message to thy family."

After several attempts, Sarah finally repeated his name correctly and understood that he was from Virginia.

"It would be difficult for a message to find its way so far, but surely not impossible. In God, all things are possible," she smiled.

Alec struggled to say more, but the woman cautioned him against too much exertion. Finally, his energy spent, his head lolled back on the bed, and he was quickly asleep.

Chapter 31

Lawrence Hampton nervously drummed his fingers on his desk, unable to concentrate on his work. It had been a week since Juliet had been informed of her husband's death, and things were not exactly going as he had hoped. The girl was almost like a corpse herself, and nothing succeeded in rousing her from her sullen silence. Why, she had not even eaten much more than bread and broth since that day. By the time Harold arrives, he thought, she will be little more than a scarecrow! And how, in heaven's name, could he prepare her for Harold's arrival in just a few weeks, much less ever convince her to go through with the wedding? The most recent note from Harold confirmed his plans to arrive the first of April. Perhaps she would listen to Frances. He had urged the girl to talk with his daughter, and at this very moment she was with Juliet, hopefully breaking through to her. Damned regrettable, this depression of hers. Lawrence Hampton never liked having to alter his plans. . . .

Upstairs in Juliet's room, Frances was doing her best to draw Juliet from the wall she had built about herself, closing in all her feelings, all her pain. ". . . and I thought perhaps we could go shopping today," Frances was saying, receiving the familiar blank gaze in response. Sighing her frustration, she went to stand close by Juliet, who was near the window, and after a few moments she began to cry. She tried to hold it back for Juliet's sake, but she could not. The long days of loneliness and uncertainty, the emotional hardships of the war were catching up with her. And Juliet, who was so much stronger and braver than she could ever hope to be, even Juliet had buckled and fallen under the weight of her hurt. How could she bear it? She needed Robert. She needed Allan. She needed her mother. She needed someone! But there was no one here to help her. She felt so alone.

As a sob shook her slender frame, something in Juliet responded to the need, a distant voice reminding her of a promise made long ago. "Don't cry, Frances," she said quietly. "Please don't cry."

Frances shook her head slowly, and her voice cracked with sadness. "I loved Alec, too, Juliet!"

With a suddenness that Frances found frightening, Juliet broke down into hysterical tears. Once she had begun to cry, she cried until she fell to her knees in utter exhaustion. Frances sobbed with her, taking her head to her breast and doing her best to give comfort as she rocked her like a small child.

"Why did he have to die?" Juliet asked, painful sobs tearing at the words. "He promised me he would come back! He promised me!"

Frances took her face in both hands, struggling to find the words that would ease Juliet's heartache.

"Robert told me once that you never backed away from a challenge. This is the greatest challenge you will ever have to face, I think, going on without him. But there are people who want to help you; you don't have to do it alone! Your father has been so very worried about you!"

Juliet closed her eyes, knowing that Frances was right. She owed it to Alec's memory to go on living, and she owed something to her father, too, if no one else. But she had no strength left in her; she was so tired! Frances helped her into bed after extracting a promise that she would eat dinner when it was sent up to her, or after she awakened. Tiptoeing out of the room, Frances wearily leaned her weight against the door. She drew a deep breath to steady herself, then made her way downstairs to Hampton's study to inform him that Juliet was finally facing her loss and would now begin trying to live with her grief.

Keeping busy seemed to ease the pain, and as night was still the most difficult time to cope with the loneliness, Juliet filled her evenings with social engagements and slept late into the day. She also spent a great deal of her time with the Reverend Helscher and found her charity work more rewarding than ever. The first days of March were exceptionally warm, and Juliet and Frances used them to good advantage, making numerous shopping expeditions in town. Loaded down one day with various packages, Frances, Juliet, and Rachel made their way along the crowded walkway to their carriage. As she handed over her parcels to the coachman, Juliet was hailed by a friendly voice. She whirled about to face a breathless Michael Alford, who had just completed a lengthy sprint to talk with her.

"Miss Hampton!" He smiled warmly, ignoring the timid, almost fearful look that crept into her face as memories of their last meeting flooded her mind. He took hold of her arm and steered her from the heavy flow of traffic. "I am so happy to see you looking so well! I had heard that you were ill."

"I am quite well, thank you," she managed coolly.

"I can see that you are!" he said. "I had hoped that I might stop by your home some day. I thought perhaps you might enjoy riding with me."

"That is very kind of you, sir, but I think not." She refused with a curt finality, turning away just in time to catch Rachel's disapproving stare.

"It's not really kindness, Miss Hampton," he hastened to assure her. "It's selfishness. I would truly appreciate your company."

Juliet turned to face him once more. "Thank you again, Lieutenant, but I am very busy, and I simply could not find the time."

Her behavior was hardly encouraging, but Michael was persistent. "I thought perhaps it might help you to be with someone who knew about your loss. That way, you would not have to hide your feelings."

Juliet eyed the man coldly. She did not appreciate his attempts to invade her privacy, and she wanted to make that perfectly clear. "I have my father and a good many dear friends, Lieutenant, with whom I share my feelings. I feel no obligation to share them with a casual acquaintance, which is all that you are to me. Good day."

She turned away from him one last time and let the coachman assist her into the carriage. She was concentrating so on

regaining her composure that she missed the scowl that darkened Rachel's brow.

Michael Alford was not one to lose heart after a single cold
rebuff, particularly one from a beautiful young woman. When
he discovered that Juliet was in attendance now at nearly
every important party, he went about securing invitations to
those same functions. The first few had proved difficult for a
mere lieutenant to obtain, but he had then spent the entire
evening heaping lavish attention on women who were generally ignored, thrilling them with his gallant charm. He sang
ballads of his own composition, played guitar and flute, and
had enough poetry committed to memory to serve any and all
occasions. In short order he made himself a most entertaining
addition to a party, and his name soon appeared on everyone's guest list.

It was not long before Lieutenant Alford felt sure enough of
his position to make his play for Juliet Hampton. At first he
asked her to dance, nothing more. But soon he was singling
her out from the crowd, dancing with her several times in one
evening, drawing her into conversation, and finally, after repeated refusals to do so, she agreed to join him in a game of
cards. She lost to him the first few hands, and she presently
found herself deeply engrossed in the game, analyzing his
moves, remembering what cards had fallen. Never had she
met an opponent who matched her so evenly. Remembering
what he had said to her when they first met, she forced herself
to learn something from every loss. Each match proved a
challenge, each victory was well won, usually as the very last
card was played.

Late one evening when Michael suggested a friendly wager
on their game, Juliet smiled her approval. "But would you
take money from a woman, sir?" she teased him as he dealt
the cards.

"Of course," he answered smoothly. "But certainly not
from you, Miss Hampton. You have something far more precious than money that I want."

Juliet's smile faded as she reached for her cards, pulling
them into a neat stack, which she pointedly left on the table.

"I am afraid I am not ready to play that game, sir," she said
quietly, her eyes carefully averted.

"I was speaking of your time, Miss Hampton," Michael

chided playfully. "As you see, the cards have already been dealt. If you lose this hand, you will be forced to find the time to go riding with me."

"And if I win?" countered Juliet, lifting her cards from the table.

"Why, then, we shall be forced to play yet another hand, of course."

As Lawrence Hampton watched the private exchange between his daughter and Lieutenant Alford, his face mirrored his disapproval. The sound of her laughter grated on his ears. The time had come to speak with Juliet, to give her the letter from Harold he had received weeks ago and swear it had only just arrived. And then they would have an earnest discussion about what she intended to do with the rest of her life. Certainly, if he let her know exactly what this marriage could mean, she would be unable to say no. But as his eyes fell on the young soldier gallantly rising to kiss his daughter's hand, a seed of doubt was planted in his mind. Not long ago there had been another man who had stood in the way of his plans. He hoped that such effort and expense would not be necessary a second time.

Chapter 32

The morning dawned perfect for a ride. Before the clock had chimed ten, Michael was tapping his foot in the Hampton's parlor, anxiously waiting for Juliet to join him, and she soon entered the room, laughingly announcing that she intended to pay her debt. As they rode out into the country, Juliet led most of the way, anxious to test her horse's limit as well as her own, for it had been a long time since she had taken a good hard ride. When she finally slowed to allow her mare a well deserved rest, Michael caught up with her, spouting a long string of protests.

"If I had known just how well you could ride, Miss Hampton, I never would have suggested such a thing! Can we rest for a moment? I don't know which has suffered more from this race—my horse or my pride!"

Juliet laughed as she slid from the saddle into his arms, pulling swiftly away from the look in his blue eyes as they touched. With a wistful sigh he took a seat beside her on a long, flat rock. He observed as she brushed at the hair that had escaped her simple coiffure, then impulsively caught her hand to keep her from binding the strands blowing free. She flashed him a quizzical look, which he answered by quoting a poem.

"As my curious hand or eye
Hovering round thee, let it fly!
Let it fly as unconfined
As its calm ravisher the wind.

Do not then wind up that light
In ribbands, and o'ercloud in night
Like the sun in's early ray;
But shake your head, and scatter day!"

"Sir, you are a poet!" Juliet sighed, mimicking the fluttery dramatics of a coquette.

"In this case, not I, unfortunately, m'lady. But I am certain that Richard Lovelace had none more fair in mind when he wrote that."

Juliet frowned, remembering suddenly another time when that same poet had been quoted by a very different man. Seeing that her smile had gone, Michael became concerned.

"What is it, Juliet?"

"It's nothing." She shook her head. "Nothing."

"You were remembering him, weren't you?"

"No . . ." She tried to deny it, to forget all the memories that crowded painfully back into her mind, but she found that it was simply no use. "Yes," she admitted softly. "I was thinking of Alec. There . . . there is another poem Lovelace wrote. It reminds me so much of him."

Michael thought a moment and then knew with a certainty which poem it was. He began to recite it.

". . . Yet this inconstancy is such
As you, too, shall adore;
I could not love thee, dear, so much
Loved I not honor more."

The tears glistening in her eyes told Michael that he had been right.

"It's all right, darling," he whispered, pulling her close. "It's all right."

"But it isn't all right, Michael! I cannot forget! Everyone says that I will learn to forget him, but I cannot!"

"Shhh! Who ever told you that you have to forget? Don't you know that you will never forget him?"

Juliet looked up at him, confused. "But—"

"Hush, love! People never really forget anything that hurts them so deeply. Think back to the first things you can remember about your life, your childhood. Have you really forgotten

316

the things that hurt—even so many years ago? Of course you haven't! You've simply learned to live with them. It's all part of growing up, Juliet. We are shaped by the things that hurt us, so how could we ever forget the things that have made us what we are?"

She searched his face for a long moment before she answered him. "I think you are the first person who understands exactly what I feel, Michael. And you are the last person I ever expected would understand."

Michael laughed at her admission. "You will discover that I am a man of many hidden talents, as well as my more obvious ones, my love."

Juliet swallowed back her tears and then, in a deliberate change of mood, playfully jumped from his embrace and scampered toward the stream, returning promptly to heave a cupped handful of cold water on his head. He looked very funny, she thought, with his hair dripping and rumpled, for she had never seen him before with a single strand misplaced. He made a face at her, and she laughed out loud, feeling very much like a mischievous child.

"Madame, take care!" he warned direly. "I was raised in the streets of London, and I am very good at defending myself."

"The streets of London?" she repeated with a doubting smile. "You make it sound as though you were raised a beggar, sir! What of the father who saw to it that you learned to ride properly?"

Michael turned serious. "My mother was an actress, Juliet," he stated simply, "and my father was married to someone else."

Though she did her best to hide her shock, Juliet's cheeks grew hot, and she found it difficult to face him squarely. "I . . . I'm sorry, Michael. I didn't mean to pry. I thought . . . ."

He smiled easily. "It's quite all right, believe me. It's something that I've necessarily learned to live with." He glanced up at the sun and reluctantly marked the quick passage of time. "If I'm to return you home before noon, we had best mount up and be off."

They rode back to the house keeping an easy gait in order to enjoy the lighthearted banter that was so much a part of their relationship. As they reached the last expanse of meadow be-

317

fore the house, a pleasant-faced woman dressed in the simple garb of a Quaker was staring wide-eyed at the huge main door of Hampton House. This was no doubt the place of which young Captain Farrell had spoken, the place where a Miss Hampton was supposed to reside. The captain had made it clear to her that Miss Hampton's father was a Tory who was not, under any circumstances, to be given the message she carried. She took a deep breath and held it as she grasped the heavy brass ring and rapped it hard upon the door. James answered the summons, masking his distaste with a polite bow. "Can I be of service, madame?"

"Thee be truly kind, sir," the woman responded with her own bow, somewhat in awe of both the man and the stately structure before her. "My name be Sarah Merriman, and I would like to see a Miss Hampton, Miss Juliet Hampton please, sir."

James smiled tolerantly as his gaze ran over the woman's worn but clean clothing. "Miss Hampton is not at home, madame. And her charity work is done through the church. Might I suggest you speak with the Reverend Helscher?"

The woman shook her head. "Thee misunderstands, sir. I must see Miss Hampton herself. Juliet Hampton. I have a message for her."

"To be perfectly honest, madame, Miss Hampton is an exceptionally busy young woman, and I cannot say when she might find the time to see you, if ever." Sarah opened her mouth to protest, but James paused only a moment before adding, "Miss Hampton plans to be married soon, you see, and her fiancé will be arriving from England any day. I am quite sure you understand. I am sorry I could not be of service. Perhaps another time."

With a polite nod James closed the door, leaving the Quaker woman staring after him, frowning her disappointment. What could she tell Alexander Farrell now? she wondered as she trudged down the long curved drive.

She neared the road with her eyes fixed on the ground, unaware of a pair of riders fast approaching. As Juliet turned her horse to enter the drive, her mare reared, just barely missing the woman and frightening her to within an inch of her life. Juliet struggled to keep her seat while an anxious Michael rushed to the scene.

"I am sorry!" Juliet called to the woman. "I didn't see you. Forgive me." With a brief, warm smile, Juliet turned and slapped the reins, once again leaving Michael pulling up the rear.

"Juliet Hampton!" he scolded. "Why don't you learn to be more careful! Don't you realize that a horse is a dangerous animal?"

Instantly forgotten by the two, Sarah Merriman looked on, her eyes filled with regret. She ought never to have come here, but she had wanted so much to help Alexander Farrell. Well, what she had to tell him would not be very helpful. Miss Juliet Hampton was going to marry a man who would arrive in New York any day now. And in the meantime, another one was obviously keeping her very well occupied.

Chapter 33

With a crisp salute that was promptly returned, Michael placed a neat pile of completed paperwork before Major Lewis. "I believe I have done everything that you requested, sir," he stated, "and I was hoping to finish early today. I have a most interesting diversion in mind for the remainder of the afternoon, you see," he confided with a sly grin.

The major, a long-faced man who appeared to wear a somber expression even when he smiled, idly rifled through the work, taking note of the neat penmanship and the even rows of figures. He found Lieutenant Alford a very likable young man, and though he certainly would not have trusted him with his wife, or mistress for that matter, he bore the man no grudges for his success with women.

"That diversion would not be, by any chance, Miss Juliet Hampton, would it?" the major asked.

Michael smiled and shook his head. "I see that every tongue in New York has already been set wagging!" he sighed. "But the gossip is fairly accurate in this case, sir. I admit to seeing quite a bit of the lady in question."

"And do you think that wise, Lieutenant? It is common knowledge that her fiancé is due to arrive any day now."

"Sir, forgive me, but I am a bit confused. Since when did romance have anything to do with wisdom?"

The major chuckled as he nodded in agreement. "Still, Lieutenant, I feel that I must warn you. Someone is very, let us say, concerned about your recent 'friendship' with Miss Hampton."

Michael's mouth twisted wryly, knowing full well that the "someone" was Juliet's father. "Major Lewis, you are fairly well acquainted with me, and I think you know that I am a man very slow to make enemies. But in this particular case, I feel I must follow my heart, even at the risk of making a very dangerous one."

"Are you trying to tell me that you are in love with the girl, Lieutenant?"

"And if I were?"

Major Lewis narrowed his eyes, and he took a deep breath. "I can do nothing more than warn you, Lieutenant, and I do so for your own sake. Very few women are worth the trouble they bring."

"This one is, sir," Michael assured him.

With a sigh, Major Lewis dismissed his subordinate. He did not envy the young man his current position, for he had experienced his own obsessions with the fairer sex, and in retrospect, he realized that he had made his share of mistakes. If Michael had fallen in love with this girl, he would be forced to face the consequences, and at this point the outcome did not appear very favorable.

Clothed in nothing more than a thin shift and grasping a bright orange silk gown to her breast, Juliet whirled about her room, humming a song she had sedately danced to the evening before. With a laugh she added a few pirouettes that were every bit as improper as her present attire, ending her performance with an exaggerated curtsy. She giggled at Frances's pained expression, then tossed aside the gown and put on a robe before taking a seat on the bed alongside her.

"Out with it, Frances," she ordered. "You think I've gone mad, don't you?"

"Certainly not! It is only that . . ."

"That what?"

"Well, it's only that you have been seeing so much of Lieutenant Alford lately."

"What if I have?" Juliet challenged.

"But everyone thinks that you are engaged to marry Lord Harold."

"I am engaged to marry Harold," she affirmed.

"Then . . ."

"Then what?"

"You know very well what, Juliet! I don't understand you at all! How can you marry Harold when you told me that you never loved him? And why are you seeing Lieutenant Alford if you've decided to marry Lord Harold?"

Juliet rested her elbow on her knees and propped her chin in her hand. "I'm sorry, Frances. I suppose I owe you some explanation. It's just that I get so angry sometimes at the gossip! I want to break away from it all, to do exactly what I want to do, and the rest of the world be damned!"

Frances showed no little amazement at Juliet's shocking choice of words, but Juliet did not pause long enough to notice. "I am going to marry Harold for so many reasons that I could not possibly tell you all of them. A part of it is because I want to please Father. He says that I could be a great help to his business, making purchases, keeping records . . . he's even taken the time to show me the way his records are kept and how to figure a profit. He thinks I could add quite a bit to his cash flow."

"But your father is already wealthy," Frances pointed out.

Juliet sighed at Frances's innocence. "Yes, but he wants more. He has always been an ambitious man, and he has convinced me that my life with Harold need not be as boring as I had once anticipated. It can be as challenging as I want to make it, and he has promised to help me."

"Is that what you really want from life, Juliet? To work with your father? To amass a great fortune?"

Juliet was suddenly angry, and her tone became bitter. "Of course it's not what I want from life, Frances. I want Alec!" As tears burned her eyes, she repeated the words softly and with regret. "I want Alec!" She blinked away the weakness and continued a moment later with surprising calm. "But Alec is dead, and I was left behind to do the best I can. Harold is not a demanding man, Frances, and he will not expect too much from me." She smiled and faced the troubled blue eyes squarely. "I shall have a fine home and a great deal of work to keep me busy. It will not be a difficult life, Frances."

"What about loneliness?"

Juliet sighed and looked away. "The loneliness. Yes. That will always be difficult, I think. But I shall have to face that anyway, no matter what I do, no matter where I go."

"Juliet, you talk as if you could never love anyone but Alec."

"I could not," she replied firmly.

"You don't know that!"

"Oh? Then answer me this, Frances. Do you think you could ever love anyone besides Robert?"

Frances had no choice but to concede the point. "Then what about Lieutenant Alford? I'm no gossip, but I would be blind not to see the way he looks at you."

"Michael is a dear friend, nothing more."

"A friend?" Frances scoffed. "The man is in love with you, Juliet."

"I suppose he thinks he is, but Michael is not the kind of man who could love one woman for any length of time. He has been very good for me, Frances, and I need someone who can help me to smile again." Juliet's eyes grew warm as she thought of Michael's blue ones, their corners nearly always crinkling with laughter. "Michael is very good at smiling," she said softly. She shook her head as if to dispel the vision and continued in a more rational tone. "But he would not be good at a lifelong commitment, and as I told you, I really don't want that anyway. Harold is the only sensible choice, if, indeed, there is any choice at all."

"But the gossip, Juliet!"

"I don't care about the gossip!"

"Well, Harold might care! He's due to arrive any day now."

"I am well aware of that, Frances. But I am perfectly capable of handling Harold, and I don't intend to let him run my life—now or after we are married. I shall not cheat him; I intend to be a good and faithful wife to him, to give him an heir, to make him happy. But I shall not end a friendship now, which is destined to end of itself soon enough, just for the sake of silencing a few malicious tongues!"

The defiant gleam in Juliet's eye coupled with the tenacity of her words convinced Frances that further argument would be futile. Giving her friend a quick pat on the hand, Juliet strode to her wardrobe and drew out her riding habit.

"Help me on with this, Frances. Michael should be here any moment."

Lieutenant Alford arrived within the hour to find Juliet waiting for him in the parlor, and they eagerly made their escape from the house. Juliet planned to be back in time for dinner, an appeasement to her father, who still insisted that she had a reputation to protect. He had come just short of demanding that she stop seeing Michael, realizing that a direct order would alienate her more than anything else he might do. Unknown to her, he had sought out alternative methods of persuasion, seeing to it that Michael was counseled by his immediate superior and also given double his usual workload. But he would soon be informed that those alternatives had failed.

At the crest of a rolling hill, Juliet paused to admire the countryside, breathing deeply of the fragrant air and turning to find that Michael had kept pace with her in climbing the long grade. "Your riding has improved, Lieutenant," she teased.

"I have never been one to lag behind in the pursuit of such a lovely creature as yourself, my love."

Juliet laughed at his flowery compliment, then pointed out a small white cottage surrounded by neat lines of freshly plowed ground. "Robert and I used to ride here when we were children and pilfer everything from strawberries to carrots from that poor old man, just out of meanness! I remember one time we ate so many green apples—I suffered for days after, I can tell you!"

Michael clucked his tongue, frowning his disapproval. "Personally, I was a perfect child, docile and mild-mannered. Yet over the years I have managed to become something of a rogue. While you, my dear, seem to have been quite full of the devil in your youth, only to emerge as an angel in your womanhood."

"The angel feels the urge to try her wings," she grinned. "I propose a race—to the line of evergreens at the far edge of the meadow." Without pausing to see if her challenge had been accepted, Juliet slapped the reins and leaned low in the saddle.

Michael had ceased to be amazed at her uncanny ability to keep her seat even at breakneck speeds, and he also took off in short order. When they reached the evergreens, Juliet admitted aloud that the contest was a draw, though she silently assured herself that if propriety permitted a woman to ride astride, she certainly would have been the victor.

She dismounted into Michael's waiting arms, breathlessly repeating her words of a few moments before. "Sir, your riding has indeed improved."

Michael's blue eyes crinkled boyishly, while his mouth twisted into a wry grin. "Madame, I have yet to win a contest with you, and as you well know, if I were forced to ride side-saddle, I would still be finding my way from the stables."

"Michael, you are the only man I have ever known who is willing to admit that a woman has bested him!"

"That is because, my dearest Juliet, I intend to prove myself in the most important contest of all. I intend to win your heart."

Juliet pulled away from his casual embrace and strode thoughtfully about the great evergreens. She threw back her head, closed her eyes, and breathed deeply. The evergreens had been fortunate to survive the winter, for a great many of Manhattan's lovely trees had been burned to warm the sorry hovels of victims of the fire. Michael followed close behind, trying to guess at her mood. He had so little time before her fiancé arrived; he had to decide with care which approach would win her.

"Juliet," he said at length, "are you afraid of me?"

She whirled about to face him squarely, answering with mild surprise. "I would not keep company with a man I feared."

"Good," he said, taking a step toward her. "I do not want you to be afraid of me, darling," he continued, pulling her gently closer until their bodies nearly touched. "I would never hurt you. You know that, don't you? You know well how much I love you."

He tilted her chin upward, and his lips gently brushed hers, then pulled away. Juliet closed her eyes and relaxed in his embrace, though she could not help the comparisons that rushed to her mind. Michael was not quite as tall as Alec, and his body, while firm, lacked the solidity and power of Alec's form. She had thought Alec stronger than any other force in the world, and when he had held her, she had felt invincible. Michael's arms about her felt warm and pleasant, but . . . She turned away from him and took a seat on the thick, soft grass, and Michael settled himself comfortably near her. He plucked a tiny flower, all but hidden in the grass, reciting appropriate words from a familiar poet.

"Haste, Haste to deck the hair
Of the only, sweetly fair."

He placed the tiny blossom in her hair, letting his hand linger to test its softness before finally drawing her head to his own. His voice was low, sensuous, barely audible. "I want you, Juliet. More than I have ever wanted a woman before, I want you."

His lips took hers in a demanding kiss, his tongue deliberately exploring her soft, yielding mouth, releasing a tide of passion he had long kept tightly reined. The taste of paradise was bittersweet, however, for Michael instinctively knew that the passion was one-sided. For Juliet, also, there came a strange mix of feelings, few of which she had expected. Michael's kiss, like his embrace, was a pleasant, affectionate gesture that had been intended to be much more. She had never realized until this moment how truly personal a kiss was, that her response to Alec had been an intimate sharing of the deepest part of herself, a part that no longer existed now that he was gone. The magical, romantic element of her life that had wanted to believe in dreams and miracles and in love had died along with him, and she found that realization quite painful and difficult to accept.

Though his pride had been dealt a sore blow by her indifference, Michael attempted to lighten his disappointment as was his custom, with a smile. "It seems I may have played a card out of turn."

Juliet sighed and shook her head. "I warned you that I was not ready for such a game."

He tilted her head back, fastening an unusually sober gaze on her. "You have given me little choice, my love, with Harold due to arrive any day."

"That is something different, Michael."

"How so?"

She attempted to pull away from his hold, but he held her firm until she finally answered. "My marriage will be a business agreement, a marriage of convenience, I believe is the term."

"Whose convenience, Juliet? Harold's? Yours? Or your father's?"

"I shall not deny that he had a great deal to do with it, but it is convenient for me also."

He scoffed at her words. "You have certainly borne your loneliness well since you last saw the man."

"I did not say that I was in love with him," she admitted. "But I don't think I shall ever love anyone the way I loved Alec. I don't think I would want to, even if it were possible."

He lifted her hand to his lips and kissed it tenderly. "Juliet, I know that you loved Captain Farrell better than you love me, and yet, it is not between the two of us you choose. Certainly I can offer you more than a man you care nothing about! I haven't his money or his title, but I have saved a good deal and I intend to have a title of my own some day." He turned her hand to press a warm kiss to her palm, then her wrist, as his eyes earnestly held hers. "And I am quite persuasive in matters of romance, my love, so that what you do not feel at first, I am certain that you—"

"Michael," she interrupted him, "are you offering me a proposal of marriage, or one of another sort?"

"Which of the two would you find more appealing?"

She could not help but smile at his answer—it was so typically Michael. "Don't you see," she asked him, running a hand affectionately along his jaw, "that neither of the two could ever work?"

"No," he answered in all seriousness. "No, Juliet. I do not see that at all."

"Michael, be honest with me, and with yourself as well. Do you really want to be tied to one woman for the remainder of your life? I am very demanding in matters of love, and I shall want children."

"I would enjoy meeting your demands, my sweet, and children should not be too great a hindrance to our life together."

Juliet shook her head, for his answer made it all the more obvious. "You really don't understand, do you? Michael, you say you love me, but I know you well enough to see that what you love is the challenge of having me. If I let myself believe that you were a different kind of man, if I were to surrender myself completely to your charm, you would soon lose interest in me and leave me for a new challenge. I could never make you happy, Michael. You would only resent me for having destroyed your freedom, for forcing you to give up your meanderings. Do you really want to give up your elegant parties for a house filled with children? Your banquets and luncheons for an honest day's work to keep us fed? I would be unhappy, too, every time you turned that boyish smile on another woman. Even if you never strayed, it would hurt me to know that you wanted to do so."

"Then what of now? We have today. We could find pleasure in each other for a time at least. I can imagine nothing sweeter than the feel of your flesh against my own. . . ." His eyes roamed with appreciative regard over her slender form, while his hand caressed the down at the back of her neck. "I promise you, it would be sweet for you, too."

He kissed her gently at first, then more and more intensely, a kiss that reflected the growing frustration of his mind and body. His hands moved to her shoulders, forcing her back against the soft bed of grass, then touching intimately the soft rise of her breast, stirring her passion with surprising suddenness. But his touch was not Alec's, and even with her eyes squeezed tightly shut, battling a powerful desire to respond to his urgings, she could not help but feel that she was betraying her love for Alec, and herself as well. When she forced herself to turn away, painful tears stung at her eyes.

"No, Michael," she sobbed. "I cannot! Please, please, Michael!"

He relented with a sigh, knowing full well that a part of Juliet had wanted him as he wanted her. "Tell me, Juliet, what do you intend to do about Harold? He will claim certain . . . rights as your husband. . . . Or perhaps your father has neglected to inform you of those."

Juliet swallowed hard to ease the burning in her throat. She had not wanted to hurt Michael, but his bitter tone told her that she had. "I do not love Harold, Michael, but I shall not be the first woman who did not enjoy her duties in bed. After I have given him a child, however, I am certain that his needs will have been sated. He is the kind of man who is easily led, one who knows nothing of making a decision for himself. He could do far worse in choosing a wife. I intend to be faithful and to treat him fairly. And if I manage his life for him, I take nothing from him that will not be taken away, in any event, by someone else," she added, in an attempt to justify her plans.

"But you and I are a different matter, Michael. I could not give myself to you for the sake of pleasure. It would somehow betray what I felt for Alec, what I still feel for him. I am not the kind of woman who loves totally today and forgets easily tomorrow." She sighed and relaxed against him. "You have been a great help to me these past weeks, and I have learned quite a bit about survival just from observing you—the way you laugh at life, never taking it seriously enough to be hurt by what it brings. You have made me happy, Michael, the only real happiness I have had since Alec died, and for that I shall never forget you."

Michael forced a smile. "For the first time in my life, I find myself regretting my sorry lack of nobility." He gave a short laugh. "It seems, Juliet, that you are destined to be unlucky at love. Captain Farrell chose Honor for a mistress, and in doing so lost you; while I chose to forget her, and likewise lost you. And Harold? I fear he shall have neither lady, though he will probably never realize his misfortune."

He sighed away his injured pride and bestowed a brotherly kiss on her forehead. "If we are to be only friends, then so be it. I'll not forfeit what little time remains for us for the sake of making a point. In the past, I have never encountered a woman who wanted the truth from me. They wanted to be lied to, and I willingly yielded to their wishes. But I say this to you in all honesty, the feeling I have for you goes far deeper than a mere challenge. You are a truly exceptional woman, and a match for me in everything. I deeply regret that it was I who brought you so much unhappiness in telling you of Captain Farrell's fate." His conscience urged him to a further admission of his guilt, but he had never been a particularly brave man, and he simply could not face hatred and resentment from the woman he loved.

"You must not blame yourself for that, Michael," Juliet told him. "I would have learned the truth sooner or later anyway."

"Yes," he agreed distantly. Hampton would have seen to that, even if he had refused the job.

"We had best be returning now, I think, or I fear your father will be distressed about the time we've spent together."

"Has he spoken with you about that?" she asked in surprise. She had never mentioned his disapproval to Michael.

"Not directly," he replied, lifting her into the saddle. "But I'm sure he is less than happy about the gossip that's been about of late."

A frown crossed Juliet's brow as she took the reins from Michael. She had done her best to explain the situation to her father, but even knowing that he did not understand, she had not expected him to interfere. Their heated words came swiftly to mind as her mare pranced happily toward home. . . .

"Harold will, of course, be informed immediately of your indiscretions with the young lieutenant. The gossips will have a field day unless you put a stop to it now."

"Put a stop to what?" she demanded hotly. "Michael and I are friends. I enjoy his company, and that is all."

"You must admit that appearances are deceiving, my dear," he returned sarcastically.

"I am not concerned with appearances."

"Then, my dear, you are a fool."

Juliet sighed her exasperation. "Father, I can handle Harold. I have told you that I shall marry him. Please do not ask me to give up my freedom any sooner than is necessary."

"May I remind you that the man is very wealthy and comes from a fine old family? If it were ever discovered that you had been married to one of the rebels, you realize that he would probably never even consider marriage to you. And if he believes that you have bedded the handsome young lieutenant, whether you have or not, you will surely lose him to someone a bit more clever.

"Juliet," he said in a more indulgent tone, "I am only trying to prevent your making another mistake . . . one that I may not be able to rectify."

"I do not consider my marriage to Alec a mistake, Father, and I never have! I only admit that I ought not to have lied about it." She drew a deep breath and smiled at the irony. "But if I had been honest, then the fact would have been public by now, and I would not be planning to marry Harold."

Silence fell briefly, for Hampton realized that he had erred. He did not want to risk making a second error in his anger.

"I shall see Michael as I please, Father, and I shall handle the consequences as they arise."

She was about to leave the study then, but her father's voice stopped her.

"Did you know, Juliet," he said slowly, pointedly, "that the man is a bastard?"

She spun about and lifted her chin. "A matter he had very little to do with," she returned. "Surely you do not condemn him for something that happened before he was born!"

"I am not condemning anyone!" he was quick to proclaim. "I am merely saying that the issue of an immoral union most certainly bears the scars of his origin. Society places us all into categories, and justly or no, one's parentage must be considered in an evaluation of any person. Like it or not, the accident of birth determines not only who, but what a person will be."

"And did it determine Lawrence Hampton?"

Her father's eyes had grown so cold at her bold accusation that Juliet trembled now just remembering them. Still his voice had answered her with an ease that belied his anger. "We shall discuss this at another time, Juliet. I do not wish to argue with you, and I am late for a business engagement. . . ."

As Michael and Juliet returned the horses to the stables behind Hampton House, she contemplated the man who was her father. His inability to trust her, even at what she felt was the closest point in their relationship, made her wonder if her own trust in him had been misplaced. It was a frightening thought and one she shook off quickly. He was only concerned for her happiness, she assured herself, and when he saw her safely married to Harold, he would relax and be the loving parent she had dreamed of as a little girl.

After dinner that same evening, Frances was called from the parlor where she and Juliet sat chatting about the party of the evening before. She had a "visitor," James announced formally, with an incongruous wrinkle of his nose that caused Juliet to giggle.

Just outside the main door, an unkempt man shuffled nervously, ragged hat in hand, waiting for the lady he had been instructed to see. He repeatedly cast worried glances at a sorry excuse for a cart, drawn by a horse that seemed to match it suitably, which was parked in the center of the long, curved drive. Sitting in the cart was a small boy of between three and four years of age, with enormous blue eyes, wide and dazed, who rocked slowly and monotonously to and fro, as if to some unsung melody.

"Can I help you, sir?" she asked.

"I be lookin' t' find Frances Church. Ye be she?" he asked suspiciously.

"Yes, sir, I am. But I don't believe we've ever met before."

"No, we 'ent." He gave a jerk of his head and announced, "I only be doin' an errand o' mercy, ye might say. The boy here said t' be kin o' ye."

Frances gasped and nearly fainted, now recognizing Edgar, but definitely not his clothing, which was badly soiled and torn.

"Edgar!" she called out, immediately rushing to the boy's side. "What are you doing here? Where are your mama and papa?"

Frances's eyes grew fearful, and her hands began to shake, for not only did Edgar fail to recognize her, but he continued with his rocking, and his eyes never even blinked. "Edgar? Edgar!"

"The boy be mad!" the stranger announced with brutal frankness. "Been that way since they murdered his kin."

Frances let out a scream of anguish that brought nearly everyone running from the house, then fell against the wagon crying hysterically. While Juliet and her father cornered the man and demanded to know what had happened, James assisted Frances into the parlor, reviving and settling her with a snifter of brandy.

As the man had told Frances, Allan and Mary were dead, murdered by the irregulars who roamed the area north of Manhattan, burning and plundering in the name of the war. "Skinners" and "Cowboys" they were called, depending on the side they claimed to be fighting for, but both were feared and hated by the people who had settled in the area, and with good reason. It became apparent soon enough that the man expected to be paid for his "errand of mercy," and Hampton dealt out a meager wage for the purpose of seeing the man gone. He begrudgingly accepted the money, all the while complaining what trouble the boy had caused him, and to the relief of all took his leave.

As Juliet cuddled the little boy close, she knew a greater bitterness for this war than she had ever known before. Dear God! When would it be finished? How many more people would have to die? She had thought that Alec's death had numbed her to sorrow, had made her callous to whatever the future might bring. She had been very, very wrong.

Chapter 34

Shaking her head sadly after the departing wagon, Sarah Merriman returned to her cottage, empty now that Captain Farrell had left for his home. The other young men she had nursed back to health she had sent off with hope, with a joyous anticipation of a second chance at life. But this black-eyed, soft-spoken gentleman had been different from the others. His will to live had seemed rooted in hatred and resentment ever since that day she had tried to deliver his message to Juliet Hampton and had failed.

Sarah had not intended to tell him about the pretty young equestrienne or her handsome companion. She had merely related her encounter with the "gentleman in black" who gave answer to her knock at the door of Hampton House.

"He told me that she be a very busy lady and that it be impossible to see her at this time," she had said, hoping that he would let the matter drop.

"You did not see her then?"

Sarah's smooth face had drawn into a frown, and she had sighed her reluctance to answer his question. Alec, puzzled at first by her manner, had realized all too quickly that she was holding something back.

"You did see her, didn't you?" he accused.

Biting her lip, Sarah had been torn between the truth that would surely cut deeply and the lie that would lay so smooth. "I . . . I am not certain it be her," she managed. "I saw a young woman. . . . She did not notice me until her horse reared . . . and just as quickly, she be gone."

Alec leaned back to study her, drawing a long breath. What had made the generally open, candid Sarah Merriman so reluctant to admit to a near collision with a young woman on horseback?

"What did she look like, this woman?"

"I saw her but a moment," Sarah replied hesitantly.

"But you did see her," he insisted. "What color was her hair, were her eyes?"

"Her hair be dark," Sarah had admitted, "and her eyes, brown. . . ." She had frowned and shaken her head, amending, "Not exactly brown . . ."

"A golden color?"

She nodded.

"It was her." He had paused only a moment before asking the question she had feared most he would ask. "Was anyone with her?"

Sarah Merriman had turned away.

"So. She was not alone," Alec surmised. "And from your face, I would say that her companion was a gentleman. What did he look like?"

Sarah had timidly raised her eyes, surprised at the calmness with which the man had accepted the news. When he had spoken of the woman, it had been from his heart, and he had called out her name in his feverish delirium. Surely he loved her deeply!"

"Tell me, Mistress Merriman," he had repeated, "what her companion looked like."

"He be fair, sir, as well as comely. Young, a score of years and five, I would judge, and he be a soldier, a King's soldier . . . he be wearing a uniform—"

"A lieutenant, Mistress Merriman?" he asked calmly, interrupting her recollections. "A handsome blue-eyed lieutenant with a dazzling smile?"

She had nodded, puzzled by his knowledge. His eyes were frighteningly bright, their black depths like hot, glowing coals, but still his voice seemed smooth, unaffected. His voice betrayed nothing, but his eyes . . . As Sarah gazed in fascination at those eyes, she was struck unexpectedly by the tremendous anguish that lay beneath his shallow facade of indifference. Her Jacob was like that, too. He had never shed a tear or shown any sign of grief when their son had left them

336

to join the fighting, though he had felt the hurt as deeply as she, perhaps even more. It reminded her of a boiling pot with a tight-fitting cover. With no outlet for his pain, the pressure would grow ever stronger and be more and more difficult to contain. At least Jacob had his faith, she thought, but Alexander Farrell was not a man of religion. She shyly lay a hand on his arm and offered what she could in the way of comfort.

"She be a beauty, sir, and thee be a fine gentleman. But that not be any guarantee that she be the only woman for thee. And she be promised to another, sir. The gentleman in black told me so, that her intended be arriving any day now." She smiled her sympathy, doing her best to encourage him. "Thy heart will mend in time. Place thy trust in the Lord. All love be rooted in Him."

He had given no sign of having heard her, and she had taken it as a hint that he wanted to be left alone. In the days that followed, Alexander Farrell had rapidly regained his strength, and when Jacob had heard of a man of their faith making preparations to travel south, Sarah and he had decided that the rest of Alec's recovery would be best facilitated in his own home.

And so it was that two men in Quaker's drab clothing with horse-drawn wagon departed the island of Manhattan on that fine spring morning.

As the days passed by, Frances and Juliet began to despair of Edgar's ever returning to normalcy. Though now he seemed to hear and see what was going on around him, he responded to nothing, not to the long hours of attention the two women lavished on him, not to the special confections they conjured up in the kitchen, not to the new toys Juliet hoped would please him.

One day, as they sat in the garden trying to interest him in a red ball that they rolled about on the grass, Michael Alford arrived carrying a small wicker basket. Juliet smiled and ran to meet him, flashing him a puzzled look as she noted the basket. They had not planned a picnic for today, and it was already late afternoon; her father would be home at any time.

"Michael! We weren't expecting you."

"I can only stay a moment. I left a stack of papers on my desk for which I shall most certainly face a court-martial! But

I have something here that I couldn't wait to deliver." He smiled mysteriously.

"Oh? What is it?" she asked, raising her brow and eyeing the basket.

"It isn't for you," he said with a teasing grin.

She pretended to pout, her curiosity duly aroused.

"It's for Edgar. How is he today?"

She sighed sadly, and her words reflected her concern. "There's no change, Michael. Frances and I have tried so hard, but he doesn't even seem to know who we are. And he hasn't said a word."

She reached out for the basket, but he pulled it just out of her reach. "Tell me what you brought for him, Michael."

"A surprise," he taunted with a smile, delaying until he had her thoroughly vexed. Finally he lifted the hinged cover of the basket to reveal a tiny dog, the smallest Juliet had ever seen, covered with kinking white fur. Two coal-black button eyes peered timidly from beneath the white fluff, and Juliet giggled with pleasure.

"Michael! How darling! Wherever did you get him?"

"I never reveal my sources," he said in mock seriousness, lifting the tiny bundle from the basket into Juliet's arms. "But it is a she, and ladies do have a way of seeking me out. . . . Most ladies, that is," he added pointedly.

Juliet brushed the long, soft coat, grinning until the pup licked at her chin. With a wrinkle of her nose, she set her on the walk, and at once the pup's sharp eyes caught sight of the bright red ball. Off she ran to play.

"Good day, little stranger," Frances smiled, patting the tiny creature's head. "My name is Frances, and what might yours be?"

"Her name is Sprite. It rather suits her, don't you think?"

Frances returned Michael's contagious smile as the dog licked eagerly at her hand. As if realizing that she had not yet captured every heart, Sprite turned toward the small boy whose eyes followed her brisk movements with detached interest. Tail wagging furiously, the pup timidly approached the boy, stopping after every three or four steps to eye him for any sign of response before proceeding. Cocking her head, she studied the strange glazed blue eyes before her small pink tongue tasted zealously at his hand. She seemed confused by his lack of response, and she began to whimper her frustration. She moved to lick his face and still received no reply, so she took a seat on the boy's lap and whined softly against him. All eyes riveted on the pair, and each widened in amazement when Edgar's tiny hand moved to comfort the puppy who lay in his lap.

"Nice doggie," he said softly.

Tears of joy flooded Frances's eyes as she ran to Edgar's side, while Juliet threw her arms about Michael and tenderly kissed him. Her eyes were brimming with admiration and gratitude; Michael had hoped for something more.

"You are wonderful," she whispered.

"Are you only now discovering that?" he answered lightly. "I really must be going, my love," he said with an anxious glance about to see that no one had observed Juliet's sudden show of affection. "Duty calls." With a halfhearted salute, Michael turned and left.

"Thank you, Michael!" she called after him. "I shall see you tomorrow evening."

Michael turned and nodded, hoping that he would catch up on his work sufficiently to attend the party the following evening. He had an idea that Lawrence Hampton was responsible for the substantial increase in paperwork suddenly dumped on his desk. But Michael Alford had never been too busy to enjoy a lady's company, and he certainly did not intend to be now.

Chapter 35

Juliet's heart was a jumble of clashing emotions as the day of Lord Harold's arrival drew near and her last days of freedom slipped away. She was certain she had made the right decision in choosing to marry him—there was so little, really, to decide. But knowing that she was right did nothing to dispel the loneliness she was already feeling in anticipation of being deprived of Michael's company, of leaving her home behind. She had come to love them both more than she had ever realized.

The day of Harold's arrival, Juliet chose to wear a flattering silk gown in a bright shade of green, remembering that green was Harold's favorite color. She took great care in her toilet, preening long and thoughtfully in an effort to calm a surge of deep, conflicting emotions. Just two short years before, she had longed for this day, had naively considered it the ultimate triumph—that an English lord thought her such a prize that he would humble himself to travel to the colonies just to claim her for his bride. Now it all meant so very little to her. It was a cold, hard bargain struck: Harold's money, his title, his power in exchange for accepting the heavy anchor of a loveless marriage. In spite of her resolutions to focus only on the future, Juliet found herself remembering the man who had first employed that analogy. The image of his strong, dark face was never very far from her mind. He had been hers so briefly, yet he would always be her captain, gentle, knowledgeable, unafraid. She found herself dwelling on her memories more and more as the moment of truth drew nearer.

She tried to be responsive to her father's light conversation as the carriage carried them toward the quay where Harold's ship had docked just a few hours before. She forced an expression of what she hoped was joyous excitement when she first glimpsed the man she was to wed. But the smile nearly froze on her face as he drew nearer, and as she appraised him objectively it struck her how ludicrous it was that such a man would attempt to take Alec's place. He was short of stature, hardly as tall as Juliet herself, and totally lacking in grace as he stumbled clumsily down the gangplank.

"My dearest Juliet!" he intoned emotionally. He bent low over her hand and pressed it to his lips. "My heart has anticipated this moment since the very day you left our beloved England."

The hand which had seized hers was cool and slightly damp, and at the touch of his lips she felt her stomach twist with revulsion. He stood there for what seemed an eternity awaiting her response, lingering over her hand, smiling slightly as he gazed at her adoringly. She battled a strong urge to jerk her hand away. Then her eyes briefly found her father's, and she suddenly knew what she was expected to do. "I have felt the isolation of these past months as well, my Lord," she said softly. "So many things have happened in the time we have spent apart."

"Indeed! The world is in an uproar! Who ever dreamed there would actually be a war with these bumbling colonials!" he raved, not even realizing his faux pas. "But I am here now, my dear, war or no. I have braved the dangers of maritime travel, have risked my very life to come." A tirade ensued in which he related in detail some of the terrible deprivations he had endured on his journey.

Juliet forced a smile and tossed out comments of feigned sympathy and gratitude for the sufferings he had borne, feeling very much a hypocrite. The lies were difficult at first, but she had known that they would be. It would not be so hard once she grew accustomed to the role she was to play.

The initial aversion she felt for Harold did not last out the carriage ride home. In spite of his self-centered, tactless arrogance, he was too simple-minded a man to be hated. He was a lamb, so easily led, so spineless that Juliet actually pitied him.

Harold had little to complain about in his quarters at Hampton House. One of the senior officers had readily relinquished his suite of rooms in the west wing to accommodate the visiting nobleman. Harold spent little time in his quarters, however, for Juliet spent the first few days showing him the sights of the city, and the wealthy citizens of New York, always looking for an excuse to socialize on a grand scale, clamored to welcome him with parties and balls that filled the calendar up to the very day of their wedding. The first of these parties was given by the Robertsons, who spared no expense to impress the visiting dignitary.

Lord Harold Medford proved a difficult man to impress. Smiling primly after each of countless introductions and wallowing in the esteem regarded his title by the people of New York, Harold nonetheless was reminding himself that most of them were not *real* Englishmen. Mother had reminded him thoroughly of that before he sailed. Mother had also reminded him often enough that Juliet was not a blueblood, but looking at those haunting golden eyes, that sweet, fetching smile, just hearing that soft, refined voice convinced him that he had been right in choosing her to be his bride. Besides, Margaret had told him that Juliet would make him a perfect wife, had she not?

Proudly escorting his intended on his arm, Harold fully enjoyed the interest they aroused about the ballroom. Everywhere ladies whispered behind their fans, jealously eyeing his Lordship and the vision of loveliness beside him in pale yellow silk. Was it his imagination, or did the room actually quiet as that handsome young lieutenant strode toward them?

Placing a palm lightly on Harold's satin lapel, Juliet drew his complete and undivided attention. "My Lord," she said intimately, almost in a whisper, "this is the gentleman of whom I spoke. My dearest friend, Lieutenant Michael Alford."

The two gentlemen nodded congenially toward one another.

"My Lord," Michael said respectfully, "it is indeed a pleasure to finally meet the man of whom Miss Hampton is so fond. It is my sincerest hope that we shall become close friends."

"Yes," Harold agreed distantly, anxious to move on. Having been carefully tutored at arrogance all his life, he felt out of place dallying with a mere lieutenant, though Juliet had spoken very highly of the man. Still, she would revolve in an entirely new and much more elite circle of friends once they were married, and he would have to speak with her about that. . . .

Much later in the evening, after spending a considerable amount of time paying court to other women, Lieutenant Alford again approached and made bold to request a dance with Juliet.

"My Lord," he smiled, "surely you would not begrudge me a single dance with your future bride."

Harold gave consent with a timid nod, although as the dance ensued he felt somehow jealous of the handsome man in uniform whose movements on the dance floor were superior to any other man's. And his Lordship's were not the only eyes that burned green at the sight. Lucretia Robertson, the thin, raven-haired daughter of the host and hostess, had waited months for Lieutenant Alford to show her the slightest encouragement, but now, as he smiled into those warm golden eyes, she realized that Juliet Hampton still held his heart.

Lucretia made her way through the crowd that lined the periphery of the dance floor toward Lord Harold, who frowned thoughtfully as he sipped at his glass of wine. When the music was over, Michael would return Juliet to her fiancé, and to Lucretia, who stood armed and waiting.

As the couple approached, slightly flushed and laughing gaily, Lucretia moved into position, a tight smile twisting her lips. "Why, Juliet! I am truly surprised that your fiancé is so generous—sharing you when he has only just arrived."

Juliet flashed her a winning smile, then turned warm eyes on Harold. "I am extremely fortunate to have found a man so considerate of my love of dancing. Even when he is exhausted from his long voyage, he sees to my tiniest whim."

"But I would think that the lieutenant would be exhausted by this time also, having danced nearly every dance with me," she bragged, though Michael's frown warned her to stop. "And besides, it would seem to me that your whims were seen to quite well *before* your fiancé arrived."

With a quick smile at Juliet and Harold, Michael made an excuse about obtaining refreshments, took Lucretia firmly by the arm, and led her away to the dining room.

"What do you suppose she meant by that?" Harold asked with a frown.

"Why, I suppose she was referring to the way my father has spoiled me since I came home," Juliet managed, trying to disguise her uneasiness.

"Mmmm," he mumbled doubtfully.

Juliet's days became a hectic succession of parties and teas and dress fittings and attending to the final arrangements for a grand reception at Hampton House on the eve of their wedding. She had little time to feel regret or sadness as she plunged into a social whirlwind that took up every moment of her time. She saw Michael at many of the parties but spent little time with him, until one evening at the Harris home, when he managed to draw Lord Harold into a conversation about the wonderful attributes of the English countryside. Harold eagerly seized the opportunity to expound on the history and prestige of his own estate, and Michael, remembering that Juliet had said her fiancé was easily led, prodded him to go on and on. Turning his charm on the man, Michael fast won his friendship, all the while humbly catering to his superior airs.

Late in the evening, Michael casually suggested a trip to the gaming tables, adding in the same breath that he was certain Harold's glib tongue and quick wit would make him an impossible opponent for a simple lieutenant. Harold promptly proclaimed himself an excellent card player, and the two were soon engaged in a match that found the young nobleman victorious. He was so seriously intent on playing his hand that he was unaware of the knowing glances Juliet and Michael exchanged after each of his obvious misplays. For the first time in many days, Juliet found herself smiling easily and actually enjoying the party. Her pleasure was short-lived, however, for Lucretia

Robertson was also in attendance, and was anxiously plotting her revenge.

After observing Juliet and Michael for the entire evening, Lucretia caught sight of Juliet alone, within earshot of several notorious gossips. She eagerly seized the opportunity at hand. "Juliet, dear!" she called, glancing about to be certain that every ear was straining to hear their conversation. "I'm so happy to catch you alone at last! Why, between those two gentlemen vying for your time, it's difficult to remember which is your fiancé and which is your . . . well," she smiled amiably, "exactly what is Lieutenant Alford?"

"A friend. A dear friend of mine as well as Harold's," Juliet returned with apparent ease, aware of the eyes upon her.

"Well, I did want to take this opportunity to give you some advice—as a friend."

"Forgive me, Lucretia, but Harold is waiting and will surely be wondering what's become of me." Juliet turned away, only to be caught and firmly pulled back to face the woman.

"All the same, Juliet, for your own good, I must offer you this advice. There is quite a bit of gossip about that you and Lieutenant Alford are something more than just friends. If I were you, I would take care that your fiancé does not become too suspicious. There are too many people who would enjoy filling his ears."

"Thank you for your concern, Lucretia," Juliet answered with an icy smile. "But I am quite sure that Harold's devotion is above being swayed by malicious gossip."

"All the same, my dear, it is certainly a risky business— cuckolding one's husband *before* one is married. I would take care if I were you."

"What a pity that one so knowledgeable in the ways of romance finds herself without a man and unable to employ such fine advice herself!" Juliet retorted, her icy smile still in place.

With a gasp of horror, Lucretia spun about and quickly made her exit. Juliet's eyes, burning almost red with anger, scanned the faces of the audience that had observed the confrontation, challenging any further comment. One by one they turned away, having witnessed quite enough to set their tongues wagging. But a single set of eyes did not turn from hers, meeting her squarely with an accusation of their own. Juliet was in no mood for admitting that she might have made a mistake, so, with a defiant lift of her chin, she turned away, ignoring the warning in her father's steel-blue eyes.

Chapter 36

It was springtime at Beau Rêve. Everywhere buds were swelling, leaves were bursting forth. The smell of cherry blossoms filled the light air with sweetness.

Alec paused to rest at the crest of a hill and took in the sights and smells of home. His trip from Manhattan had been a nightmare—endless days of rain and nights of cold; of following mud-steeped roads; of living with the constant threat of being ambushed by irregular troops. And always the thoughts of her, thoughts that had tormented him far more than a month of being jostled about in a Quaker man's crude cart. He had traveled alone, on foot, for the last forty miles, and now he was on the brink of total exhaustion. His eyes drifted slowly, almost indifferently, over the familiar grounds.

The tall pillars that flanked each of three entrances to the mansion were in sore need of paint, he noticed, and the entire building, once a brilliant white, was now a darker color, approaching gray. But what had he expected? he chided himself. Hadn't he learned by now that a dream would fade without the proper tending? His eyes roamed the paths about the house, the well-worn patch to the kitchen, the stables, the quarters. For all he had changed, everything else went on as it had been, even after two long years of war. The Negroes were planting in the fields; his mother was looking over the gardener's shoulder, giving careful instructions about the placement of every herb and vegetable in her kitchen garden; the windows were opened wide, and Mother would have organized an army of house slaves to beat every carpet, strip and air every bed, wash down every wall and scrub every floor. Everything here was familiar to him, even the feeling that he did not really belong. And now, he thought bitterly, he probably never would.

Alec took to the footpath, remembering. Justin, who had been so young, so trusting, so full of life. Justin, whom Alec had loved as fiercely as a man can love his brother. He could never forget the good times, the carefree springs of racing and wrestling with Justin, the treasured lessons in planting and horse-breeding from his father. Though Beau Rêve remained, those people were only memories now, marked by two nearly identical white crosses in the family graveyard.

Alec reached the paddock and paused, gazing blankly about in his reverie, seeing yesterday as clearly as if it were today. . . .

It was just barely spring at Beau Rêve. The earth was yawning and stretching but had not yet been fully awakened by the mild breezes of the new season. A giant black man everyone called Sol led a high-strung stallion into the paddock with difficulty, for the late yearling protested every step of the way. Waiting there was a handsome youth, dark of hair and eyes, who took the long line from the slave and with easy confidence led the horse to the center of the paddock. Shaking his head, Sol retreated to the stables, mumbling his frustration. No sense in asking why, Alexander Farrell just had a way with horses.

Young Alexander gave the line a good amount of slack, and with a click of the boy's tongue, the horse began lungeing about, first left, then right. Looking up in some surprise when a feminine voice called out to him, Alexander encountered the sparkling green eyes of none other than Cassandra Collins. She waved to him, giggling and fluttering her long dark lashes, doing her very best to break his concentration on the task at hand. With a grimace of distaste, he pointedly ignored her. At eighteen years of age, Alexander recognized trouble when he saw it. It was too bad that Justin could not have recognized it as well. His brother had acted as foolishly as the other smitten men, following Cassandra about the colony like a lovesick puppy until finally last year, her father had given consent that the two should marry. Beau Rêve and Tamarack, the Collins' plantation, shared a common border, and it seemed a natural union for both families. Before arrangements for the wedding were even finalized, however, Cassandra had lost all interest in Justin, eyeing a greater and far more interesting challenge in his younger brother. Aware of the obvious, Alec had done his best to ignore her bold flirtations, but she had only made it more and more difficult for him to do so. As she leaned against the paddock fence, calling him, taunting him, teasing him, she finally succeeded in arousing his ire. How he longed to slap her face, to tell her that she would never be good enough to call herself a Farrell. She was not only spoiled and selfish, he thought, but she had no honor. And honor to a Farrell was everything.

He sought about for some outlet for his seething anger, eventually settling on a foolhardy attempt to break the young stallion. He called out to Sol and ordered him to prepare the horse for mounting, ignoring his protests that Mast' Jerome was always present when one of his finer animals was saddle broken. While the stallion whinnied nervously and shuffled about in the tight stall, Sol lifted the saddle into position and tightened the cinch. Alec stroked the young horse's soft muzzle and spoke to him in a low, calm voice until he settled down a bit. Then Alec made his way around to the side of the stall, hoisted himself to the top rung, and eased himself into the saddle. Sol, eyes nearly popping out of their sockets, reached a trembling hand up to Alec, giving him the reins. Alec leaned down to draw a gentle palm over the stallion's neck, all the while maintaining his quiet drone of reassurances. Then, with an almost indiscernible nod to Sol to release the stall gate latch, Alec and the horse moved out.

The next moments were thrilling ones, filled with the raw struggle of man's will against beast's. Alec was tossed about in a dozen different directions at once as the stallion reared and kicked and bucked violently to win his freedom. But by some strange miracle Alec kept his seat, and eventually the mighty stallion quieted, pranced hesitantly about under the tight rein, and finally admitted to defeat.

Wiping the sweat from his brow with his sleeve, Alec reveled in his victory, hardly noticing that Cassandra was shouting her approval and excitedly applauding his accomplishment. When he finally did look in her direction, his eyes met not hers, but Justin's, and the jealousy there struck him like an unexpected blow.

Without a word, Alec dismounted and led the horse quietly back to the stable. But Justin had seen the admiration flashing in those wide green eyes, and he needed to prove that he was every bit the man his brother was. Justin ran after Alec, insisting that he, too, would ride the stallion. Alec's angry scowl only deepened his brother's determination, until he reluctantly handed over the reins and took hold of the bridle, allowing Justin to mount. His eyes drifted over to Cassandra with a look of utter disgust. She knew as well as anyone that Justin was not a great equestrian. And then, while she stood smugly observing Justin's obvious play to win her favor, Alec released his hold on the bridle. . . .

The images faded. The paddock was empty. Captain Alexander Farrell stood alone. His face was contorted in a terrible mask of pain, his eyes burning, his lips quivering out of control. With tremendous effort he forced himself to turn from the paddock and walk on.

He drew deeply of the spring air and recognized the sweet scent of lilacs. Once that smell had reminded him of his mother, but now it called to mind a very different woman. His eyes rose to the second floor window of the room he had dreamed of sharing with her. Without ever being here, she had given this place a reason for existence . . . and taken it away again.

Hard at work directing the early planting of her kitchen garden, the mistress of Beau Rêve wiped her hands on her apron, and her dark eyes scanned the rolling green hills. Her gaze paused momentarily on an unfamiliar figure in dark clothing slowly approaching the house, almost dismissing him for a beggar as did the slaves. She made to return to her work, then suddenly straightened as realization dawned.

Pale and visibly shaken, Colette Farrell raised a trembling hand to her mouth and walked dazedly toward her son. Nearing him, she lifted her skirts and ran to him, throwing her arms about him, unable to hold him tightly enough to convince herself that he was really there. Finally recognizing their master, the slaves began to shout excitedly and cheer with wild enthusiasm, while the plantation bell clanked out a loud and joyful "welcome home."

Tears rolling unheeded down her cheeks, Colette searched his face as if to prove that he was really there. "The letter . . . from Frances . . . said that . . . oh, thank God! Thank God that you are home, Alexander!"

She lifted her hand to touch his face, a face thinner and paler than the face in her memory. But it was the look in his eyes that she found most disturbing, a look of tortured sadness, of torment, of emptiness. What had happened to his quick smile, to his taunting grin, to the playful gleam that had always twinkled in those eyes, so like her own? She lifted a corner of her apron to wipe away her tears, reining her own emotions out of concern for him. "What is it, Alexander?" she asked him, reaching up to take firm hold of his shoulders. "What is wrong?"

He let out a ragged breath and shook his head, embracing her tightly as he attempted to answer. "Nothing is wrong, Mother," he forced out hoarsely. "I have been . . . ill . . . and the journey here was hard—" His voice broke off, and he released her abruptly to turn away, to rub a hand tersely over his eyes. He expelled a long breath, and when he spoke again it was in a smoother, much more controlled voice. "It is good to be home," he said, avoiding her eyes.

She forced a smile though her eyes were uneasy as she took his hand. "Of course you must be exhausted. Come inside, Alexander." She led him into the house, ordering a hot bath prepared and giving special instructions for a dinner in celebration for her son's homecoming.

During that dinner, after Alec had slept and changed into clothing of his own, Colette did her best to draw him into conversation. But he remained distant, detached, revealing only a very sketchy tale of what had happened in New York, offering perfunctory comments about the war, and making only brief, impersonal remarks when she brought him up to date on the lives of friends and acquaintances. He was openly evasive when she questioned him further about his capture, his escape, his illness, even his long trip home, and he became angry when she pressed him a bit harder. She simply could not reach him. His food went untouched, though he drained the decanter of wine served with dinner, and when they moved to the parlor, he continued to drink heavily. Reluctantly, after hours of waiting for her son to talk, Colette retired for the night.

It was a few hours before the break of dawn, but Colette Farrell could not sleep. She rose and left her bedroom, wandering to the parlor, where a single light still glowed. There she found Alec sprawled out on the couch in a drunken stupor. She retraced her steps and returned with a quilt, covering him as she had when he was a little boy. Perhaps his pain would ease in time, and then he would be able to talk about it, she thought, tenderly brushing a stray lock of his hair back from his brow. It was only a question of waiting. At the touch of her hand, Alec stirred in his sleep and murmured a name unfamiliar to her. Colette waited and listened, hoping that he would say more. But quickly he relaxed, and once again all was quiet. She frowned thoughtfully and pressed a light kiss to his temple. Then she extinguished the lamp and returned to her room.

The sun had taken to the western side of the sky before Alec became fully aware of where he was and how he happened to be there. Colette had stationed a sentry of sorts, a young Negro boy, at the door of the parlor, who was to inform her immediately when Alec came awake. She was there before he even had a chance to rise, with a tray of steaming coffee and hot rolls and butter.

"Delilah will be happy to fix you breakfast, Alexander," she said, lowering the tray to the table nearest him. She poured him a cup of coffee, straight and strong, while she diluted her own with a dash of cream. He accepted the brew but turned away from the rolls and gave no sign that he wished to have anything else.

"Well, perhaps Delilah's cooking has lost some of its flavor since you've been away. But you'll soon be a scarecrow if you don't eat something, Alexander."

"I shall eat when I am hungry, Mother, thank you," he answered softly. His head throbbed painfully as every sound, however slight, touched his ears.

"Of course you will," she humored him. She cleared her throat and decided that the time for coddling was just about finished.

"There are a great many things we must discuss, Alexander, though I do not wish to burden you when you've just arrived home. Things have not been easy here while you've been away. The taxes have increased, prices have gone sky high, and we've lost quite a few field slaves to the war. I cannot see how we'll make ends meet, even if we have a good year."

She waited for him to comment, but he seemed very interested in his coffee at the moment, so she continued. "Wade Collins has offered me a nice sum of money for the purebred horses. Had you not returned, I would have been forced to sell them. But now you're here, and the decision will be yours. I thought to keep Madame. She'll foal within a few months, and besides, I could not bear to sell her, unless—"

"Sell them all, if you must," he interrupted sullenly.

"Very well," she replied patiently. "The matter is settled then." She took two long sips of her coffee, then plunged on. "As I told you, Alexander, these years without you to manage the plantation have been difficult. I have completely exhausted any cash your father and I had saved, and our credit has become—how shall I say?—questionable. Still, there are supplies I need in town—paint and glass and the like—and I have no way of paying for them. I should like to know if you might offer some solution to this problem." She hesitated before making a suggestion. "I am fairly certain that if you were to go with me, no one would question our ability to repay a debt. It is only the thought of extending credit to a widow, and an old one at that, that makes Mr. Linchen nervous—"

"I am going back to the army, Mother," Alec announced.

Colette placed her cup on the saucer and set it aside, folding her hands in her lap. "Alexander, you have done your duty for your country. Now it is time to do your duty for your home. You can join the militia—"

"Militiamen lose more battles than they help win," he scoffed. "My place is with the real army—the Continentals."

"Your place is here, Alexander. Beau Rêve needs you. I can't run it alone. Haven't you been listening to me? How long do you think it will be before I am forced to sell more than the horses? The furnishings, the house, the land?"

"I know that you will do the best you can."

"No, Alexander." She shook her head. "No. I shall not work this land with my bare hands for your sake when you don't

355

even care enough to help me. It is impossible for me to supervise a major planting, keep the house, and feed and clothe the slaves by myself. No one person can do justice to such a task. Beau Rêve is your birthright, Alexander. You are all that remains of six generations of Farrells in Virginia, and the beautiful dream of your ancestors depends entirely on *you*, not me. If you truly do not care what happens to this place, then leave it freely once more, but do not look back . . . ever! I shall sell it and be gone from here long before you return. I have no desire to spend the remaining years of my life trying to save something you don't want!"

Alec stood up and walked to the window. The sun filtered through the small panes of glass and danced on the carpet beneath his feet. His eyes beheld the view beyond, the Rappahannock's lazily rolling current, the willow trees bending so low near the shore. From his earliest days he had known a passionate attachment for this land, for the rich Virginia soil that nurtured the peaceful life of a planter.

"What do you want of me, Mother?"

"I want you to be happy, Alexander."

"You ask too much," he said with a sad smile.

"And you give too little," she returned.

He faced her squarely. "I love this place, Mother. You know that well enough. But . . ." He hesitated, as if considering just how honest he ought to be. "But I cannot stay here, not now. Someday . . ."

"Alexander, you have been away a long, long time," she reminded him. "If you leave here again, I must have something, some show of good faith that you want me to hold on to Beau Rêve while you're gone." She knew very well that her son had returned home penniless; he had even lost Cheval. But her words were a bluff, calculated to force Alec into staying on, at least for a time. He bluntly called that bluff.

"How much?"

Colette cocked her head, as if she did not understand the question, but he only repeated it.

"How much?"

"Two thousand pounds. It will pay the taxes for the next two years, buy everything I need to maintain this house, and provide a cushion for emergencies."

"Fair enough. I shall have it for you before I leave."

Colette did her best to hide her disappointment. "Would you care to tell me how you intend to do that?"

"Of course." Alec's eyes grew cold and hard as he laid his cards on the table. "I believe my 'fiancée's' father will provide me with a loan. And I am certain that his daughter can convince him to be very generous about the terms."

"You talk as if you intend to marry her, Alexander," Colette stated with mild surprise.

"I do. She's waited all these years, hasn't she? Well, if she can hold out just a little while longer, she'll have bought herself a husband. Or, rather, her father will have done it. Provided, of course, that the war doesn't interfere. Just think! She's waited seven years! She must be twenty-two years old by now."

"And prettier than she was at fifteen," Colette remarked. "She's had numerous proposals in your absence."

"I'll wager she has," he commented with a wry smile.

Colette had lost one hand; she dealt another.

"Alexander, would you like to talk about whatever it is that's bothering you?"

"Nothing is bothering me, Mother. What makes you think that?"

Colette smiled indulgently. "Well, it could be the fact that you haven't eaten a thing since you've been home . . . or it could be the fact that you drank yourself senseless last night . . . or perhaps the fact that you've suddenly decided to marry a woman I happen to know you abhor"—she raised her brows and stared at him accusingly—"for money."

Alec sighed and looked away. She knew him so well. "There is nothing to talk about," he answered firmly.

"Who is Julie?"

Black eyes, narrowed, flew to her face. "How did you know about her?"

"Last night you said her name in your sleep."

"What else did I say?" he asked with obvious concern.

"Nothing. Who is she, Alexander? Did you care for her? What happened . . . ?"

"Nothing happened! Nothing!" he insisted hotly. "She's dead! Do you understand me? Dead! And nothing will bring her back!"

Colette was silent, shocked by his outburst. Obviously the wound was fresh—and deep.

He turned away and calmed himself before adding in a much subdued tone, "Please do not ask me about her. I never want to hear her name again."

Chapter 37

With her wedding date set for May twenty-first, one month away, Juliet was caught up in a whirlwind of parties, charity balls, and evenings at the theater, as well as preparations for the elaborate receptions planned at Hampton House to celebrate the wedding. She had barely a moment to herself, with Rachel spending several hours daily preparing her hair according to the latest dictates of fashion and helping her to dress in a style befitting the future wife of a nobleman.

Lawrence Hampton meanwhile ground his teeth and struggled to hold his tongue. In one short month he would see Juliet safely married to the Lord Harold Medford. He could foresee only one problem that might prevent the marriage from taking place, and that was a public scandal. Each time Hampton saw Michael Alford his resentment burned; the young man was the one loose thread in his plan, a thread that threatened to unravel a fine tapestry. Everything else had fallen neatly into place, or so it had seemed until the twentieth of April. On that day the *Springstorm* returned to dock in New York Harbor. And on that day Lawrence Hampton was informed that another loose thread had not been clipped off as cleanly as he had thought.

Late one evening during the last week of April, Juliet sat before her vanity in her night rail brushing out the curls Rachel had worked so long to effect that afternoon. Frances had joined her and sat curled up on the bed, hugging her knees to her chest and listening to the latest news of the war. Michael always kept Juliet well informed, unlike most men who confined serious talk on that subject to other men.

". . . and they say that Dr. Franklin has captured every heart in the French court—wearing a fur cap and frontiersman's garb! Michael says the rebels have a great deal of French backing already: money, ammunitions, even officers. But they haven't become complete and full allies yet, and, of course, England would just as soon have it remain that way."

Frances sighed. "Did he say how much longer he thought it might last?"

Juliet tossed the brush on the vanity, then walked to the window.

"No," she whispered. She wistfully committed to memory the view of the city she loved. It would not be long before she left this place and so many memories behind.

"I got a letter from Mama," Frances said, changing the subject. "Apparently she had not gotten my letter as yet. She doesn't know about Allan. . . . Juliet, I've been thinking a great deal about what I shall do after you leave—"

"You'll stay here, of course," Juliet assured her. "I have already spoken with Father at length, and he expects you to stay, as well as Edgar."

Frances smiled her gratitude, but an odd sadness marked her eyes. "It will be strange here without you. And difficult. I've come to depend on you for so very many things."

Juliet walked to the bed and took her friend's hand. "You will see quite enough of me, I can assure you of that. I intend to visit home often, and after you and Robert marry, he might even persuade you to come and visit me."

Juliet turned back to the window; she did not want Frances to see how difficult the prospect of leaving was for her to face. Three years ago she had come home from school planning to stay here only a few months. Now she was twenty years of age, and those three short years had shaped her far more than the prior seventeen. She had learned to accept herself because a man had seen past a practiced, arrogant facade and loved her for what she was. She had found a dear friend who loved her in spite of the contrasts in their characters, and another friend—who would have been more—who had taught her how to deflect the blows of life with a half-step backward and a smile. And she had learned so much about that great mystery who was her father, only to find that she still knew so little. She no longer feared him as she had when she was a child. He could never hurt her as deeply as he had done then. Where his love had been important to her, Alec's had been crucial, and if she had learned to accept life without Alec, then she knew there was nothing she could not face. She begrudgingly admitted that life was still worth living—Michael had shown her that. How she would miss him! She sighed, for he had not made an appearance at the party this evening, but perhaps that, too, had been for the best.

A movement on the road approaching Hampton House caught her eye, and as the rider galloped up the half-circle drive and stopped before the main entrance, Juliet's face lit up with recognition.

"It's Michael!" she said to Frances, who went to the window to observe beside her.

"Why, it cannot be! It's after midnight!"

Juliet frowned, seized by a sudden uneasiness. With a single motion, she took hold of a wrap thrown carelessly over a chair, and when a quick glance assured her that no one was about in the hallway, she left the room to approach the top of the stairs. Frances, wide-eyed and whispering nervous protests about propriety, was left to hope for the best in Juliet's room.

"I should like to see Miss Hampton, please, James, immediately. The matter is urgent."

Juliet strained to catch every word and leaned forward as far as she dared to catch a glimpse of Michael.

"I am sorry, sir, but Miss Hampton has already retired for the evening. As I'm sure you are aware, the hour is late. Perhaps in the morning—"

"James," Michael said with an insistence that seemed contrary to his nature, "the matter is urgent. I want to see her now. If you tell her I am here, I am certain she will see me."

Juliet stepped forward and had opened her mouth to speak when her father's cool voice kept her from doing so.

"Good evening, Lieutenant Alford. You are calling rather late, don't you think? My daughter has already retired. If the matter is as urgent as you say, perhaps I could be of some assistance," he offered, a bit too cordially, Juliet thought.

Michael took a deep breath, and when he spoke his voice

sounded odd and dull. "Yes. Perhaps it would be best if I spoke with you. The matter is private, sir," he said with a pointed look at James. "Could we move our meeting to your study? I find myself in sore need of a glass of wine."

"James, we are not to be disturbed, do you understand?"

With a stiff nod, James turned away from the two men and began to climb the stairs, extinguishing the lamps. Juliet rushed back to her room and carefully closed the door behind her, wincing at the soft click as it shut. She paced the room nervously, ignoring Frances's questions completely. She tried to imagine why Michael had come here at such a late hour and what matter could be of such urgency that he would confide in her father. The two had been less than friends these past weeks.

Finally, in exasperation, Frances stood before Juliet, hands on hips, demanding a reply. "Juliet, *what* is going on?"

Juliet answered with hard-won casualness. "I have no idea. Michael is here on business, I assume. He and Father are in his study." She paused a moment. "Why don't we go to bed, Frances? It's been a long, long day, and I'm very tired." Juliet stifled a yawn and removed her wrapper, pausing before the bed lamp until Frances made a move to leave. With a sigh and a puzzled raise of her brows, Frances lifted a candle and made her way back to her room.

Juliet hardly waited for Frances's door to close before she crept out into the hallway. She began to descend the stairs one at a time, careful not to make any noise. With only one oil lamp burning low in the hall, Juliet made her way stealthily along the wall toward her father's study. She stretched a shaking hand out to touch the doorlatch, then opened the door very, very slowly. Why, there is no one here, she thought, stepping in to view her father's desk and empty chair. At that moment a hand clamped tightly over her mouth, cutting off the scream that threatened to escape, while an iron grasp held her cruelly immobile despite her attempts to free herself. Just as suddenly a voice she recognized as Michael's hissed in her ear.

"Don't scream! Juliet, promise me that you will not scream!"

She relaxed in his arms and nodded, but her eyes were fearful and wide when she finally faced him.

"Michael! What is it? You said it was urgent . . . where's Father?" Juliet glanced about the study and gasped. Beside her father's desk lay a lifeless form heaped on the floor. Michael held her fast, preventing her from going closer.

"He'll recover, Juliet, I promise you. He's not hurt badly, only knocked unconscious."

Her face reflected her horror. "Michael, what have you done? Have you gone mad? Why have you done this?"

Michael leaned wearily against the wall, but his hold on her still restrained her from going to her father. He pulled her close and breathed a ragged sigh. Then he gathered his courage and faced her squarely as he did his best to explain.

"Juliet, I haven't much time. I . . . I lied to you, Juliet. Your father paid me to lie to you, and I did."

"Michael, what are you saying?" Her eyes searched the familiar face, strangely distorted with tension and pain.

"The truth! The sad truth. Your father hired me, long before I ever met you, to find Captain Farrell and to report my findings back to him—but not to you! I was to convince you that Farrell was dead, no matter what had actually become of him."

"No! No!" She shook her head in disbelief, but Michael held her tightly and insisted that she listen to what he had to tell her.

"I found him, Juliet. He *had* been captured; he *was* in prison, here on the island. But he was to be sent . . . to another prison, and he escaped. I . . . I don't know if he survived the escape, but—"

"Alec is alive?" she repeated in amazement. Again she could not bring herself to believe him. "No! No!" With an effort, she pulled away from Michael, backing away from him in horror. "Michael, how could you?"

He shut his eyes in a gesture of great pain, then faced her. "Juliet, my mother was an actress, and I, unfortunately, inherited that talent. Your father knew that Captain Farrell was alive, Juliet. He knew what he was doing to you, but he wanted you to marry Harold. Not for your happiness . . ." He gave a short laugh. "He told me at first that I was lying to you for your own good, that you would ruin your life if you waited for a rebel who was rotting away in prison." He laughed again. "But I have recently learned that your marriage to Harold will mean ever so much more than just a title to your father. The Medfords have controlling interests in businesses, shipyards, a fair amount of land near Liverpool . . ." He shook his head as if to banish the thoughts that tortured him. "Imagine the power, Juliet. An empire for your father. He pictures himself an emperor, I think. I came here tonight because your father had decided that I also jeopardize his plans. So he . . . arranged to have me implicated as a spy."

Juliet's mouth flew open in protest. "Michael! Spies are . . ."

"Hanged," he finished for her. "Yes. It would have been a neat way to remove me from the picture, don't you think? But your father made one mistake. He forgot that I am a generous man when it comes to purchasing interesting information. And I found the fact that I was to be arrested extremely interesting."

"The neckchain," she choked out. "I never told you about the neckchain. . . ."

His hand found its way to her cheek, where the tears had begun to spill, and he tenderly smoothed them away. "He knew about the neckchain. He described the medallion to perfection. He has used you, Juliet! And lied to you, and cheated you of the man you love. And I . . . I helped him to do it." He blinked back tears of his own before he could continue, his voice straining against his anguish. "I did not know you then, my love. And when I realized what I had been a partner to, it was too late!"

She was sobbing now; still she shook her head slowly as if to negate his words.

"Juliet, believe me, for I speak the truth at last. I am sorry! Believe that above all else! My most heartfelt regret is that I have hurt you . . . and lost you!" His voice broke off, and he swallowed hard. "Perhaps someday you could learn to forgive me for what I have done."

His hand drifted from her cheek to the back of her neck, under the thickness of her hair, pulling her mouth to his own. His kiss was slow, deep, mingling the salty taste of her tears with the sweetness of her lips. He knew all too well that this kiss would be his last from her.

Reluctantly he broke away. "Did anyone see you come here?"

She shook her head, unable to speak or even to raise her eyes to meet his.

"I must go. Please don't alert the others. But if you should desire to see my blood spilled, I could not blame you."

In the lengthy stillness that followed came the vague realization that Michael had gone. How long she stood there, minutes or hours, she would never know. She left the study and trudged up the shadowed stairs as if in a dream. She had not even bothered to see if her father was still breathing. Her mind was flooded with a single thought, and there was simply no room for anything else.

Alec was alive!

Chapter 38

There was so little time and so much to do, Juliet thought as Rachel finished fixing strands of pearls in her hair. Only three weeks until her wedding. Three weeks and she would be leaving Manhattan forever. She was certain now that she would never return to this house, this city, this island.

Frances joined her in her room, twirling about with a smile as she modeled a new gown of sky blue satin, demure, lacy, and utterly suited to Frances. She had not attended many parties of late, for it had become her custom to remain with Edgar until he had drifted off to sleep. He was improving remarkably, quickly returning to the same little impish boy he had been before the tragedy. Still, he was fearfully possessive of his aunt now, and cried whenever she left him alone. But this afternoon Juliet had asked his permission to take Frances to a party, and they had struck upon a bargain. In return for going to bed at an early hour, Juliet would take him riding with her out in the country.

"Aunt Frances," he was saying, for he had joined her in Juliet's room, "you look like a princess! And you are a princess, too!" he said to Juliet.

Juliet smiled as Frances curtsied before him, and he answered with a stiff bow. The two began to dance while she hummed an appropriate song.

"Why, Edgar," Juliet said, clapping her hands in appreciation of his performance, "you are truly ready to escort a young lady to a ball!"

Edgar nodded solemnly. "Aunt Frances taught me the minuet, and now I only need a proper suit of clothes. Could I come to the great party before you marry Lord Harold?"

Juliet's smile faded quickly, though she did her best to maintain it. "We shall talk about that later, Edgar. Now off to bed with you. And remember our bargain."

Edgar whirled and ran halfway out of the room, then stopped short and turned back to Juliet, a frown deeply creasing his little brow.

"Is something wrong?" she asked him.

He shook his head. Then, as if the courage finally came to him, he nodded. "I wanted to ask you . . ."

"Yes? You wanted to ask me what?"

"Aunt Juliet, does it hurt to get married?"

"Of course not," she smiled.

"Then why do you look so much like it hurts?"

His childish honesty came as a mild shock to her, and she glanced about at Frances, who seemed suddenly interested in the lace flounces at her sleeve.

"Edgar, we shall have to discuss this at another time. Now it's off to bed with you."

He gave a quick sigh of resignation and trotted off to bed, leaving Juliet gazing thoughtfully after him.

"Very perceptive, isn't he?" Frances asked.

Juliet ignored the comment, and when she spoke her tone was serious. "Frances, I have been wanting to speak with you for several days now about a matter of some urgency." Juliet's eyes strayed for a moment to a far corner of her room, where Rachel silently worked with Juliet's wardrobe, checking for stains or tears in any of her new gowns, packing away ones she had already worn. Juliet knew that the task might have been performed at another time, that Rachel often used her work as an excuse for eavesdropping on private conversation. Frances took a seat on a chair near the vanity and waited for her to go on.

"I have been thinking about Edgar, about his life here in New York. Have you considered what might become of the child if something were to happen to you? Of course my father would pay to see him tended, but that would never be adequate for a child who has already experienced so much tragedy."

"What are you trying to say, Juliet?"

"Only this, Frances. As long as we are both here, Edgar is reasonably secure in his future, for we both love him dearly. But when I leave here he will depend entirely on you for his love. And I don't think that's a good idea. If you were to become ill, he would have no one but the servants. If Robert were here, of course, everything would be different."

"He will come home someday . . . soon," Frances said hopefully.

"Frances, this war has already lasted longer than anyone anticipated. There are no signs of it ending soon."

Frances rose and turned away, wringing her hands. "What else can I do, Juliet? I suppose I could send Edgar to Mary's parents, but they are older, and their home is very small. Edgar told me that he did not like living with them."

"What about your parents, Frances?"

"But they're in England!"

"Yes! And they have a fine home there and friends, and most important of all, they are away from the problems of the war. In her last letter your mother wrote that they planned to remain in England, did she not?"

Frances nodded. "But Robert—"

"Robert will find you," Juliet insisted. "And I know that he would understand your decision to leave here, in light of the circumstances. For the sake of Edgar, I don't see that you really have any other choice." Juliet bit her lip, hoping that Frances would not realize that there was one other option open to her. "I shall be in England, too, Frances, and I must admit to having selfish motives for wanting you to go. But primarily my concern is for Edgar. He must be our first consideration."

Frances nodded tearfully, and Juliet plunged forward. "I was speaking with Captain Charlington just the other day. He has an absolutely lovely ship, the *Cooper*, which will be sailing for England the fifteenth of May. He assured me that the accommodations were luxurious, and I believe that in deference to Harold, he would give you the finest cabin."

"The fifteenth of May?" Frances repeated, stunned. "Why, that's before your wedding! How could we possibly leave so soon?"

"Frances, Edgar has very little to do in the way of preparation. You are the one who will have difficulty in packing."

"But why so soon? I . . . I should have to consider it before I make a decision."

"Frances, you told me once that you were very afraid of sailing, but for Edgar's sake, you must make up your mind to overcome that fear. And the longer you delay your decision, the more difficult that will become. There is another reason for haste, though I did not want to hold it over your head. My father is an extremely busy man, and my wedding plans have taken up a considerable amount of his time. I should hate to burden him further with a request to arrange your journey, but if you leave right away, I can arrange everything myself. Captain Charlington is willing to be very accommodating for a friend of Harold's."

Frances felt suddenly as if she were trapped. If Juliet said that she must go to England for Edgar's sake, if Juliet said that Robert would understand, if Juliet said that she must leave immediately, then she must do exactly that. But the very thought of leaving New York, of being so far away from Robert, of getting aboard a ship broke her heart and brought a nauseous feeling to her stomach as well. Still, she had little choice in the matter. She must somehow find the strength to carry it out.

With a slow nod Frances gave her assent, and Juliet breathed a sigh of relief.

"But I find the air rather chilly so early in the morning," Lord Harold complained. "And I have no real interest in riding, as you know well, Juliet."

"Harold, you have seen such a small part of my home since you've come here, and there's so much to see! The meadows, the trees . . . oh, Harold!" She sighed and leaned against him ever so lightly, her hand stroking the lapel of his elegant satin suit. "If you don't wish to see it, of course . . . if you have no interest in my home . . ." She seemed close to tears as her voice trailed off, and Harold quickly reversed his position.

"I shall adore seeing the island, my dear!"

She planted a brief kiss on his cheek, then spun away. "I shall inform the groom to have our mounts prepared at dawn," she told him as she made her exit. He nodded reluctantly after her and watched as she hurried off to the stables.

Inside the stables it was both dim and cool, and Juliet squinted and carefully surveyed the interior to be certain that Jay was alone. There were a good many soldiers usually lolling about, and for several days Juliet had taken note of the time that found most of them occupied with other tasks. Her painstaking observations had just been rewarded.

"Jay, Harold and I wish to go riding tomorrow at dawn, weather permitting." She took another quick look around and added in a very low voice, "And I need to speak with you. Are you alone?"

At his nod, she went on in a whisper. "Jay, I am in need of your help, and I have so little time to explain. I plan to leave this place, and I must do so secretly. Not a single soul must know of my plans. They will involve a great deal of sacrifice . . . and risk. Will you help me?"

The bottom tip of the sun was still hidden below the horizon when Juliet tugged playfully at Harold's hand. "Come quickly!" she urged him. "The groom will have our horses saddled, and I do want to get away while the morning is fresh."

Harold stifled a yawn and reluctantly trudged behind her. "I do believe it looks as if it might rain," he suggested hopefully.

"Nonsense! It's an absolutely glorious day!"

He blinked the sleep from his eyes and resigned himself to this trial for the sake of true love. The wizened groom led two mounts from the stable, and Harold lifted Juliet into the saddle. How heavenly the feel of her small waist, her slender limbs, her easy grace! He paused to return her smile, absolutely captivated by a pair of warm golden eyes framed by thick, dark lashes. Perhaps this adventure would prove worthwhile after all, he mused, taking to his own horse. He and Juliet would have some time alone, at least. There had been so precious little of that!

"Have a care, Miss Juliet! Be takin' no chances!" the old groom called after the pair.

Harold turned around to frown his disapproval at the man and nearly slipped from his saddle. Such a show of concern

371

from a mere servant was hardly proper—not that servants in the colonies did anything well. Still, this was such an obvious breach of propriety! Harold decided then and there that he would mention it to Juliet's father.

They began traveling at a pace closely akin to a walk and had reached a lush green meadow before Juliet loosened her hold on the reins, finally giving Amber enough slack to run. After only a few moments of giving the horse her head, Juliet pulled fast on the reins. The unexpected command confused the mare, accustomed as she was to racing to the meadow's edge. Juliet frowned and sighed when the mare slowed smoothly to a halt. Again she gave Amber her head until she had torn through the remaining stretch of meadow, then jerked abruptly back on the reins. Harold, who had fallen a good distance behind, watched on in horror as the mare reared in frustration. Then, as he clumsily urged his horse onward to offer what he might in the way of assistance, Juliet was hurled to the ground. His hands were trembling, and he was making strange, mewling sorts of noises as he dropped beside her lifeless form.

"God in heaven!" he cried out, lifting his hands dramatically toward the sky. "God help us!"

Knocked breathless by her fall, Juliet slowly and painfully began to move, testing each muscle for bruises—or worse. To her relief she found that the thick grass had served her well. She had sustained no serious injury. She moaned and rolled her head from side to side, but Harold did not notice. He knelt beside her, sobbing aloud, his face buried in his hands. Juliet opened her eyes and frowned in annoyance. She closed them again, calling out to him in a weak, tremorous voice.

"Harold . . . Harold . . ."

Though he kept his hands upon his face, his fingers spread apart and he peered doubtfully down at her. His eyes widened, and he slowly lowered his hands, but he was yet afraid to touch her. "Juliet," he whispered nervously, "you aren't . . . dead, are you?"

Juliet clenched her teeth to keep her anger from coming to the fore. She fluttered her eyelids as if it took tremendous effort and forced her voice to sound pained and wan. "You . . . you saved my life, Harold." She groped for his hand. "If . . . I had been alone . . ."

Her words seemed to propel him to action. An arm worked its way behind her back and supported her efforts to sit up. She leaned against him.

"Oh, Harold, how could this have happened? It felt as if the saddle slipped right out from under me."

"Now, now, Juliet. You were simply riding too quickly, and . . ." He paused, and a puzzled frown pulled at his brow. His eyes caught sight of the horse, grazing a short distance from them, who had indeed lost her saddle.

"Why . . . why . . . the saddle did come off! It actually came off the horse's back!"

"But Harold, how could it possibly come loose like that?" she asked him.

Harold's mind was fast at work. He left her side and found the saddle, which had fallen nearby, inspected it for a few moments, and called out his findings.

"It's the cinch . . . worn completely through." He fingered the torn edge of the cinch, where the leather was cracked and dried, then frowned and shook his head. "This saddle looks to be fairly new. The rest of the leather is smooth and clean. But this—"

"But that's impossible, Harold! Jay has been our groom for years, ever since I was a child. He has always taken care of our riding equipment conscientiously. How could he have made such a careless mistake?"

"How indeed!" Harold repeated bitterly, recalling the impertinence of the man. He returned to help her to her feet, catching her when she swayed weakly and nearly fell once more. "Juliet, that man is directly responsible for this accident! Had you been thrown earlier, you might have been killed! You are extremely fortunate to have been thrown where there was enough foliage to break the fall. I shall personally see to it that the man is discharged immediately."

Juliet meekly allowed Harold to lift her into his own saddle. He took Amber's reins and led her back to his own horse. Three times he tried unsuccessfully to heave himself, one-handed, into position behind Juliet. It was one of the most uncoordinated endeavors she had ever seen. Waging a difficult battle to suppress a giggle, she took the reins from him, and finally, with the support of both arms, he managed to take the seat behind.

"But Father, Jay has worked here for as long as I can remember, and he has made only one mistake!"

"A fatal one for his occupation . . . and a near-fatal one for you, I might add."

"But you cannot simply discharge him after all these years of service!"

"I can and I must, Juliet," Hampton responded coolly. "Lord Harold has insisted that I do it immediately."

"But he's old, Father! He will never be able to get a position suitable to his capabilities!"

"His capabilities have not been proved of late, Juliet. The soldiers have done most of their own work, they tell me, and that leaves little work for Jay."

"But he stayed with us, even when all the others left! His loyalty ought to be worth something!"

"He was paid for his services," Hampton remarked, taking a seat at his desk and turning his attention to the stack of papers there. But Juliet was not to be put off so easily as that.

"You intend to dismiss him then?"

"Tonight."

"You leave me no choice. I shall have to speak with Harold."

"Why ever would you speak with Harold?"

"He is the one insisting that Jay be discharged, is he not? He said that he would do so after my fall, but I didn't think he was serious! I am very fond of Jay, and I tried to explain that to Harold, but he wouldn't listen. I ought to have known that he wouldn't. His mother has carefully instructed him to look down on anyone in service, particularly here in the colonies. Well, he will simply have to choose between his mother's advice and mine! I shall not allow his arrogance to ruin Jay's remaining years! Not after so many long and faithful years with our family."

"Juliet, calm yourself," her father ordered.

"I am calm. But I am also determined to help Jay."

She turned and made as if to leave the room, barely taking a single step before her father's stern voice called her back.

"Juliet Hampton, come back here and sit down. You will discuss this matter with me before you do anything."

Juliet paused with her back toward her father, as if considering whether or not to obey the order. Hampton waited for his daughter to make the next move. He felt ill at ease with her now, as if she had somehow changed from an innocent pawn into a formidable opponent. The transition had occurred at about the same time as Lieutenant Alford's unexplained disappearance from New York. There were rumors about that he had been a spy, a coward, a deserter, and some believed him simply the victim of foul play. But none of these rumors seemed convincing to Juliet, and Hampton had been forced to question whether his decision to keep Michael's last visit to the house a secret had been a wise one. Perhaps Juliet had seen him arrive or depart, or one of the other servants besides James might have witnessed his arrival and mentioned it to her. It was too late at this point to confide in his daughter. His decision had been made when he had woken at dawn with a splitting headache and had promptly informed James that no one was to know of the late-night visitor. Lieutenant Alford was gone, and he would not be coming back. The fact that his name had been linked with his daughter's these past months would soon be forgotten.

Juliet finally took her seat, chin held high and eyes flashing. Hampton drew a long breath and leaned forward, placing folded hands comfortably on his desk.

"Juliet, you are to be wed in a few short weeks. It would be unwise to stir up trouble with Harold now, for any reason." She opened her mouth to protest, but he went on. "Hear me out! I propose a compromise. I shall discharge Jay, but I shall be extremely generous in the terms of that dismissal."

"What do you mean?"

He met her eyes squarely for a long moment. He had no desire to risk her further displeasure. "I propose to give him, say . . . a few hundred pounds . . . with which to travel to another location and begin a new life."

Juliet lowered her eyes and kept her face carefully void of expression. Her father's generosity had been greater than she had hoped, but she could not appear too eager to accept. She forced a sigh and gave a halfhearted nod.

"I suppose that it would insure his remaining years."

"You speak as if the man were near death, Juliet. He is in fact barely forty-five years of age. They tell me General Washington is the same number . . . thank goodness you have no sympathy for his remaining years, or I might well be penniless!"

He chuckled at his own humor, while Juliet bit back an angry reply.

"Very well. I shall see it done. Of course, Harold need not be informed of our agreement."

She nodded coldly.

"As we have begun to discuss things," he continued, "I may as well ask you about Frances." His eyes narrowed. "Why have you suddenly decided that it is so important for Edgar to leave New York?"

She could not keep her mouth from twisting into a bitter smile. So Rachel had already reported that to her father! Her father gave her smile an incorrect interpretation.

"It is really not Edgar I am concerned about, Father. It is Frances. I suddenly realized that I would miss her terribly, yet I know that she would never leave New York for my sake, or her own. Edgar is the only reason she would agree to sail for England, so . . . I used him."

His eyes searched her face, questioning not her unselfishness, but her ability to employ such deception. "Why so soon? Before the wedding?"

"Isn't it obvious? The longer she has to consider, the less likely she will be to go through with it." She paused, formulating her next words carefully. "In truth, Father, there is a second reason. Frances knows that I was married to Alec, and before the wedding there will be a rush of parties . . . and a great deal of drinking. If she should let something slip . . ." She shifted uneasily in her chair. "I am extremely upset about Michael's disappearance. My nerves are stretched so tightly that I cannot even sleep at night. It seems that everything that can go wrong has done so. And now, there is this matter with Jay . . ."

"Which has been resolved," he concluded. "You ought to have told me about your troubles sooner, Juliet. I am certain that a physician will be able to cure your insomnia. I shall send for one in the morning."

"But I am not ill!"

"I realize that. I shall tell him simply that you are a nervous bride-to-be, and he will prescribe laudanum to assure that you get your rest."

Another problem neatly solved, Juliet thought. Without thanking him, she withdrew from the study, leaving her father uneasily drumming his fingers on his desk. Something was not right here, he was thinking. Something was just not right.

Chapter 39

It was nearing the hour of three on the afternoon of May fourteenth, and Frances and Edgar were ready to depart on the *Cooper*. In the carriage on the way to the docks, Juliet tried not to notice the pale, almost greenish hue to Frances's complexion. How she wanted to confide in her, to tell her that the trip would be so much shorter than anyone guessed.

Her arm linked through Harold's, Juliet dutifully smiled at him at proper intervals, renewing her thanks for accompanying her to see her friends off. At the docks Juliet was the last to bid a tearful good-bye to Frances, knowing that if her plans went awry she would not be seeing them for a very, very long time. At the last possible moment, she removed from her bodice a letter that had been folded into a tiny square. She pressed it into Frances's hand and closed her fingers so tightly over the letter that her hand ached. Juliet blinked her tears away and bore into Frances's blue eyes for a long moment.

"Frances," she whispered gently, "I wrote you this letter last night. It says so many things I could never tell you before. Read it, Frances, as soon as you are alone. Read it and know that you must be strong; you must not be afraid. Everything will work out for the best." Juliet kissed her cheek and squeezed the hand holding the letter one last time, as if to remind her of its import. Then she turned away and ran to the carriage, unable to hold back tears of tension and exhaustion any longer.

* * *

It was quite late, and most of the sailors had retired for the night when Frances timidly approached Captain Charlington. His brown eyes perused her frail form completely, taking in the angelic features, the innocent blue eyes. It would be a long voyage, and Miss Church could prove a most interesting diversion. But to the business at hand. Something seemed to have distressed the lady, something even more, perhaps, than the queasiness that she had not been able to hide since setting foot on this ship.

"Can I be of assistance, Miss Church?" he offered gallantly.

Frances began in a voice straining fearfully. "Oh, Captain, I regret so informing you of this, but—"

"What is it, Miss Church?" he asked, solicitously taking her hand.

"I . . . it's Edgar. He's not well."

The captain chuckled. "Seasickness is a common ailment, madame. I assure you it won't last."

"You misunderstand me, Captain. Edgar is not seasick. He is seriously ill! He is burning with fever, and . . ." She stole a glance at him to be certain she had his full attention. "He . . . he has a rash. It's very light, and probably not serious," she said without conviction. "Children are prone to rashes, and it only covers a very small portion of his chest. Still . . . he was exposed to the pox a few weeks ago, and—"

He dropped her hand as if it were a hot iron. "The pox, you say?"

"I don't want to alarm you unnecessarily, sir. Perhaps it is another ailment . . ."

"Exposed to the pox, you say?" he repeated incredulously. He swallowed with difficulty and began to shift his weight nervously from one foot to the other. "Miss Church, if your nephew is ill, I feel it would be best for all concerned if he received immediate medical attention."

"I agree, sir. Have you a ship's physician?"

Captain Charlington ran a finger about his collar and cleared his throat. "Uh, yes . . . but . . . I . . . I cannot vouch for the man's ability. However, it would still be possible for me to dispatch a dinghy to see you both safely ashore. I realize that this would mean a change in plans, but we must consider the boy's welfare first, above our own inconvenience."

"Of course you are correct, sir," Frances relented. How

right Juliet had been in predicting his reaction, she thought. "But what of our baggage?"

"I shall see to it," he assured her.

She nodded and turned as if to leave, then stopped and faced the captain once more. "What of the fare, sir? I am already indebted to Mr. Hampton for so many things. How shall I explain . . . ?"

"I shall reimburse you, Miss Church. But let us lose no time. The boy should receive immediate care."

He swiftly set about waking a dozen or so sailors and put them to the task. As Frances had hoped, not a single sailor stopped to investigate the boy's condition. Everyone kept his distance, fearful of infection.

It was well after midnight when Frances and Edgar, seen safely to a hired coach by one of the sailors who had rowed them ashore, gave their destination to the coachman—an inn several miles south of Manhattan that neither of them had ever seen or heard of before.

The weeks of preparation at Hampton House reached their culmination at the gala reception and ball on the eve of the wedding. No expense had been spared for the celebration of the long-awaited event, and the gifts were piled high. The actual church ceremony, it had been decided, would be tastefully small, but it would be followed by a second elaborate reception, after which the couple would be sailing immediately for England.

As the carriages lined up in the long, curved drive and spilled over far down the road, Hampton House welcomed more guests than ever before. A practiced smile fixed to her mouth, Juliet endured being cajoled, complimented, flattered, toasted. She watched the free flow of alcohol and was careful to carry a full glass about with her at all times. No one noticed that she had scarcely sipped at it at all. It was nearing the hour of ten when she saw her opportunity and coaxed Harold into the garden on the pretext of taking the night air. She frowned painfully as she looked into his pale blue eyes. Who was it that had called him an innocent lamb to the slaughter? He had certainly been accurate in the description. She shook off her feelings of guilt and reminded herself that if she did not wield the ax, someone else would.

"Harold," she sighed, "we have had so little time together! So little time for me to know you, for you to know me."

"Nonsense! We shall have years together! The rest of our lives," he answered brightly.

"I know . . . and yet . . . I have told no one else of this, Harold, but these past few days I have been doubtful of . . . of my ability to go through with the wedding."

Harold's jaw slackened considerably, and the whites of his eyes completely surrounded the blue. "Juliet! You cannot be serious! Tomorrow is our wedding day!"

Juliet blinked back the tears she forced to her eyes. "Harold, I am so afraid! When I think of leaving this place, of never coming back . . ."

Harold fumbled clumsily at her chin and brushed at the tears that had dropped to her cheeks.

"I have not been able to sleep," she choked out. "I feel as though I am doing the wrong thing with my life. Have you ever had a feeling like that?"

"Uh, no . . . no, I haven't," he stuttered nervously. He had no idea of how to cope with an emotional female.

"Perhaps it is only that I am tired. So many things to do, so many parties, packing . . . and I miss Frances dreadfully!"

"Yes! I'm certain that's it! You are simply tired!"

"Oh, Harold, do you suppose that I could slip away, now, early? And retire? This week has been so hectic! But Father will be angry if I retire while all these guests are here in our honor." She sighed deeply, stealing a glance at him to check his reception of the idea. His brow knit in concentration. He would have liked to solve this problem, but Juliet was right. Her father would certainly be angry if she left her own party so early.

"Perhaps if you were to accompany me to my room," she suggested. "We could talk there for a short time. Father should not mind if I want a moment alone with you."

"Juliet!" he gasped, truly scandalized. "That would hardly be proper!"

Juliet sniffed back a fresh flow of tears. "How could you think such a thing? If you do not care about my feelings, my health . . ."

"Of course I care! Come," he told her with determination. "I will take you to bed." When he realized what he had said, his face reddened painfully, and his eyes nearly protruded from their sockets.

Juliet placed a hand lightly on his arm and whispered sweetly, "I know of no other man I would trust with my honor, Harold. You are a perfect gentleman."

He would have led her through the crowd to the main stairway but she directed him another way—through the kitchen to the back stairs, ignoring the puzzled looks they received from the help, as well as the smirks and knowing nods when they were recognized. No one, not even Father, would disturb the eager young lovers on the eve of their wedding.

Once in her room, Juliet lost no time in offering Harold a beverage she had prepared in advance, heavily laced with the sweet-tasting potion the physician had given her to induce sleep. Hardly a quarter of an hour had lapsed before Harold's head teetered precariously and dropped to his chest. Then his body slumped forward in a heap to the floor. Juliet quickly began to undo the fastenings on her dress, but her nervous fingers made it so difficult that in her impatience she tore it apart. She pulled angrily at the elaborately arranged coiffure, her haste making ever more tangles to be brushed out with brisk, painful strokes. It was an hour before she stood before the looking glass, little resembling the fine lady who had been the toast of the party downstairs. She made a final check of her costume and decided that it would pass, except for the queue. It was decidedly too long. She bit her lip and ran to get a pair of shears from her bureau, wincing as she clipped her hair to a more suitable length. She could not think about it now; she had to go while she yet had the time. She slipped a note into Harold's hand and closed his lifeless fingers firmly about it in an attempt to ease her troubled conscience. Then she checked the hallway, pulled her tricorn low on her head, and edged through the hall toward the west wing. Moments later she was dropping to the ground from a low branch of the thick oak tree. She ran from shadow to shadow until she reached the stables. Slipping a bridle over the mare's head, she then hoisted herself onto the mare's back.

She kept the horse under tight rein until she had cleared the Hampton grounds, then slackened the hold and flew through the night, heading south. When she had found the inn that Jay had spoken of several weeks before, she would set the horse free and take up her journey with Frances, Edgar, and Jay. They would travel all night to make a fair head start, but their greatest protection lay in the fact that if anyone were in pursuit, they would be searching for a single young woman, not a young boy in breeches and hat.

Part II
Virginia, 1781

Chapter 40

A troubled frown knitting her brow, Juliet stared out over the familiar view of rolling grass and river flowing languidly in the midday sun. September had brought no break in the moist summer heat, though the evenings had begun to cool this past week, providing some small measure of comfort. Still, within an hour of the sunrise the air became so heavy and motionless that moisture clung to everything; clothing matted itself to skin damp with perspiration, and any physical labor required double the usual effort.

A soft moan and stirring from across the room brought Juliet swiftly to the woman lying there on the bed, but she relaxed, seeing that the woman slept on. Her smooth skin was dreadfully pale, almost transparent, and felt hot under Juliet's gentle hand. She wrung out the cloth in the dish nearby and moistened the parched, burning skin of the sick woman's face, then briefly touched the cloth's coolness to her neck.

Juliet sighed wistfully, remembering the days when Colette Farrell's countenance had beamed with a smile befitting one of far fewer years than she. Her smile had been only a small part of the woman Juliet had come to know and love, and from whom she had learned so much. Juliet's eyes touched the simple wooden cross affixed to the wall above her bed, wondering at the peace and strength Colette had found in her faith. At this moment there was little room in Juliet's heart for faith. The sickness had wreaked havoc on the plantation. Though most had recovered, as she had, within a few days of its inception, others had not been so fortunate. The fever had its worse effect on the very young and the very old. The past few weeks Juliet had spent night after sleepless night keeping vigil in the servants' quarters, helplessly watching tiny black children gradually weaken and die. She had offered what comfort she could to the grieving parents, but little could be done to ease the devastating loss of one's own flesh and blood. And only two weeks before, Juliet had known a terrible personal loss when Edgar had succumbed to the fever. Juliet had never seen death before, but she would never forget her last glimpse of Edgar's wide blue eyes, void of the impish twinkle she had known and loved. She had felt helpless, uncertain, and more than anything she had been afraid. Frances had taken ill almost immediately and had been prostrated with grief ever since. And now Colette lay struggling for her life.

Juliet summoned what remained of her courage to hold back her tears as she thought of Edgar's tiny white cross in the family burying ground. This was not the time for tears! She had to, somehow, hold everything together until Alec came home. Surely he would come soon! Even General Washington had found the time to stop at his home at Mount Vernon just a few weeks before. Alec had to be within a few days of home! Juliet strained to keep tight rein on her emotions. The previous week, in desperation, she had swallowed her pride and written to him, begging him to come home at once, explaining that his mother's health was failing rapidly. The only thing that remained to be done was to hope and pray that he received the missive in time. She had sent Sol, though she could ill afford the loss of his excellent services, to Mount Vernon, where, she hoped, someone would be able to help him find the army and Alec. She remembered well the difficulty of finding one man among so many, but she pushed the despair firmly from her mind. She took up the bowl and cloth and left the bedchamber to follow the long hallway to the back stairs.

As she traced the well-worn path out the back door to the kitchen, the smell of steaming poultry struck her nostrils. Delilah was busy preparing a light broth as Juliet had instructed her to do for those sick with the fever. The sturdy woman's deep brown skin glistened with sweat as she worked with slow, deliberate efficiency. Delilah was a large woman of almost forty, with an angular jaw and strikingly large features. She could manage everything from a simple bowl of porridge to an elaborate dinner for half a hundred, systematically ordering each step of the preparation as well as the serving. But where she was a capable general, she was a timid commander-in-chief. Beau Rêve needed a mistress, a woman to take charge of the house and to give orders. And these past few weeks the responsibility had fallen entirely on Juliet's shoulders.

"We be mighty low on flour, Miz Juliet. The stream's down to a trickle, and that ol' mill jus' ain' a grindin' nothin'."

Juliet sighed and did her best to hide the discomfort she felt as she entered the kitchen. The freshly stoked fire burning in the room made it feel like an oven, despite the opened windows. "Have you finished with the broth?"

"Yes'm."

Juliet ladled out a small portion for Colette and informed Delilah that someone ought to be sent to take a bowl of it to Frances, also, and to see that she ate every bit.

"I'll check on Frances myself later this afternoon, but I don't want to leave Colette alone."

"How be Miz Colette?" Delilah asked with some concern.

"The same."

"Don' you worry none now. My Sol be deliverin' that letter quick as anybody can, and he bring back Mist' Alec afore you know it." The woman's chin rose with pride.

Juliet sighed and attempted a smile. "I am certain that he will. That is exactly why I sent him."

She left the kitchen and stopped at the dipping well to put fresh water into the washbowl. Then, arms full, she retraced her steps and returned to Collette's bedside. Juliet pulled a chair close to the bed and again sponged the woman's skin. She lifted her head and spooned small portions of broth into her mouth, but much of the effort was wasted. The liquid slipped from lifeless lips and dribbled down her chin. At length Juliet set the bowl aside and wiped away what had been spilled. She was so tired, so very tired! Sleep had been an elusive stranger these past weeks. As she closed her eyes, the same troubling thoughts crowded her mind, and with them, the same unanswered questions, the same despair.

Had it really been over four years since her arrival at Beau Rêve? The journey here had been six endless weeks of hardship, of traveling crude, unfamiliar roads, always with the fear that they were being followed. During that time Juliet had almost grown accustomed to sleeping on the rough wooden bed of a cart as it creaked and bumped along the rutted roadways. She and the others had often been drenched by a sudden rain or chilled by the dampness of a misty night. Roadside inns were few and far between, most were hardly fit places for ladies, and none offered what could be termed comfortable accommodations.

They had arrived at Beau Rêve well after nightfall, travel-weary and on the brink of total physical exhaustion. To Juliet it had seemed almost as though their journey had ended in paradise. At her very first look at this house, illuminated by a full silver moon, she felt that she had come home. The setting was serene, with lush greenery all about, and the pleasant noises of locusts and crickets blended with the quiet rush of the river as it flowed languidly past. And Colette. She would always remember her first glimpse of the woman whose eyes were so like her son's that Juliet felt an immediate attachment to her. Colette, clad in a nightgown and wrapper, had rushed to take a weary Frances into her arms, listening to her breathlessly relate the news that her letter had been a mistake, that Alec was alive, before she nodded and told her of his recent visit home. And then she had apologized and eagerly turned to welcome the others, seeing to their immediate comfort with a warmth that made them feel like family, though she knew them only as Frances's friends.

Juliet smiled, remembering her initial tour of the grounds. She had been taken to the various outbuildings and told the function of each: the kitchen, the spinning house, the salt house, the smokehouse, the washhouse, and so on. It had seemed to Juliet that there were a hundred of them, and she was certain that she would never be able to remember which was what.

"It's like a city!" she had cried in awe. "Surely you do not oversee everything yourself!"

Colette had assured her that she did indeed, from the planning of her kitchen garden to the management of the shoemaker's shop. Everything and everyone at Beau Rêve ultimately depended on her. Juliet had shaken her head in wonder. "I could never begin to undertake such a task."

"Why not?" Colette had returned with a smile that reminded her so much of Alec. "Are you afraid of a challenge?"

It had been the beginning of a strong bond between the two, strengthened by their sharing of everyday life, of common joys and sorrows that brought them closer together. Colette, as she had asked Juliet to call her, was more than willing to teach the younger woman every phase of plantation life. She welcomed her help, finding her not only eager and willing to learn, but capable as well. While Frances was content to sit mending, writing letters, and, most of all, caring for Edgar, Colette taught Juliet tasks she found far more interesting than anything her own mother had taught her or things she had learned at school. Juliet smiled, remembering . . .

The first hard winter the plantation residents had slowed their normal hustle-bustle to a quieter pace. One afternoon about six months after her arrival, Juliet had spent several hours in the library with Colette, who made entries into a large book, explaining each as she went along. Juliet watched for a time, but her eyes constantly strayed from the neat columns of figures to her surroundings. In the past months she had been far too busy to spend much time in the house, and with the advent of the cold weather, this room had been closed off for the sake of saving fuel. But today the hearth held a glowing fire that dispelled the natural chill, and while Colette was intent on her paperwork, Juliet went about inspecting titles of the leatherbound volumes that lined three walls from floor to ceiling. She noticed a group of miniatures on the far wall and immediately advanced for a closer view.

One portrait was of a man in an elaborate powdered wig. Though the face was unfamiliar to her, something in the eyes, the set of his mouth, the firm line of his jaw reminded her of Alec. Under the first portrait was another of a man whom Juliet guessed to be Alec's father. Under that were a pair of miniatures, side by side. She stared at the artist's conception of her husband as a young man, and frowned as she examined the other, who had to be Justin.

Colette raised her eyes to see Juliet's deep contemplation of the portraits of her sons. Suddenly a realization dawned. Juliet . . . Julie . . . could the two be the same? She watched as the girl raised a timid finger to touch the small painting like a child, hoping that a touch would somehow give it life. Unknown to Juliet, she saw the tears collect in her eyes and the effort it took for her to blink them away. Colette's brow mirrored her confusion as she closed the book. How could this be?

Juliet had admitted to meeting Alexander, of course, at the Churches' home in New York. But there was far more emotion here than befitted a casual acquaintance. When she had arrived at Beau Rêve so late that night, Frances had been bursting with the news that Alexander was not dead, only to find that Colette had seen him not two months before. Now that she thought about it, Frances had faltered several times during her introduction of Juliet as her "close friend." But she had been so tired after such a long trip that Colette had overlooked it. Then, too, she did not believe Alexander's explanation that his "Julie" was dead. The hurt in him was something more than an inability to accept the death of a loved one, of that she was certain. But what, then, had happened between these two young people?

"That is Alexander, my son," she said aloud, noting that Juliet immediately withdrew her hand. "You met him in New York before the war, I believe."

"Yes," she answered hastily, directing her attention to the remaining portraits. "Who are the others?"

Colette rose and went to stand beside her. "The first is another Alexander Farrell, my son's grandfather. He obtained the patent on this land long before this house was built. He had another plantation in the Tidewater that was left to his eldest son."

"The Tidewater?" Juliet had heard the term used, but it had never been explained to her.

Colette removed an oversized book from a shelf on the adjacent wall. She opened it and folded out a neatly drawn map of the colonies. "Here, this is Virginia Colony. Here is the Chesapeake Bay. The Tidewater is the coastal region, the area first colonized. Here is Jamestown, the first English settlement." She turned to a second, more detailed map of the area. "Where the Tidewater includes the lowlands, Virginia's middle section is more or less a plateau, or a raised area, and it is commonly called the Piedmont. Beyond the Piedmont are the mountains. Here is where we are, Beau Rêve. You see, it is marked."

Juliet studied the map, nodding.

"Much of the land in the Tidewater that has been used for growing tobacco year after year is worn out. This is why so many men have moved away from the coast, why they buy up patents on thousands of acres of new land, because they know that the land being tilled now will eventually be useless. A few years ago, when the King decreed that no more Virginians could settle beyond the mountains, many felt that it threatened their future and the future interests of their children."

She paused, then closed the book, noticing that Juliet's eyes had strayed to Alec's portrait. "Have you thought about what you will do when the war is over?"

Juliet lowered her eyes and drove all expression from her voice. "I have an aunt in England. I thought I might go there—"

"Nonsense! Surely you've considered marriage! You are young and bright and very pretty, and I am certain that some young man will be clever enough to win your heart. And he will be a lucky man indeed!"

Juliet swallowed hard. How she longed to spill her heart out to this woman, but she had no choice but to keep her secret. She had learned the night she arrived that Alec had been home just weeks before and had renewed his longtime romance with his fiancée, Cassandra Collins. And she had met Cassandra, who visited Beau Rêve at least once a month to see if there had been any word from him. Unfortunately Cassandra was very beautiful. Her hair was a soft, silvery blond, always arranged in the latest style, and her green eyes were even brighter than the silks and satins she always wore.

"I had planned to marry a man in New York," Juliet said finally, "but I realized that I did not love him. So I left and came here with Frances."

"And I thank God that you did. I cannot tell you how much help you have been to me, Juliet. You have been the daughter I always wished for, and I tell you now that as long as I am alive, you will have a home here at Beau Rêve." She put an arm about Juliet's shoulder. "Somehow I feel you belong here."

Juliet blinked back her tears and once again resisted the temptation to tell Colette the truth. Colette Farrell was the mother she had never known, but she was Alec's mother first.

If it was in Alec's mind to forget her, then he would do so without his mother's knowledge. And if he had eagerly courted Cassandra in the brief time he spent at home, how indeed could she claim any hold on him at all? But neither could she leave without ever seeing him, without ever knowing for herself that what Cassandra claimed was true.

Colette also studied the portraits, and an uneasy silence began to settle between them. When she finally spoke, her voice was calm and only slightly wistful. "This other young man was Justin, my firstborn son. He looked very much like Alexander, and yet he was very different. Justin fancied himself a writer, an artist, while Alexander was content to work the land and to breed his horses. And there was another difference. Perhaps because it is in the nature of a writer to want to share what he feels with those he loves, Justin had no fear of sharing his most heartfelt thoughts, his deepest sorrows. But Alexander . . ." She frowned and shook her head. "He often reminds me of a treasure box with a key that has been locked inside. You must have the key to open the box, but you must open the box to get the key!" She smiled at Juliet, but her eyes remained sad.

"What happened to Justin?" Juliet asked, unable to contain her curiosity.

"There was an accident. He tried to ride one of Alexander's horses, and he was thrown . . . his neck was broken." She paused, and the trace of pain was sharpened as she remembered. "I think that Alexander felt guilty about Justin's death, but there were others present who swore it was no fault of his. He never told me what happened or how he felt about it; he never once spoke of it to anyone I know of."

Juliet sighed. "Perhaps he confides in Miss Collins?"

Colette gave a short laugh. "Cassandra Collins would be the last person Alexander would ever confide in! My son is usually perceptive when it comes to people, and he knows exactly what Cassandra is."

Juliet's eyes widened in amazement. "Are you saying that he does not love her? But he intends to marry her!"

"Yes," Colette agreed slowly, "but I think not because he loves her. The marriage was originally arranged by my husband. It is considered a natural arrangement here for the young people of neighboring plantations to marry, though

394

their feelings are usually taken into consideration, of course. Some people say that all the planters in Virginia are 'cousins,' and there is some truth to the statement.

"I am certain that when Jerome spoke with Cassandra's father, he had no idea that Alexander would be so vehemently opposed to the union. And he was considering other things at the time. The tobacco crop had failed for two years running after Justin's death, and Jerome saw the marriage as a simple solution to everything."

"And Alec did not?"

Colette smiled, noting that Juliet had used her son's familiar name. "No. In fact, he refused to honor the agreement made by his father. He left home, went to Europe for a time, and only returned after Jerome had passed away. Alexander loved his father, but he could never find it in his heart to forgive him. He felt that Jerome had betrayed him, and, unfortunately, Jerome was equally as stubborn." She sighed very deeply and tried to smile. "I prayed that time would heal the rift between them, but Alexander refused to return home until after his father's death, and he has never been one to talk about the past. I wonder sometimes if it is because he cannot deal with it honestly. . . ."

"He must have changed his mind since then. Cassandra makes no secret of the fact that they intend to marry when he returns."

"Yes," Colette agreed wryly. "She is certainly persistent in this matter, but I think that it's only that Alexander is the first man she ever wanted and failed to win, with her charm or with her father's money. Those green eyes of hers have no effect on his heart, and well she knows it!"

Juliet dared not show her eagerness to believe what Colette had just told her. "Perhaps you are mistaken, Colette. Cassandra was very encouraged when Alec was home last spring. And there is no denying that she's a beautiful woman."

"I believe that Alexander renewed his courtship of her for another reason, Juliet—a financial one."

Juliet's heart fell. With all her might she tried to believe Colette's words. But one thing she knew for certain. Alec would never compromise his principles for the sake of money. Besides, hadn't Colette's entire tale of the past reinforced what she already knew? No; if Alec planned to marry Cassandra, then he must love her. But what of his wife? Did he intend to forget the vows spoken in haste on that summer's morn in New York? Did he expect her to do the same? She stared at the miniature and suddenly realized how little she knew of her husband. He was indeed like a treasure box with the key locked inside. . . .

The sleeping woman stirred, and Juliet's thoughts of the past scattered momentarily while she saw to her patient's comfort. Several moments later, she settled in her chair once more, remembering . . .

The day was crisp and cool, and the dry leaves rustled as the wind shook the trees. Colors were splashed everywhere on the landscape. The sky was a brilliant blue, the trees were red and brown and gold, and the grass was only slightly less green than it had been in the summer's heat. Out in the stables, Juliet stroked the stallion's soft neck and offered him a carrot. She laughed when he grunted his thanks. "I regret to inform you that there won't be any more carrots for a long while, Spaniard," she told him. "The frost last night finished off the kitchen garden. But it looks to be a fine year for apples. Every bough in the orchard is drooping with them. Do you like apples, Spaniard?"

He snorted his approval, and she laughingly patted his neck. "Good boy!"

"Ain' never seen nobody get along with horses like you do, Miz Juliet—sep maybe Mist' Alec. Too bad you ain' a man, else'n you could break this 'n an' that's a fact!"

"Don't tempt me, Sol," she smiled. "He's the most beautiful horse I've ever seen! Even prettier than Cheval, don't you think?"

"Yes 'm. I sho' do. But he sho' is a difficult animal! Ain' nobody gonna' break him—not till Mist' Alec gets home, leastwise."

Juliet sighed her frustration. A few years ago, Jay could have broken Spaniard, she was certain. But his body was painfully twisted with rheumatism, so that all he managed lately was keeping the tack in good condition. He left the heavier work to the younger slaves assigned to the stables, and on cold or wet days even his lightest tasks went to Sol.

"Well there, Miss Hampton!"

The voice that called the greeting was cheery, but it was

not one that Juliet welcomed. She tossed a glance over her shoulder, and her worst suspicions were confirmed. Wade Collins had found her, despite her attempts to avoid him. Ever since their first meeting a few months before, he had made it a point to accompany Cassandra on her visits to Beau Rêve, though his avid admiration for Juliet had not been at all encouraged.

"A fine animal," he commented. "I intend to buy him—as soon as Mistress Farrell sets the price," he added importantly.

Juliet's reply was cold. "I doubt if she will ever sell him, Mr. Collins. Spaniard is the last of his line."

Wade laughed, and his green, catlike eyes sparkled much like his sister's. "Everything at Beau Rêve is for sale, Miss Hampton."

Juliet's eyes grew hard, and her mouth tightened. "In that you are mistaken, sir, I can assure you."

"Perhaps," he relented. He had failed to impress her with his money, but surely she would stand in awe of his natural ability with horses. "The horse is of little use here, you must admit. If I took him to Tamarack, I could have him broken in less than a week."

"And break his spirit as well, no doubt," Juliet taunted.

"A horse's spirit is of no use unless he knows who is master," he said without a smile. "And he would learn that quickly enough from me. Not that he would ever be a great horse like Caesar, but he could cut a fair figure, with the proper training."

"Caesar?" she repeated incredulously. "Why, he's a cow-hocked gelding compared to Spaniard!"

Wade's green eyes widened, and a muscle in his jaw began to twitch. "Obviously you know nothing of judging horse-flesh, Miss Hampton. This horse could never equal one born and bred at Tamarack."

"This horse could run circles around any horse from your stables, and if you cannot see that, then *you* are the poor judge of horseflesh, sir"—she poked a forefinger at his chest—"not I!"

"Miss Hampton," he gritted out, "it is fortunate that you are a lady, or I would be forced to call your bluff! In deference to your gender," he added generously, "I shall attempt to forget the insult."

"It was no insult, sir," she assured him tersely. "It was a mere statement of fact. And I should be happy to stand behind my statement, if you care to make a wager to that effect."

"I do not wager with women, Miss Hampton."

"And why not, Mr. Collins? Are you so afraid of losing?"

He straightened under her sharp gaze. "Certainly not! But I am a gentleman, Miss Hampton. I could not even consider it." He paused and brushed at the lapels of his beige broadcloth coat. "Besides, everyone knows that you are penniless—as are the Farrells." He looked pointedly at her drab homespun gown.

Juliet clenched her fists so tightly that they hurt. "Well, everyone happens to be wrong, Mr. Collins!" she flung back. "I have money, gold as a matter of fact. And if you were truly the gentleman you claim to be, you would stand behind your convictions as I do mine!"

She had turned on her heel and taken all of two long, angry strides before Wade answered her challenge. "I accept the wager, Miss Hampton."

She stopped in mid-stride, and a slow smile crept over her face. "Are you certain that you will not mind losing to me, Mr. Collins?"

His jaw tightened visibly. He was accustomed to sedate, simpering plantation belles who quietly and efficiently catered to their menfolk. The audacity of this woman was scarcely to be believed! Well, she deserved to lose her money, if indeed she had any, and if she did not . . . Well, now! That would be an interesting proposition! She would have to pay one way or another, and Wade, being a congenial man, would be happy to accept a payment other than gold.

"The terms will have to be worked out, Miss Hampton. How soon will your horse be ready to race?"

It was ludicrous, he thought with a cocky grin. There wasn't a soul on Beau Rêve capable of training the beast. The best she could hope for was that Alec would be home in time to break him, as well as race him, and that was a doubtful prospect, to be sure!

"I shall need a month, no more. Shall we say All Hallows Eve?"

"That is agreeable. And we must set the price of the wager, Miss Hampton." His green eyes glittered as he looked her over, trying to fix a price.

"The gold jewelry I have is worth nearly a hundred pounds. Being a gentleman, I am certain that you are willing to give me odds." Michael had taught her quite a bit about gambling during their short friendship, and she put that knowledge to good use now. "Say, four to one?"

"Four to one?" he gasped. This woman was a bit more knowledgeable in the matter of wagering than he had thought. Still, if the wager was a sure thing, what difference the odds? "You drive a hard bargain, Miss Hampton. But, of course, you are correct. You deserve to have odds."

"And the distance . . . let us say, one mile. Is that agreeable?"

He nodded, and his smile faded in the face of her confidence.

"Why then, Mr. Collins, we only need decide the place and the time. Shall we say dawn, the straight stretch of road near the river. Do you know the place?"

Again he nodded. "Fair enough."

"It is settled then. Until All Hallows Eve." She turned and was nearly out of the stable when she called brightly over her shoulder. "Good luck, Mr. Collins. You will certainly need it."

The day following her confrontation with Wade, Juliet was up before dawn and dressed in the less than feminine apparel that had already served her as wedding gown and traveling garb. She had told no one of her foolishness, recognizing that it was that. She knew well enough that Colette would never agree to her trying to break Spaniard, particularly after what had happened to Justin. But once the horse was broken she was certain that Colette would agree to the race. If she refused . . . Juliet put the thought quickly from her mind and made her way to Jay's quarters adjacent to the stables.

"Why, ye be demented!" he broke in frantically as she began to explain. "Ye always had ye a temper, but ye never before did such a thing as this!"

"Will you help me or not, Jay?"

He shook his head in disbelief. "And if I not be helpin' ye,

ye be trying to see to it yeself." He heaved a heavy sigh. "All
Hallows Eve! Why, ye haven't a prayer!"

"Yes or no?"

Without ever giving her a direct answer, Jay made his way
to the tack room and began to gather the necessary equipment.

"Ye be fortunate that he be familiar wi' a bridle an' wi'
bein' led about. We be startin' wi' the horse in the paddock,
wi' leadin' him about on this. This here be a lungeline. It
be for teachin' the horse to move around his master." He
frowned his disapproval and pointed an accusing finger.
"That be ye," he said gruffly before shuffling past her.

She hurried after him, observing as well as listening to
every word he said. First he wrapped the horse's front legs securely in long strips of white cloth. "To keep him from
injurin' himself," he explained. "We be using a halter for
lungeing. It be better for him than a bridle."

He fixed the lungeing line to the halter and led the horse to
the center of the paddock before he handed it over to Juliet.
"Now take up the slack so he be movin' in a tight circle, jus'
big enough t' be comfortable for him t' turn about. No! Not
like that! Never roll it around ye hand. If he takes it in his
mind t' run, ye'll be pulled right along." Juliet pulled lengths
of slack and held them in the palm of her hand as Jay directed. "That's it. Now, I be usin' the whip at first till he gets
the feel o' takin' orders from ye. Talk to him firm now, so he
knows ye mean business."

It was a much slower process than Juliet had ever imagined. By the end of the first week, with nearly two hours invested each and every morning, Spaniard was responding in a
way that only slightly encouraged her. She began to use the
whip herself while Jay looked on, and Spaniard obeyed her
commands to walk, trot, canter, and stop. By the middle of the
second week, Jay agreed to add the saddle but still refused to
allow Juliet to ride. At the beginning of the third week, Juliet
was getting nervous.

"I've got to race him in less than two weeks, Jay!" she
pleaded. "And I don't even know how he runs!"

"If ye want t' see him run, take ye a look when I turns him
out t' pasture! If ye climbs on him too soon, it's not riding ye'll
be doin'."

Finally, with only a week and a half to go before the race, Jay gave the nod for Juliet to take to the saddle. "Don't be so anxious there! I want t' see ye calm and serious. Remember, if he gets excited or smells yer fear, there'll be no racin' him at all." His eyes narrowed, and he cocked his head to give Juliet a sidelong glance. "An' I not be wantin' t' explain his poor trainin' t' Captain Farrell when he be comin' home."

Properly reprimanded, Juliet sobered and quietly followed Jay to see Spaniard saddled.

"Ease yeself down now. Don't plop. That's it . . . easy. And talk t' him."

In the enclosed stall, Juliet leaned down to stroke the stallion's neck and spoke in a low, calming tone, assuring him that there was no cause for alarm. With a firm hold on the bridle, Jay opened the stall and coaxed the horse to take his first few steps with the strange weight on his back. The steed neighed nervously, and his eyes were wide and fearful, but he followed Jay with very little protest. Out in the paddock, Jay led him about the perimeter two complete times in either direction. Then he released his hold and slowly backed away. Now it was up to Juliet.

With a click of her tongue he was moving for her, slowly and timidly at first, then in a trot. When she signaled for him to stop, pulling back tersely on the reins, he mistook the command and reared, sending Juliet promptly to the ground. Then he raced to the far side of the paddock, as if realizing that he had done something wrong. Juliet got up, brushed herself off, and advanced to the horse's side. She reached out to stroke his neck as she encouraged him.

"We haven't much time, Spaniard, and I am not the greatest rider in the world. But you're a better horse than Caesar. It's that simple! You'd like to prove that, wouldn't you? You'd like to show that Wade Collins?"

Jay was nearby and made to take hold of the bridle once more, but Juliet shook her head. Easily, quietly, all the while talking to the horse, she slipped her foot into the stirrup and lifted herself into the saddle.

Spaniard had flown through the air the day of the race. He had moved with such grace and power that Juliet had wondered if his hooves ever touched the ground. She had never really considered that the race might draw a crowd, but people had flocked to the Old River Road until they lined both sides far beyond the finish line. She would never forget Wade's face when she arrived that morning wearing breeches and a jacket. Or the way Colette had stood proudly in the crowd cheering her on, while most of the women had immediately lifted their noses in the air and returned to their carriages to wait for their husbands, absolutely scandalized. Spaniard and she had won the race handily, taking not only money but a good helping of pride from Wade Collins. . . .

The money had been a godsend. It was spent now, almost to the penny, and when the taxes came due next year . . . She squeezed her eyes tightly shut and tried not to think about that. Surely Alec would be home by then! The war could not go on forever!

She smiled a sad smile, remembering that Robert had thought to be home before the end of 1776. Both she and Frances knew now that neither he nor Alec would be home until the very last battle was decided. But it had already lasted an eternity! At first each piece of news had brought pangs of despair: the British victories at Brandywine, Monmouth, and Charleston; the betrayal of the cause by Benedict Arnold. Or bursts of hope: particularly the battle of Saratoga, where Burgoyne's surrender had finally nudged the French into a full alliance with the colonies, bringing a real hope for a quick end to the war. Yet, four long years later, that hope still had not been realized. Instead the fighting had edged ever closer to Virginia, with bloody and sadistic Indian attacks on the western frontier, raids on Chesapeake coastal plantations, and Benedict Arnold's sacking of the city of Richmond. There were continual pleas for contributions of money and jewelry, shortages of leather and tools, horses and wagons. Following the battle of Saratoga, there had been four thousand prisoners of war sent to be quartered in nearby Albemarle County. Thomas Jefferson, who had since been elected governor of Virginia, and his wife, Martha, had become friendly with many of the Hessian officers, including a certain Baroness Riedesel, who was traveling with her general husband. The baroness had shocked the women for miles about by riding astride like a man. Juliet chuckled, remembering Cassandra's condescending attitude as she related the story of the baroness. She would certainly like to meet this woman someday.

Juliet rose and went over to check on Colette. The older woman's eyes opened, and she smiled weakly at Juliet.

Juliet returned the smile and tested Colette's brow with her palm. It was noticeably cooler. She lifted one of Colette's hands and held it in both of her own. "I was so afraid that you . . ." She shook her head and blinked back her tears. "I sent Sol to bring Alec home."

Colette gave a feeble nod.

"Delilah made fresh broth. Would you like some? It might help you regain your strength."

Again the nod.

Juliet rose and hurried to get a bowl of broth, smiling all the while she descended the stairs.

Juliet slipped quietly into Frances's room and nodded a dismissal to the young slave who sat at her bedside. She stretched her palm over Frances's brow, which was cool, though her skin remained terribly pale.

Frances's eyelids fluttered wearily open, and worried blue eyes searched her face. "Aunt Colette! She is not—"

"She is much improved," Juliet smiled, taking firm hold of her hand. "She will recover now, I am certain of it. How are you feeling?"

Frances looked away, blinking repeatedly as her eyes filled with tears. "I still cannot believe he's gone, Juliet. I know it in my head, but my heart refuses to believe."

Juliet squeezed her hand tightly in unspoken understanding, even as her own grief sharpened.

"I keep thinking over and over that this has all been a terrible dream, that I shall wake one morning and find him still here. But then I wake up. And he is . . ." She could not bring herself to say the word.

"I know, Frances. I know so well what you are feeling. Sometimes death is so impossible to understand. Sometimes I want to scream with anger and bitterness at the injustice of it all!" She let out her breath and shook her head. "But that would accomplish so little," she said helplessly. "It would never bring little Edgar back to us."

Frances sobbed aloud at that, and Juliet gathered her

quickly in her arms. "I'm sorry, Frances," she crooned softly. "I should not have spoken in anger." A small, sad smile touched her lips. "Colette told me once that I ought not to question why. 'Never ask God to explain His workings,' she told me. 'Accept what life brings, do the very best you can, and He will take care of the rest.'" Strangely enough, Juliet drew strength from the words, even as she repeated them to Frances.

"Aunt Colette is right," Frances said, a small white hand wiping the tears from her cheeks. "We must not dwell on things that are not in our power to change."

Juliet gently aided Frances in settling her head back against the pillows, studying the frown that still pulled at Frances's brow. She gnawed indecisively at her bottom lip. "I sent Sol to deliver a letter to Alec," she began. Frances's eyes opened wide in surprise. "I wrote him of her illness because I feared the worst," she explained, feigning indifference that Frances did not quite believe. "I thought he would want to know."

"Then he must also know that you are here," Frances concluded.

Juliet nodded. "And you. I asked him to get a message to Robert, if at all possible." There was a sudden glow in Frances's eyes at the mention of his name. "Rumor has it that the bulk of the Continental Army is not so far from here." She smiled and gave Frances's arm a pat. "You may see Robert far sooner than you think."

Frances's blue eyes were wistful as she half smiled in return. "It has been so very long since I have seen him, Juliet. Not since New York . . ." Her voice trailed off as she remembered their farewell, and Juliet's eyes clouded with memories of her own. There was a long silence.

"I think of your father sometimes," Frances said suddenly. "I wonder if he ever really realized how much he hurt you with his schemes. And Robert, too."

Juliet bit back the bitter response that sprang to her lips even after all the time that had passed. She had no doubt that her father had known exactly what he was doing. She knew now that he was a totally callous man, a man willing to destroy anyone who stood in the way of his plans. She shuddered to think how near he had come to destroying her.

"I am certain he did not realize it, Frances," she lied, knowing that in her innocence, Frances could conceive of no one so evil. "I am only surprised," she went on thoughtfully, as much to herself as to Frances, "that I have never heard from him these past four years. Surely it must have occurred to him that we would come here. Father is so very clever, and it is the logical place, after all. . . ." Her voice trailed off as Frances covered her mouth to stifle a yawn.

"I never thought of that," Frances said sleepily.

Juliet promptly pushed her own thoughts aside and briefly pressed a cool compress to Frances's brow, cheeks, and neck. "Rest now. You will need your strength when Robert comes home."

Frances yawned again, her eyes closing, her cupid's-bow mouth curving into a small smile. "When Robert comes home," she repeated to herself as she settled her cheek against the pillow.

Captain Alexander Farrell lay on the tattered remains of his woolen blanket, alone in his tent, oblivious to the sounds of raucous merrymaking taking place outside. Though the light was dim, his eyes scanned the letter he had received only a few days before. So Juliet was at Beau Rêve, nursing his dying mother. He was not looking forward to such a homecoming, even though the battle fought here at Yorktown and Cornwallis's surrender of an entire British army could well mean an end to the war. Regardless, it was the end of fighting for Alec. He had no choice but to leave for home.

How had she gotten there? he wondered. But more important, why had she come? Had she grown tired of her handsome young lieutenant? Or had he grown tired of her? Perhaps she had left to be rid of Lord Harold. He must have arrived in New York expecting to be married soon after Alec had left. One thing was certain. She had kept their marriage a secret. Sol had explained simply that she was a friend of cousin Frances, though he had not spared words in his admiration of her. "She be doin' a fine job, seein' t' the plantation, Mist' Alec. But it ain' been easy wi' the fever takin' everybody sick. . . ."

Alec threw an arm over his forehead and wondered if he would ever see his mother again. He had left her with a nearly impossible task over four years before, though if anyone were capable of running the place alone, surely that person was Colette Farrell. Pride, determination, and courage were second nature to her. Alec had always been proud of those qualities in his mother, for he had known so few women who possessed them. He remembered their last meeting, and the painful distance that had separated them more than the miles between them did now. Yet he knew that his mother had understood. No matter how he tried to conceal his feelings, his mother had always been able to see through to the truth.

"Use this war if you must, Alexander," she had told him when she bid him farewell. "Rid yourself of the hate you feel and return to Beau Rêve to start again. I shall hold it for you, and I shall pray for your safe return. . . ."

How had she known that he returned to Washington's army for a much different reason than that he had joined for in the spring of '75? Oh, the cause was every bit as honorable and just as it had been before, but Alec's motives were no longer so honorable. ". . . Loved I not honor more," he thought, remembering the poem. He was no longer the man who had quoted that phrase. He had blatantly courted a woman he despised for money, ignoring the vows he had made to Juliet less than a year before. Of course, he rationalized, she had broken them first; but marriage promises were not made contingent on the fidelity of one's spouse. Legally and morally, whether or not either or both chose to ignore the fact, Juliet was still his wife. And though she had betrayed his trust in her; though she had danced the nights away and playfully ridden about Manhattan with her lover while he stared at the dank walls of a prison; though she had played the coquette at his home while the army, half-frozen and starving, had struggled to survive at Valley Forge; though every part of him wanted to despise her, still he loved her. His arms ached to hold her.

He kneaded his brow, so tight with tension and frustration. After four long years of being a soldier, of facing death or worse, being captured again, there was nothing that had frightened him as much as the prospect of facing Juliet once more. Would she run to his arms, he wondered, expecting him to forget her indiscretions? By God, he would not do it! He would never forgive her for what she had done! He crumpled the letter and angrily tossed it aside, hating it for what it represented. It was time to go home, to fight the most difficult battle of all, and one that he could not afford to lose. But was there really any winning? he asked himself bitterly. The taste of revenge is never so sweet as one might imagine. Certainly it would never be as satisfying as those brief moments of ecstasy he had known with Juliet so long ago. He shut his eyes and did his best to forget the image that always haunted him . . . the hurt little girl whom he had held in his arms, the temptress whose passion had equalled his own, the soft, yielding woman who had given herself to him in love and who had sworn to be his alone. Once her love had made everything in his life fall together in a simple design, but the pieces no longer fit. They lay in shattered fragments on the ground like a fragile pane of glass, never to be repaired.

Chapter 41

In a small nook of a room that was used as a study, Juliet sat with Colette discussing the necessary chores to be done about the plantation. The chill brought on by the evening air, the sounds of axes ringing in the distance, the rustling of the dying leaves, all reminded them that it would not be long before winter. Juliet was bringing Colette up to date.

". . . Peter has three men chopping and splitting firewood, as you can hear. Jake took the cart and enough help to collect the wheat at the west field, and I sent six slaves to pick the last of the grapes. When they finish with that, there are apples falling from the trees. . . ." She sighed, and Colette picked up immediately where she left off.

"The entire kitchen garden must be gone through. Whatever is salvageable should be taken to the greenhouse; seeds must be properly stored for spring planting, and the herbs and flowers dried. The first frost will come any day now. . . ." Colette sat back. The list seemed endless, and she was already tired, though it was not yet noon.

"Colette, you must rest before lunch. Everything will be done, I shall see to it," Juliet said with a reassuring pat on her arm. Then she added with a smile, "Alec should be home any day now."

The other nodded and gave a tired smile. "I believe Cassandra's daily visits have done more to sap my strength than the fever did."

Ever since Cassandra had been informed of Alec's summons to come home, she had made it a point to visit every day, making afternoon "tea" a trial both Juliet and Colette would have preferred to do without. Not only did Juliet dislike Cassandra, but she realized now that she would have little chance to discuss anything with Alec on his homecoming, for Cassandra intended to be right there, waiting.

"I'm looking forward to this winter," Colette was saying. "I believe I shall enjoy those dark days when there is little to do but watch the snow fly across a frosty windowpane. But most of all I look forward to having my Alexander home where he belongs. This time, I intend to see that he stays."

"Perhaps my brother, Robert, will come here as well," Juliet said hopefully. "I miss him dreadfully, and Frances has been so despondent since Edgar died."

"I'm looking forward to meeting your brother, Juliet. Does he resemble you?"

"More in temperament than anything else, I think," she answered thoughtfully. "But he is very, very special, Colette! He would be able to make Frances smile again—and he always made me smile!"

"Ah, this war has cost us dearly, every one of us! It has taken our men and scattered them about the colonies, leaving us to fight our own battles, to live on bits and pieces of information, never knowing for certain where our loved ones are, how they are, when they will be coming home. . . ."

Juliet nodded. "Sometimes I envy Mistress Washington, joining her husband at winter quarters every year since the start of the war. I think I would rather face the battles right alongside the men than be left behind to face the uncertainty we have known." She paused, then lifted the two empty cups that sat on the small desk and moved them to the tray. "I shall give Delilah your orders for dinner, and I shall take Polly and Jim and whoever else I can find and start them to work on the kitchen garden. You lie down," she ordered. "And remember, you'll be entertaining this afternoon."

Colette sighed. "To think that I once took for granted a simple cup of tea in the afternoon. Now 'tea' brings to mind a weak cup of coffee and a visit with Cassandra."

Cassandra arrived at half past two, dressed in a magnificent gown of bright green satin that matched her eyes to perfection. Her hair was arranged in a fashionable mass of silvery curls that more than did justice to the gown. Juliet's labors kept her occupied for well over an hour after Cassandra's arrival, and when she finally joined the group in the parlor she was exhausted. She took a seat with a freshly poured cup of coffee and half listened to Cassandra discussing the hairstyles currently worn in France. Juliet frowned, glancing at Frances and Colette. They, as nearly every woman in Virginia, had taken to wearing homespun as a patriotic gesture as well as a measure of practicality. Each wore her hair in a simple style that could be easily arranged and maintained. Yet on Cassandra rattled, as if she were seated among women dressed like herself. Her gown was lovely, Juliet admitted with a twinge of jealousy. It was cut provocatively low, and it curved to accent her small waistline quite snugly. Juliet wondered if Alec preferred a more fleshy woman, comparing her slender figure to Cassandra's more generous curves. But her thoughts scattered when the plantation bell began to ring, though the day's work was far from finished. She frowned and rose to see to the reason for its premature signal, but had scarcely taken a step when the excited cries reached her ears.

"The massuh be home! The massuh be home!"

Juliet froze in her tracks, suddenly fearful of her first confrontation with her husband in five years. Not so Cassandra, who brushed eagerly past her and made her way out the door to be the first to greet him, leaving the others far behind.

Alec swung down from his horse and found himself in Cassandra's smothering embrace. Her lips struggled to reach his in an ostentatious show of her devotion. "Oh, Alec! Darling! I've waited so long for you to come home! Now we can plan our wedding!"

"Would you mind terribly if I said hello to my mother first?" he asked dryly, not bothering to return the embrace. She made him feel like a sack of goods, bought and paid for, not yet delivered.

With a flutter of her long lashes and a coy smile, Cassandra reluctantly freed him, but she linked her arm possessively in his before he took another step. "Of course, dear."

He disengaged her hold on him to embrace his mother as well as Frances, but Cassandra quickly resumed her position at his side before he greeted Juliet. Juliet waited timidly on the threshold, fighting to conceal a treacherous tide of emotions when she saw the man she loved in the arms of another. Dark eyes locked with gold for a single breathless moment before Juliet felt the color draining from her face. He might as well have struck her full across the face; she felt very much as if he had. His black eyes on her were cold and hard, and the gleam in them was odd, out of place. Juliet remembered that look, remembered it all too well. Her father had looked at her that way when he had been very angry or upset, when his true feelings for her had come to the surface. She felt a sickening lurch in her stomach at the memory, and a rash of long-forgotten feelings clutched at her composure. Her father had not loved her. He had thought her a pawn to be used for his own selfish purposes. Facing that had been one of the hardest things in her life; facing Alec's cold stare made it seem easy in comparison.

"You know Miss Hampton, don't you, Alec? She's a friend of your little cousin, Frances."

"I believe we've met," he said slowly. His black eyes pierced her like a well-honed blade.

"Yes," Juliet managed, lowering her eyes. She felt as if he were accusing her of something, some terrible crime, yet she could name no reason for his indictment. She had spent long, lonely years here, doing everything in her power to make Beau Rêve a home for him, only to find that he had indeed chosen another woman to share it with him.

"We were having coffee in the parlor, darling," Cassandra cooed as she brushed past Juliet once more, this time with Alec on her arm.

Juliet could scarcely breathe for the burning tightness in her throat. How she loved him! She needed him so! She longed to throw her arms about his neck and feel his warm, hard body against her own. She was so shaken from the rejection that she could hardly hold back her tears. She turned and trudged toward the stairs, but Colette took hold of her arm.

"Juliet, you did not finish your coffee."

Juliet shook her head, momentarily unable to answer.

"Come, child. I cannot tolerate Cassandra's ramblings alone."

Juliet swallowed hard and followed her into the parlor, vaguely realizing that Frances was also close to tears. Somehow that made it even more difficult to be strong. Her weakness had to be terribly obvious, she knew, for she was trembling so violently that she could scarcely walk to her chair. In the parlor Cassandra was already serving Alec a cup of coffee. She took a seat so near him on the small couch that even Colette frowned her disapproval, though Alec seemed very comfortable.

"From the note I received I expected to find you at death's door, Mother. You seem to have made a miraculous recovery."

"Thanks to the excellent care I received, my recovery was indeed miraculous," she answered with a smile for Juliet that went unnoticed. "Tell us, Alexander," she said, eagerly changing the subject, "what is the news of the war?"

"The best news of all, Mother. It is over."

"Over!" Frances cried, rising to her feet. "It's truly over? Then Robert will be coming home!" She was smiling, forgetting for the moment that Alec's behavior was unforgivable.

"Yes. He ought to be here within a few weeks. I left almost immediately after the battle at Yorktown, where Cornwallis surrendered his entire army thanks to the French fleet that bottled up the Chesapeake."

"Then there is not a single reason to postpone our wedding! Of course, I shall have to order a dozen new gowns, but Papa will pay the seamstress to work day and night and—"

With a cold smile Alec lifted Cassandra's perfect white hand to his lips and kissed it lightly. "My dear, I have no doubt that you are anxious to be wed, but as I have been home less than a quarter of an hour, I believe the plans should be discussed at a later time." She opened her mouth to protest, but he touched his forefinger to her lips and repeated his request, and his dark eyes left no room for further argument.

From across the room Juliet watched the casual contact Alec shared with Cassandra and felt as if she would be sick. She stared without interest at her cup of coffee, but did not dare drink it for fear she would not be able to keep it down.

As a silence fell, Cassandra noticed that Alec's eyes had drifted to Juliet, and she made a hasty attempt to dispel any interest he might have in the woman. Not that such a drab thing could ever compete with her, but Wade saw something very attractive in Miss Hampton, and after all the time she had invested in Alec, Cassandra intended to take no chances.

"It's so good to have you home, Alec! After so many years of seeing strangers here at Beau Rêve—"

"Strangers?" he repeated blankly.

With a pointed glance at Juliet she gave a delicate laugh. "You know what I mean . . . guests."

"Neither Frances nor Juliet is a guest," Colette reminded her. "This is their home."

"Oh, Colette, you are such a generous person to share your home with those in need! It's a shame that the war has taken so many men and left so many unfortunate women . . . unprovided for."

Juliet bit back an angry retort, allowing Colette to make a more appropriate reply. "Things will be very different now that our men will be coming home. And though I have come to think of Juliet and Frances as the daughters I never had, I have fears that they will be married and gone from here before another summer passes."

"Really!" Cassandra returned with a smirk. "Why, Miss Hampton! I had no idea that your heart belonged to a man fighting the war! And after you led my brother Wade down the primrose path! Why, he'll be so disappointed!"

Juliet's jaw tightened. With tremendous restraint she rose from her chair and politely excused herself to see to dinner. Once on the familiar path to the kitchen, her anger dissolved and was replaced by a strange numbness. She forced her feet to function and her mind to revise the menu for dinner, but as she informed Delilah that Cassandra would be staying, she suddenly broke down into hysterical tears.

"Did that woman give you some sass?" Delilah asked her, a thick arm quickly squeezing her shoulders in an attempt to comfort her. "Don' you worry none now. Mist' Alec home, an' he don' take no sass from nobody."

"I . . . I feel a little sick," Juliet choked out. "Would you make my apologies at dinner?"

Delilah put a hand to Juliet's brow. "You done lost yo' color, that's a fact. You ain' gettin' no mo' fever, I hopes." She shook her head. "You been workin' a mite hard, Missy, now you go right on t' bed. Don' worry 'bout nothin'. Lilah will take care o' everythin'. Go on now!"

Juliet ran from the kitchen to seek the refuge of her own room. She flung herself across the bed and cried, long and hard, but even hours later when the tears had stopped, she felt despair and heartache. She had waited, hoped, prayed for this day, never allowing herself to consider what would happen if Alec refused to admit she was his wife. She had trusted him as completely as she had loved him, and now she felt completely empty. She jerked about anxiously at the sound of someone entering her room, then relaxed, seeing that it was Frances. Her friend came and took hold of her hand.

"Oh, Juliet! I cannot believe that Alec would do such a thing! I . . . I know how you must feel . . ." Frances began to cry, and Juliet forced herself to hold back more tears of her own.

"Sometimes things don't work out the way we planned, Frances. You mustn't cry. It won't help things at all."

"But . . . you are his wife! He . . . he cannot simply . . ."

She knew that Frances was trying to be kind, but she found her pity almost unbearable. "It isn't the end of the world, Frances. Just think! Robert will be coming here any day!"

Frances nodded while the tears continued to roll down her cheeks. "Can I get you anything?" she asked, wiping the tears from her face as she rose from the bed. "Delilah saved you a plate from dinner."

"No, thank you, Frances. I'm not really hungry."

"I told Sol to bring up a nice warm tub. That always makes me feel so much better!"

Juliet sighed and nodded, knowing that Frances would feel happier if she could be of some help. And with a rueful glance at her hands, which still showed traces of that day's work in the garden, Juliet had to admit that she might enjoy a hot bath. A quick smile flashed across Frances's face before she hurried out of the room.

After a lengthy soak in the tub, Juliet rubbed the ends of her long, dark hair between a towel and brushed out the tangles incurred in her vigorous shampooing. She rummaged through her wardrobe, seeking out some piece of clothing that might lift her spirits, but her finest gown was a plain black dress with a full hooped skirt that she had slipped in with Frances's garments when she had helped her pack to leave New York. Her homespun gowns were simple and drab in both color and style, with a row of buttons down the front of a fitted bodice, half-sleeves with turned-back cuffs, and a skirt that hung almost straight from the waist. She had nothing capable of competing with any one of Cassandra's fine dresses. She wistfully thought of the scores of gowns she had left behind in New York without a second thought. If only she had brought along the dress she had chosen for her portrait sittings so long ago. At least it had made her feel like a woman . . . and Alec had noticed. . . . No, she chided herself. It was over. He had made that clear this afternoon. She sighed deeply and gave up the search, taking a plain shirtlike nightgown and tossing it over her head.

She walked to the window, unlatched it, and felt the cool night air flow into her room. The sky had darkened to a deep blue velvet, and the stars were tiny blinks of silvery white. So many times she had comforted herself with the thought that Alec rested under that same sky, dreamed under those same stars. Now that he was under this very roof, he was farther away than he had been in all that time. Juliet drew a deep breath and tried to forget the hurt. She had to think about the future, of where she would go and what she would do, but her mind refused to dwell on those things. She thought instead about the last time she had held him, kissed him, given herself in love to him. She thought about his smile when he had told her that he loved her, of the times he had made her furiously angry because he had seen the truth, of the weakness he had stirred in her, as well as the strength. She blinked back the tears that burned in her eyes. She did not feel very strong now; she felt defeated, and the memories only made her feel more so. But she would not cry anymore, she resolved. She would begin again without him. She had thought to do that before; she would do it now. She curled up in the chair nearest the window and propped her chin in her hand. Cassandra's carriage was just leaving Beau Rêve, but it really made no difference now. She had to think about tomorrow, and she had to leave this place as soon as she possibly could.

Chapter 42

In the library Alec poured himself another glass of brandy while Colette arched a disapproving brow. "Is that necessary, Alexander?"

He ignored her comment except for an annoyed scowl. "You look tired, Mother. Perhaps we ought to discuss this tomorrow."

"I would rather tonight, Alexander," she answered, opening the ledger book to the list of current entries. "I have already waited four years. As you can see, we have barely been able to—how did your father used to say it?—keep our heads above water. Certainly Beau Rêve needs a man's guidance to turn a profit."

Alec snorted derisively. "To hear Sol tell it, Miss Hampton ran the place perfectly while you were ill. It's obvious from the books that her management left quite a bit to be desired."

Colette's dark eyes met her son's squarely. "If you choose to place the blame for our financial woes on someone, then please position it accurately, Alexander: half on your shoulders and half on mine. Had Juliet not been here during my illness, I have no doubt that we would face a longer and colder winter than we have ever known before. She acted as I would have done—"

"And managed to show the greatest loss in four years," Alec dryly pointed out.

Colette fixed her stare on her son's bitter expression. She was more than a little puzzled by his insistent condemnation of Juliet. "I never knew you to be so reluctant in giving credit where it is due."

"Nor was it ever my custom to engage in excessive flattery."

"Alexander, please look at the entire picture before you pass judgment. The money you left ran out. It's that simple. Taxes have been raised time and again, and you ought to know what's happened to the value of a Continental note. We grew no tobacco these past years because there was no one to oversee the project, and there was no market for it anyway —or did you forget that we were at war with England? You must realize that there were repairs to be made, necessities to be purchased, and that we had little money. But we have not been forced to sell off any land, or slaves, and we even managed to keep Spaniard—"

Alec's head jerked to attention. "Spaniard?"

"Madame's colt. She foaled just after you left."

"Spaniard?" he repeated, raising his brows to indicate his disapproval of the name.

"Juliet thought it an appropriate name for one so proud and dark and arrogant, and I had to agree. He is one of the finest horses ever bred at Beau Rêve."

Alec's scowl deepened as his attention returned to the entries in the book, and he briefly tallied a rough estimate of their finances. "Did you take a loan, or did the storekeeper extend you credit?"

"Neither," she answered with something akin to pride.

His puzzled eyes rose to meet hers. "Mother, I left you with two thousand pounds, but the expenses show that you have spent well over twenty-three hundred. Would you like to tell me where the remainder came from?"

"Let us say, a windfall," she answered with a slight smile. "I am very tired now, Alexander, and I am going to bed." She kissed his forehead and left the room, ignoring the exasperated frown he wore as she serenely made her exit.

So Juliet had run the plantation during his mother's illness, he thought. It was no small feat, but then, he had never questioned Juliet's capabilities. But it irked him to find that she had won every heart at Beau Rêve, from his mother's down to the smallest slave's. Exactly what was this game she was playing? he wondered as he refilled his glass and just as quickly emptied it again. Whatever it was, he intended to find out, and before she managed any more surprises—like informing Colette of their marriage. He drained the last bit of brandy from the decanter, left the library, and made his way upstairs to Juliet's room.

At the sound of someone at her door, Juliet jumped to her feet. She trembled and waited for Alec to be revealed in the low lamplight. With effort she straightened her stance and lifted her chin. She would not stand before him in shame, nor would she attempt to arouse his pity.

The voice that broke the silence was cold and heavy with sarcasm. "Good evening, Miss Hampton. We missed you at dinner this evening."

"I do not believe your welcome home was at all lacking in warmth, Captain Farrell," she answered, attempting to match his tone. "There was little for me to add."

"But surely a wife who has waited faithfully so many long years for her loving husband's return would do more than retire to her room with a headache!"

"That I cannot say, for I see no loving husband."

"Nor see I a faithful wife!" he spat out. He paused for a moment, and once again his voice came icy and sarcastic. "I am certain you fully enjoyed the attentions of Wade Collins in my absence. Is that why you came here? Had you grown tired of the British officers in New York?"

She frowned indignantly. "I left New York because my father became most insistent that I marry Harold. He even . . . he even lied to me, convinced me for a time that you had been killed. When I finally realized to what lengths he would go . . ." She swallowed a large lump in her throat and finished simply and quietly. "I could think of nowhere else to go."

Alec's eyes drifted over her. Her eyelids were red and slightly swollen, and he knew that she must have been crying. But she was not crying now. She was standing ramrod straight, pretending to be brave, though her lip trembled as she spoke, and her voice sounded small and shaky. His scathing regard burned every inch of her. "Do you honestly expect me to believe that you have had no other male admirers in my absence? That you have taken no lovers?"

"Lovers?" she repeated incredulously.

"Does it surprise you that I should know about them? Such news travels very quickly, my love. Have you no denials of the stories told about you?"

Her temper exploded with a suddenness that surprised him. "I attempt no explanation at all! You ought to know that it is folly to shout one's innocence over the testimony of a thousand gossips!" She shook her head in disbelief. "And now, after you have already chosen to accept their word as truth, you expect me to deny it! I will not!" Her throat grew tight, and tears began to sting her eyes. "To think that I remained here all this time, waiting for your explanations of why you said nothing of our marriage to your mother, of why you courted Cassandra Collins . . . *after* we were married!"

"It was easy enough for you to forget the vows spoken that day, my love. I merely followed your lead. But I hardly expected to find you here, and especially not playing the part of 'belle of the county.' 'Led Wade down the primrose path' I believe was the expression Cassandra used. And Wade was not the only young man anxious to win you, was he?"

"I encouraged no one!" she denied hotly. "You gave me little choice but to play the part of an unmarried houseguest! How could I claim to be your wife when you had so recently promised that title to another?"

He laughed, a hard, brittle laugh that cut her deeply. "I am certain you encouraged no one, Julie. You merely flashed those innocent golden eyes, raised your chin, and gave a single challenging smile. But that is enough, my dear, to cause any man to fall victim to your charm . . . as I did."

She shook her head and tried to laugh. "Would you care to view the wardrobe with which I enticed the entire male population of Virginia?" She made her way across the room and flung open the closet for his inspection, running her hand over the homespun gowns. "I hardly know which to choose, I have so many . . . any of which is sure to fire the passions of every man I encounter! And my hair. Would you care to know how long it has been since it was arranged like Cassandra's? I have had no time for such things, you see. I have spent every day here learning, and working, and doing what had to be done, praying that some day you would come home to me. . . ." Her voice faltered, and though she blinked, a single tear escaped her eye and slid over her cheek. "To me!" she whispered again. She turned away from his hatred, unable to bear it a moment more. It was as if the dam that had held back a deluge of emotion had burst, and she fell against the wardrobe, sobbing helplessly.

The sight affected Alec in a way her words had not, dissolving the years into nothingness and spawning a need to hold her, to comfort her, to love her, as strong as he had ever known. He rushed to her side, and his arms drew her near, but she twisted angrily about to be free of his embrace.

"Is it so easy for you to forget my lovers?" she cried. "A few tears and all is forgiven? Well, I cannot forgive you so easily, Alec! Leave me in peace! Cassandra will be more than willing to warm your bed!"

His hold on her tightened, and his anger returned. "You are still my wife, Juliet. There is little either of us can do to alter that fact. And you have a document to support your claim on me—"

She abruptly ceased her struggling and stood aghast at his accusation. "If I had such a document in my possession, do you actually think I would use it to hold you?" She searched his eyes, unable to believe that this was the man she had loved so completely. "Once I thought you knew me, but I see now that I was mistaken. Love is based on trust—"

"A harlot is hardly deserving of trust," he scoffed.

The indictment was too much. She slapped him across the face with every bit of her strength, and without pausing, drew back to strike him again. His fingers encircled her wrists to stop her, then tightened their grip until she cried out in pain. He twisted her arms behind her back and brought her body flush against his own.

"Don't touch me!" She stubbornly met his spiteful glare.

"Come, Julie! Surely your husband deserves the same consideration as the others." He took a cruel hold of her chin and forced it back abruptly. When she twisted her head in an attempt to avoid his searching mouth, he became at once savage, insulting, brutally intent on imposing his will. Tears burned in her eyes, and it hurt her deeply to know that he would take her this way, without love, only to satisfy a selfish, vengeful lusting. But something inside her welcomed his kiss, and a desire of her own was swiftly awakened by his passion. Her heart began to beat at a frantic pace, and she longed for him to take her, even while she hated him for doing so.

His hand touched her breast, conjuring up long forgotten passion that thundered throughout her body. He stripped the gown from her shoulders and let his eyes drink the vision before him. So many nights he had dreamed of her thus, her hair tossed about in shiny waves, her shoulders smooth as velvet, her breasts soft and heaving, her lips full, parted, beckoning. She trembled and shrank away from his gaze, but for a single moment her pleading eyes met his. He had expected a defiant woman; he saw only a fearful, hurt little girl. He gathered her into his arms once more, her fresh flow of tears stirring a new tenderness deep inside him. His hurt, his anger, his pride were swept aside by a stronger emotion, and his passion rose like a wave at high tide, helplessly rushing toward the shore. The desire for revenge was drowned in a yearning long denied, a longing to share the magic of the past, a need to possess her in the fullest and most satisfying expression of love. His lips smoothed over her dampened cheeks.

"I love you, Julie. I love you so . . ."

It was enough. She had no more heart to fight him. Her arms slipped about his neck, and she held him fiercely, wanting him more than she had ever wanted him before. His fingers wound themselves in her hair, and his kiss was answered with an intensity that drove everything else from his mind. He touched her and held her and made love to her with a wild, frenzied haste, filling her only to leave her hungering for more. Blindly they struggled toward the scorching light of fulfillment until a white fire exploded in their veins and disappeared, leaving man and woman alone in a separate world, joined as one.

Long moments later heartbeats slowed, heavy breathing stilled. Gradually Juliet became conscious of Alec's even breath on her shoulder. She moved to nestle against his chest and pressed a kiss to the hand that took hold of her own. He cupped her chin in his hand and lifted it until she faced him, her eyes bright with tears. Her voice was soft, yet tight with emotion.

"Is it so easy to believe that I would betray you?"

He pressed a finger to her lips, silencing her pleas of innocence. The past was forgotten in the peaceful aftermath of their lovemaking, and the warm glow in her eyes made him want to leave it buried. "It is past, Julie. We shall not speak of it ever again."

"Cassandra?" Troubled eyes searched his face.

"That, too, is past. It never really was."

"We did not know if you would ever be coming home," she choked out. "You never wrote . . . we did not even know where you were!"

He pressed his lips to her forehead before pulling her against him once more. "It's over, Julie. I'm home," he whispered against her hair. The air about her was filled with the fresh, clean scent of lilacs and spring. He sighed deeply, having found peace for his troubled mind and heart. In the comfort of each other's arms, they easily gave themselves to blissful slumber.

Several hours later Juliet woke to find his eyes upon her. She clutched the sheet to her breast as he leaned to kiss her, smiling with utter contentment as he pressed her back into the pillows.

"Julie"—his mouth touched her cheek, her ear, her throat—"did you say that you no longer possess proof of our marriage?"

"Only here," she answered, tenderly pointing to her heart. "I have the ring, but I am afraid the paper was left behind in New York. I was in such haste to leave that I took nothing with me, except a few things I slipped in with Frances's things. When I found that Father had lied to me about you, I was afraid to leave Frances and Edgar behind in his care. So I set out to get all of us here, and I was very careful that no one guessed my plans. I couldn't have done it without Jay's help."

"In that case, my love, I cannot remain here a moment longer."

In the face of her wide-eyed stare, Alec gave a wry smile. "There would be good cause for anyone to doubt that we had been married these past years. And for the sake of your reputation, I shall be forced to keep a promise I made to you long ago. A large, formal wedding—"

"A small, intimate one would be far more suited to my taste," she smiled. "Though I would like to wear a gown this time."

"And I shall most certainly invite my mother."

She sighed and held his hand to her cheek. "Stay a little while longer."

"I must go, Julie, and quickly. There is very little that gets past the house slaves. The place will be buzzing by morning."

She pulled his head close and stroked his hair. "Stay then. I care not what anyone thinks."

"The offer is most tempting, I must admit. But there are others to be considered—"

"Like Cassandra?" She pulled back her hand, and her voice was sharp.

Alec lifted his head in amusement. "Yes, as a matter of fact. I think it would be proper to break my engagement to her before I marry you . . . again."

Her eyes shone with sudden devilry, and she rose to her knees, letting the sheet that had shielded her modesty drop. She lifted slender arms to encircle his neck, and his eyes widened in surprise as she leaned forward, pressing herself full against his firmly muscled chest. "I think it would be more exciting to let all the world believe we live in sin!" she announced with a wicked grin.

Alec drew a difficult breath and hastened to disengage her arms from about his neck. Her unexpected boldness aroused him far more swiftly than he had imagined possible. He stood up and cleared his throat, trying to control an ever augmenting desire to stay. "What about Mother?" he asked in a strangely tight voice.

Juliet gasped and retrieved the sheet to cover her nakedness, pulling it up with a jerk. "Colette! Alec, you must go before Colette finds you here! She would never believe the truth!" Her brow puckered with dismay. "She says that we must refrain from all appearances of evil."

Alec's brows rose sharply. "Don't tell me that Mother has made a convert of you in my absence!"

"Will you go!" she ordered shortly.

He shook his head and muttered a curse as he gathered up his breeches and shirt, donning the former abruptly while tossing the latter over his arm. Then he deliberately resumed his seat on the bed, ignoring Juliet's anxious protests.

"I do not live my life according to Mother's rules, Julie, and neither do I expect you to do so. However, in deference to her age and beliefs, we shall not confront her with a situation I'm certain would cause her undue distress." With a meaningful gleam in his eye he bent to kiss her bare shoulder, while his hand moved to a rather intimate position on her thigh. She held her breath and backed away, pulling the sheet tightly up to her chin while his voice continued like a leisurely caress.

"Neither will I have Mother effect a change in my wife. I have never fancied myself married to a saint."

"Alec," she pleaded, drawing herself up and doing her utmost to stop the spread of warmth surging in her veins.

"I shall go," he agreed, planting one last brief kiss on her mouth. He bounded from the bed and with a few long strides was gone. Juliet relaxed and slid between the covers, and was asleep before she heard the last of his footfalls in the hall.

Chapter 43

Juliet woke with the sunrise, refreshed in spite of missing half the night's sleep. She stretched like a contented feline and smiled at the memory of passion spent in this very bed, as well as the knowledge that Alec would not be leaving her ever again. She hummed all the while she was dressing and brushing out her hair, and smiled brightly at her own reflection. The world was suddenly a wonderful place and she felt beautiful in spite of her coarse, plain dress and the simple style of her hair. She made her way to the dining room, where a pot of hot coffee had already been placed on the buffet. Colette was seated at the table, making up the day's menu. Alec sat opposite, listening to his mother's comments about what chores ought to be done. When Juliet's eyes locked with his, the light blush in her cheeks deepened noticeably, and she turned away to pour herself a cup of coffee. She mumbled a greeting and took her seat.

"Good morning, Juliet." Colette greeted her with a smile. Her sharp eyes just caught the warm look that passed between the two. Something had apparently effected a change in his son's opinion of Juliet since the previous evening. "I hope you slept well," she remarked.

"Yes," Juliet answered as her eyes drifted once more to Alec's. "Very well."

Colette shook her head and returned her attention to her menu. The night before, Alexander had refused to even acknowledge that Juliet was human. This morning, well, it was almost as if they were newlyweds! At the thought the cup slipped from Colette's trembling fingers and sent a million tiny droplets flying about the room. No! It could not be! Alexander would never take advantage of a fine young woman like Juliet Hampton. Or would he?

Juliet and Alec were momentarily attentive to Colette and the spilled cup of coffee, but once the mess had been cleaned up, their attention was again divided between their coffee and each other.

"What do you intend to do today, Alexander?" Colette asked, finding the silence most unsettling.

"I plan to ride to Tamarack."

She lowered her quill. "There are things to be done here that need your attention. Could you perhaps postpone your visit to a less hectic time? Winter will be here before we are ready for it, I'm afraid, unless we do what must be done to prepare for it properly. I'm certain Cassandra will understand. She will probably be busy ordering her trousseau anyway."

"I need to see her today," he stated firmly.

"She will keep, Alexander. There are quite a few things more pressing than an overanxious bride-to-be."

"I can think of none!" he remarked with an odd smile. He flashed Juliet a sidelong glance that made her blush a bright pink. "I shall leave directly after breakfast," he continued as Delilah entered the dining room with a tempting platter of eggs, ham, and cornbread.

Having completely lost her train of thought, Colette's fingers drummed noiselessly on the table. Her eyes narrowed as she watched her son down a robust portion of the fare with obvious relish, all the while sporting a contented half-smile. His eyes met hers evenly, innocently questioning her close scrutiny. Not satisfied, she turned to Juliet, who also ate heartily and seemed unduly happy this morning. As brandy-colored eyes caught sight of her accusing glare, Juliet's already pink cheeks turned an even hotter shade of crimson, and she became completely engrossed in emptying her plate of food. Colette resolved to have a heart-to-heart talk with her as soon as Alec left for Tamarack, then forced herself to return to the task at hand. If Alexander meant to waste this day, she certainly did not.

By the time the chores for the day had been dealt out, Alec had left for Cassandra's. Colette caught Juliet alone and insisted that she sit down to a second cup of coffee and a chat. Everything else could wait.

Juliet was itching to be about her work, having lingered over breakfast long enough. The easy conversation that usually flowed between them was absent. Colette took a sip of coffee, cleared her throat, and made to broach the subject directly yet tactfully.

"Things should be much less hectic here now that Alexander has returned."

"There will be less for you to worry about, I am sure."

Colette nodded. "There will probably be parties now, and visiting and socializing, just like before the war. It will be a good opportunity for you to meet some fine young men."

Juliet had no reply for that, and became suddenly interested in her coffee.

"You do not return Wade Collins's affection, do you?"

Her eyes lifted in surprise. "I find him a boring braggart— nearly as tiring as his sister!"

"Juliet," Colette scolded gently, "if Cassandra is to become my daughter soon, then we must try to speak of her more kindly. Perhaps we have not been as understanding as we ought to have been. The times have been difficult, but if Alexander means to make her mistress of Beau Rêve, then we must quietly accept the fact."

"Accept the fact?" Juliet's voice rang with sudden emotion. "Accept a woman whose idea of work is to get up in the morning and let someone else fix her hair!" Her eyes widened in realization of what she had just said, and she bit her lip to keep from revealing more.

"Do you find it upsetting that Alexander plans to marry her?"

Juliet longed to say yes, but reason cautioned her to silence. Alec would tell his mother about them in his own way, in his own time; she had already said too much.

"Alec must do what he must do," she answered quietly, her eyes lowered.

"And what do you suppose that will be?" Colette asked pointedly.

Juliet's bewildered eyes rose to meet the question. Could she possibly know?

"You must know that I am very fond of you, too much so to

want to see you hurt. And I cannot help but fear that your devotion for my son will lead you to that end."

"Is the bend of my heart so obvious?" Juliet asked in a tiny voice.

"To me it is, because I know you so well, perhaps better even than I know Alexander. Nothing would delight me more than if he shared your feelings. I could choose no woman to make him a finer wife. Yet the decision is his own, and he will make it as he sees fit. In the meantime, I shall not see him taking advantage of what you feel."

"Taking advantage?"

"Juliet, you must realize that all men experience temptations of the flesh. And you, my dear, are enough to tempt any man. Yet a woman must always keep in mind that promises made in a moment of pleasure are never as honest or as binding as those spoken before God. A virtuous woman must remain pure until after a man has proved himself worthy of her . . . which, of course, means marriage."

Juliet nodded, though she dared not raise her eyes.

"Juliet, I must ask this question for your sake, and I expect an honest answer, however difficult it may be. Has Alexander ever . . . have you ever allowed him to . . . ?"

To Juliet's utter relief, Frances chose that moment to enter the dining room.

"I hope I am not interrupting anything," she said timidly, eyeing the pot of coffee.

No!" Juliet answered a bit too quickly. "I was just leaving, as a matter of fact. Goodness! Where does the time go?"

"You look much better this morning . . ." Frances's voice trailed off as Juliet brushed by her, leaving her puzzled by her eagerness to be off.

Colette sighed and shook her head. Juliet was being evasive, which was a further indication that there was cause for concern. If Alexander had taken advantage of her, he was bound by honor to marry her. Colette would feel no remorse if this were the case, but she wondered if Alexander would admit to his guilt, and if he would consent to doing the honorable thing.

When Alec tossed his reins to the skinny black boy at the Tamarack mansion, it was nearly noon. Cassandra had risen only moments before his arrival and greeted him sleepy-eyed in the parlor wearing a frilly, flowing concoction of lace and ruffles and bows. She smiled and stifled a yawn as she eyed his entire form deliberately, seductively. In answer, Alec's tone was brusque.

"Cassandra, I must speak with you, and afterward, I would like to see your father—"

"Oh, Alec! You're always business, business, business!" She smiled and lifted a hand to trace the V-shaped opening at the neck of his shirt where his chest was bared. "Papa's ready to leave for Devonhill, but if you need more money, darling, I'm afraid you'll just have to wait until after we're married." She smiled and let her green eyes meet his before coyly fluttering her lashes.

Alec's jaw tightened. "I did not come here for money, Cassandra."

"Then did you come to set the date?" she asked eagerly, smiling so as to show off her perfect white teeth.

"No. As a matter of fact, I came to formally break our engagement."

Her green eyes hardened until they were bright chips of emerald meeting his darker ones, which were every bit as cold. "You're joking, Alec. You owe my father a great deal of money—you have to marry me! Or you will lose Beau Rêve!"

"I am not joking, Cassandra," he returned easily. "And as for the loan, I have a year to repay it. A year from the date of my return, if I recall the contract correctly."

"You cannot do this!" Her voice rose to a shrill protest. "You can't! I've waited all these years! I'll be the laughing stock of the whole county! I could have had my pick of beaus, but I waited for you! You promised!"

His voice in reply was brittle. "I never promised you marriage, Cassandra. My father made the promise, not I."

"But when you came home, you asked Papa for a loan, and you acted as if—"

"I admit to misleading you that day. It was wrong of me, and for that I apologize."

"Apologize?" she wailed. "You . . . you . . ." She broke down into hysterical tears, fully expecting to win her way with them. "You let me wait all this time!" she sobbed. "You cannot just throw me aside! Alec, I love you! I need you!"

Alec sighed and lifted a skeptical brow. "Please, Cassandra. Your anger is more palatable to me than your 'devotion.'"

Her tear-stained face was the picture of innocence. "I don't know what you mean, Alec. I love you! I have always loved you!" She slipped her arms around his neck and fell against him, sobbing.

Alec's brow darkened ominously. "Even when you were promised to Justin?"

"Yes! Yes, even then!"

He drew a long breath while his eyes took in the well-acted performance. "It won't work, Cassandra." He smiled stiffly in the face of her tears. "I'll admit you've been persistent, but what you've waited for has nothing to do with love. You want to own me, and I am not for sale."

Suddenly she gave up one tactic for another. "But you are for sale, Alec. Everyone is, at the right price."

He disengaged her arms and stepped away from her. "I rode here this morning to tell you this because I thought you might wish to spread your own tale of how our 'agreement' was terminated. I don't care what reason you give."

For a long moment she stared at him in stunned silence. She simply could not believe that this was happening. No one would dare make a fool of her! Not Cassandra Collins!

"I'll see you crawl, Alexander Farrell!" she snarled. She lifted a glass curio from a nearby table and hurled it toward his head with all her might. It missed its mark by a fair distance and smashed against the marble mantel. "I'll see Beau Rêve burned to the ground! I'll have you ruined! My papa will ruin you!"

"Cassandra, please reserve your childish tantrums for someone more appreciative of them."

"You'll be more appreciative!" she warned with a vengeful smile. "There's no way you'll pay back the loan in a year, and I'll see to it you have no credit—not a penny!"

"Cassandra—"

"You'll pay for this! I promise you, you'll pay!"

Alec smiled wryly as he watched her hurried exit from the room. Things had gone pretty much as he had expected, but still he waited politely in the parlor, certain that Clay Collins would be joining him soon. The word ought to have reached

434

him by now that Cassandra had thrown a fit, and he would be swift to investigate the cause.

Clay was a short, heavy man whose quick smile gave the illusion of easygoing joviality. What hair remained atop his head was thin and white, and his eyes were bright green and dancing in a rounded face of rough pink skin. He was a very successful planter, a shrewd businessman, and an eager drinking partner, but he had two major flaws. The first was a penchant for gambling, which had lost him at least as great a fortune as he now boasted of holding; and the second was his inability to deny his children anything. They asked; they received. It was as simple as that.

When he entered the parlor he greeted Alec with a warm handshake, though the concerned glance he tossed over his shoulder reminded Alec not to expect too much. "Well, Alec, Ol' Goliath came running to me with news that you and Cassandra had a falling out. What happened?" As he spoke he poured two glasses of claret and offered one to Alec, a frown wrinkling his brow when he caught sight of the broken glass at the base of the mantel.

"I'm afraid I was at fault, sir. You see, I broke our engagement."

Clay's shaggy eyebrows jerked upward. "Indeed!"

"It's best to face the fact now, sir. Cassandra and I are simply not suited to one another."

. Clay sipped at his wine for a moment, his eyes thoughtful. "You've been a long time coming to this decision, Alec. Perhaps there's a reason for your sudden change of heart." His mouth curved up at the corners. "Could it be that another woman has captured your fancy?"

Alec hesitated, at a loss for words. Clay was quick to recognize his advantage. "You needn't tell me her name if you don't wish. Wade's been filling my ears with it these past years anyway. I just had a feeling about that girl . . ." His voice trailed off wistfully as he remembered her. Alec stood yet speechless, for he certainly had not planned to admit his love for Juliet so soon after breaking off with Cassandra.

Clay tossed a cautious glance over his shoulder before continuing in a conspiratorial tone. "Now I can certainly understand a man's preoccupation with that woman! I remember the day of that race." He paused and chuckled. "I'll never forget the sight of that round little derriere in those silly breeches! Why, there wasn't a man among us who wasn't plotting to have his way with that wild bit of fluff!"

Alec could barely force the question from his lips. "The race?"

Clay's brow rose, and his eyes twinkled in amusement. "You don't know about it? No, of course not. There's been a war on!" He let out a booming laugh, slapping Alec good-naturedly on the back. "Well, sir, the story will surely be told you a hundred times over now that you're back, but I feel almost honored to be the first!

"My Wade set his sights on that little firebrand, and she challenged him to a race at the Old River Road. Drew quite a crowd—half the county, I'd guess—everybody wondering who would ride that black horse called Spaniard. I think most of us expected to see you there, come back just to prove Beau Rêve's claim to the fastest horses in the state. Instead that stallion sported quite a different rider!" He paused to let out a long, hard laugh.

"Wade was so sure of himself until he saw her on that horse! When his tongue came untied, he said, 'Why, Miss Hampton! Surely you don't intend to ride him like that! It isn't proper!' and she said, 'I would consider riding sidesaddle, Mr. Collins, if you will do the same. Otherwise, I am sure that you would not want me to give you an unfair advantage. . . .' Brazen as brass, those gold-colored eyes of hers were!"

Alec downed his glass of wine in one gulp, and Clay quickly refilled it, losing none of his good humor despite the other's dangerously dark expression. "Anyway, I can understand your preference in ladies." He glanced about before adding in a much lower voice, "But don't ever tell Cassandra I told you so."

Alec forced back a desire to follow Cassandra's example by sending his glass flying across the room. He would deal with Juliet when he returned home, but for now he had to be about business. "Sir, I would speak with you about the debt I owe you," he said in a controlled tone. "I hope that it will be possible to see it repaid within the year, but you realize, as a planter, that such things are contingent on many factors of chance. Should it be a poor year for crops, or should a blight take the tobacco—"

"Alec, I like you. We're neighbors, and I want to accommodate you further. But you know that Cassandra is a determined young lady, and she is also my daughter. The terms of the loan are already more lenient than I would have considered giving to anyone else. To be perfectly frank, I agreed to the terms on Cassandra's urgings, certainly not as a matter of good business. I am fairly certain that she would no longer plead your case, and as a businessman, I cannot extend the loan."

Alec gave no sign of his disappointment and offered his hand to Clay. "Then the debt shall be met in full within the year, sir."

Chapter 44

Alec strode angrily up the steps and into the main house, letting the door slam behind him with force enough to send a tremor through every wall. Colette, arms filled with freshly ironed linens just returned from the washhouse, started at the sound, then quickly moved to confront her son in the hallway. He mumbled a greeting and abruptly brushed past her, leaning into each room he passed to check for Juliet. He, too, was ready for a confrontation, but certainly not with his mother.

"Alexander," she said firmly, blocking his path to gain his full attention. "We need to have a talk."

"Later, Mother." He neatly sidestepped her and moved on. "Where is Miss Hampton?" He opened the parlor door and glanced about, finding it empty.

"As a matter of fact, Alexander, that is exactly whom I have it in mind to discuss." She spread her arms to prevent him from passing her again in the narrow hall.

"Mother," he growled, "I am not in any mood to be crossed! Now where is she?"

Colette pursed her lips and raised her brows. Alec's temper had never intimidated her in the past, and she would not allow it to do so now. Sensing the stalemate, Alec turned with a snarl and strode to the front stairs. He had ascended half the flight when Colette relented.

"She's in the kitchen, Alexander."

Alec made an about-face and hurried to the kitchen. Every minute added fuel to his already raging anger, and he was fairly bursting now with the need to have this out with her. The kitchen was warm and fragrant with the spicy scent of apple butter and currant jelly, but Alec's flaring nostrils were immune to the pleasurable aroma. Delilah scurried about, keeping one girl stirring the kettles, another checking for nicks or cracks in the freshly polished jars, and another filling them to the proper level and sealing them with hot wax.

"Where is Miss Hampton?" he grunted.

"Miss Ha—oh, Miz Juliet gone to the house. We almost done with this cannin', an' she keepin' a record o' what we done, so she can make better next year."

Alec let out a sigh through clenched teeth and went back into the house. The library! If she were going to keep some kind of account, she would be doing it there.

Juliet stood behind the desk, bending over to make notations on a lined piece of parchment. She had recorded which vegetables had done well, which plants had produced to excess and which were already in short supply, and had thoughtfully made notations for improvements next year. Alec found the door to the library half-opened and entered unnoticed, taking in a rather stunning display of decolletage as his wife bent low, her front-fastened homespun dress open well below the curve of her breasts. She stroked the line of her jaw with the softer end of the quill and suddenly caught sight of Alec in the doorway. Her eyes lit up, and she tossed the quill aside to hurry to his arms, oblivious to the scowl that darkened his brow.

"I missed you!" she said brightly, touching a quick kiss to his tight mouth before hurrying back to her paperwork. "I shall be finished here in just a moment, darling. I want to do this before I lose my train of thought." She resumed her former position and lifted the quill from the desk.

Reaching an arm behind him, Alec slammed the door with such force that Juliet started in amazement, once again dropping the quill. He advanced on her with slow, angry strides, giving her ample time to digest his angry expression.

"Did Cassandra give you a bad time?" she asked in a tiny voice.

"No," he returned quietly, almost pleasantly. "Cassandra reacted exactly as I knew she would, with tears and a tantrum . . . nothing I couldn't handle. I wish that I could say the same of my wife." His face bore an odd expression, an angry half-smile that Juliet found puzzling as well as frightening.

"Did I do something wrong?" she asked innocently.

"Oh, no," he answered in that same quiet voice. "Unless the story Clay Collins just told me happens to be true. But I'm sure that it isn't! I mean, you certainly would never have done what he said you did!" The sarcasm was heavy in his tone.

Juliet gulped. "What did he say?"

"Only that your wardrobe includes an outfit of clothing you neglected to show me last evening . . . a rather unique outfit"—his voice became loud as he leaned forward across the desk—"suitable for riding astride!"

Juliet's head jerked back with each word. Her eyes were wide, but she made no move to answer the accusation.

"Well?" came the booming voice.

"Well, what?"

"Do you mean to tell me you have no reason, no explanation for such behavior? What in heaven's name did you think you were doing? Parading before half the county in a pair of breeches! Did no one ever instruct you on the rules of propriety?"

The desk stood between them, Alec bracing an arm on either side and leaning so close that Juliet had taken a step backward and even flattened herself against the wall. "Alec . . ." she began in an even voice.

"You actually raced a horse? Dressed like a man?" He shook his head, leaving her a small opening to speak.

"It was a fair wager, Alec, and—"

"Wager, madame? Did it not occur to you that a lady does not gamble?"

"I only did so once!" she protested, suddenly bolstered by a righteous anger of her own. "And if you had been there, you would have done no less! That Wade Collins said that their Caesar was the better horse. Why, any fool could see that he was no match for Spaniard!"

"Then why didn't someone else race him?"

"Who? Jay is old and crippled, hardly able to do him justice! Sol is too heavy, and besides, he was afraid he'd be thrown . . . and with fair cause. So Jay helped me break him and—"

"*You* broke him?" Alec gasped in disbelief.

"I certainly was not going to lose the wager simply because he was a bit skittish of the saddle at first!"

Alec straightened, and his eyes roamed over Juliet's deceptively delicate form. "You made the wager *before* he was broken? Madame, you give me good reason to doubt your sanity!"

Juliet drew herself up with an unmistakeable measure of pride. "I won."

"Won?" Alec laughed and rounded the desk. "Won, madame? That is a matter of opinion! It seems to me that you have come up even at best—having bartered your reputation for a stupid race!"

Juliet stiffened and stood her ground, though Alec was advancing on her like a vengeful hunter. "It was not stupid! And I don't care what is said about me. It was a fair race, and I won it! I think you're angry because I bested a man!" Her eyes narrowed, and she pointedly added, "And I'm proud of it!"

"And what of me, madame?" Alec tossed back at her. "What of your husband? Gave you no thought to my feelings?" His voice became a bellow. "Was it beyond your grasp that I might not approve of my wife dressing and acting the part of a boy?"

"No one knew I was your wife!"

"You knew it! You might have at least remembered that you are a woman!"

The insult bit deep. Alec had always reassured her of her femininity, had made her acutely conscious of her womanhood. Now he reminded her very much of her father, telling her to be more like Frances . . . or, worse, Cassandra.

"In the future, madame," he continued in a cold, clipped tone, "I shall expect you to conduct yourself with more thought to the consequences. And I will personally burn those damned breeches of yours, so that there will be no question as to the wearer in this household!"

"Oh, no you will not!"

Alec's jaw slackened momentarily. No one crossed him when he was really angry, as he was now—no one!

"Oh, yes I shall!" he hissed through clenched teeth. "And furthermore, I shall extract a promise from you that you will never, under any circumstances, wear breeches—ever again!"

Juliet crossed her arms over her chest, stuck out her chin, and fixed her eyes to a point on the ceiling. "That, sir, will prove an even more difficult task to accomplish." Her tone was low, but there was no mistaking the challenging note in it.

It was too much! Alec was beside himself with fury, and his voice became silky smooth and dangerous. "If you fail to obey my order, Juliet, I shall be forced to do what your father was so remiss in doing when you were a child. Turn you over my knee and—"

"You wouldn't dare!"

"You have from the count of five."

Juliet snorted derisively, though a quick look around gave her true cause for alarm. She was backed into a corner, with Alec blocking the only exit around the desk. She bit her lip and stared at the wall.

"Four."

Well, she certainly did not intend to give in! Let him count from five if it made him happy.

"Three."

"Alec, if you dare to touch me, so help me, I'll . . . I'll tell Colette!"

He raised a brow, and his eyes gleamed like two glowing chips of coal. "Two."

Fear was beginning to tingle at the back of her neck. She had to get out of this and quickly! But there was no way out, no way but . . .

"One."

Gathering her courage, she lifted her chin and attempted an arrogant exit, but Alec was in no mood to allow for dissension, even if such boldness surprised him. As she made to brush past him, he caught hold of both her wrists.

"No!"

She bent her head and bit his hand, but he spun her about and took a new and even fiercer hold, twisting her hands behind her back.

"Alec, let me go!"

He half dragged, half carried her over to the large leather chair, and though she continued her furious struggles, he pulled her with frustrating ease across his lap. Then he systematically began to deal out the promised punishment. She screamed and kicked and twisted and fought, all to no avail. A single hand was sufficient to hold both of hers in an iron grip, and his second landed with painful regularity on her hindquarters. Rendered utterly helpless and realizing as much, she abruptly ceased her struggles, and Alec sensed that her defiance was at an end. He was wrong. He had scarcely slackened his hold at all when she wriggled free and darted away, but he was up and blocking the exit long before she could effect an escape. Once again he advanced on her with a stiff, haughty stride, which she matched step for step in a backward direction—until her back was to the wall. She looked about in some confusion, and a moment later his hard-muscled arms flanked her, preventing any further flight. She faced his hardened eyes for all of a moment before two large tears welled up in her eyes and spilled over her cheeks. She bit her bottom lip to stop its trembling, but her chin remained high and determined. Alec knew that look well; Juliet had no intention of admitting defeat.

"Damn but you're stubborn!"

"I am not a child, Alec! And you will not see me give in because you treat me like one!"

He sighed his exasperation. "Then what ought I to do? I will not have my wife scandalizing the family name merely to prove a point to a rejected swain!" His voice slowed and softened. "This is our home, Julie, the place where I hope to raise our children. I would not have my wife a permanent topic for idle gossip."

Much like a small child, she buried her face in his chest and sobbed against him. Unnoticed in the flood of emotions, Frances opened the door to the library, curious about the odd noises that had filtered through to the hallway as she passed. Every bit as quickly she pulled it shut again. She understood nothing about Alec and Juliet's behavior, but she had certainly learned to stay out of it. Eventually they would work things out for themselves . . . she hoped.

In the main hallway she passed by Colette with a somewhat dazed expression in her wide blue eyes. She had ascended nearly all the stairs before she realized that Colette was speaking to her.

"Frances! Are you well? I asked if you'd seen Alexander."

"Oh, yes," she replied blankly. "He's in the library."

Alec lifted Juliet's chin and tenderly gazed at her tear-stained face. "You hurt me!" she accused him.

"It was not my intention. But I will have your promise that you will not wear those breeches again." His voice was gentle as he held those lovely, childlike eyes.

Her lip trembled as she met his gaze. She loved him so, she would do anything to please him, but not because he had bullied her into submission.

"Julie," he pressed sternly, then sighed and relented. "I ask for your promise."

"I promise." She blinked back a fresh onslaught of tears. "Alec . . . do you think . . . ?" She twisted a strand of his hair around her finger and looked away. "Do you think Cassandra is very, very beautiful?"

He laughed until he met her earnest gaze. "Yes," he replied soberly, "she is quite a beautiful woman."

Juliet took a painful breath and looked away from him, until she heard him whisper hoarsely at her temple, "But you, my darling, put her to shame."

Her eyes flew once again to his face. "Oh, Alec! I love you so!"

He bent his mouth to take hers and savored the way she returned his kiss, contemplating the moments they would share alone that evening. He sighed as his finger touched the row of unfastened buttons on her bodice. "Madame," he whispered, "how can you expect me to contain my ardor when you are so careless about your attire?" His head dipped to the valley between her breasts, and the feel of his hot breath set her head to spinning.

Neither of the two heard the door open or saw the amazed expression on Colette's face as she witnessed their zealous show of affection. For a time she was so taken aback that she considered leaving them and confronting Alexander alone later. But when he began to work the buttons on Juliet's dress, she abruptly made her decision and loudly cleared her throat. The eyes that met hers were at once surprised and embarrassed, and their speechless shock at being discovered gave her ample time to take in Juliet's tear-stained face.

"Would you care to explain your behavior, Alexander?" she demanded quietly.

Alec cleared his throat. "Mother, I do not think you would believe my explanation."

She smiled sweetly. "I would like to hear it, all the same."

Alec shrugged and gave up any hope of finding the right or best way to tell a very long, very involved story. "We intend to be married."

Colette's eyes hardened, and her voice was stern. "That would certainly seem appropriate in light of what I've just seen. Yet I cannot help but recall that you also intend to marry another."

"No longer," he returned. "My visit to Tamarack today put an end to that."

"Indeed!" Colette was honestly surprised at the announcement. For a space of time she eyed the couple suspiciously, Juliet, blushing furiously and still unable to meet her eyes, and Alec, who seemed unaffected by the discovery, casually slipping his arm around Juliet's waist and urging her near. "I shall not ask you, Alexander, how all this came to be. I only hope that you and Juliet are as well suited to one another as you appear to be. However, I will insist that you reserve such displays of . . . warmth for a time more appropriate—*after* you are married."

She turned to leave the room, adding over her shoulder, "I would speak with the Reverend Foster, Alexander. He will want to publish the banns several weeks prior to the ceremony."

Alec's eyes snapped with sudden realization. The game was up, and he knew that there would be no possibility of a secret rendezvous with his wife under his mother's watchful eye. "Mother!" He hurried after her, thinking to inform her that he had no intention of enduring several long weeks of celibacy. After all, Juliet was his wife! But he found himself in a quandary, for unless he wanted to make a complete confession there was no way to protest her ruling. And he could hardly begin to explain to his mother the happenings of these past years.

"Yes, Alexander?" Her voice was sweet and expectant.

Alec sighed as he reconsidered his course of action. Perhaps it would be for the best if they did begin anew, if the promises made in the past were forgotten, as well as the bitterness and the hurt. It would not be the first time he had forced himself to bury the past. . . .

He gave a halfhearted smile. "I shall be getting in touch with the reverend as soon as possible."

Chapter 45

On a bright, frosty November morning, Robert Hampton arrived at Beau Rêve. Heedless of the cold, Frances ran out to meet him the moment she saw him approaching, flinging her arms about his neck almost before he had dismounted, kissing him with joyous abandon—until she realized that a crowd of smiling observers had assembled at the window. She drew back abruptly, breathlessly blushing her embarrassment and letting out a gasping, "Oh!" But before she could retreat to a wholly proper distance, Robert's long arms scooped her up, sweeping her off her feet.

"Have you completely lost your senses, Frances?" he scolded sternly as he strode toward the house. "You'll catch your death of cold!"

She seemed about to cry for a moment, but then she noticed the twinkle in his eye. "Oh, Robert! I'd brave the cold of February if it meant I'd touch you one moment sooner!" She tightened her arms about his neck and kissed him again, heedless of Juliet, Alec, and Colette, who had now flung open the door and stood waiting in the hall. Alec caught Juliet's eye as the kiss continued, and he raised a brow in mock disapproval. In response she gave him an impish grin and cleared her throat loudly.

At the sound Robert's head jerked up, and it was he who broke their embrace, placing Frances's feet on the floor and bestowing a proper kiss to her brow before he stepped forward to greet the others. His mouth was a wide grin. "Juliet—"

At the sound of his voice, Juliet bounded into his arms.

"Oh, Robert!" she cried, holding him tightly, her voice catching with emotion. "I am so happy you've come home!"

"Home?" he repeated doubtfully.

Her eyes still tear-filled, she grinned up at him and nodded happily. "This is to be my home, Robert. The master of Beau Rêve has asked me to become his wife. I do hope you approve."

His eyes darted from Juliet's to Alec's and back again in wide surprise, for Alec had spoken so very little of his sister in the last years that Robert had assumed the romance had ended. "Approve! Juliet, your announcement has just saved me from performing a service far more difficult than anything the army ever demanded of me."

She raised an inquiring brow, bracing herself for his teasing. "What task is that?"

"The task of finding a suitable husband for my hot-tempered, shrewish sister!"

Juliet managed a suitable pout before she giggled and belatedly remembered her manners. She proceeded to introduce Colette to her brother, then suggested that all would be more comfortable in the parlor.

Frances took a seat beside Robert on the settee, her eyes gazing up at him with open adoration as the others found their seats. For a time the conversation was light and laughter-filled, but as Robert questioned Juliet and Frances as to the past, the room grew quiet and the atmosphere somber. Juliet's voice was soft as she mentioned Edgar's death a few months before. There was a space of silence as the memory of the little boy with the face of an angel sharpened in each person's mind. Some moments later Colette rose and excused herself from the group, insisting that Juliet remain to visit with her brother while she saw to the preparation of a suitable luncheon.

"Years ago I heard a rumor that your nobleman actually came to New York to claim you, Juliet," Robert began after Alec's mother had left them. "I am pleasantly surprised to see that you came to your senses before he wed you. But I am curious as to how you came to be here."

Frances and Juliet exchanged a brief glance before she carefully responded, "I very nearly did wed Lord Harold, because at the time I falsely believed that Alec had died. When I

discovered the truth, of course, I didn't go through with it."
Her eyes left Robert momentarily to smile at Alec. "I was
hopelessly in love with someone else."

"I cannot suppose that Father was thrilled with your decision," Robert remarked wryly.

Her smile faded abruptly, and her eyes grew hard. "Knowing full well my feelings, he did everything in his power to see
me wed Harold. He was almost obsessed with the thought of
gaining control of the Medford family holdings. He thought
nothing about what he was destroying in order to get them."
Noticing the troubled frown on Frances's face, Juliet forced a
change in her tone. "In truth, Robert, I am relieved as well as
surprised that I have not heard from him in the past four
years."

"And you will not hear from him in the future." She tilted
her head, looking at him dubiously. "I heard over a year ago
from a reliable source that Father was killed in a fire at
Hampton House." Frances uttered a startled cry, and Juliet's
eyes flew to Alec's. His sober gaze told her that he was unaffected by the announcement. He had heard a rumor to that af-
fect months before.

"Was the house totally destroyed then?" Juliet asked.

"I assume so. Though I could glean very little reliable information about the fire itself, or about the settlement of Father's estate. I heard all sorts of stories, most of them rather
bizarre."

"What do you mean, Robert?" Juliet pressed him. "What
kind of stories?"

Robert spoke hesitantly. "That Father had gone mad, that
he had neglected his business and begun to drink heavily, to
gamble away vast sums of money. Some say he sold most of
his holdings to cover his debts. There was even a story that
several men in his employ began to embezzle ridiculous
amounts of money when they recognized his condition." He
snorted and shook his head. "So much for idle gossip. I am curious as to what happened to his property, though. But needless to say, a trip to New York to make inquiries would have
been impossible during the past year, for either of us. I intend
to write a letter to Father's solicitor, now that the war is
ended, notifying him of our whereabouts. But I wouldn't put

it past Father, mad or not, to have neatly eliminated the both of us from any inheritance."

"I don't know if I would even want a share of his money," Juliet said seriously. Then she sighed and stretched a hand to Alec, who gently squeezed it in understanding and support. She forced a smile for him. "I am only relieved," she said softly, "to know that it has all finally ended."

Chapter 46

It was a crisp winter morning, the previous day's sun having removed the last remnants of the Christmas snow. In the cheery warmth of the parlor, the deceptive brightness of the new day beckoned. Juliet longed for spring, though this past month had been without a doubt the happiest of her life. She and Alec had been married in early December in a quiet ceremony in this very room, and she had indeed worn a gown, Colette's own wedding gown of stunning silver brocade, the skirt draped exquisitely over a magnificent quilted blue petticoat. A striking contrast to the lad who had searched for Alec among the troops of Manhattan!

Alec quietly approached Juliet as she gazed dreamily out the window, and he pressed a kiss to her temple. She smiled and relaxed against him, so completely contented in his arms that she knew she must be dreaming.

"Thinking of spring?" he breathed against her temple.

"How did you guess?" She lifted her eyes to his.

He shrugged. "Mmm . . . I've been doing the same for the past few days, ever since the sun grew brighter. We've still a good bit of winter left, though, I'm afraid."

She turned and lifted her arms to encircle his neck. "I've enjoyed this winter for some reason"—she touched a kiss to his mouth—"or other . . ." She kissed him again and smiled, nestling against his chest.

"I thought we might go riding today."

"Oh, Alec! Could we?"

"What I had in mind was a ride to Rosewood. Some of the

land there was cleared and tilled two decades ago, but a lot more is still virgin timber."

"Rosewood," she repeated thoughtfully. "That's to the southeast, isn't it?" He seemed surprised that she would know the location until she added, "I saw the notation on the map in the library."

"I have to admit those maps of Father's have served a purpose." His brow furrowed. "Are you certain you wish to brave the cold?"

Juliet pulled away from him, anxious to be off. "Very certain. I'll go change clothes right away."

It was almost two hours later when Alec assisted Juliet in dismounting at the sight of an old plantation house that had long ago burned to the ground. Two stone chimneys rose starkly out of the rubble; they had flanked the modest structure at either end. Juliet examined what remained of the house. The few charred beams that still lay about were soft and rotted, and the flat stones that had served as steps to the cellar now led nowhere, having filled in with mud and debris. The place had a feeling about it, an eerie chill that was more than the whining of the winter wind. But it was a lovely setting for a home, or rather it would be, once spring clothed the hill with greenery. The view was breathtaking. One could see the blue haze of the mountains in the distance, and the miles and miles of hills in between.

"Beau Rêve takes in all the land to that second rise." Alec pointed to a ridge that crested to a large level area. "Next week I thought to bring the field slaves up here and scar the trees before the sap rises. Then, in a few years, we shall have firewood as well as a cleared field. If I plant as much tobacco as I hope to come spring, I shall need to clear a good deal of land for the coming years. There's been so little of it planted during the war that for now I can use what land was cleared long ago—though there is a good deal of brush to be taken up and plowing to be done."

"Who lived here, Alec?"

"I never knew the people. The fire destroyed this place when I was just a babe, and sometime later, when Father bought up the tract, there were a thousand stories being told about the people who had perished in the fire and the spirits they had left behind to haunt the place. Justin and I used to—" He stopped abruptly and turned his attention back to the hill in the distance.

"Justin and you used to what?" she asked quietly.

He shook his head. "We used to come here when we were younger, in spite of all the stories. We'd spend the night out, hunting and talking and dreaming. . . ."

"Do you know you never speak of him?"

His eyes held an odd hardness that she did not comprehend. "I do my best not to remember."

"But why? I mean, you loved him. I know that you did. He was a part of your life. You cannot just forget someone whom you really love—"

He stopped her with a stern glare. "Julie, you know nothing about Justin, or about my feelings for him. If I choose to forget him, then I shall do so." His words were sharp, and they cut deep. Hers in turn were soft and pleading.

"I should like to know about him, Alec. I should like to know about your father, too. But more than anything else, I should like to know you."

"You already know me. If you must know more than I choose to tell you, then ask my mother. She does not seem to mind digging up the past. I do." He drew a deep breath. "It was a mistake to bring you here. The wind is much too strong today to enjoy a ride. It's time we started back."

Juliet began to protest, but something made her stop. An argument with Alec would solve nothing, and she was much more hurt than angry at his silence. When he turned to lift her into her saddle, he paused, noticing her downcast expression. "Julie," he said, lifting her chin, "I love you. That's all that really matters." He kissed her, his gentle prodding of her mouth finally awakening the response he sought. "Come, there are other things I wish to show you, and we shall need to be home before dusk."

Dinner at Beau Rêve had become a wonderfully noisy affair the past few weeks. Robert's arrival had brought the smile back to Frances's face and a pinker, healthier glow to her cheeks. When Alec and Robert were not reminiscing about life in the Continental Army, Juliet and Robert were arguing about some misadventure in their childhood. In the talk of the war, all either veteran seemed to remember of late were various practical jokes, wrestling matches, and evenings of excessive drinking after a victorious battle. There seemed to be no end to the bantering back and forth. It was truly amazing that so much food was consumed along with the nonstop flow of conversation.

Juliet listened and smiled as Robert and Alec matched exaggerated tales, each one more so than the last, but something was missing in her enjoyment this evening. Time and again her mind wandered to that place called Rosewood and to a painful warning that she did not really know the man she loved so dearly. Colette had said that Alec felt guilty about Justin's death, and that he had not discussed it with anyone. But his refusal to do so this afternoon had been no less disturbing to Juliet. She was not just anyone. She was his wife, the woman he loved and supposedly trusted. It was a poignant reminder of the distance he had placed between them from the very beginning; there was a part of himself he still refused to share.

She quietly lingered over a second cup of coffee, observing the easy smile and quick wit that so thoroughly covered Alec's deepest feelings. He had been angry at his slip in mentioning Justin, as Juliet had once been angry at his mention of her ill-fated romance with Allan. She had never wanted anyone to see that she had been hurt at losing him, and it had been very irritating when Alec had stumbled on the truth. But now that she loved him, she was no longer afraid of her feelings. On the contrary, she felt a very real comfort in sharing them with him. Why was it that Alec refused to do the same?

"I said, if you drink any more coffee, you will be awake the entire night—which may not be so bad a situation at that!" Alec smiled meaningfully into her blank stare. "Julie, are you there?"

She swallowed and suddenly realized that all eyes were focused on her. "I'm sorry. I was just thinking."

"Would you care to tell us what about?" Robert inquired with raised brows.

Her eyes met her brother's, then moved on to touch Alec's with significant seriousness. "The past," she answered simply, noticing that his casual smile immediately disappeared. "I'm very tired. I suppose it was the ride in the cold air. I hope that you will all excuse me. . . ."

456

Juliet sat curled up in a chair near the fire, chewing pensively at her fingertip. She told herself over and over that she was being silly, that her worries were unfounded. Still they refused to be pushed aside. When she heard Alec enter the room, she remained seated, and her gaze stayed carefully on the warm orange and yellow tongues that licked at the logs in the fireplace. She listened to him rummaging about the room, readying himself for bed, tossing his clothing across the back of a highbacked wing chair as was his habit. At length he approached her and stood before her, a hand braced on either side of her chair. He leaned close and smiled into her troubled countenance. "Are you attempting to tell me, madame, that you have already grown tired of married life and prefer to spend the night in a chair? Will I be forced to coax, cajole, and plead for your favors in the future? Perhaps the winter air has brought a sudden chill to our romance," he suggested with a teasing smile.

"It was not the winter's air, Alec. It was an even colder reminder that you do not trust me."

He seemed mildly surprised at her comment, but he remained untroubled. "Julie, darling, I believe I have told you more than once—the past is better forgotten."

"Then why is it *you* cannot forget? Oh, you refuse to speak of it, but it's hardly the same thing."

Her statement met its mark, and he straightened abruptly and left her to search out a bottle of brandy kept in the room to ward off the chill on the coldest winter nights. He took a deep draft, then turned to face her squarely, his expression firm and severe. "You would do better to steer clear of things you do not understand, Julie."

"But I want to understand, Alec!" she insisted, coming quickly to stand before him. "I love you! And I want to know you. Is that so much to ask?" Her voice was softly beseeching, and as she spoke, a slim hand slipped around his neck and toyed with the fringe of his dark hair. "Alec?"

He set the brandy aside and pulled her close, kissing her gently, thoroughly. His lips traced the curve of her cheek, then brushed against her velvet skin of her ear. But she held back, not responding in the manner to which he had become accustomed.

"I need you, Julie. I want you—now. . . ." His voice was hoarse and low, and she recognized a desperate hunger in his tone. His mouth was eager, insistent, anxious as it drifted from her lips to her throat and shoulders. His urgency touched a like emotion in her, and Juliet found that she, too, suddenly ached for the reassurance of their physical union. The magical blending was dramatic yet simple, the satisfying of an almost animal craving that implied the deepest of human emotions, a momentary forgetting of self to become a part of another, and in return to be made whole.

Juliet lay entwined in the comfort of her husband's arms, her doubts forgotten as Alec nuzzled her hair. "You see, my love. The past does not matter. Nothing matters but here and now, and the love we share today."

Chapter 47

Suddenly it was spring! Everywhere bits of green struggled from their resting places in the moist earth or moved to
clothe the naked boughs of winter. The air, still cool, was no
longer biting. It picked up the fragrances of fresh foliage and
April rain and was truly a delight to inhale. Beau Rêve bustled with activity. Everyone had had enough of the long
winter. Windows were opened, and the women spent every
waking hour shaking out the musty odors of a closed house,
dusting the soot from every fixture, scrubbing every room,
floor to ceiling. Alec spent each day, dawn to dusk, supervising the preparations for planting. Fields not used during the
war years had to be cleared of saplings as well as brush and
the ground turned. Though his pride forced him to stubbornly
refuse Robert's oft-repeated offers of help, many days found
Alec laboring in the sun right alongside the slaves, seeing to
it that all was done perfectly. So much depended on the success of this crop.

The tiny tobacco seeds were an expensive investment, but
seeds for the next year's planting would be recovered from
this year's crop. Planted in long beds of rich soil, they would
be protected by cheesecloth until May, when they could be
safely placed in the fields, in rows three feet apart. Every
field slave toiled with a vigor that reflected Alec's own drive.
The work was long and hard, and would continue until after
the harvest.

A letter from Elizabeth and Edgar Church found its way to
Beau Rêve, giving their blessing for the forthcoming mar-

riage of Robert and Frances. They had decided to live out their days in England, but they begged their only daughter to consider a honeymoon there, having included a very generous gift of money to help the couple begin a new life. In a ceremony at Beau Rêve much like Alec and Juliet's, Robert and Frances were joined as husband and wife.

The entire state of Virginia celebrated the coming of spring, made all the more sweet because now the country was at peace. Alec was kept so busy by his work that most of the grand socializing was avoided. But finally one invitation came that could not be refused. Oliver and Rosalind Delancy resided at a plantation called Devonhill, a full day's journey by coach from Beau Rêve. They were longtime friends of the Farrells, Jerome having attended William and Mary with Oliver, and Rosalind having known Colette since her girlhood days in Williamsburg and remaining a dear friend all these past years. In a brief personal note, Rosalind had extended the invitation to everyone at Beau Rêve, in particular to Alec and his bride, whom she declared was, "the talk of every party, even more so because you have kept her hidden."

In spite of pressure from Alec and Juliet, Colette immediately declined the invitation, admitting only under prodding that the trip would be far too much for her. Though she rarely let it show, she had never completely recovered her strength from her bout with the fever the autumn before. She did, however, insist that the others attend in her place and enjoy a visit with the Delancys, and Alec finally agreed.

Excitedly, Frances and Juliet made plans to attend, coercing Robert into driving them into the tiny town of Leighton, about two hours away, to look at the latest fashion dolls recently arrived from France. Frances made several purchases, including material for half a dozen new gowns, as well as many suitable accessories. Robert had returned from the war with enough money to see them through, and the Churches' generous wedding gift helped them as well. Juliet refrained from buying anything, ignoring Alec's orders that she do so, knowing full well that the cost of tobacco seeds along with the payment of taxes must have exhausted most of what he had saved from his meager soldier's pay. Alec repeatedly refused to discuss finances with her, but she knew that he could not have returned from the war with unlimited funds, and judging from the way he was driving himself to reap a profit this year, she felt that frugality ought to be observed. On several occasions Colette offered Juliet her choice of older gowns, which had been carefully packed away and which, though dated, could be altered to the newer, more fashionable styles. Frances had already promised to perform the miracle on two or more of them if time permitted.

It was during one of the several tedious sessions of measurement that Frances came to realize what Juliet had known for weeks: that Juliet was with child. "I simply cannot understand it, Juliet!" Frances had cried in exasperation, her blue eyes flashing. "I measured so carefully! The fit ought to be perfect! Why, it's almost as if you—" Her cupid's-bow mouth formed a perfect circle of stunned surprise as Juliet met her eyes and gave a guilty nod. "Oh!" she gasped, quickly giving her a hug. "Are you absolutely certain? Why haven't you told me before? And Colette! Why, she will be totally . . . totally . . ." Frances shook her head, unable to find a word to describe such happiness. "And Alec! And Robert!" Her smile suddenly disappeared. "Should you be on your feet so much, Juliet?"

Juliet laughed at her doting manner. "I am perfectly healthy, Frances," she assured her friend. "And I haven't told anyone because . . ." Her eyes grew troubled. "Oh, Frances, Alec has so very many things to occupy his mind these days!"

"But the news will please him so much!"

"And give him just one more thing to worry about," Juliet argued promptly.

Frances scowled with disapproval. "I understand what you're saying, Juliet, but I still think that you ought to—"

"I have thought the matter through quite thoroughly, I can assure you. And I have decided to keep it a secret, at least for a little while longer. I know that I can trust you to keep this confidence, Frances," she went on, her expression growing stern and leaving little room for argument, "even from Robert."

Reluctantly Frances nodded agreement.

It was a simple matter for Juliet to conceal her morning bouts of nausea. She simply rose at a later hour, after Alec had already left for the fields. She found that she needed the

461

extra rest, and indeed, she often made an excuse to steal a few moments of sleep before he returned home. Her usually boundless energy seemed to slip away long before the day's work was finished, and for the first time since arriving at Beau Rêve her motivation to see a task through to its end was lacking. Still she refused to trouble Alec with more worries than those in which he was already involved, and kept the trials of early pregnancy to herself.

Having prepared herself for the journey to Devonhill, Juliet gnawed at her lip, studying the reflection in the full-length looking glass and wondering if her condition would be apparent to any eyes besides her own. Despite the tight lacing she had just endured, she still felt self-conscious about the slightest curve just below her trim waist. And the newer fashions were certainly no help! Gone were panniers and hoops, and here were draping skirts puffed only in the rear, calling all the more attention to a slender abdomen. Frances had lent her a new burgundy-colored caraco, a jacket with a tight, form-fitting bodice flaring from the waist, which was long in the back and short in the front to accent the newer cut of the skirt. She sighed, then pulled in her tummy and held her breath, but still it seemed hopeless. If anyone noticed, it would certainly be disastrous!

Colette's soft voice came from across the room. "You cannot tell."

Juliet whirled and stared aghast at her. "Frances told you," she pouted.

Colette smiled. "No one told me. I just happened to notice one day a few weeks back that you weren't coming to breakfast anymore. And then I noticed that you'd taken to napping before dinner. And now I see you holding your breath in front of a looking glass. It does not take a genius to come to some conclusion. Have you told Alexander?"

Juliet drew a long breath and frowned. "Not yet."

"I thought not. Are you waiting for some special time?"

"Not exactly . . . It's only that he has been so very busy, I . . . he has enough to worry about."

"You are too considerate, my dear," Colette confided with a twinkle in her eyes. "Nary a complaint from you about the trials of childbearing! You could be a bit more difficult. The least you might do is shed a tear or two."

Juliet did not understand exactly what Colette was trying to say, but it brought on a timid confession. "I do feel like crying sometimes, Colette. I wake up in the morning every bit as tired as when I went to sleep, and I tell myself every morning, 'Just get up and begin moving about, and you will feel much better!' So I get up and begin moving about, and instead of feeling better I feel worse! And when I smell breakfast . . ." Her skin actually paled at the thought. "Please don't tell Delilah I said that," she added.

"Well you sound very healthy to me," Colette smiled. "That is exactly the way I used to feel."

Though it was certainly not what she wanted to hear, Juliet forced a smile and took Colette's hand, gazing with open affection into her lovely black eyes. "I do wish you would reconsider going to the party, Colette. Mistress Delancy will be so disappointed."

"Rosalind will be enchanted with the new mistress of Beau Rêve, I'm sure. Please tell her for me that I will visit someday soon, won't you?"

At that moment Juliet heard Alec call for her from the foot of the stairs, and his tone told her he was most anxious to be off. "When are you going to tell him?" Colette queried in a hushed tone.

"I . . . I don't know. I thought perhaps while we are away, while his mind is not so taken with the planting."

"Well, don't wait too long, Juliet. He will be very pleased with the news."

"Do you think so?"

Before Colette could answer, Alec once again called to Juliet. This time his voice was something akin to a bellow, so with a quick hug and a fond farewell, Juliet lifted her skirts and flitted from the room.

Devonhill's manor house reminded Juliet quite a bit of Hampton House. It was a large Georgian-style brick structure, a full three stories in the central portion, two full stories in either of the two adjoining wings. Four gigantic oak trees that nearly dwarfed the massive building stood before it, one on either end and one on each side of the central portion. The house was situated atop the slope of a hill that was terraced and outlined with a flagstone walk and well-tended shrubbery. There was also a delightful flower garden to the rear of the house, which was Mistress Delancy's pride and joy.

The entire county and more, it seemed, had turned out for the grand party at Devonhill. The stables overflowed until horses were tethered and tended on the outer perimeter of the building. Every guest room was filled. Nowhere in the house could one find a quiet corner. Several guests who had traveled long distances would be staying a few weeks or even longer, but Alec and Juliet would be staying only three days; Alec had said that it was all he could spare and had agreed to attend only out of a deep feeling of obligation. Robert and Frances had accompanied them to the party.

Alec assisted Juliet from the carriage, wondering at the beautiful image before him. He had spent every hour of late thinking of Beau Rêve, but for these next three days he intended to force all that from his mind. This would be a holiday, a reprieve, a chance to squander time on his lovely wife, who certainly deserved the attention. She had not complained once about his long hours of toil, or about his falling into bed most nights too tired to think of anything but sleep. Neither had she complained about missing innumerable balls and parties, or about the fact that he could not afford to allow her the unlimited wardrobe she had been accustomed to in New York. It would be a pleasure to rekindle the flame. Indeed, he was already burning with a hunger for her and rued the time he had to spend socializing and sharing her with others.

The four made their way inside, and the women were immediately shown to their rooms to prepare for the formal dinner that would precede the party. Juliet felt the need to rest, but there was simply not time, so she did her best to relax while the young Negro girl assigned to help her in her toilette unpacked and saw to the pressing of her gown. She became abruptly conscious of the young girl's staring at her in a strange, almost fearful way, and grew more and more anxious about being presented to Alec's friends. She knew well enough that there were stories told about her, particularly with regard to the race and her relationship with Wade Collins. But would they like her? she wondered. Would they compare her to Cassandra? And would anyone dare broach the delicate subject of her unusual attire the day of the race? Her stomach felt like lead, and she knew that she would never be able to keep a bite down at the formal dinner.

The young black girl lifted the flame-colored silk gown over her head. As had been the fashion for many years, a good bit of bosom was bared by the low neckline, but a slightly more daring cut had come into vogue with the new decade, a style that extended the neckline out over the shoulder. Frances had altered the dress to perfection, Juliet had to admit, though she still lamented the newer style of skirt, which she feared might make her condition obvious. She had little time to waste on worry, however, for after a brief smoothing of her hair, swept up and away from her face with a few long curls falling over one shoulder, it was time to be off.

She nervously held her breath during Alec's serious and rather lengthy scrutiny. Then his face broke into a roguish grin and he remarked that he would much rather retire before dinner and have such an exquisite creature entirely to himself. A measure of her confidence restored by his compliment, she gracefully descended the stairs on her husband's arm. There were many people milling about in the hall at the bottom of the staircase, and every eye lifted to take note of the handsome couple about to join them. A hush preceded a great deal of whispering, but Juliet held her smile, finding that her rigid social training was finally put to good use.

She was polite, proper, cultured, intelligent; not at all what most of those who had heard the stories about her had expected. One by one she impressed them with her wit and her ability to converse with an assurance just short of arrogance; the pride she felt in Alec's gaze encouraged her more than anything else. He remained by her side through dinner, and afterward, when they danced, everyone else in the crowded ballroom seemed to disappear. They were once again at the Churches' spring party, sharing the same excitement they had shared years before. Their dance had barely ended when Alec was coerced by Oliver Delancy to join a few of the gentlemen in the gaming room.

"I can understand your preoccupation with this pretty young thing, Alexander," he smiled, "but we want to discuss politics. You've always been level-headed, and, more important, you have a way with words. I was hoping to convince you to run for the state congress this coming year. . . ." He did not give Alec a chance to refuse as he slapped him heartily on the back and led him off to the gaming room, leaving Juliet standing alone.

Wade Collins was quick to seize the opportunity, having eyed her all through the banquet like a starving pup. Juliet danced with him, then forced a smile, thanked him, and promptly took her leave. She made her way through the crowded perimeter of the room toward Robert and Frances, but while she was still quite a few feet away, an oddly familiar voice made her spin about in surprise.

"You certainly are looking as beautiful as ever, Mistress Farrell."

Juliet could scarcely hide her amazement as she met the dancing blue eyes, the dazzling smile, the playful challenge in his voice, and she found herself fighting an urge to fling her arms about his neck. "Michael!"

His wry smile seemed to recognize her dilemma, so he quickly placed a properly gallant kiss on her hand. "Shall we dance?"

She began to protest. She was unfamiliar with the gavotte, the newer and quicker variation of the minuet being done to this particular song, but Michael only laughed away her arguments, leading her to the dancing area. "You've been observing long enough, I'd say. Just follow me!"

Her concentration was intense for a few moments, until she became confident in the graceful succession of movements and was able then to turn her thoughts back to her partner. He had gained weight, but it became him, and the firmer, more muscular frame was, as always, extremely handsome. He sported the latest fashion, a high-waisted, double-breasted, cutaway coat of dark blue with sloping tails, large collar, and turned-back cuffs. Tight black velvet breeches extended below the knee, and his hair was unpowdered, pulled into a queue and secured with a crisp black bow.

Michael was equally enthralled with her appearance, noting the becoming flush in her cheeks and appreciative of her smooth complexion, unmarred by decorative patches or the heavily scented starch many women had taken to wearing as face powder. If anything, she was even more beautiful than he remembered, with the red silk gown baring a tempting feast of creamy shoulders and rounded breasts. Her eyes shone every bit as bright and golden as a harvest moon, matching the smile in his own blue eyes.

They were unmindful of the brows raising here and there about the room, for their mutual regard seemed far too intimate for a young bride and a casual acquaintance. Robert, too, was perplexed by what he observed, for the man was unfamiliar to him, yet Juliet's gaze was both candid and warm.

"Do you know that man dancing with Juliet?" he inquired of Frances at a moment when they were out of earshot of anyone else.

"Oh my," she gasped, "I do believe it's Lieutenant Alford!"

"I simply cannot believe it!" Juliet said at length, exchanging a sunny smile with him. "How on earth did you get here?"

"I might ask the same of you, my love," he returned. "Both of us have come a long way from Manhattan."

"Yes," she agreed, turning away from him as the dance continued. Her eyes idly scanned the crowd, catching sight of Robert and Frances, the bright colors of silks and brocades and satins, the smiling faces, the groups of people intent on conversation . . . until they suddenly riveted on a pair of steel-blue eyes burning with hatred. Juliet stopped in midstep, absolutely paralyzed with fright. Her knees weakened, and her vision blurred. She did not fully realize what was happening, as Michael helped her make a graceful exit, propelling her out into the cooler evening air. She leaned heavily against him for several moments, then turned away and braced herself on the portico railing.

"Juliet?" His voice carried his concern. "What happened?"

She made a weak attempt at a smile, but when she spoke her voice was small and shaky. "Michael . . . I . . . I thought . . . that I saw my father in the crowd."

"You really did have a scare, didn't you?" He smiled down at her tenderly, noting the tears she was trying hard not to let fall. "It's all right, darling. There's nothing here to hurt you."

She forced a nervous laugh. "I feel very silly."

"Well, you don't look a bit silly. You look absolutely ravishing."

His remark brought something that passed for a smile to her lips. "You haven't change a bit, Michael Alford!" She scolded lightly.

"Oh, but I have. You see, I've become a very successful man here, in the land of the 'country gentlemen.' I find myself very much at home with these colonial aristocrats. I've always fancied myself an aristocrat, you know."

"But how did you come to be here? In Virginia? At this particular party?"

His blue eyes lit up, and his dimples danced as he unwound the story of the years since he had seen her. "When I left New York and deserted the army, I had a single destination in mind—the west, the frontier, where I was fairly certain to be safe from your father's lies. Believe this or not, I actually made a go of it in that godforsaken wilderness—killing savages and wild animals and that sort of thing. I gradually worked my way back to the periphery of civilization, hoping to hear that the war was finished. Before that welcome news reached my ears, I was told another, far more intriguing story about a horse race in Culpepper County, Virginia, a few years back. They say that a beautiful young lady rode like the wind on a fiery black stallion, and actually bested a man!" Juliet felt a hot blush in her cheeks as he continued. "Before anyone told me, I knew immediately that it had to be you. So I came here as quickly as I could, hoping against hope that I might claim you for my own. Instead the war interfered time and again, and I nearly ended in the thick of battle. By the time I reached this vicinity, I was informed of your recent marriage to Captain Farrell, who had apparently survived the war with honor." His smile became bittersweet. "Are you happy with him?"

She smiled and answered without reservation. "Very."

"Then I am happy for you. I was concerned when I heard about the considerable debt your husband contracted with Clay Collins—" At Juliet's suddenly confused expression, Michael stopped, realizing that he had said too much. But her reaction surprised him, for Alec's debt had been a subject thoroughly discussed among the gentlemen at recent parties, as Juliet herself had been.

"I know I ought not to have mentioned that, and I apologize for my faux pas. If you are happy, that is what really matters." He smiled warmly, enjoying the smile she returned. "And is Captain Farrell happy about the child?"

Juliet's eyes flew open with a start. "How on earth did you know?"

He chuckled, deepening the boyish dimples in his cheeks. "I guessed! It is to be expected of one newly married, is it not? But Juliet, if there is one subject I know well, that subject is women. You are not the swooning type, my dear, no matter what you think you've seen, not in front of so many people anyway. You've far too much pride. Well? Is he happy about it?"

"Alec does not know yet, Michael."

It was Michael's turn to be surprised.

"He's very busy and has enough to occupy his mind of late," she explained.

"Indeed," he replied with unmasked skepticism. "I hope that he is not taking you for granted, my dear."

"No, it isn't that. I am happy, Michael, really I am!" Even as she did her best to convince him, she felt a pang of hurt at not being informed of Alec's debt to Clay Collins. If Michael had mentioned it, then it had to be common knowledge. He was not one to let a confidential tidbit accidentally slip out.

"I've been told that his mother is something of a religious fanatic," Michael remarked, changing the subject.

Juliet laughed outright. "Whoever told you that?"

"Why, Miss Collins. She's an expert on Captain Farrell, you know."

"Well, don't believe a word she says. Colette is wonderful! You would absolutely fall in love with her, Michael."

"As easily as I fell in love with you, Juliet?" His blue eyes were no longer playful, and his tone was at once serious. Suddenly ill at ease, Juliet avoided his searching gaze. "I apologize, my love. It was not my intention to cause you distress, and I know full well that such a remark was improper. But have you forgotten all about me so quickly? It should not surprise you to find that I am not a man of honor."

"That's not true, Michael. If it were, you would never have come back to the house that night to tell me the truth about Alec."

"That, my dear, was a matter of love, not honor."

"The two are very closely akin, I think. Had you not risked coming there to tell me, I would at this moment be married to Lord Harold."

"Ah, yes! Lord Harold! Whatever happened to him?"

"I don't know. I left Manhattan as if I were leaving the cities of Sodom and Gomorrah. I was afraid to look back."

"I would set a fair wager that you left Harold a sweet, soothing farewell note to ease his smarting pride, did you not?"

She gave a timid nod, more than a little embarrassed by his correct conjecture. He knew her better than she had imagined.

He sighed thoughtfully. "Thank God you left before the fire. When I heard about that, I was frightened for you, though I knew in my heart that you had left your father's house after finding out about Captain Farrell."

"Do you know much about the fire, Michael? Robert heard so little that made any sense."

"I only know that it took place well over a year ago, I forget exactly when. I met a gentleman recently come from New York who told me a wild story about the whole affair. He said that your father had gone quite mad, had lost nearly everything, and had even set Hampton House afire himself."

"But did he say for certain that my father was killed?"

Michael considered for a moment, wanting to reassure her after the frightening experience she had just had, but not wanting to lie. "From what I have been told, your father was living in the house at the time of the blaze and assumed burned to death." He lifted her hand in both of his own and raised it to his lips.

"I ought not to have brought up this subject. I seem to cause you undue worry no matter what I say this evening." He smiled into her eyes. "I shall have to practice all of my charm to rouse you from the depths of despair. Though I have a simple solution in mind, my love. I shall challenge you to a race on that fiery black stallion—" He stopped abruptly and passed a meaningful eye over her stomach. "Perhaps I had better settle for a quiet game of whist. . . ."

Alec had endured at least a dozen introductions to important gentlemen in the gaming room before he became absorbed in a heated conversation in one corner of the room.

". . . It was not his fault that Virginia was left with so few militiamen to defend its soil," insisted Jack Parker, a tall, gray-haired gentleman.

"Then, pray, whose fault was it?" returned Clay Collins.

"General Washington was crying out for men! Jefferson merely gave his all for the cause!"

"But a governor's first duty is to his state, not the commander-in-chief of the Continental Army! I, for one, say that he was wrong to leave Virginia open to British assault. And obviously the Congress agrees with me."

Alec sipped thoughtfully at his wine, paying close attention to the climate of the discussion before he spoke in words both easy and convincing. "As I understand it, the charges leveled against Mr. Jefferson have been dropped. George Nicholas could not even face him with the accusations—he pointedly refused to do so. And, of course, Jefferson was re-elected to the assembly without a single dissenting vote. I would say that wherever there is a problem there will be someone looking for a scapegoat. The problem is past now, fortunately, and the past is best forgotten. Thomas Jefferson is too great a statesman to be condemned for the troubles a long and hard war heaped on the state."

"Well, well, well." Clay eyed the man who had just effectively ended a good discussion. "We have certainly missed your insight in our debating, Alexander. This is the first social engagement you've attended since you came back from the war. What on earth could be taking up all of your time?"

"I am a planter, sir, and I have obligations to fulfill, as you are already aware."

"I thought it might just be a reason other than work," he suggested slyly, nudging him with an eldow. "Like maybe . . . pleasure."

Alec's jaw tightened, and sensing his discomfort at being the center of attention, Clay made to further it. "Tell us, Alexander, how did you manage to win the lady's heart in so short a time after your return from the war? Why, my Wade did his best to court her the whole time you were gone, only to be rejected time and again."

"There is no explanation for romance, sir," Alec answered with apparent ease, though he bristled at the idea of discussing any aspect of his relationship with his wife publicly.

The alcohol had flowed excessively throughout the long

evening, and many of the gentlemen in the parlor were feeling less inhibited by propriety than usual. Wade Collins, having heard his father's remark and still stinging from the rejection dealt him by Juliet, was feeling particularly courageous. He left the wagering table and made his way rather unsteadily across the room.

Clay let out a hearty chuckle. "Well, you are indeed a lucky man, Alexander! It isn't every day a man marries one so fair yet so determined. I envy you your prize!" He took a sip of his drink and noted the baleful green eyes of his son. "Poor Wade! He made the mistake of wagering with an opponent he most certainly underestimated, and lost not only the wager, but the woman as well."

"A mistake easily understood," Matthew Culver chimed in. "Who, indeed, expects such things from a woman?"

"The error was made in wagering with a woman at all," another voice added. "Any woman!"

Wade's nostrils flared at the affront. "But she is not just any woman. If you had been offered a chance to possess so tempting a prize, I am quite certain you would have taken the risk. To me, the loss of a few hundred pounds was nothing when pitted against the pleasure of claiming one so fair."

Alec stiffened, and his eyes hardened dangerously to chips of black onyx. It suddenly occurred to him that the money Juliet had won in the wager had been the "windfall" his mother had been so evasive about explaining to him. And he had never known what it was that Juliet had wagered to match Wade's money. Seeing the change in Alec's manner, Clay immediately sobered enough to soften his son's crude insinuation. He gave a nervous laugh.

"Wade, I think your mind is befuddled by an overabundance of drink. The story you always told me was that the young lady wagered her jewelry against your gold. Is that not correct?"

Wade's eyes flicked over a dozen anxious faces, a normally jovial pair of green eyes taken with sudden seriousness, and an alarming threat that gleamed ever brighter in Alec's eyes.

"Yes," he answered begrudgingly, only because he felt backed into a corner. "But I never saw any jewelry, and I naturally assumed—"

"You assumed what?" came the silken question, at odds

with the ominously darkened brow. Alec's fingers, which encircled a crystal wine goblet, went white as he steeled himself for the reply.

Wade's green eyes met his with an impertinent stare, but it vanished in the realization of his precarious position. He drew a long breath and swallowed a good deal of pride with the remainder of his drink. Then he deposited his glass on the nearest table and abruptly left the room.

Alec's stony glare fastened on the retreating figure that disappeared into the crowd. Then he made a brief excuse to the other gentlemen and also took his leave. He circled the entire perimeter of the ballroom, his eyes scanning the scores of faces but not finding the one he sought. Feeling a familiar pressure as someone took hold of his arm, he spun about hopefully, but, instead of Juliet, he confronted another pair of sparkling green eyes. Cassandra flashed him her most fetching smile and playfully tapped her fan on his chest, but she failed to arouse the slightest interest. His eyes still sought another.

"You might at least act happy to see me," she pouted, "or request one tiny dance with me, for sentimentality."

"Later, perhaps," he answered distantly. He finally located Robert at the far wall and took a step in that direction, only to find himself restrained by an arm linked possessively in his own.

"Are you looking for someone?" she inquired sweetly, ignoring the scowl brought on by her boldness.

"I am looking for my wife, as a matter of fact," he replied, carefully disengaging his arm.

Cassandra stepped directly in front of him, blocking his path and tracing a finger over the neat lapel of his dark brown broadcloth coat. "Oh, Alec! You could find the time for one little dance with me! Particularly now . . . while your wife is so well occupied."

"Occupied?"

Cassandra nodded, her green eyes wide and seemingly innocent. "It seems to me that if she can take a moonlight stroll with that handsome gambler friend of Papa's—" Before she could say another word, Alec removed her hand from his lapel and stiffly made his way to the door, pausing momentarily until his eyes adjusted to the dim light outside.

He stayed carefully in the shadows, studying several pairs who wandered about the portico, until his eyes came to rest on Juliet's pert profile and moonlight-splashed hair. He was painfully aware of his wife's seductive attire, of the way the soft light turned her skin to a creamy ivory that beckoned a man's caress. Even now it stirred a hunger in him that he had never known for another. She lifted troubled tawny eyes to the man who stood opposite, and the man took tender hold of her hand, raising it to his lips. Every muscle in Alec's body twitched with restraint. Still smarting from the insinuations in the gaming room, he found himself choking with jealousy at the stranger's familiar handling of his wife. As he cautiously approached the pair, his temper just barely under control, Juliet's face brightened, and the man threw his head back, laughing.

The shock of recognition riveted Alec to the spot for a split second and sent an explosion of violent indignation shuddering through him. He had killed this man a hundred times on the battlefield as he aimed his gun at the approaching redcoats, his hatred feeding on the thought that his shot might forever close those laughing blue eyes. And a thousand nights he had spent dreaming of seeing him crawl, his life's blood pouring out as he lay in the gutter with the rest of the rotting, stinking filth. But this was no dream. This was here and this was now, and the man whom he hated more than he had ever hated anyone was with the woman he loved, holding her, touching her, laughing with her.

In an instant Alec closed the distance between himself and Michael, jerking him about to face his thunderous rage. A single smashing blow to his jaw sent Michael sprawling backward, buffeting him painfully against the portico railing. Alec ignored Juliet's attempts to stop him, reaching out to grasp Michael's ruffled cambric shirt and sharply pulling him to his feet.

"Stop it! Alec, please!" Juliet pleaded desperately, her hands struggling in vain to loosen the cruel hold he had on Michael. For scarcely a moment his black eyes lifted to hers. Juliet's face mirrored her confusion as well as her anguish, but at a single accusing glare from Alec, she clutched a hand to her trembling lips and fled.

The sudden commotion on the otherwise quiet portico had

kindled the interest of many, who now crowded closer to investigate the trouble. It was the curious onlookers who forced Alec to release Michael, who promptly collapsed on the floor. Alec's voice was a slow, deliberate snarl forced through clenched teeth, coming the moment the attention of the others had faded. "If I ever see you touch my wife again, so help me, I shall kill you!"

Alec straightened and pulled tersely at his wrinkled waistcoat. Michael, a trickle of blood oozing from his mouth, raised himself carefully, then shook out his kerchief and dabbed cautiously at his lip, finding one entire side of his face a dull, throbbing ache. He winced, testing the movement of his jaw, and found it in one piece despite the pain.

Alec's black eyes raked him in disgust. "If the Delancys were not such dear friends, I would call you out here and now. Consider it your good fortune that I give you this reprieve, for their sake." He pointedly turned his back, but had scarcely taken a step when Michael found his voice.

"Captain Farrell!"

Alec stopped in mid-stride, fists clenched tightly at his side. Michael spoke quietly to his back. "I owe you a debt, sir, having wronged you in the past for my own gain. I pay that debt now by arming you with the truth. The promise I made you that night was never kept, though it was Juliet's choice, certainly not mine. Your hate for me is justified, Captain, but Juliet is innocent. I swear to it! And in doing so, sir, I consider my debt to you paid in full."

Alec drew a deep breath, and his mouth tightened to a thin white line. The man was a liar. Without a backward glance, he walked on.

Juliet paced the entire length of the guest room she and Alec were to share, her mind a turmoil of conflicting emotions. Her breath was coming in short, difficult gasps, and she felt weak and shaken. She wished that she could cry, but there came no release for the tension winding like a spring inside her, tighter and tighter and tighter. She jumped as the door was slammed, rattling the tiny glass curios that lined the mantel. Alec's stern glare burned into her, and she struggled against a sudden fear. He poured himself a generous snifter of brandy from the decanter on the bureau and took a lengthy draft before he spoke with biting bitterness.

"Madame, I have already accepted the fact of your infidelities in my absence, and I generously agreed to overlook them." Juliet's eyes widened in disbelief. His words became more forceful as he approached her. "But I will not be cuckolded publicly, and if you dare to attempt such a thing again—"

"Again?" Juliet flew into a rage. "Alexander Farrell, you are a fool! You dare accuse me of—"

A harsh laugh cut her short. "Come, Juliet! I am not blind!"

"Oh, but you are! You see what you want to see. If it will make you happy to believe that I have been unfaithful to you, then do so. You obviously have no interest in hearing the truth."

"The truth?" He gave a derisive snort. "I saw more than enough to form my own conclusion, my dear. Do you really think to convince me that Lieutenant Alford is not your lover?"

Juliet's eyes mirrored her amazement. "You know him?"

Alec's lip curled in a mocking smile. "Does that surprise you? I suppose he forgot to mention his dealings with me, the fact that he tried to see me shipped safely off to a prison out of the country. Out of the way, so that he might have you. He told me that same night, from his own lips I heard it—'Juliet will marry Harold, and I shall be her lover.' "

Even as Alec repeated the words, the pain of betrayal sharpened, and he hurled his glass across the room. Juliet was suddenly torn between her righteous anger at being falsely accused and her desire to ease the torment she saw in his face.

"I forgave you!" he continued bitterly. "I was ready to forget it all, to begin a new life with you, in spite of what had happened! But I am not willing to share you, Julie. Not with anyone! You are my wife, dammit! I will not share you!"

There was nothing she could say. Alec would never believe her innocence, no matter what she swore. He was insane with jealousy; it had turned him into a stranger.

"We shall return to Beau Rêve in the morning. I shall give the excuse that you are not feeling well and make our apologies to the Delancys. Be prepared for an early departure." He paused almost as if he expected an argument. Receiving none, he turned and with quick, angry strides left the room. It was many hours later when he finally returned to seek his rest, smelling of strong liquor and not saying a single word to Juliet. He turned his back to her the moment he slipped into bed.

The following morning at dawn, the Farrells left Devonhill. The long carriage ride home was a sharp contrast to the one taken but a single day before. Robert and Frances had elected to stay behind, having accepted Alec's explanation that Juliet was not well, and having received several generous offers of transport back to Beau Rêve.

Juliet huddled in her own corner of the coach, chilled by more than the damp air. She fixed a stony gaze at the passing scenery, stealing a hopeful glance now and again at Alec, who likewise seemed preoccupied with the view from the opposite window. The silence was heavy, tense, nerve-wracking. There seemed no end to the road they traversed. When the carriage finally jolted to a stop before the familiar white house, Juliet felt no elation. She had hoped to find a new closeness with Alec during the time away, to prove herself an asset among his friends. She had not even told him about the baby, and she had good cause to wonder now if he would welcome the news.

Colette was surprised by the premature return of the carriage. She lifted a lamp from the table and went to meet them at the main door. "You returned earlier than expected," she remarked, confused to find that Alec and Juliet alone had returned from Devonhill. Her eyes attempted to read the odd expressions in their faces.

"Juliet wasn't feeling well," Alec explained tersely. "I should like to speak with Sol before he retires for the night. If you will excuse me . . ."

Colette's brow knit in a perplexed frown as she watched him exit. She turned to Juliet for explanation, only to find that she was halfway up the stairs. "Juliet!" She lifted her skirts to follow, fearful that some mishap might have befallen the unborn child.

Juliet proceeded to her room, heedless of the call, and curled up into her favorite chair. She fixed a dazed stare on the empty hearth. "Juliet?" Colette was becoming quite disturbed. "Where are Robert and Frances?"

"They decided to stay the week at Devonhill," she answered quietly.

"And you decided to come home. Is it the child?"

Juliet's face tightened at the question. She shook her head, unable to mouth the words.

"Did you tell him?"

Again she shook her head, then bit her lip to stop its trembling. Colette studied her for a moment, then bent to take her hands. "Juliet, did you and Alexander quarrel?"

As the first tear escaped her eyes, she pulled away from Colette's offer of comfort and covered her face in her hands. Colette sighed. "Juliet, both you and Alexander could practice better control of your tempers. You have that fault in common. You often react in a flare of emotion without considering the consequences. Angry words spill out so easily, and one can never take back what has been said. Tell me now, what did you quarrel about?"

Juliet met Colette's kind gaze. "I don't want to involve you in this, Colette. There is nothing you can do."

"Perhaps you are right. In the end, you must settle things with Alexander, and he with you. But Juliet, I would tell him about the child. If for no other reason, then simply because he has a right to know." She placed a hand on Juliet's shoulder and gave it an encouraging squeeze. "Things will work out. Trust in God." She rose. "I shall leave you now, but if you feel the need to talk, please come to me."

As Alec came up the stairs with Juliet's trunk, he saw his mother leaving their bedroom. Just like the two of them, closing ranks, he thought angrily. Well, let the harlot blind everyone else with her wide-eyed innocent stare. He knew better. He delivered the trunk to her and gave a mocking bow before he retired to the parlor and finished off a decanter of brandy, falling into an exhausted sleep. He rose at dawn, cramped and weary from a fitful night's slumber in a parlor chair. He changed to his casual attire without disturbing his wife, then went to the dining room for a much needed cup of coffee.

"Good morning, Alexander," Colette called cheerily.

His reply was a growl, which, as usual, failed to affect his mother's bright disposition. "Did you sleep well?"

A scowling glare answered her inquiry.

"It's good to have you back, Alexander. Things were ever so quiet while you were away." She hesitated. "Is Juliet feeling better?"

"That you will have to ask her," he snapped.

"Alexander, Juliet is your wife. I should expect you to see to her comfort if she is not feeling well."

"Mother," he ground out, "I've no doubt at all that Juliet most thoroughly informed you about what happened at Devonhill. And if you want to believe her story, then do so. But do not expect me to play the fool merely because you have chosen to do so."

"Alexander, Juliet told me nothing of what happened at Devonhill. But I find it difficult to believe that she would play me for a fool, or you."

Without another word, Alec drained the remainder of his coffee and left the dining room.

Chapter 48

Robert and Frances returned to Beau Rêve a week later, but the high spirits of the past had vanished. Dinner became a quieter time, with a few forced smiles interspersed in a heavy silence. Alec made it his habit to retire to the library directly after dinner, ostensibly to do planning and paperwork, but to Juliet it was obvious that he did so to avoid a confrontation. Late each night when he finally came to bed, she would smell the heavy, sweet odor of brandy and would accommodate him by pretending to be asleep.

Nearly a month after the party at Devonhill, Juliet gathered her courage and followed him into the library after dinner. He poured himself a brandy and took a seat at the desk, ignoring her presence.

"May I speak with you, Alec?" she asked rather formally.

"I'm busy, as you can plainly see," he said brusquely, opening the ledger and removing the quill from its holder.

"It will only take a moment."

He raised his eyes to hers for a long moment, then returned them pointedly to the book of accounts. Her throat tightened painfully at the affront.

"It's important," she stated quietly.

He tossed the quill aside and settled back in his chair, frowning and toying with his glass of brandy. Juliet felt the bulk of her determination ebbing away under his expectant, annoyed gaze. She met it squarely at first, but when the words she had gone over time and again refused to come, she lowered her eyes in despair. She had no choice now but to tell him; he would know soon enough even if she remained silent.

"I am going to have a baby," she said softly.

She stole a hopeful glance at him, but he sat motionless, taken by surprise. Then that same hateful expression crossed his brow as he took a long swallow of brandy, and his eyes narrowed on her once more.

"Well? Do you know which of us is the father? Or as your lawful husband do I unquestionably lay claim to that honor?"

Juliet felt that she could scarcely breathe. It was everything she could do to stumble away. But Alec was still so filled with hatred and bitterness that he did not realize the full impact of his blow. Before she reached the door, he moved to block her path, refusing to allow her to leave. She had no strength to meet his accusing glare.

"Please, Alec. Let me pass. I shall not trouble you with this again."

"Oh? And exactly what do you intend to do, my dear? Where do you intend to go?" His voice was mocking, further wounding her.

"I . . . have . . . an aunt in England . . ." Her voice was so tiny that it was barely audible.

"Your aunt in England? The proper Lady Farmington?" He laughed. "You would expect her to take you in, and in your delicate condition? Come now! Surely you've had a better offer than that! Perhaps Lieutenant Alford—"

She flew at him, screaming her anguish and pounding her fists in hopeless defiance against his chest. "Damn you to hell, Alexander Farrell!"

He caught at her arms and pulled her against him. She struggled helplessly against his strength, and then, suddenly, their eyes locked, and each stopped fighting the other.

"Dear God!" he whispered. "Is the taste of revenge always so bitter? I am sorry, Julie. I wanted so much to hurt you, as you hurt me. But no one wins this spiteful game." He breathed a ragged sigh and pressed his lips to her hair, then lifted her into his arms and carried her from the library to their room. For a long time he held her. His mind wandered to the past, to the stolen moments they had shared in New York, to the magic of their first kiss, to the wondrous joy he had known in sharing the fullness of their love. And now, a child.

His child. They were bound even closer, having shared in the creation of a new life. But still there were doubts, questions with answers he could not face, a past he could not reconcile with the future.

She lifted her eyes to his. "Oh, Alec. What are we going to do?"

He drew a long breath. "We shall begin again, Julie. I love you."

She lifted a hand to trace the hard line of his mouth. "Another new beginning, Alec?" She sadly shook her head. "It would only be as the last."

His expression grew sullen. "What then? I shall not allow you to leave me for your Aunt Cecilia—or anyone else."

She pulled away from his embrace, and her mood was at once firm. "You do not own me, Alec, no more than I own you. When I married you I sought to be more than a possession. I thought to be a wife, an intimate and necessary part of your life." She paused, and her voice rose until it cracked with pain. "I loved you so much! It all seemed so easy, like a beautiful dream. But instead we have come to this nightmare, and it frightens me, Alec! It makes me wonder if I love you still. . . ."

Alec sighed and ran a finger along her arm. "It is difficult for me, also, Julie." His voice was low. "Alford makes no move to disguise the fact that he desires you."

"And am I guilty because of it? What of Cassandra's affection for you? Now there is a public display of desire, certainly! Yet I trust you, Alec, while you distrust me at every turn."

"What do you expect of me? Shall I yet trust you when you turn to another? To a man who would have seen me rot in prison?"

"I had no thought of seeing Michael that night. And I only left the crowd with him because I nearly fainted. I . . . I suppose it was the child . . . or the fact that I was so very tired. . . ." She raised determined eyes to his. "Michael is a dear friend of mine, Alec, nothing more. At a time when I was without you, when I thought my life had ended, he made me smile. In New York there were many who thought otherwise, and I did not trouble myself to change their opinions, but they were wrong. The whole while I believed you to be dead, I came to know him and to love him in a way I cannot explain to you.

But it was never the same love I feel for you, Alec, and I never gave myself to him, even then. I swear it!"

"You love a man who was a party to your father's deception and to your husband's torture? Knowing what he is—a liar! A deserter! A man entirely without honor!"

"Yet a man who risked his life to confess his part of the plot to me."

Alec snorted derisively. "He owed you far more. A simple confession does not erase his guilt."

"I won't argue the point. I don't claim that what I feel for Michael is logical, yet neither is what I feel for you. Love is a thing of the heart, not of the mind, and I cannot hate him merely because you ask it of me. I do know, Alec, that the trouble between us goes much deeper than what I feel for Michael, or any other man. You once accused me of building a wall around myself, of keeping everyone at arm's length and of hurting them by doing so. I know now why it was so easy for you to see that wall, because you've done exactly the same thing."

He stiffened at the accuracy of the accusation. "You know I love you, Julie—"

"I know that you want me, Alec. That's much different from love, much easier and less complicated, requiring far less effort, far less giving, and very little trusting." Her eyes glittered with emotion. "It leaves me empty to know that it's all you are willing to give me."

"What do you want of me?" he asked, his voice subdued.

"I want to share your life. That means more than sharing this house or sharing your bed. It means that I want to share your troubles, your failures, your self. If you cannot trust me with the things that have hurt you in the past, then how can you trust me in the future? That is something I learned when I thought you had died, Alec, that the past is the foundation for the future. We are molded, shaped by what has happened, and if we cannot accept it—"

Abruptly he released her and turned away so that she could not see his face. Long moments passed before he spoke, and even then the words came hard. "Many years ago, my brother fell in love with a beautiful woman. I never understood the way he overlooked her blatant flirtations with other men, the desperate way he tried to be something he was not to please

484

her. I hated him for it! I thought he had no pride. And now . . . I find myself doing the very same thing."

Juliet burned at the comparison. "I have a pride of my own, Alec, but my love for you comes first. I am not Cassandra. I have never betrayed you, and if you knew how much I loved you, you would know that I never could."

She moved to put her arms about his waist and leaned against him, her tone soft and pleading. "I'm not asking you to be something you're not. I love what you are, Alec, and I will never love another man as I love you. If you truly want to begin with me again, then let our love be a deeper thing, a bond of faith and trust as the basis for the future. You must believe that I have been faithful to you and that I always shall be. Then no other can come between us, Alec, for our love will truly make us one."

He took hold of her wrists and pulled her to him. His fingers brushed her temple, then felt the softness of her hair. He brought his mouth to hers, and his kiss was questioning, almost timid, until her lips warmed and parted beneath the easy pressure. Then suddenly it became demanding. He worked the buttons at the front of her gown and pulled it from her shoulders. He frowned and drew back as he saw that she was tightly laced in a corset.

"A woman in your condition ought not to utilize such silly contraptions!" he reprimanded firmly. He turned her around and tore at the lacings. "I would insist that my child be given room to breathe."

Juliet smiled happily and was much relieved at having the binding pressure at her abdomen removed. He pulled her against him once more and let his hungry eyes roam over her still slender form, clad only in a chemise and a plain cotton petticoat. His mouth bent to the high curve of her breast, his breath burning her skin until she trembled with desire.

The long weeks of loneliness, of tension, of anger were all but shattered by the devastating tenderness of his mouth, his tongue, his searching hands. Her body, warm and totally responsive, arched instinctively toward his. Yet he seemed almost reluctant to satisfy her, as if he wanted desperately to make the moment last forever. Juliet's grasp on his broad shoulders tightened as she began to pulse with the need to be taken. She clung to him, crying aloud with joy and fulfillment as their mutual surrender was finally complete.

Much later, when Alec's chest rose and fell with the regularity of deep slumber, Juliet carefully lifted her head to study his troubled face. She brushed a stray lock from his brow, and her fingers gently smoothed the furrows there. She sighed, wondering what uneasy thoughts disturbed him even as he slept. Would he ever learn to trust her? Would he finally learn to live with his past instead of trying to bury the hurt under an endless succession of new beginnings? She pressed a kiss to his forehead. "I love you, Alec," she whispered. "There has never been anyone else."

Chapter 49

Juliet yawned and stretched contentedly, then bounded from the bed when she realized that the sun was already high in the sky. She slipped on her petticoat and dress, wincing as she forced the last button to close over her rapidly thickening stomach. Turning sideways, she frowned at the reflection in the looking glass. There was simply no hiding her condition any longer. She would have to speak with Frances about altering the remainder of her house dresses, she thought, wishing for once that she had taken greater interest in sewing than in horses. Her frown deepened. What would she do without Frances and Robert? Just the night before, Robert had spoken of returning to New York, where he hoped to find employment among old acquaintances who knew of his experience in Father's business. He had sent off dozens of letters in the past weeks, and made frequent trips to Leighton in the hopes of collecting some response. Frances and he missed the life they had known in Manhattan, and Robert dreamed of building a home for her there that would equal the one that had burned during the war. But that would take a good deal of money, which Robert did not have at the moment. Someday . . . he had said.

Juliet ambled down to the dining room to find that Delilah had left the coffee warming on the buffet over a small candle. She poured herself a cup, then carried the pot out to the kitchen. The bees were humming about the freshly opened fruit blossoms, and the sun was both hot and brilliant. The day was a pleasant cross between spring and summer, she thought happily as she breathed in air that whispered of lilacs and primroses and tiny violets.

In the fields the planting had begun. Still refusing to accept any help from Robert, laughingly reminding him that he was a houseguest and a gentleman, and certainly not a planter, Alec directed the careful placement of the plants himself, then divided the fields into large plots, each for a single slave to tend. The fields of wheat and corn took far less tending than the tobacco, and where a slave might cultivate fifteen or twenty acres of the former, he could handle but one or two of the latter. Once the tobacco plants had grown a bit, they would need to be weeded and the soil around each plant opened up to allow rain to reach the roots. Each field hand would fight incessantly against insects and tobacco worms, removing them by hand from each plant. Later, unnecessary sprouts would have to be trimmed and the tops cut to prevent the plants' going to seed. The work was only beginning, yet there was more on the horizon for Alec.

One Sunday, after returning from the weekly excursion to church services, Alec had spoken with Juliet about his own plans for the future.

"Oliver Delancy spoke to me some weeks ago about running for the assembly. I would like very much to do that, once Beau Rêve shows a fair profit. Father was a member of the House of Burgesses many years ago, as well as his father before him, the man for whom I am named. I remember that this house was opened to a constant stream of visitors during the three days of election, and I can remember going with Father as he rode about the county, politely requesting everyone's vote. It was all very proper and honorable, and I was quite in awe of the entire idea. I can still remember how proud I was of him then, and I think our son might feel the same."

"Oh?" Juliet remarked with a raise of her brows. "You seem awfully certain that the child will be a boy."

"Oh, he will be," Alec returned with confidence. "Boys run in the Farrell family. We are—all of us—men, you see. My father, and my grandfather, and his father—"

"And what about your Aunt Elizabeth?"

Alec feigned surprise. "Why, she is a Church, didn't you know? Ask Frances."

"Well, then, what about me? And your mother?"

"You, my dear, are the luckiest of all women." He playfully kissed the tip of her nose. "You succeeded in marrying a Farrell, which is a greater feat than winning any election! The position has lifetime tenure."

"And in doing so, I became a Farrell, did I not?"

He placed a finger to her lips and ended the argument with an insistent whisper. "It will be a boy!"

Juliet smiled as she remembered that conversation. More and more Alec was thinking of their child, and he was mentioning bits and pieces of his past in planning for the future. More important, he was sharing both with her. She folded away the freshly laundered linens just brought in from the washhouse, for the house was understaffed now, with every available slave hard at work in the fields. But things were going well; the plants were sturdy, and the weather was fair. Everyone at Beau Rêve was happy and hopeful and looking forward to both a bountiful harvest and a new baby. As Michael had told Juliet years before, luck runs in cycles. Take gambles with your luck when it is good, he had said, for it would stay that way for a spell, until it changed.

Unfortunately the same was true of bad luck, as Alexander Farrell was soon to find out.

The days grew longer, and the June sun brought a hazy gray tinge to the brilliant blue sky. The air became hot and humid. Mornings dawned in veiled mists, and the sunsets were accompanied by a heavy fall of dew. Crops thrived in the moist summer heat, while the cows lolled about in the thick green pastures, searching for a spot of shade.

Juliet had begun rising early again with Alec and Colette, so that her work might be done in the cooler morning hours and her rest taken during the sultry afternoons. This morning the last of the strawberries had been picked from the kitchen garden and enough mint gathered to make a refreshing round of drinks for this evening when Alec returned home.

The sun was always low when the plantation bell sounded to end the day's work, and it usually roused Juliet from her nap in time to dress for dinner and help Colette with the last-minute preparations in the dining room. When she woke this June evening, it was with a sudden start to find that the sun had all but disappeared from the horizon. She was late. And something was wrong, she could feel it. She hastily pulled on her dress and with a sense of impending doom, rustled down the stairs. On finding the dining room empty, she rushed to the parlor, where she found Colette pacing the floor and Frances peering nervously out the window. Juliet's wide eyes searched Colette's face, and her voice was anxious.

"What's happened? Where are Robert and Alec?"

"We don't know, Juliet," she responded with forced calmness, belied by the deep furrows at her brow. "Alec didn't come home this evening, nor did the slaves working the tobacco fields to the west. Robert went out to see what has happened, but he hasn't returned yet."

"Why didn't you wake me?" she cried, looking out the window over Frances's shoulder.

"There was nothing to be done. There was no reason to alarm you unnecessarily."

"But what could it be, Colette? Something must have happened!" Juliet bit her lip, suddenly realizing that Colette and Frances were every bit as worried as she was. But worry served no useful purpose, and the time would be better spent in some constructive task. "There is mending to be done," she said quietly. "Let us see to it now—the time will pass more quickly."

It was hours later when the sounds of horses brought each of the women to her feet. Their nerves were frazzled, and they ran expectantly toward the main door, trying to still the apprehension that had been building for the entire evening. Juliet flew to Alec's arms, heedless of the soot and grime that covered him from head to toe, while Frances rushed to Robert's side sobbing, and Colette sighed wearily, leaning heavily against the wall. Alec gingerly disentangled his wife's loving arms.

"There was a fire at the mill," he explained, stripping off the soiled and tattered remains of his shirt. His voice was tired and despairing. "We kept it from spreading, but the mill was an entire loss."

Confusion flooded Juliet's face. "But the mill was not in use today. There's been barely enough rain the past week to turn the wheel once around. How could a fire have begun there?"

Alec's eyes bore into hers for a long moment, warning her

490

against saying any more. Catching his gaze, Colette quickly rose to the occasion. "Dinner will be well done by this time, but I am certain you are famished, as we are. Frances? Juliet? Shall we retire to the dining room and see to it? Alec, Robert, you will want to clean up and change."

Throughout dinner, Juliet was forced to keep her suspicions to herself, but as soon as they had retired to their room, she pressed Alec for answers.

"The fire was set."

"Set? But why? Who would . . . ?"

"I would like to know that as much as you, Julie."

"Are you absolutely certain it was not an accident? I mean, something might have caused it to start—"

He cut her short. "Julie, you said it yourself. The mill was not in use, and fires do not start all by themselves." He tossed his clothing in a pile near the chair, then plopped on the edge of the bed and drew a lengthy breath. Juliet quickly donned her night rail and slipped beneath the light blanket, waiting for Alec to join her. But he sat there dejected, his head bent, his shoulders drooping, so she rose to her knees and reached to knead the tightness from the back of his neck.

"It will all work out, Alec," she said quietly.

He lifted his head and stretched under the soothing pressure of her fingers. "You don't understand what this means, Julie."

Her hands stopped their massaging. "Then explain it to me."

"It means that we shall have to build another mill. . . . It means time and labor lost. It means expense. . . . We can't afford to build a new mill, and when the harvest comes, we shall be hard-pressed to do what must be done."

She rested her cheek against his bare back. "Is it the money you owe Clay Collins?" She felt him stiffen. He had not to this day mentioned that to her.

"How did you know about the loan?"

"It doesn't matter how I knew, though I wish it had been you who told me. It's why you've been driving yourself so hard, isn't it?"

He half turned to face her. "That loan was a mistake, Julie. I ought to have stayed here and worked instead of leaving and going back to the army—at least for a year, enough to see the place producing again. It was all Mother could do to keep Beau Rêve with the taxes rising, the number of slaves shrinking . . . you know as well as anyone. I came back here and I saw it all, and I dumped it promptly back in her lap." He shook his head. "I could not stay here without you. I was convinced that you'd conveniently forgotten your marriage vows when the war was going badly. In my heart I knew that I was making a mistake, leaving you in your Father's care. I ought to have waited to marry you, as Robert waited, until my military obligations were finished. But I wanted you, and I left you to face the consequences of our marriage all alone, because I had to have you. Just as I left my mother here, knowing that it was wrong, that it was the easy way, not the honorable way."

She slipped into his lap and lifted her arms about his neck. "You acted out of hurt and anger. I have often done the same."

"But we all pay for our mistakes, Julie, and the price for mine may be the loss of Beau Rêve."

"Lose Beau Rêve?" The idea had never even occurred to her.

"I could sell Spaniard, though I dearly wanted to breed him, and I doubt that he would bring enough to cover the debt, at any rate. There are the slaves, but they are a necessary part of the workings of this place, and besides, they have been loyal to us and served us well, even while the war dangled a promise of freedom before their noses. And then there is the land. I could sell a part of this plantation, but it would be like selling a part of myself."

"Alec, you won't be forced to do any of those things," she said firmly. "This will be a fine year for crops. The weather's been fair, and you have worked hard. Everything will work out, I am sure of it!"

"Julie," Alec began, his words slow and measured, "how well do you know Michael Alford?"

Juliet was confused by the abrupt change in subject. "How well?"

"I was wondering if he might be the kind of man to carry a grudge. I struck him at the party, and this might be his way—"

"Michael? You think that Michael set that fire?" Her denial was intense. "No, Alec! He would never do such a thing. I am certain he would not."

"I can think of no one else who would want to see me ruined."

"What of Clay Collins? If Cassandra asked for the moon he would try to deliver it. And she does have cause to hate you."

"Yes, but Clay has already done her bidding. I can't secure a loan from anyone in the entire county. He's made certain of that. Everyone seems to owe him a favor—if they don't owe him money, that is."

"It wasn't Michael," Juliet insisted one last time. "Everything will work out, Alec. Who once told me that a Farrell laughs at disaster and scoffs at impossibilities?" Her encouraging smile warmed him, and he made an attempt to return it.

"Who did tell you that?"

"You did! And you were right!" She placed his hand on the life stirring inside her. "I do not believe in Fate or luck anymore. I believe in life and in love. Those are really the only things that matter."

He pulled her close. "Where would I be without you, Julie?"

"I cannot say for certain," she answered him with thoughtful seriousness, "but I believe you would be married to a green-eyed blonde."

At that he laughed and rolled her onto the bed. "If I had married her, I would most surely get more sleep than I do now!"

It was two weeks to the day after the fire at the mill that a second disaster struck at Beau Rêve. Alec woke several hours before dawn to the smell of smoke touching his nostrils. He threw on his clothes and opened the door to the hallway, but the smell was not there. He closed the door once more, puzzled. No one kept a fire burning in this heat, and it was not the smell of wood burning anyway, it was more like . . . As the thought struck him, he ran to the window and leaned out. There was a strange orangish glow in the western sky, and with the subtle movement of the heavy summer air the smell was growing stronger. Without disturbing Juliet, he rushed out of the room to get Sol and the other field slaves, but a sick feeling took hold of Alec as they hurried to the scene, and he knew at once that their haste was useless. They worked to keep the roaring fire from spreading past the fence line, but they were forced to watch the countless hours invested in the tobacco fields go up in smoke.

Alec returned to the mansion house in utter depression. A loss of such magnitude would have been difficult to absorb in a good year, but when coupled with the loss of the mill and the debt to Clay coming due, he knew there was no way short of a miracle to make ends meet. He would have to sell part of Beau Rêve and very probably take on another debt to cover the costs of next year's planting. He contemplated the view from the window. Tomorrow he would begin again, supervising the clearing of a new field for late wheat. He had to keep the slaves working at their full potential and be absolutely certain that enough wheat and corn were harvested to feed the plantation this winter. But try as he might, his mind would not keep to the future, to planning the task at hand. Someone had it in his, or her, mind to ruin him, and it would not take many more "accidents" to do just that.

Time and again he asked himself who might be guilty of the crime, and he always came up with the same answer: Michael Alford. He might have fooled Juliet with that charming smile of his, but he certainly had not fooled Alec. The man had no honor, and he freely admitted as much, as well as admitting his hunger for another man's wife. If Alec were to lose everything and prove himself a failure, then surely Michael would stand a chance at claiming her for his own. And yet Alec had come to realize that his wife would never leave him for the sake of an easy life of luxury. Indeed, she seemed to thrive on the challenges facing them now. But the baby might change her way of thinking; she would surely want the best of everything for her child.

Well, thought Alec grimly, the slaves posted as sentries at each field would prevent Michael from an easy end to his plans. And some day he would pay for this. Alec would make sure of that.

Chapter 50

Juliet brushed at the damp tendrils of hair that clung to her cheeks and forehead. It was a day best spent in relaxing in a spot of shade, a fan in one hand and a cool drink in another. But there were no such days this summer, she mused, scattering a handful of feed among a dozen anxious hens and dumping what remained in a single sweeping motion. She observed for a moment as the largest white hen clucked and scratched her way to an overripe tomato. The hens never ceased to amuse her with their rigid pecking order, and she had laughingly named the highest ranking of the chickens Queen Charlotte.

"I do hope you laid your share of eggs today, Charlotte, or Delilah will see you in a stew."

The hen gave a loud squawk as Juliet turned away to fetch the eggs, then, slinging the basket over her arm, she headed for the kitchen. She was just about to enter when she noticed a small cloud of dust rising above the road to the house. She paused, wondering if Alec was returning home early. A frown pulled at her brow, and she mouthed a silent prayer. "Please, God, don't let anything else go wrong. Alec's worked so hard!"

She left the eggs with Delilah and proceeded directly to the house. In her room she splashed water on her face and combed her hair before going back downstairs to meet Alec. But he had not yet entered the house; in fact, someone was knocking at the main door. Juliet hurried to answer it.

When she opened the door, her eyes widened in surprise as

she stared at a familiar figure. "Michael! I . . . what are you doing here?"

"I bring you news, my love. News of every sort! And I needed to have a look at you, to assure myself that you were doing well. That husband of yours is far too stingy about sharing your company."

Juliet's hand rose self-consciously to her rounded form, and she glanced nervously over her shoulder. "You ought not to have come here, Michael. Alec is not at home, and Robert and Frances have gone to town."

Michael's eyes twinkled mischievously. "Do you mean that I have actually stumbled upon the most advantageous of all situations? I have dreamed of such a circumstance, but I never dared to hope—"

Juliet cut him short. "Michael, I am not alone. Colette is here."

"Ah! That is all the better! To be entertained by two charming ladies—who could ask for more?"

Juliet paused indecisively. She would enjoy a few hours of lively conversation with Michael as much as anything else she could think of, but she knew Alec would hardly be receptive to the idea. And he would have a right to be angry if she dallied with another man while he labored, sweating under the blazing July sun. Still, she could not simply ask Michael to leave—or could she? Before she could make a final decision, Colette came up from behind her.

"Have we a visitor, Juliet?" She took in the handsome young man in his fine broadcloth suit.

"You must be Mistress Farrell. I have heard a great deal about you. I am Michael Alford, an old friend of the younger Mistress Farrell's from New York." He flashed her a dazzling smile, and his dimples deepened boyishly in his cheeks.

Colette raised a quizzical brow to Juliet's pained expression. "Well, sir, I believe the sun must have taken its toll on Juliet, for her to leave you standing out in the heat of the day. Come in and share some refreshment with us." She led the way to the parlor, directing Michael to a comfortable chair with a nod. Juliet followed her and also took a seat, protesting unsuccessfully when Colette left to get cool beverages for the guest.

Michael rose immediately from his seat, straining his eyes

at the parlor door to be certain that Colette was on her way to the kitchen. "Are there any servants about?" he whispered, rising and approaching Juliet. She shook her head. "Good. I had hoped to speak with you alone. Are you well?"

"Yes," she answered nervously, finding his closeness unsettling.

"The news about the fires at the mill and the tobacco field is all over the county. Is it true that they were deliberately set?" At her nod he became troubled. "Who would do such a thing?"

Juliet swallowed and stared at her hands, primly folded in her lap. "Alec thought . . . it might be you."

"Me?" Michael was incredulous. "I certainly hope you told him I wasn't the type. I've already done quite enough to arouse Captain Farrell's ire! And it's not my habit to make enemies; I much prefer making friends."

Her eyes were wide, distressed. "Then why did you come here, Michael? Alec will think . . ." She bit her lip and turned away from his searching blue eyes.

"Alec will think what?" She did not answer. He touched his hand to her cheek, forcing her to face him. "Don't you know why I came here, Juliet? I came because I'd heard the news and I was very worried about you. I've been worried ever since your husband laid me low at the party that night. I'd half expected to see you sporting a blackened eye and swollen jaw! He's a mean devil when he's angry."

Her eyes met his with a hint of skepticism, and her mouth held a reproving smile. "If you were so very concerned with my well-being, Michael, and fearful that my husband would abuse me, why did it take you so long to come? In three months I could have been beaten to death a hundred times over without you ever having known."

"True. But I'm afraid it took me the better part of that time to work up the courage to come here," he admitted. "I am not normally eager to face a raging lion in his den."

"And you also knew that Alec would never really harm me."

He begrudgingly returned her grin. "Yes, I suppose I did. But I did need to have a look at you. These past weeks I've been tormented, knowing that you are so very near, yet so impossibly out of my reach."

"Michael—" she began.

"So I came to bare my heart to you one final time," he went on smoothly, "to beg you to go away with me, to promise you a life of silks and satins and laces and parties . . ." He paused to kneel before her, taking hold of her hand and sweeping it to his lips.

She promptly snatched it away. "Michael, please." Her voice reflected a growing impatience. "I am a married woman. I am expecting a child."

"You mustn't interrupt, my love," he scolded playfully, his eyes bright with amusement. "Now where was I? Oh, yes. I was pleading for you to reconsider my offer of lifelong love and devotion, perhaps even fidelity." He attempted to take hold of her hand once again, but she had had enough.

With an uneasy glance at the doorway, she rose and brushed abruptly past him, trying to calm herself as she stood before the window. He watched her for a moment, then rose also, slowly, while a great deal of the light in his eyes faded away. He went to her and slipped his arms about her. She tensed but did not pull away.

"I knew that you would say no," he whispered against her hair. "You've far too much honor to leave him while things are going so badly. 'To the bitter end,' I believe is the expression. And the end is bitter, is it not?"

She lifted her eyes to meet his, and her words came slow and deliberate, though they were laced with tenderness. "I love Alec, Michael. I have always loved him. And I am happy with him, regardless of what you may think. I tell you now in all honesty that the reason I stay with him is because I cannot live without him."

He looked at her for a long, long time, but her eyes did not waver. Then he gave a reluctant nod and smiled, though his eyes remained sad.

The pleasant tinkling of glasses rattling on a tray gave Michael and Juliet time to resume their seats before Colette brought the refreshments into the parlor. She offered them politely about, then gracefully took a seat near Juliet.

"Tell me, Mr. Alford, how did you and Juliet come to know one another? Are you from New York originally?"

"No. Actually I'm from England. I was serving in the British Army in New York near the beginning of the war, and that was when we met." He eyed Juliet for half a second, then proceeded casually. "We knew each other but a brief period before I left His Majesty's service and made my way to the frontier. Fortunately for me, the ragged Continentals played havoc with the polished troops of Britain—which meant that I had managed to desert from the correct side."

Colette choked on her drink. "You deserted?" It was beyond her that someone would freely admit to such a dishonor. Juliet held her breath, hoping fiercely that he would tell no more.

"Yes, Mistress Farrell. I am sorry to shock you, but you see, I was never really cut out to be a soldier." His smile was warm and completely disarming. "My talents lie in other directions. I am a poet of sorts, a musician, a gambler . . . and I am very good at charming beautiful women, madame, which I intend to prove this afternoon."

Colette raised a brow and matched his even gaze. Why, the man was a rogue, a scoundrel! And straight forward he admitted as much! Yet who could condemn him when he'd already done so thorough a job of that himself? He was no hypocrite certainly! Those mischievous blue eyes and that boyish smile were enough to melt a woman's heart. She could not help but wonder if more than a friendship had existed between this young man and Juliet before Alec came along . . . or perhaps after Alec came along. Colette frowned, realizing that she did not know much about Juliet's life before she had come to Beau Rêve.

"Well, I seem to have rendered the two of you absolutely speechless," he remarked wryly, sipping at his julep. "A feat I could never manage to accomplish in New York."

Juliet could not suppress a smile at that. It had been a game between them to have the last word. "Times have changed, Michael. I haven't the time for parties anymore, or balls or cards, and I haven't even been riding in months."

"Don't tell me you've become thoroughly domesticated? Miracle of miracles! I never thought I'd see the day!" he teased.

"There's so much to be done here, and I enjoy the work, too. It's different, and challenging as well."

"And you were always one to rise to a challenge, that much will never change."

Colette was amused by the fast, lighthearted interchange. "I agree with your appraisal, Mr. Alford—"

"Michael, please."

She nodded, finding that calling him by the more familiar name came easily to her. "I agree, Michael. Juliet is always eager to accept a challenge. Before Alexander returned home, I don't know what I would have done without her help." She paused. "Do you know my son Alexander?"

Again she noticed that he flashed a sidelong glance at Juliet before answering. "We've met. I found Captain Farrell to be . . . an honorable man." He said the last in an oddly bitter tone, so that it was certainly no compliment, yet neither could it be taken as an insult.

"Shall I tell you the news?" he asked, abruptly changing the subject. "Cassandra Collins is finally to be married." He paused dramatically and raised his glass to his lips as he enjoyed their undivided attention. "To me." He grinned as surprise flooded the faces of both women. "It's true. She finds me irresistible, and she's a very determined woman."

"How do you feel about her?" Juliet blurted out.

"Well, she's comely enough," he understated. "And I think that we are a good match. We deserve each other, one might say."

"Do you intend to live here in Virginia, Michael?" Colette asked.

"As a matter of fact, I have just today made up my mind to stay here. I hope to buy some land just west of Tamarack. I know of a few tracts for sale. . . ."

"You will become a planter then?" He nodded. "Forgive my curiosity, but what did you do in the interim? I mean, between the time you left New York and the present?"

"I suppose you might say I was a professional gambler, though I certainly did not start out to be one. I believe there's something in the air hereabouts. Every man I meet seems anxious to wager on everything! And I am a lucky devil! I admit to playing a fair hand of cards, though Juliet was every bit as good. The only woman who ever bested me, though I don't deny there were occasions when I allowed others to win." His blue eyes flickered over her wistfully.

"Michael won three out of every four hands, and that was when he wasn't paying attention," Juliet corrected.

"Don't you believe a word of it, Mistress Farrell. In truth, it was nearly always a draw, and each game taxed my powers to the limit. Take care not to stumble into a game with her, unless, of course, you don't mind losing." With a hint of a challenge in his voice, he posed a question. "Tell me, Juliet, have you ever played cards with your husband?"

"Why, no, I never have."

"I would advise against it then. Captain Farrell does not strike me as the type of man who might take losing to a woman graciously."

Juliet was quick to defend him. "You misjudge him, Michael. If I were to better him, it would most certainly be a temporary condition, for he's not one to easily admit defeat."

"I find it easy to admit the obvious," Michael returned smoothly, his eyes solemnly holding Juliet's. "But I find it nearly impossible to resign myself to the concessions which come with defeat."

An uneasy silence fell at that point, and it was not long afterward that Michael declined Colette's invitation to dinner and took his leave.

Alec strode into the house, his shirt flung over his shoulder, his skin every bit as brown as his leather breeches. In the dining room Colette was instructing a thin young black girl in the proper setting of the table for dinner.

"Good evening, Alexander," she called cheerily.

He smiled, gratefully accepting a tall, cool julep from her. "Where is Juliet?"

"She is still resting, I think. We had a visitor today."

"Oh?"

"Yes. An old friend of Juliet's from New York. Michael Alford."

At the mention of his name Alec's eyes grew hard and cold, though he sipped at his julep and his voice remained calm. "What did he want?"

Colette shrugged. "I believe he came to tell Juliet that he is going to marry Cassandra Collins."

"Indeed?" His lip curled into an odd smile. "They deserve each other."

She smiled. "Do you know, Michael said exactly the same thing?"

"Michael?" He repeated the name with obvious distaste.

"Yes. I found him very charming, though certainly a roué. You do not approve?"

Completely ignoring his mother's question, Alec finished off his drink and proceeded to his bedroom. He tossed his shirt across a chair, pausing as he saw Juliet on their bed. He drew near, his gaze softening despite his inner turmoil. She looked like a child, her face untroubled, her body curled up like a kitten. He turned away and went to the washstand, where he splashed cool water on his face and neck.

Juliet started from her sleep at the sound. She relaxed, recognizing Alec's tanned back, then she remembered what she had to tell him. She fingered the hem of the pillowslip, wondering how she could best approach the subject, how she could tell him the truth without bringing on another ugly confrontation. When he came to stand before her, she peered doubtfully up at him, then away. He took a seat on the bed, leaning to kiss her cheek, while his fingers smoothed over her shoulder and arm. She slipped her arms about his neck, loving the feel of his hard-muscled chest against her. How she loved him! But how she hated the way jealousy changed him! She steeled herself, and her words came in a rush.

"Alec, I have to tell you something. Michael Alford was here today."

"I know. Mother told me."

Her eyes were wide and searching. "And you're not angry?"

"Did you invite him?"

"Of course not."

"Then I have no cause to be angry with you. My anger is directed at him, or to be a bit more cogent, my hate."

"He denied setting the fires."

"And you believe him?"

For a long moment she hesitated. Slowly she nodded, and though his jaw tightened, he did not turn away. "That is your privilege, my dear. But when I catch him in the act, I do hope you will not argue with seeing justice done."

"You would see him hanged?"

"I must admit the thought gives me pleasure."

Juliet sighed and looked away. "You hate him for other reasons, Alec."

"That I do not deny. I cannot admire a deserter, a liar, a man who covets another man's wife." He took hold of her shoulders, but his voice was gentle. "Let us not discuss this now. I made a promise to trust you, and I am doing my best to keep it—though Michael Alford seems to enjoy making things difficult for me."

"He is going to marry Cassandra."

"Yes." Alec's lips twisted into a cruel smile. "Mother told me. What a match! The pair of them—handsome, charming, rich, and totally corrupt. They should make each other very miserable." He noted her troubled frown. "Come, Julie. I shall not see them make us the same."

He rose and began to dress for dinner, and after a moment she did the same. His feelings for Michael were as rancorous as before, but he had made no move to accuse her without reason. Trusting had become a part of his love, and that was certainly encouraging, yet the burning hatred he felt for Michael kept her from feeling any elation. Michael would be their neighbor when he married Cassandra, and there would be no avoiding him in the coming months. A feeling of foreboding came to her, the dread knowledge that such bitterness eventually demands vengeance. She chased away the thought, but much like a weed that has taken firm root, it was destined to return again . . . and again . . . and again.

Chapter 51

Two long, hot weeks later, the Rappahannock still lay steaming in the July sun. Juliet squinted as her eyes scanned the hills. She wiped the sweat from her forehead with her apron as she returned to the shade of the house. Sighing her relief, she took to the nearest chair and rested her eyes as well as her aching feet. She did not know how Delilah managed day after day in the heat of the kitchen. Or indeed, how she had managed these past years herself. The heat affected her much more now than ever before. The child had grown rapidly inside her the past few weeks and seemed to stir about in her womb the entire night with nary a flutter during the day. She smiled, with a hand to the life inside her, so quiet now. She was looking forward to having this baby. It was all so mysterious! How she longed to hold the babe in her arms, to rock him, to cuddle him, to sing him to sleep!

She stirred from her daydreams when she heard a knock at the main door and half rose to answer it, then relaxed as Frances rustled past her through the hall. Frances and Robert had decided to stay until after the baby was born, but they were already making preliminary plans for their departure. Because a letter had arrived from Elizabeth Church mentioning the failing health of Frances's father, the two had decided to go to England before going to New York. Besides, Manhattan was still occupied by British troops and would be until a peace treaty was signed, and no one knew when that might be.

"Juliet, there is a man here who wants to see you." Frances's voice was uneasy and her eyes troubled.

Juliet rose to see about her visitor, but Frances stopped her. "What's the matter, Frances?"

"There . . . there is something about him, Juliet," she began awkwardly. "I . . . I don't think you should talk with him."

Juliet frowned, then cautiously peeked about the corner to catch sight of her visitor. He stood with his back toward her, but his clothing was obviously fine, and he appeared not at all threatening. "Frances, for heaven's sake!"

"No, Juliet. There's something about him that frightens me."

"Well, stop being frightened. Alec is near enough to the house to make us quite safe." Frances was hardly comforted by the reminder. Alec was in the fields, quite a distance away, and Robert had gone to Leighton to see if there had been any word from New York. Juliet brushed by her then, and went to see about the visitor.

He was a well-built, muscular man, though not particularly tall, and he wore a crisp, expensive suit of clothes that seemed to defy the summer's heat. "I am Mistress Farrell. Did you wish to see me?"

He nodded. "I wish to speak with you on a matter of some urgency, Mistress Farrell." His eyes strayed significantly toward Frances, then back again. "I carry a message from a friend."

Since the man was obviously reluctant to speak in Frances's presence, Juliet directed him with a sweep of her hand. "We can speak privately in the parlor," she offered. Tossing a reassuring smile to Frances, she followed the man into the parlor and closed the door securely behind them. She took a seat but did not offer one to her visitor, indicating that she considered his call purely business in nature. She folded her hands primly in her lap, curiously studying the man's face and manner. "I am anxious to know what urgent matter concerns me, sir."

"As I have already told you, Mistress Farrell, I carry a message from a friend of yours. A man by the name of Michael Alford."

"Michael?" she repeated. "What urgent message could Michael possibly have for me?"

"He wishes to meet with you, mistress, at a place called Rosewood. He has come across some valuable information that—"

Juliet was already shaking her head. "I am sorry, Mr. . . . ?"

"My pardon, Mistress Farrell. I ought to have introduced myself earlier. The name is Jacquard, John Jacquard." He gave a short bow.

"I am sorry, Mr. Jacquard, but I could not consider it. And I cannot imagine that Michael would send a messenger to arrange such a meeting. Why, Michael visited Beau Rêve just a fortnight ago. Why would he go to all the trouble of sending a messenger to arrange a meeting elsewhere?"

Jacquard gave her an almost patronizing smile, hiding his surprise. He had not been told about the man's visit two weeks earlier. It made his story slightly less plausible. But he had been paid very well to come here and would collect a second generous bounty when the madman had his way. If convincing the woman proved difficult, then he was only earning his pay.

"Forgive me if I am blunt, madame, but the incident at Devonhill a few months back is certainly no secret. And neither is the trouble you have had here of late. It is said that your husband has posted sentries about the plantation to prevent someone from setting another fire, that if he catches the man responsible, he has threatened to hang him immediately, without benefit of trial. Just about everyone hereabouts feels that he would be justified in doing it, too. In light of all this, for Mr. Alford to come here even once was foolhardy; to come a second time would be nothing short of madness."

Juliet frowned slightly. The man was right. Michael would be very reluctant to risk coming here a second time. Still . . . "I am sorry, Mr. Jacquard, but meeting with Michael is still out of the question. I cannot imagine anything so urgent that—"

"You do not understand, Mistress Farrell," he interrupted smoothly. "Mr. Alford has in his possession proof of who set the fires."

Her eyes widened in disbelief, but a look of uncertainty touched her brow. "What kind of proof?"

He shook his head, disguising the relief he felt at her sudden interest. "I cannot say exactly. You must understand that I am only a passing acquaintance of Mr. Alford. I met with him this morning to settle a gambling debt. But rather than accept payment for what I owed him—a considerable amount, I might say—he asked instead that I come here, that I arrange this meeting."

He paused, and Juliet's eyes flickered over his fine clothes, thoughtfully considering his story. He did indeed look like a gambler, and the rest of what he had said was beginning to ring true.

He gave a helpless shrug. "I know only what Mr. Alford told me during our brief encounter. Nevertheless, I got the distinct impression that his discovery may have placed him in grave danger. I attempted to press him for further information, but he refused to say more"—he stopped, then went on slowly as if to emphasize the threat in his words—"except that there is the very real possibility of another fire if you do not come."

Juliet's skin paled. Another fire would ruin Alec. She could not afford to take the chance. "When did Michael want this meeting to take place?" she inquired reluctantly.

"He said that he would wait at Rosewood until noon."

"Noon! But that's less than an hour from now."

Jacquard pulled an expensive gold watch from his vest pocket and examined it to hide the smile in his eyes. "I suppose you will be forced to hurry, Mistress Farrell. Good day."

"Juliet, you cannot do this! In your condition! I . . . I am not going to let you do this! I am going to tell Colette."

"Oh, no, you are not!" she flung back sternly, taking a firm grip of Frances's arm. "I've no time to argue or explain to anyone else. Rosewood is a good long ride from here, and I don't want to hurry. I haven't ridden in months."

"And you aren't going to now! Juliet, I have never stopped you before, but this time is different. It is dangerous—for you and the baby! Think of the baby!"

Juliet pulled on a pair of riding gloves, turning a determined countenance to Frances. "He said there would be another fire, Frances. Someone could be killed. I must go!"

"Then please at least wait for Robert. He could go with you—"

"He might be another hour getting back from town!"

"Then let's ask Colette. Oh, please, Juliet, don't do this! What will I say?"

"Tell Colette that I have a headache, that I am resting in my room. Keep the door closed, and no one will ever know. I shall be back in two hours, I promise." She attempted a confident smile. "Don't worry."

In the stables Juliet roused Jay to saddle her a gentle mount, telling him she was going to fetch Alec in the fields. She winced as she saw the pain twisting his features with every movement, and it seemed to take him all of an hour to fix the mare a proper saddle. Finally she was off.

It took a long time to become accustomed to the added weight around her middle, for she could not lean forward and give the horse her head, and the seat offered no support for her back. It made maneuvering all the more difficult, and she was forced to keep a slow pace that she would normally have considered unthinkable. She ground her teeth, wishing desperately that she knew the shorter path to Rosewood. Alec had taken her along it that day last winter, but it was a poorly cut trail, and besides, everything looked different now, with the landscape covered with thick foliage. Patience, she scolded herself over and over again. Michael will wait a few moments longer.

"Alec! Alec!" Robert galloped at breakneck speed over the dusty road that led to the newly planted field. "Al-e-e-e-c!" His cries rang with urgent excitement across the land.

Alec straightened, scowling as he lifted his hat and wiped the sweat from his brow. Seeing Robert approaching in such haste, he gingerly picked his way between the neat rows of seed. Before he had even reached the end of the row, Robert was off his horse and running to meet him, waving a piece of parchment above his head like a flag of victory.

"News! Wonderful news!" Robert gasped out.

Alec disengaged himself from Robert's clumsy bearhug with an annoyed frown. "What the devil—"

"You will not believe it, Alec," he broke in breathlessly. "I am not even certain I believe it myself!"

"Believe what?"

"It's all here in the letter. I've read it and reread it a hundred times over on the way back from Leighton. It's true! It's really true!"

"What are you talking about, Robert?" Alec demanded, exasperated. "What's true?"

"We're rich! Juliet and I have inherited a fortune from Captain Adam Barkley!"

Alec's expression was incredulous as he quickly snatched the letter from Robert's hand and scanned it, unintelligibly muttering its content until his serious expression broke into a smile and his voice became a shout, very much like Robert's. ". . . that Juliet Cecilia Hampton and Robert Lawrence Hampton are named sole heirs of said estate."

This time it was Alec who initiated the bearhug, then laughed aloud and cuffed Robert on the shoulders. "I can hardly wait to tell Juliet!"

"And Frances!" Robert cried.

The sun was just short of center sky when Robert and Alec arrived at the house, anxious to share their news. In his present state of excitement, Alec all but ignored Jay's stammerings as he took charge of their mounts. His excitement had him almost running to the house. Frances and Colette were much surprised when the two of them burst in, shouting and laughing as if they had spent the morning in a tavern. "We have news!" Robert told them after they had prodded him a bit. "Wonderful news!"

"What news?" Colette and Frances demanded simultaneously.

Alec and Robert exchanged a conspiratorial look. "The news concerns Juliet," Robert baited them, refusing to say more.

"Where is she?" Alec asked his mother with a wide grin.

"She is resting at the moment," Colette answered, missing the wide distress in Frances's eyes.

"She isn't ill?" Alec asked, his voice holding concern.

"No, no!" Frances replied a bit too quickly. "She was tired, that's all."

"You said that she had a headache," Colette reminded her.

"Oh, yes. Well, she did. But she will feel much better after her rest. We must let her sleep for a little while longer though."

Robert lightly wrapped an arm about Frances's shoulders, his smile fading somewhat when he felt her trembling against him. "Is something wrong, Frances?"

"No! No, nothing," she managed with a shaky smile. "But you and Alec must be dying of thirst. Please sit down in the parlor where it's cool, and I'll get some juleps for you."

Alec's eyes wandered anxiously to the stairs. "I believe I shall check on Juliet first."

As he took to the stairs, Frances froze in terror. Then she pulled away from Robert and flew after him. "Alec! Alec, please don't disturb her now! Wait a little while—until after dinner. She really needs to rest." She pulled at his arm, doing her best to direct him away from their room.

"I'll not wake her if she's asleep, Frances," Alec assured her. His brow darkened when she darted in front of him to block the door, and his voice became stern. "But if she is awake, she'll want to know the news."

His hand reached out for the door, and in desperation, Frances pushed him away, on the verge of hysterical tears. "Don't, Alec! Please, please, don't!"

"Frances?" Alec took hold of her shoulders and gave her a shake, then studied her face for a long moment. When he spoke again his voice was dangerously cold. "She's not here, is she?" he whispered incredulously. "She's not here! Where is she, Frances?"

Frances shut her eyes and began to cry, but Alec was relentless. He grabbed her arms cruelly, and he ground out the question one last time. "Where is she?"

"Rosewood," she said helplessly. "She went to Rosewood."

"Rosewood? Why there?" Frances shook her head, and Alec's voice was filled with venom. "She went to meet someone, didn't she? Who? Who is she meeting at Rosewood?"

"The man . . . the man said . . . that Lieutenant Alford—"

He flung her hard against the door, and she sank weakly to the floor. "Alec!" she choked out, her voice breaking painfully as she sobbed. "He said that he knew who set the fires!" But she knew even as she cried after him that he had heard nothing save that hated name.

As Alec took to the stairs with long, angry strides, his face became an ugly, distorted visage of hate. He shoved Robert aside as he was hurrying up the stairs to his wife, having heard her terrified cries. Colette stood by, a bewildered spectator, until Alec returned from the library with his long rifle. She ran to block his exit from the house.

"No, Alexander." She spoke firmly, struggling to still the fear erupting inside her. Her eyes were impenetrable as she faced his murderous glare, but he only took her roughly by the shoulders and pushed her against the wall. Somehow she managed to keep from falling, and she watched with sick dread as he crossed to the stables with quick strides. When Robert came back downstairs, she ran to him, clutching at his shirt like a frightened child. "Robert, you must go after him! You must stop him!"

"Jay!" Alec repeated the angry summons as he saddled Spaniard. "Jay!"

"Yes, Master Alec," came the quiet response.

Alec turned on him savagely. "Did you saddle a horse for Juliet?"

Jay struggled to swallow. He had never seen Alec in such a dangerous mood. "Yes, sir. She asked me t' saddle her a—"

"I want you off this plantation, do you understand me? Do not be here when I get back." He angrily jerked at the cinch, scooped up his rifle, and swung into the saddle, his heels digging deep into Spaniard's belly, his hands taking a firm rein.

Robert ran from the house just in time to see him take to the road. Without hesitation, he raced to the stables to fetch a mount for himself, hoping that somehow he would be able to find his way to Rosewood before Alec did any irrevocable damage.

Juliet was relieved as the tall chimneys of Rosewood came into view. The scene was a very different one than she remembered, for the lush greenery and thick tangled vines hid the haunting remnants of the fire; the chimneys seemed out of place in the heavy foliage. Eyeing a horse tethered to a nearby tree, she urged her mare in that direction, though as she came upon it she saw no one. She slid awkwardly from the saddle and tethered her own horse, glancing anxiously about for Michael. She called his name. She took a few timid steps and called it again, doing her best to force down the eerie feeling that she had felt at this place before.

Suddenly, seemingly from out of nowhere, a hand clamped hard over her mouth and a muscular arm banded about her rounded waist. She struggled fiercely, sinking her teeth deep into the calloused fingers, which she knew at once could not be Michael's. The arm about her tightened, forcing the breath from her. As she cried out in pain, a familiar figure stepped slowly from the thick cover of brush.

"Not so tight, John," an overly polite voice warned. "I want to talk with her a bit before the lieutenant arrives."

Juliet felt her knees go weak when she saw him. The bright sunlight became a weird assortment of black and white spots that spun about her head. The man was her father. Through a strange blur she saw him smile at her. She shook her head and fought off the dizziness as Jacquard bound her hands behind her back. "You . . . you were there. At Devonhill." Her own voice seemed distant and reverberating.

Her father tilted his head to one side and smiled as if he were pleased with her for knowing that. "Yes. I was there. Imagine my surprise at finding not only you and your loving husband there, but also our dear Lieutenant Alford!" A strong feeling of nausea grew in Juliet as he spoke to her in the eerie, singsong voice of a small child. The voice was her father's, and yet it was not. She studied his face, his steel-blue eyes glazed yet glowing, his mouth smiling, always smiling. "How kind of you all to come together like this," he went on. "To make it so simple for me to repay my debts."

Suddenly the smile was gone. His mouth tightened into a thin white line. "You deceived me!" he screamed at her. "You didn't really expect me to forget what you did to me, did you? You planned all along to leave, even while you pretended that you would marry Harold!"

His anger was gone then, as swiftly as it had come, and his eyes were wistful, his voice soft with self-pity. "I went to so much expense for you. All of your fine clothes and fancy parties. I pleaded with Harold to go after you—I begged him! But he refused. He left for England. And he took all of his money. . . ." For an instant Juliet thought he might actually cry. But then his chin lifted, and his eyes became hard again.

"So I thought to recover everything you had cost me, to win it all back at the tables." He gave a little smile. "I won my very first pound that way, you know, so many years ago." His voice became a childish whine. "But they cheated me! They took everything! Everything I had built! And the rebels won the war," he went on more softly. "Who would have thought it possible? Who would have believed . . . ?" His voice trailed off, and his eyes were glazed and unblinking for several long moments. Then his head jerked suddenly, as if he were waking from a dream. "They won't get Hampton House!" He smiled like a small boy who had just eaten a stolen tart. "I burned it to the ground," he told her proudly. He laughed, the high-pitched, hysterical laugh of a madman. "They'll never get Hampton House!"

Juliet shrank away in utter terror and struggled anew to be free of her bonds. She tried to think clearly; she knew that she had to remain calm, that she had to think of a way to escape.

Then, as if he were suddenly aware of her presence again, his laughter stopped. His voice sounded almost sane. "You must tell me, Juliet, how you came to know that your husband was still alive."

"Michael told me about Alec. That night he left New York."

The smile was back again. "I thought so. I knew that he came to warn you about me. But I foolishly let myself believe that he had given up trying to ease his conscience and had settled for getting away. That was a mistake," he scolded himself, "a very, very bad mistake."

"What are you going to do?" she asked, forcing a calmness into her voice. Her own father . . . the man whose respect had meant everything to her . . . whose love she had tried so hard to win. This man was mad—and dangerous!

"Can't you guess? I intend to pay my debts, every single one of them in a single fell swoop." The smile was replaced by a hate-filled scowl. "Your husband ruined everything for me!" he cried. "All of my plans! My son, my daughter, my home! Once I thought to have his blood—but that was far too easy an end for him! A man like that has no fear of death. Death is far too easy." He grinned as if he thought himself quite clever. "But that night at Devonhill, when you were dancing with Lieutenant Alford, it suddenly came to me—a plan to do to him exactly what he had done to me."

"So it was you who started the fires," Juliet said with certainty.

"Hardly ample payment, but it was a start," Hampton confirmed. "Now Captain Farrell will know what I have known these past years, the loss of everything that is important to him. And you have been such a help to me, Juliet, coming here alone like this. Imagine what the poor man will think when his wife is found dead in the arms of her lover—and she so far along with child! Such a tragedy!" He paused to sigh, as if relishing the thought. "Perhaps there will also be a suicide. Captain Farrell is not one who handles his jealousy well, is he?"

Juliet's last bit of bravado disappeared as she realized what she had done. She had played right into his hands. "Alec! Oh, Alec!" she whispered as she crumpled to her knees in total defeat, tears falling unchecked down her cheeks.

"Alec?" He laughed at her. "Your tears are better spent on yourself," he chided. "*You* are the one about to die. An eye for an eye, as I tally my book of accounts. Your death will satisfy the debt so completely. Isn't it wonderful that you are so well loved?"

His face and voice changed abruptly as he gave an authoritative command. "Jacquard, get that horse out of sight. Untie her hands and bind her more firmly there." He jerked his head toward a tall, thick tree. "And don't dally. Our young lieutenant will be here soon, and we do so want to surprise him."

Juliet offered little resistance as Jacquard took hold of her arms and half dragged her to the tree. He pulled her arms tightly about it with a savage jerk, flattening her back against its trunk. Then he drew a silk kerchief from his breast pocket and held it by the corner, daintily shaking it out. "I apologize for the inconvenience, Mistress Farrell, but I cannot have you warning your friend before your father has a chance to talk with him, can I?" He twisted the kerchief and secured it tightly about her mouth, then made a mocking bow before her and disappeared into the brush.

A moment later, at the sound of an approaching rider, her eyes jerked open and her strength surged. He must not be caught! He must not! Somehow she had to warn him! She strained with all her might against the thick ropes that bound her, all the while trying to scream. But the noises she managed were muffled and useless, and she could work not the slightest bit of slack in the ropes. Her shoulders ached, her chest felt so tight that it became difficult for her to breathe. She began to gnaw at the kerchief and roll her head from side to side until the fabric cut deep grooves into the sides of her mouth. Then she let out a single long sob of utter anguish at the hopelessness of the situation.

Alec prodded Spaniard along the overgrown path, angrily smacking his hindquarters with his bare hand whenever the horse hesitated. He was close now, a quarter of a mile or less from Rosewood, and he had made excellent time up until this last stretch, where the brush had grown so thick that the trail actually disappeared in a maze of vines and wild blackberries. Spaniard reared as Alec's heels dug deep into his belly. The path was nonexistent from this point on, and Spaniard had had enough of thorns tearing at his flesh. He stretched his neck around in an attempt to plead his case, snorting and neighing with eyes wide and bright. With a snarl, Alec swung down and cursed the worthless animal as he tethered him to a nearby tree. From here on it would be every bit as fast to proceed on foot, and besides, with the foliage so dense, he would have the element of surprise on his side. What explanation would Juliet have this time? he wondered. Oh, yes, Frances had tried some silly excuse about knowing who set the fires. He laughed. As if it were some great secret who had set them! He ought to have beaten Juliet to within an inch of her life. Damn her and all her pious talk about trust and love! What a fool he had been actually to have believed it!

He raised his eyes above the thick tangle of vines that had ripped a million tiny cuts in his tanned skin. The crest of the hill was not much farther. He paused indecisively, then turned to circle the hill. There was no path that came from that direction, so he would be certain to come upon them unobserved. His hand tightened in anxious anticipation on his rifle as he ducked to miss the low-hanging bough of a hawthorn tree. A single thought pushed him on, heedless of the torture such dense growth worked upon his body. This day he would have his vengeance; he would see justice done.

On approaching the small clearing just at the leveling of the hill, while still well out of sight, Alec loaded his rifle, jamming the soft lead ball down the long length of the barrel. Quiet as an Indian, he slipped from one tree to another through the clearing until the twin chimneys of Rosewood came into view. He flattened himself against the tree and strained his ears, almost certain that he heard an approaching rider. Could it be that he had arrived at their little tryst even before Michael? He edged around the tree, then darted to the next closest one to get an even better look. Sure enough, Michael was just riding up.

Alec watched him jump down and walk his horse to where Juliet's mare stood loosely tethered, dropping the reins carelessly over a thin branch. Alford gave the mare's flanks a pat, then strode about the place staring curiously at the chimneys. Alec heard him call for Juliet twice, three times. Dropping to the ground, Alec slithered along like a snake as he moved to conceal himself again in the foliage. Inch by inch he worked his way closer, pausing every so often to view Michael from the sight of his gun. He was just about in range when Michael let out a startled cry and sprinted off behind the chimneys. For an instant Alec considered relinquishing his cover to go after him. But he only had one shot, and he intended that to be enough. He needed the element of surprise to be absolutely sure. Slowly, deliberately keeping his concealment, he again began to work his way through the vines and thorns.

Completely disregarding an instinctive urge toward caution, Michael hurried to Juliet's side and started to tear at the tightly knotted gag. She shook her head and tried to shrink away from his help in an effort to warn him.

But it was already too late. "Welcome to our little party, Lieutenant." Her father came forward with a gleeful smile.

Michael started and whirled about at the sound, but before he could defend himself Jacquard got a firm hold from behind, pinning his arms tightly against his back. Michael's gaze fixed momentarily on Hampton's bright, piercing eyes, then flickered downward without expression to a pair of pistols, primed and ready, one in each of Hampton's hands.

"I deserve your justice, Hampton," he said with forced

calmness, his voice betraying none of the terror that flooded his consciousness. "But let her go. You've no reason to force her to be witness to my death."

"How gallant, Lieutenant! Spoken like a man of honor!" Hampton smiled condescendingly. "But I do not intend to force Juliet to witness your death. Rather *you*, Lieutenant, will be witness to *hers!*" His eyes glittered with triumph.

A rash of sweat beaded almost instantly on Michael's brow. "You cannot be serious! She is your daughter, man! Your own flesh and blood!"

Hampton's mood was ugly again, his words malicious. "She is his, Lieutenant. You never fully realized that, did you?"

Michael jerked violently against the hold Jacquard had on him, but the man held him fast, wrenching his arm high until his breath caught painfully in his throat.

"Patience, Lieutenant," Hampton reproved as if Michael were a disobedient child. "I should hate to have to kill you first."

Michael groaned in pain and settled an aching stare on the pistols looming ever more deadly before his face. His eyes wandered helplessly to Juliet's, and he immediately forgot his own terrible anguish, so haunting was the look of defeat in those beautiful golden eyes. A razor-sharp pang of regret shot cleanly through to Michael's soul, setting off a foreign burning in his throat, a stinging in his eyes. In his dreams she was ever laughing, ever lifting her chin in a subtle challenge, ever riding like the wind through a spring-blessed meadow. How he loved her! The wild and frenzied look in his eyes disappeared as she met his gaze for a long, poignant moment, and Michael knew that she loved him, too, and that she forgave him for everything. . . .

Annoyed by the pure and cherished affection that passed between the two of them even now, Hampton lifted the long gray barrel of one gun and poised his index finger on the trigger. Suddenly, a crack of thunder shattered the silence, and at once the childlike smile on his face distorted into a grimace of pain and disbelief. One pistol fell from his hand as he clutched convulsively at a small spot of red on his chest. He grunted and doubled over, a larger splotch of crimson at his back coming into view. The bullet seemed to have come from out of nowhere, so suddenly, so unexpectedly, that for a moment everyone froze. A split second later Alec was rushing toward them, his eyes filled with such hatred that Jacquard panicked and hurled Michael to the ground to make a run for the horses.

At that same instant, Hampton was straightening, concentrating every last bit of his strength on his shaking hands, which leveled the barrel of his second pistol at Juliet's heart.

Michael's eyes filled with horror as the gun was raised into position, and he lurched forward to block the shot. *"No!"*

There came an odd, muffled blast as the gun exploded against Michael's chest, a sickening sound of human flesh being torn asunder.

Sobbing hysterically with defeat, Hampton fell to the ground, his arms stretching toward the yet unfired pistol, somehow grasping it, lifting it into position as he struggled to his knees. But before he could take aim, Alec had him by the neck, easily wrenching away the gun and hurling it aside.

When Hampton fell backward in a limp heap, Alec threw himself on top of him, cursing him and smashing a rock-hard fist into his face again and again, actually savoring the horrid smacking sounds of his knuckles crushing tender flesh and bone, drawing a morbid pleasure from the tiny cries of pain that Hampton emitted each time he struck him. His bloodlust was such that he was not even aware that Robert was there, cutting free his sister's bonds, loosening the silk scarf from her mouth.

"Michael!"

It was Juliet's scream, so fraught with anguish and torment that finally made something inside Alec snap. He froze, his fist raised in preparation to strike, suddenly seeing the unrecognizable mass of blood and pulp beneath him, totally void of life. His head jerked up. He saw Juliet run toward another body that lay motionless in the dust. Somehow she found the strength to turn him, to lift his fair head into her lap. She shook her head and blinked back a flood of tears. "Michael?"

Her lips were trembling so that she could hardly mouth the word. She began to tenderly brush the dirt from his face, much of it caked with blood that was already flowing from his mouth. He moved his lips. It was scarcely a whisper, but she bent closer to him and entwined her fingers firmly about his hand. "I am here, Michael. Oh, Michael! Please don't die!" Her voice was no more than a frightened whimper, and she sobbed uncontrollably when she realized he was actually trying to smile.

His hand tightened around her warm, slender fingers, but his flesh was cold and his hold weak. He closed his eyes and forced out the words. "For . . . honor's . . . lady . . ." And then his hand slipped lifelessly from hers.

A violent shudder coursed through her at the icy realization that Michael was dead. She cradled his head in the crook of her arm and smoothed the hair back from his brow. Slowly, pleadingly, she raised her eyes to Alec's, but even through the blur of her tears she could not mistake what she saw: that look of shame and hatred and disbelief. His black eyes cut her deeply, penetrating to her very soul, making a vital part of her recoil. And then he rose and walked away.

Her father had won his vengeful game after all, she thought. She had lost Alec's love forever.

She pulled Michael's head against her breast and began to hum a soothing song, holding him as she had once held her favorite porcelain doll. She forgot then where she was and what had happened, and all the hurt she could not even begin to face alone. She was a little girl again, holding a cool, smooth porcelain doll, rocking her baby to sleep. She did not hear Robert's low words of comfort, did not see his horrified expression as he pulled her to her feet. It was such a nice day, she was thinking, a good day for a ride. So she smiled as Robert led her to her horse and hoisted himself behind her in the saddle. She liked to ride with Robert. She stared curiously down at her hands, which were covered with stuff that was red and sticky. She would have to wash them the minute she got home, she thought, or Rachel would be angry with her. And she did not want to make Rachel angry today, because suddenly she was very, very tired. She sighed and leaned wearily against her brother.

Chapter 52

"Juliet, please try to relax. Everything will be all right, I promise. I shall stay right here with you." Colette took firm hold of Juliet's hand and squeezed it reassuringly, though she found it difficult to smile into such a blank stare. Juliet still did not recognize her. "It's Colette, dear. Colette."

Juliet pulled her hand away and gazed suspiciously at a pair of coal-black eyes. Devil's eyes, Rachel would call them. Her stomach tightened painfully, and she squirmed, trying to avoid the hurt. She and Robert must have gotten into that old man's green apples again. They always gave her terrible stomach cramps, though she could never remember them being this bad before. . . .

She breathed a long sigh and sank gratefully into the pillows as the pain abated. She had been awake nearly the whole night with the stomachache, and every time she managed to fall asleep, the pain would come back again and wake her up. And that strange woman with the black eyes had been here, too, watching her, always watching her. . . . Suddenly Juliet was afraid. Who was this woman? Where was Robert? As the pain took hold again, she began to cry. "Robert!" She grabbed hold of the bedlinens and twisted them in her hands to keep from screaming.

A large hand lifted hers gently from its place on the bed, and she opened her eyes to a different face, a familiar one. "Robert," she sighed in relief. Then she looked at him oddly and said, "Robert, you won't tell Father that I went riding with you, will you?" Her eyes were wide and childlike.

521

"Juliet." Robert shook his head. His face looked so strange. Why, he looks almost like he's going to cry, she thought in alarm.

"I'm all right, Robert," she said with a smile. "Don't tell Rachel, though . . . about the apples, I mean." Her hand gripped Robert's with a sudden fierceness as the pain washed over her once more. Moments later, when it ceased, she heard his voice, firm and deliberate. He was saying something important, she knew. She must not fall asleep. She must listen to him, she must concentrate on what he was saying.

". . . Do you understand, Juliet? You are going to have a baby. We've sent for the doctor, and he will be here any moment. Don't worry."

Her eyes were uncertain and dismayed. "A baby?"

Robert frowned his frustration. Would she ever remember? "Juliet, try to remember. You are married to Alec; you are having his child."

"Alec?" she repeated blankly. A slight frown flitted across her brow, then deepened rapidly as the pain returned. It was getting worse, she realized, as she squeezed Robert's hand with both of her own. And she was so tired.

"Alec," Robert was saying in that same desperate tone. "Don't you remember Alec?"

Juliet blinked back a sudden flood of tears. "I'm tired, Robert, and it hurts so much."

"I know, but you must try to remember. Alec is your husband, Juliet."

He stopped his scolding as the tears began rolling down her cheeks. For two months she had been like this, completely in a world of her own. She did not recognize Alec or Colette, and she treated Frances coldly, not bothering to disguise her contempt. It was as if she were seven years old again; she even believed that she was still at Hampton House, worrying constantly about Father and Mother and Rachel. Robert's throat tightened painfully as he realized that his words were in vain. He turned as he felt a hand on his shoulder.

"Robert, Dr. Jacobi is here now," Frances whispered. "It isn't proper for you to stay any longer."

Reluctantly he rose, disengaging Juliet's fingers from his hand and leaving the room. He steeled himself as she called for him, continuing resolutely down the stairs.

In the parlor, Alec paced nervously, sipping at a brandy. His face lifted expectantly as Robert joined him, then fell as the other shook his head. His eyes rose to the top of the stairs and his spine stiffened visibly as Juliet let out a scream. He pulled his eyes away. There was nothing he could do.

"Mistress Farrell, I am Dr. Jacobi. I am not going to hurt you."

Juliet pulled fearfully away from him, clutching the sheet tightly to her chin. She braced herself for another pain. They were pure torture! Why wouldn't everyone simply leave her alone? And where was Robert? Why had he left her?

"Juliet, please! The doctor will not hurt you!"

It was Frances. Why was she here? She had told Robert to leave. How she hated Frances! She would never forgive Frances for taking Robert from her. Her eyes flew open as the doctor touched her, and she jerked violently away from his hand.

"Mistress Farrell!" The man's voice was sharp, but she was not afraid of him! She narrowed her eyes, as if daring him to touch her again. Why, he did not even know her name! Her face tightened, and she gasped as another spasm of pain spread over her stomach and around her back. The doctor was speaking again, but his words were garbled, and she did not understand what he was saying.

"The pains are very close; the child will be here soon. How long has she had the pains?"

"I heard her crying before dawn this morning, but I cannot say how long before then."

"You will have to hold her down. Perhaps we can force her to take some laudanum." He looked questioningly at Frances and Colette, then jerked his head toward Delilah, who had just brought in a pile of fresh linens. "She can be of help, also."

Juliet opened her eyes as they gathered around her bed, but her mind was a weird tangle of shadows, and as they took hold of her arms and forced her to lie still, she suddenly saw not three women and one man, but thousands of men, many of them in different-colored uniforms. They were everywhere! Soldiers of every age and description stacking rocks and digging trenches, and though she called and called, she could not find Robert. She struggled with all her might, wrenching against the groping hands that touched her flesh. Then she screamed in agony as the pain took hold once more. "Robert!" Her thoughts became a confusing jumble of pictures, of memories piling one atop the other as she drifted in and out of consciousness. She saw Father's cold expression as he listened to her mother's monotonous voice: ". . . a young lady must receive proper training . . ." As the pain ebbed away, she saw a blurred succession of vaguely familiar faces. Aunt Cecilia, Lord Harold, Frances, Allan, little Edgar, and . . . She strained against the hands that held her down, and shook her head to free herself of those faces, a sudden panic rising as the pain began again.

"No! No!" Her screams tore through the quiet house. She wanted to remember. She didn't want to remember. She only wanted . . . She only wanted . . .

"Help me! Someone help me, please! Alec!"

He took the steps two at a time and reached the bedroom in a matter of seconds.

"Blast it! Hold her still!" the doctor demanded.

Alec disregarded everyone else in the room, pushing Frances brusquely aside to take hold of one of Juliet's hands. He brought it to his lips. "I'm here, Julie. I'm here."

She fell back on the pillow, crying. "I'm afraid, Alec."

"I know, darling. It won't be much longer. I promise."

"Alec, you must leave at once!" Frances whispered urgently. "It simply isn't proper!"

"Captain Farrell, the child will be here soon. Do you wish to remain here with your wife?"

He nodded briefly at the doctor, then turned back to Juliet as both her hands tightened around his. "Don't leave me, Alec!" she cried desperately. "Please don't leave me!"

"I'm here, darling. I'll never leave you." He held his breath and stared lovingly at her face, which was blanched with pain and pinched with fear. Finally she relaxed as the pain dwindled away, but then it returned only moments later, and she could scarcely breathe. Her fingers whitened around Alec's hand, and her lips were drawn into a thin line.

"Mistress Farrell, when the pain comes again, I want you to bear down, tighten against the pain. Push the baby out, do you understand?"

Juliet stared helplessly at Alec as the pain cruelly penetrated her brief respite, and she heard his voice come soft and gentle. "Do what he tells you, Julie. I'm with you. It will all be over soon, darling."

She drew a quick breath and held it, straining with all her might.

"Good. Very good. Do the same when the pain comes again. It will not be much longer."

She wanted to tell him that she was too tired, that her limbs were like lead, that her body simply had no strength left, but when the pain attacked again she held Alec's hand and forced herself to do what had to be done. Her face twisted with the effort, but strength seemed to flow from the long brown fingers that held her hand.

Then suddenly there sprang from the silence a strange, wonderful, miraculous sound! A baby's first cry! It was small and timid at first, then it was loud! It was strong! It was beautiful! Juliet's eyes filled with tears of joy, and when Alec bent to kiss her, she saw that his eyes were also bright and wet.

"You have a son, Captain Farrell," the doctor said with a relieved smile. "A fine, healthy son."

Chapter 53

Alec stared out the parlor window, listening to the quiet peace of nighttime at Beau Rêve.

"Your wife and son are sleeping, Alexander. I suggest you do the same. We shall call you when she wakes," Colette said wearily.

When he turned from the window, his expression came as a surprise to her, but his words surprised her even more. "Could we talk, Mother?"

Colette nodded and went to close the door against intrusion. Then she took a seat near him and waited.

"I have decided to leave Beau Rêve. With the money Captain Barkley left to Juliet, she will have no problem hiring a competent overseer."

She found it difficult to hide her shock. "Leave Beau Rêve? But where will you go?"

"France, I suppose. I have not really decided that yet."

"Alexander, you have a wife and son. You must think of them; they are your responsibility."

"Don't you think I know that? I am thinking of them!" He took a long sip of brandy, and when he spoke again, it was with the same studied calmness as before. "Several years ago, when I was in London, I remember meeting a child of five or six years, no more. Every day he was there in the streets begging, and every night he went home to a filthy room and a drunken father who took what little he had made and beat him. When I discovered his plight I spoke with him. I offered to take him away from all his suffering, and do you know what he told me? He said that he couldn't leave his father, that he loved him too much to leave him all alone. Juliet is very much like that child, I think. She would sooner destroy herself than admit that her love was wrong."

Colette stared at her son but said nothing.

"Do you know that I meant to kill him? That day at Rosewood, I was going to kill him. I actually relished the thought of seeing his blood; I had dreamed of it, of seeing him crawl! I might have killed her, too, had she not been with child. I would not have listened to explanations or thought of the terrible anguish I might have caused her. I was too filled with vengeance for that! I loved her as selfishly as her father did, and I deserve to lose her exactly as he did."

"You have a chance to change now, and that is what you must do. Giving up is the coward's way, Alexander. You cannot run away from your mistakes."

"Perhaps I have always been a coward, Mother. All these years I've thought of myself as such a proud and honorable man." He laughed bitterly, and the sound stung Colette's heart. "I could have stopped Justin from riding that horse. I knew that he would be thrown. But I didn't care enough to stop him. I thought he deserved to fall, because he was acting like a fool. Oh, how easily I judge everyone! How blindly I sentence them without bothering to see what is there!"

"You are equally as harsh in your judgment of yourself."

"A trifle tardy with it, though, wouldn't you agree?"

"It is not too late, Alexander," she answered quietly. "I understand how you feel—"

"No, Mother. You could not possibly understand how I feel. You have your God, your faith. I have nothing. I can find no reason for my life. During all those years of fighting I saw so many good men fall—far better men than I! Men with families, men with faith, good and honorable men. They died while I survived. Sometimes I think it was only the hate that kept me alive. And now, when I finally realize what it has done to me, to Juliet . . ." His voice faltered. He drew a deep breath, forcing the emotion from his tone. "Why did I survive? Why not Allan or Mary? Or Edgar? Or even Michael Alford? Why me? For what purpose? Can you answer me that?"

Colette stared at her son's face, so filled with confusion and helplessness and anguish. Her own voice was strangely tight, and there was a sharp aching in her breast as she began a story she had never told to anyone before.

"Many years ago, my father bought a tract of land he affectionately named 'Ciel,' Heaven. He cleared the land and farmed it himself until he could afford slaves to do the work. He worked hard, and by the time I was seven he was a very rich man, and he and Mother began work on the home they had always dreamed of." She sighed and smiled, her dark eyes lighting up as she remembered. "It was the most beautiful home I have ever seen! Every ceiling was a work of art, each wall mural a masterpiece, the ballroom spacious and elegant! Every detail was a labor of love. It was four years before the house was completed, and even then Mother was constantly planning changes and improvements. Oh, life was so beautiful for us! I had everything I could possibly want. A loving mother, a doting father, an older brother whom I idolized, and two younger sisters whom I loved as well."

The smile faded slowly as she went on. "When I was fourteen, I remember waking one night very late. I will never know what it was that woke me, but I remember opening my eyes and thinking that there was a cloud in my room. I watched it for a few moments, that swirling gray mist hanging just below the ceiling, until I came full awake and realized that it was smoke. The smell of it was strong in the air.

"I pulled on a robe and hurried to the door, but when I tried to open it, the latch was so hot that it burned my fingers. The smoke was pouring in under the door, and I knew I could not get out that way. So I ran to my bed and pulled the linens free. I knotted them together and tied the end to the wooden arm of a chair. Then I climbed out the window and sat on the ledge, pulling the chair until it lodged firmly against the window frame.

"God knows how that makeshift rope ever held me, my fingers were trembling so!" She shook her head. "I remember that I was still a good distance from the ground. I had to let go, but I hesitated. It seemed I hung there for hours. I was so frightened! But my arms were weak and tired, and finally I had no other choice. Once I was on the ground, I ran as hard as I could to the slave quarters, screaming all the way. When they followed me back to the house, the flames were going wild! Fire shattered one after another of the beautiful glass windows and leaped so high in the air! No one could even get near the house, the heat was so very intense. I remember that I tried to run back inside, but one of the slaves stopped me." Her voice rose painfully, and she wiped a tear from her eye. "I fought him with all my strength, but Mama and Papa . . ."

She swallowed hard and did not speak for what seemed like a long, long time. When she did, her voice was still tight with her pain. "There was nothing left. Not a single portrait, no treasured memento, nothing. Only memories." She closed her eyes against a fresh onslaught of tears. "I had had everything. My life had been so simple and peaceful and secure. I had never once considered life without my family. I did not really care much about living without them. Time and again I found myself asking why. Why Mama, with her sweet smile, her gentle ways? Why Papa, who was so good and handsome and strong? Why Justin, my brother, whom I had loved more dearly than anyone else? Why Lisa and Mignon, who were so young and full of life? It seemed to me that each of them had far more reason for living than I.

"I went to Williamsburg then, to stay with friends until I could decide what to do. It was there I met your father." Her eyes held a wistful smile. "He was young and much like your brother, Justin—a dreamer, and very trusting of people. He fell in love with me long before I loved him. He spilled out his heart to me, his dreams, his plans for the future. I married him so that I could forget. I thought that if I could forget the past, then I would be a stronger person, but I was wrong. Still there were the questions. They were always with me, until I learned to accept what had happened. I could not change it. I could not forget it. I was forced to accept it, Alexander. Gradually it came to me that someone far greater and wiser than I had chosen me to live. Out of everyone in my family, He chose me, and He had a reason. It was up to me to find that reason. Their time was spent, but mine was not. I was alive. I had a husband who loved me, and soon, a son.

"I look back on it all now, and I cannot stop to ask why. Rather I see what wondrous things life holds for me still, and I hope that what is past will make me strong enough to face the future."

She rose and took a step toward him. "You have a son, Alexander. And a wife who loves you and needs you. If you cannot live with the man you are, then strive to be a better one! Life is not for cowards. It is a constant challenge, a race we must run time and time again. And love is not an easy thing; it is a decision we make day after day."

He was a tall, broad-shouldered man, and his face was dark and lined from years in the sun. But when his arms went around his mother, he was still her little boy.

"Thank you, Mama," he whispered.

Colette Farrell smiled through her tears. He had not called her Mama in a long, long time.

Chapter 54

The sun rose bright and yellow in the clear autumn sky. Alec, in a crisp white linen shirt and freshly pressed broadcloth breeches, strode deliberately toward the bed. With a warm smile he took hold of Juliet's hand and bent to kiss her forehead. "Good morning."

He noted a certain timidity in her manner as she returned his greeting. "Good morning, Alec." She smiled up at him, and her eyes were wide. "Have you seen the baby?"

He crossed to peek into the ornately carved cradle, decorated elaborately with ribbons and bows and lace. Almost lost among the frills were a tiny round face and two wee fists of pink. The baby's head was already covered with an abundance of dark, feathery hair, and Alec watched in amusement as the baby's lips parted in the shape of a diminutive O before he turned his tiny head and was still once more.

"He looks exactly like you," Juliet said when he returned to take a seat on the bed.

"He is most certainly a Farrell," Alec agreed proudly.

"I thought to name him after you, Alec," she said with some uncertainty, searching his face. Her shaky smile vanished when a frown pulled at his brow.

"Julie," he began, lifting her hand in both of his own. His voice was very soft, very gentle, as was his touch. "Do you remember what happened?"

Her voice was weak and hollow, and her eyes looked away. "Yes."

"Everything that happened?"

She nodded and swallowed a painful lump in her throat. "My father is dead."

"Yes."

"And Michael . . ."

"Yes."

She forced her eyes to his. "Are you going to send me away?"

He smiled a little at that, and his hand brushed a tear from her cheek. "No, I'm not going to send you away."

She turned her head so that her lips touched his palm, then her eyes met his once more. "That day I went to Rosewood, Alec, I thought—"

His finger at her lips stopped her. "Ssh. I know. Frances told me."

"And you aren't angry with me?"

"No."

She lifted her arms to his neck and pulled him close, her tears falling silently on his crisp linen shirt.

He drew a long breath and pushed her gently from him. "Julie, we have to talk." He rose from the bed and began to pace the room, assembling his thoughts. She watched him closely, still afraid that he might be angry, that he might send her away. It was a long time before he spoke, and then it was slowly, with much deliberation.

"Last night, when I couldn't sleep, over and over I asked myself if I could ever forget what happened, if I could ever forget that a man I . . . I hated had died so that my wife and my son might live, that I owed that same man everything." He stopped his pacing and turned to her. "And I was forced to admit that the answer was no." He drew a deep breath and gazed distantly at the bright autumn morning, at the natural beauty of Beau Rêve.

"Then I asked myself if I could learn to live a life without you, if I could leave you and everything else I've ever loved behind." He shook his head. "And that answer was also no."

He came back to sit beside her, taking her hands in his own once more. "And so I thought that rather than forgetting what had happened, I might learn from it, grow from it, perhaps become a better man because of it. And I hoped that this might be the start of another new beginning for us . . . if you want to begin again with me."

"We have the best reason of all for beginning again, Alec. We have a son."

He nodded and smiled. "Yes. We have a son."

"Had you thought of a name for him, Alec? Would you like to call him Jerome after your father?"

Alec's eyes were at once serious as he replied, "I had thought to call him Michael."

She stared at him for a long moment, then her eyes flooded with tears, and she held him tightly, loving him more than she had ever loved him before.

Across the room the child began to whimper and cry. Alec rose to go to him, lifting the tiny, weightless bundle into his arms. The baby quieted as he struggled to focus on his father's face.

"Michael Justin Farrell." Alec repeated the name slowly, testing the sound of it. He smiled. "Yes. It suits you. You are a new beginning, Michael. You have so very much to learn. I have so very many things to teach you. And I shall learn with you as well, my son. But above all, I shall love you, Michael. For love is surely the finest honor of all!"

Dear Reader:

If you enjoyed this book, and would like information about future books by this author and other Avon authors, we would be delighted to put you on the mailing list for our ROMANCE NEWSLETTER.

Simply *print* your name and address and send to Avon Books, Room 1210, 1790 Broadway, N.Y., N.Y. 10019.

We hope to bring you many hours of pleasurable reading!

Sara Reynolds, Editor
Romance Newsletter

Book orders and checks should *only* be sent to Avon Books, Dept. BP Box 767, Rte 2, Dresden, TN 38225. Include 50¢ per copy for postage and handling; allow 6-8 weeks for delivery.

The Novels By *New York Times* Bestselling Author
JOHANNA LINDSEY